Penguin Books

Against the Tide

Peter Yeldham's extensive writing career began with short stories and radio scripts. He spent twenty years in England, becoming a leading screenwriter for films and television, and also wrote plays for the theatre, including the highly successful comedies *Birds on the Wing* and *Fringe Benefits*, which ran for two years in Paris. Returning to Australia he won numerous awards for his television screenplays, among them *1915*, *Captain James Cook*, *The Alien Years*, *All the Rivers Run*, *The Timeless Land* and *The Heroes*. His adaptation of Bryce Courtenay's novel *Jessica* won a Logie Award for best mini-series. He is the author of nine novels, including *Barbed Wire and Roses*, *The Murrumbidgee Kid*, *A Bitter Harvest*, *The Currency Lads* and *Land of Dreams*.

For more information please visit
peteryeldham.com

PETER YELDHAM

Against the Tide

Penguin Books

PENGUIN BOOKS

Published by the Penguin Group
Penguin Group (Australia)
250 Camberwell Road, Camberwell, Victoria 3124, Australia
(a division of Pearson Australia Group Pty Ltd)
Penguin Group (USA) Inc.
375 Hudson Street, New York, New York 10014, USA
Penguin Group (Canada)
90 Eglinton Avenue East, Suite 700, Toronto, Canada ON M4P 2Y3
(a division of Pearson Penguin Canada Inc.)
Penguin Books Ltd
80 Strand, London WC2R 0RL England
Penguin Ireland
25 St Stephen's Green, Dublin 2, Ireland
(a division of Penguin Books Ltd)
Penguin Books India Pvt Ltd
11 Community Centre, Panchsheel Park, New Delhi – 110 017, India
Penguin Group (NZ)
67 Apollo Drive, Rosedale, North Shore 0632, New Zealand
(a division of Pearson New Zealand Ltd)
Penguin Books (South Africa) (Pty) Ltd
24 Sturdee Avenue, Rosebank, Johannesburg 2196, South Africa

Penguin Books Ltd, Registered Offices: 80 Strand, London, WC2R 0RL, England

First published by Pan Macmillan Australia Pty Ltd, 1999
This edition published by Penguin Group (Australia), 2009

1 3 5 7 9 10 8 6 4 2

Design by Cameron Midson © Penguin Group (Australia)
Cover coastal image by Australian Scenics
Typeset in 10.5/15.5pt ITC Legacy Serif by Post Pre-press Group, Brisbane, Queensland
Printed and bound in Australia by McPherson's Printing Group, Maryborough, Victoria

National Library of Australia Cataloguing-in-Publication data:
Yeldham, Peter.
Against the tide / Peter Yeldham

9780143010395 (pbk.)

A823.3

penguin.com.au

To Carl Schultz, film director and friend

*And to the waves of immigrants who made the
long journey against the tide, bringing us
new visions, this book is dedicated*

Budapest

The streets were on fire, and the barrage from the guns across the river was relentless. A thick shroud of smoke blanketed the ruined city as buildings famed for their antiquity collapsed into fragments. Burning shingles from the roof of the Church of St Paul almost hit the boy as he ran through the devastation, past corpses lying in the gutters. He was carrying two loaves of stolen bread, and fleeing for his life.

An army corporal from the *Wehrmacht* bakehouse had spotted the theft, snatched his rifle, and was trying to take aim at the scrawny figure as it sped towards the Szechenyi Chain Bridge. The corporal was a baker, not a sniper, so the shots went wild, and the boy laughed, turned to shout an obscenity and stuck out his tongue tauntingly. The German gritted his teeth and steadied his rifle. This time he aimed more carefully and gently squeezed the trigger – remembering the way he had been taught as a recruit in training camp – and his shot hit the statue of the Empress Maria Theresa an inch from the boy's head, an inch from death as it showered him with chips of masonry.

Miki turned and bolted. He headed down Rakoczi Ut towards

the river. The corporal pursued him, shooting wildly again, yelling for him to halt. The boy began to realise he was in extreme danger; any moment others would hear the shouts and then he would be the target of real soldiers, not a well-nourished baker brandishing a rarely used rifle. He summoned his last reserves to put a safe distance between himself and the corporal, racing down a laneway, turning into a street past the blackened remains of the old synagogue, a charred relic that had been doused with petrol and set alight, one of the first targets on the fearful night when the tanks rolled in.

He came to the river. As he felt the biting wind and saw the frozen banks of the Danube, he realised he was almost certain to be caught. There was no way to cross. All that remained of the imposing Chain Bridge was a tangle of wreckage that sagged into the muddy water. Shells from the advancing Russian army had destroyed all crossings between the twin cities. He was trapped on the east side in the unfamiliar terrain of Pest, where the Germans were hanging their own deserters from street lamps, and where fourteen-year-old Jewish boys could expect far less mercy.

He thought for one brief moment of Ilona waiting for him, his sister's thin peaked face at the tiny crack in the boarded window of the attic, where she kept anxious watch on the maze of cobbled streets below. She would already have a premonition of his danger. They'd had an unerring, intuitive sense about each other ever since the Germans came, since the day they and their parents had been made to leave their home and the pharmacy their father ran in the village of Eger, forced to walk out of the town with only the few belongings they could carry, bewildered and shocked by the jeers and mockery of neighbours whom they believed had been their friends.

Barely more than a year apart in age, he and Ilona had always been close, but this dependence upon each other had become entrenched since the night, only months after leaving the village, when they had run through the dark city streets vainly following a terrified group who had been rounded up – among them their mother and father – and seen them forced aboard a train, driven into overcrowded freight cars, while the SS guards used whips or unleashed dogs to round up stragglers and hasten the moment of departure.

It was like a scene from hell in which their parents were two of the helpless participants. Hiding, trying not to cry at the enormity of it, they'd heard sounds that haunted them still, and would forever; the clatter of freight car doors slamming, steam hissing, the mournful whistle of the engine haunting the night as the train rolled out of the loading yard. Neither of them had the least idea where it was going, but they had heard people whisper the names of places, strange foreign names harsh on the tongue, like Buchenwald, Bergen–Belsen and Auschwitz. No-one knew precisely where these places were, or what happened there. What Miki and his sister did realise was that nobody came back from these journeys, and that night had been a grief-stricken, desolate parting in which they were unable to say goodbye. In terror of being taken themselves, they could only huddle together and watch the cattle train disappear into the dark.

In the months since then they had accepted that they were orphans. The only remaining members of their family. With this awareness had come their almost psychic affinity. Ilona would by now have guessed his predicament and be anxious for him. He thought of trying to swim the river, but the water was icy and dangerous with drifting debris. Not only that; it would make his hazardous expedition futile, for the precious bread he had managed to steal would be ruined.

At least he had outrun the corporal. There was no sign of him. The sudden wail of air-raid sirens came too late to warn of an attack as bombers swept across the city, scattering their load of high explosive indiscriminately, bracketing the Catholic cathedral in the square. The building seemed to tremble, then it shuddered and began to break apart as he watched – an awesome sight to see six hundred years of sanctuary collapse into dust and rubble. A cyclist was passing. He stopped his bike to stare, ashen-faced, at the wreckage.

'It's terrible,' Miki said, 'barbaric. What can we do?'

'Nothing,' the man replied, about to ride on.

'We can say a prayer.' Miki sounded devout and shaken. 'I think we should at least do that.'

He knelt reverently, crossed himself and bowed his head. He glanced at the man, but for a moment there was no response. Then the cyclist gave a nod and stepped from his bike. He placed it carefully on the ground behind him as he dropped to his knees, murmuring a prayer while shutting his eyes to avoid the sight of the great church's destruction. Miki picked his moment to perfection, and moved like a flash. Before the man had time to realise what was happening, his bike was being ridden away through the swirling bomb haze.

'You dirty thieving little bastard,' the cyclist shouted, and tried to chase him, but realised it was hopeless.

'Look,' Miki shouted, sitting upright in the saddle and waving both his arms at him. 'No hands.'

~

'No hands,' old Mr Gutinsky chuckled. 'That young Miklos, he makes me laugh, he's a card.'

'Oh, he's a card, all right.' Ilona gave the old man his slice of bread. There was only enough for one modest slice for each person, and it would have to last for two days.

'And on the way home, at the market when he don't need the bike no more, he sells it.'

'Very clever, my brother,' she said disparagingly, but the old man was too busy chortling to realise that she was angry. She knew it was pointless to find fault with Miki; Mr Gutinsky and the others relished his escapades, and it was their admiration that encouraged him.

'Clever like the fox,' Mr Gutinsky continued. 'Very smart to trade the bike like that, to dispose of the evidence and buy potatoes and carrots.'

'Yes,' she said. She was glad about the vegetables. If they could steal a bone with any meat on it, they could have the semblance of a stew. 'Enjoy your bread,' she told him. 'Make it last.'

'Not so easy, little Ilona, to eat slow when you're so hungry.'

'I know. But try.'

'Also – although it hurts me deeply to have to say this – the bluddy Germans, they make good bread.'

'They do, Mr Gutinsky.'

'No hands,' the old man chuckled again. 'I really like that boy. I don't know what we'd do without him.'

'No,' Ilona said, 'nor do I.'

That night, when it was completely dark, they climbed the flimsy ladder, removed the skylight and crawled out. They slid down the slate roof to a refuge behind the chimney pots. Above them clouds obscured the stars, as searchlights vainly chased bombers across the sky. The air was fresh, a blessed relief after the atmosphere of the tiny enclosed room, where seven people shared a space that had once been a scullery.

All the houses still standing were crowded with people – illicit occupants – packed into whatever tiny spaces they could find. Nowhere was too small or cramped for human beings to shelter from the snow and the shrapnel, despite the perils. If a house was hit by shells, few inhabitants on the upper floors survived. The only safe places were in the basements and cellars, but these were already filled beyond normal capacity, and Jews were not welcomed there by fellow Hungarians. The sight of the yellow stars they were forced to wear would bring instant hostility, and the likelihood of ejection.

The stars made it impossible for the Jews to live in safety or obscurity. They could not find refuge except with their own, always in the most dangerous or uncomfortable places. The order to wear the star had been one of the first issued, when Hitler had lost patience with his recalcitrant ally, and occupied the country. It was one of the risks Miki took when he went scavenging; he always unstitched it, and Ilona sewed it back on when he returned. He hated the star; it was like an unsightly birthmark that made him feel blemished.

They huddled close to each other for warmth. The city stretched below them, its ugly wounds veiled by drifting smoke. From their vantage point they could see glimmers of light, the dying flames from the incendiary bombs glowing like scattered gypsy campfires.

'You're upset, Iluska.'

'I'm upset,' she agreed.

'I got back, didn't I?'

'Some day you won't, if you go on taking such risks.'

'Don't say that.'

'I have to say it. Who else will? They're happy and pleased now you're back, laughing at your antics. But a few hours ago they were afraid, and most were crying. They thought you'd been caught.'

'They should know better,' Miki said, on the defensive.

'I thought it too, Miklos. I was afraid every bridge had gone, and there was no way back. I worry because sometimes you're stupid. You get excited and show off.'

'Me?'

'Yes, you,' she insisted. 'You know your trouble, don't you?'

'What's my trouble?'

'You think the Germans are all fools. And by now you ought to know they're not. If you go on believing that, someday you'll take one silly risk too many.'

Miki said nothing. He had decided, after the luck of finding the Franz Joseph Bridge still standing and pedalling thankfully across it, that the less she knew about the day's events the better. Ilona worried far too much for a girl of fifteen. He would never say so, but sometimes he felt she acted more like his mother than his sister.

'Are you going to tell me what really happened?' she asked.

He looked at her. Secrets between them were impossible. Only he would try not to mention how close the bullet had been – or that the grit from the Empress's statue had filled his eyes, and he would most definitely not mention it had made him wet his pants with sudden fear.

'A mad old German pastrycook chased me and tried to shoot me. Only he couldn't aim straight. I thought I'd have to swim the river – if I didn't freeze first. Then I had some luck – I stole the bike while the owner was saying his prayers. He certainly answered mine.'

He watched her face clear into a smile. She put an arm round him, and hugged him tight.

'You fool,' she said fondly. 'We love you, Miki. That's why we were all so worried and frightened. When people knew you were safe, they cheered. Most of the women cried again – and some of the men, too – but this time with relief and joy.'

'The men cried?'

'Quite a lot of them. Like Mr Gutinsky. All the old ones care for you. I hardly know how to say this,' she paused and took his hand, fumbling for words, 'but you seem to give people a feeling of hope. It's very important – to have hope. We've got precious little else.'

'I don't do much,' he said, embarrassed and unsure how to respond, but inwardly proud.

'You do,' she said. 'You steal food for us, take risks, you're bright and cheeky, and you know all the latest rude anti-Nazi jokes. You make us laugh. Make us feel alive. You scavenge books to read, and batteries for the radio, and pamphlets that tell us the war might soon be over. And you do mad things like insult Germans.'

'Which is stupid, I know it is. But sometimes I can't help it.'

'Sometimes we need it. Only be careful. Without you, my Mikloska, I don't know if we would survive.'

Mikloska. It was a term of endearment she rarely used, and hearing it he felt a wave of affection for her that caused him to swallow a lump in his throat and brought him close to tears.

'You would, Ilona. You'll survive.'

'We both will. We have to. We're all that's left. No family; no aunts, uncles, cousins, just us. We'll find somewhere else, a better place than this, and start again.'

'Where?' Miki asked.

'America? Canada?'

'You think they'd let us in?'

'They must.'

'I don't think so,' Miki said, with the insight of a fourteen-year-old, wise in the ways of living by his wits.

'Of course they must. We helped get food to the partisans,' Ilona argued, 'so that makes us allies of the British and Americans. And it can't be long, only a few weeks before they get here.'

'They won't come.' He knew that for certain.

'What do you mean, they won't? The English short wave on the BBC said the Allies will liberate all of Europe. Liberate means to set free. Of course they'll come.'

'Why do you believe what you hear on the BBC? The Russians will be here first. Everyone, every single person except you, knows they'll win and take over in Hungary. It's only a matter of days. When they do, we'll become Russian.'

'Not me,' she insisted. 'I won't be a Russian.'

'We'll have no choice,' Miki said.

He looked up at the canopy of sky. The clouds had shifted, and a faint crescent moon shed light on their rooftop. Dew was falling like soft rain; it was growing cold. They could see the street below, the wreckage of burnt-out vehicles stripped of seats and tyres, overturned and vandalised. All the buildings that remained standing lacked windows; hardly an apartment or a house had any panes of glass in this most bitter of winters.

Miklos shivered. Ilona nodded, acknowledging the cold. Even wearing all the clothes they possessed, it was no longer possible to ignore the freezing temperature. They would have to go below, back to the cramped room and the people they lived with. Five others in their hiding place, eight in the room adjacent. All older, frightened people. He and Ilona were the only young ones among them. In another time, in a different place, they might have been considered as children. But not here. Perhaps it was why they so often came up to the rooftop, where they could make plans for the rest of their lives like real children, and dream their dreams. It would be nice to think they could some day go to America or Canada, but there was no point in make-believe.

Or was there? If Ilona believed, then anything was possible.

He gazed fondly at his sister, at the outline of her face with its fine almost Slavic cheek bones. Her dark hair was cropped short, but he knew it could be long and wavy if she were allowed to grow it. Here it was not safe to have long hair or to be pretty. *She could be beautiful one day*, he thought, *if anyone ever gives us a chance to live.*

The city of Pest was recaptured in late January, and two weeks later came the last battle for the inner heart of Buda. Trying to break out westwards and flee towards the safety of Austria, the remaining German troops were caught, cut off, and brutally massacred. The slaughter took place in the neighbourhood of the once-elegant Castle Hill, within sight of the ruins of the citadel and the palace of Archduke Joseph, and lasted for two savage days and nights.

Afterwards the citizens emerged from the houses and cellars.

Ready to celebrate the end of occupation and a year of German terror, they found a new nightmare. Wild mobs of Soviet soldiers rampaged behind the fighting troops, and pillaged their way through the twin cities. Drunk and violent, totally out of control, they pack-raped girls and women no matter how old or young, shot people on sight, or threw them into public cages as collaborators. The soldiers broke into homes, looted the contents, then set the houses on fire. Citizens were stopped on the streets, forced to strip naked and robbed of their clothes. The same indignity could as easily happen in shops and cafes. A wristwatch or the cheapest piece of jewellery became dangerous to wear. The city boulevards were unsafe by day, and empty and lifeless at night.

As civilian administrators took control, and the Soviet official bureaucracy began to rule the country, an illusory attempt was made to restore normality. *All those between the ages of eight and sixteen will report to their nearest school, and be enrolled.* The notices were distributed widely, tacked up in public places, and impossible to ignore.

'We can't stay here,' Miki said. 'It'll get worse.'

'We can't go,' Ilona said.

'We must.'

'Go where?'

'Anywhere.'

'Miki, think about it. East is Russia, west there's Austria and Germany. And the war with Germany still isn't over.'

'South, to Yugoslavia.'

'That's hopeless.'

'Not if we can find a partisan group.'

'The partisans are fighting each other. In the north, Ukraine and Slovakia, the Nazis are in control. Everywhere around us is too dangerous.'

'We must get out of this country,' he insisted.

'We can't. The war may go on for months yet, even longer. Now the BBC Radio says the British and Americans are only halfway to Berlin. You want to risk being taken by the SS? Miki, be sensible.'

They argued about it for most of the night, and by morning Ilona had prevailed. They decided to be sensible.

'Remember,' the teacher said, 'that you are an inferior Magyar race. Your speech, Finno-Ugric, is the language of peasants. I intend that you will all learn to speak in Russian.'

There was silence in the classroom. The schoolteacher cast his gaze across the assortment of students, all sizes and ages from eight years old to sixteen, and it lingered on the slim figure of the girl in the front row, the one who excited him. He knew little about her, except that her first name was Ilona, and he fully intended that before long he would have her naked in his bed.

He needed some consolation for being ordered here to teach this bunch of orphans and misfits. And all because he spoke passable Hungarian. He had applied for a position at the Lenin Academy in Moscow, proudly listing his six languages, and instead the bastards had sent him to this slum in this third-rate country to teach these dregs. Little Ilona would have to provide solace for that.

The conquest of her would be easy enough. The pretext of adopting a favourite pupil, praising her work and giving her extra food rations was a tactic he had adopted in the past, and it had always proved infallible. It must happen soon, he decided, conscious of his own need and the outline of her young breasts beneath her shabby blouse.

'How can we learn Russian,' a boy's voice said, 'if we're so inferior? If we're a bunch of peasants?'

The teacher knew who it was without even looking.

'Stand up when you speak,' he shouted, and watched Miklos rise to his feet. There was always one in every class, a clown to whom the other children responded with laughter, and it was essential such behaviour be dealt with before it spread. He deliberately slowed his walk towards the boy to instil maximum fear in his victim. It was invariably effective, prolonging the impending moment of punishment, allowing the offender's imagination to run riot. At least it always had been until now. But this particular youth showed no trace of fear. His eyes looked bold with what seemed dangerously like derision as he watched the Russian approach. Surprisingly for his age, he was almost the same height as the teacher.

They stood facing each other.

'Name?'

'You know my name,' Miklos replied.

'Now let's see if you can remember it,' the teacher said, and waited for the expected laughter, but the class remained still and silent, unmoved by his sarcasm and watching the encounter.

'Ferencz. Miklos Ferencz.'

'So you're a peasant are you, Ferencz? A yokel?'

'I'm a Hungarian. You say we're inferior, but what are you? I'll tell you what you are, you Russians. Barbarians and liars.'

'What?' He felt utter disbelief. 'What did you say, boy?'

'You heard me. Liars.'

'You're insane! Retract and apologise. It might – just might – reduce your punishment.'

'Like hell I'll apologise. We all know you're liars. Everyone knows. You called yourselves our allies, but after you killed the Germans, you started to kill us. You promised life would be normal again, that we'd be free, which was another lie. Freedom doesn't exist anywhere under Soviet rule.'

'How dare you,' the teacher said. 'How dare you speak to me like that!' He glimpsed the alarmed face of the girl, Ilona, but before he could wonder why she was exhibiting such concern, his victim was talking again. Scornfully. Deriding him. Speaking as no brat his age had ever dared, fashioning words like poisonous barbs to attack him.

'Weeks ago we came out of hiding to greet your soldiers, to welcome them – believing all the things your radio told us, that they were friends. We brought them flowers and called them comrades and saviours. They trod on the flowers, and spat on our welcome. And then it began all over again, just like the Nazis – the same arrests, the torture, the rapes. If we're peasants, your people are pigs. Cruel and savage, like wild animals. And your kind, the scholars and teachers, are worse than the soldiers, because you pretend you're civilised. It's an insult to think you could teach us anything.'

The teacher could not believe he was hearing this. He realised to his horror that the class was applauding. *Actually applauding this attack on his people.* Using all his force, he slapped the boy's face. It was like a pistol shot, louder than if he had slammed his heavy ruler on one of their wooden desks, and he heard the collective gasp of indrawn breath with some satisfaction.

But he hardly had time to register this. A split second later the boy hit him back – hit him as hard as he could. The teacher felt the pain as his cheeks flushed and his eyes watered. He stepped backwards and almost fell, stunned by the blow, and with incredulity and outrage heard the class cheering and the shouts of encouragement.

'Hit him again. Hit, Miki. Hit him, hit him,' they chanted. The boy smiled, a cold and angry smile, but instead of attempting this he did the unexpected, lashing out with his foot, the cap of his boot sinking into the soft junction of the teacher's groin. The thrust of the pain was so intense the schoolmaster was rendered breathless, helpless. He doubled up, aware only of Miklos brushing contemptuously past him, the girl Ilona standing, the boy taking her hand and the pair of them running from the classroom together, while the rest of the students clapped and cheered his downfall.

'Come back,' he shouted vainly, and the children, recognising his ineffectual anger, banged their desks and shouted with laughter, creating uproar.

'You bunch of ignorant Hungarian bastards,' he yelled at them in Russian, but they paid no heed, for they did not know or care what he might be shouting in his own strange language. He moved painfully to the window, trying not to hold his injured testicles or show the extent of his agony.

'You bitch,' he yelled at their retreating figures. 'You filthy cheating bitch.'

The fury he felt at the boy's attack was as nothing to the rage caused by the girl's betrayal. For she had betrayed him. He had made his feelings plain – for weeks now she could hardly have been unaware of this – yet she had chosen instead to escape with this delinquent.

There was no-one to tell him they were brother and sister.

He could not telephone the police to stop them, for the line was still out of order. It was typical of this place. However, he would send an urgent message to the local commissar to contact the State Security Office, and broadcast their descriptions. The hunt would be thorough. Those who insulted authority must be taught a lesson. It was pointless to run, as they would very soon find out. The borders had been shut tight for weeks, and they could not possibly escape.

Somewhere in the dark, a man coughed. His cigarette glowed as he inhaled, then he flicked the stub and they watched it arc and drop into the water, extinguished and swept away in the narrow stream. A dog barked in the distance. A field telephone rang. It was answered by a voice inside the hut, where they could see lights and the reflection of a fuel stove and the warmly clad figures of other border guards. It was only an outpost; further down the stream would be a main barracks where the guards lived and the tracker dogs were kept. Like the hut near them, it would be within the high perimeter fence of barbed wire. The wire was only fifty metres away from where they stood, but they knew it was electrically alarmed, and the approaches to it were boobytrapped with landmines. The farmer had told them this – about the alarms and the mines – after giving them food and letting them sleep in his hay shed. In the morning he had drawn them a map of the area, but reiterated his warning that there was no way through, not here. Not if they wanted to stay alive.

The guard stamped his feet and swung his arms vigorously

to ward off the cold. They realised he had propped his rifle against a tree in order to do this, but he was at least six metres from where they were standing, and it would be impossible to seize the gun before he grabbed it and started shooting. It was a wonder, despite them remaining motionless in the thick foliage, that he had not already sensed they were there. He had been little more than a breath away, at least twice in the past hour.

It had been ten days. Sleeping in ditches and tracts of forest during daylight, moving slowly westward by night, wondering if the rumours they had begun to hear – that Hitler was dead and the German army had surrendered – might possibly be true. They could risk talking to few people, and no-one they asked was sure. Twice, apart from the friendly farmer, they were given food and water, the rest of the time they had to steal it. Sometimes, when they ventured near the main road, army vehicles passed. Once a group of Russian soldiers in a truck pulled up and emptied their bladders at the side of the road, while they made noisy and raucous jokes in their own language. They aimed their streams of urine towards a clump of bushes down the embankment, unaware of the hidden, frightened and drenched children on whom they were pissing.

As it became more dangerous, and it seemed certain they would be caught by a stray patrol or blunder into one of the random checkpoints, they tried to keep their fear at bay by making plans for the future. If it was not to be America, Miki said, he favoured Israel. They'd all heard, long ago in the ghetto, that the British were leaving Palestine and there would be a Jewish state. Perhaps, perhaps not, Ilona argued; we've been hearing talk of a Jewish state since we were babies. Their first real choice had always been America, and the better they spoke the language, the better their chances of acceptance. For this reason she insisted they talked only in English, and told him she had found out that Ilona when translated meant Helen. They began to call each other Helen and Michael.

A match flared as the border guard lit another cigarette. A voice called an order, and he answered. He stamped out the cigarette with a muttered curse, and moved away downstream. They heard him work the bolt of his rifle as he went. It was time. They had only a few hours before dawn, and there would not be another chance.

From the map the farmer had drawn, they knew the stream originated in the mountains high above them, and descended steeply down through the pine forest. When the snows thawed in the spring it became a fierce torrent, too deep and dangerous to cross. For this reason there were no landmines or electrified fences way up there, but to reach the narrow causeway where a crossing might be possible, they had to make their way upstream for almost two kilometres. Until the mountain snow thawed, it was possible to walk in the river itself, which would be less than waist high – it was the quickest way – although the water would certainly be freezing, the farmer had promised that.

For the rest of it, he said he could only guess. He pointed out that they got no local weather news now, not on the state-controlled radio. The winter had been long and bitter, the spring was late. The snows might have begun to melt in the past day or two; if they had, it would unleash a deluge, a flash flood, and should they be caught by this, they might not have time to climb out and would very likely drown. But it was the only way to cross; there was no other.

Michael took her hand. They moved carefully through the bushes and found the bank that led to the stream. They slid down it into the swirling water and thought their hearts might stop as the icy cold enveloped them.

PART ONE

1947–1951

Chapter 1

Last night he dreamed of it again: the armoured cars and troop carriers drove in convoy through the orchard, down an avenue of flowering fruit trees. Pink and white blossoms, like a delicate tapestry, filling the air with the fragrance of a spring day. In lush grass amid the rows of trees, tethered cattle grazed contentedly.

It was mid-April, 1945, and in two days' time he would be twenty-one years old. At home in the Weald of Kent, his old man would go down to The Oak and sink a few, and no doubt after a while declaim, 'For young Neil, on his twenty-first. Silly bugger could've stayed home on the farm, been in a protected occupation, instead of riskin' gettin' his balls shot off, fightin' for King and country.' And his cronies would all line up for another round of bitter, raise their glasses, and drink to Neil coming home with all his equipment intact, so some day there'd be a grandson.

Neil smiled. There had been times in these past two years when his dad was right. He had joined in haste, to escape the drudgery of their meagre small-holding, but often, in the bitter fighting across France and Germany, he would have gladly settled for the chores on their Wittersham farm. As if in memory of that, he could hear what seemed to be a tractor cutting hay in a distant field beyond the orchard; it might easily have been Kent, and the feeling of rural tranquillity in this pastoral landscape suddenly made the war seem far away.

It felt unreal.

There had been no fighting now for two days, forty-eight rare and precious hours in which they had killed no-one, encountered no enemy, heard no gunfire; heard nothing except the same recurrent rumours that a cease-fire was imminent. If it made them all feel full of optimism, it also made them afraid. No-one wanted to be killed in these final hours – if they were to be the final hours – but there seemed little chance of violence or ambush here in this remote, idyllic place, which the war had somehow miraculously left untouched.

Bees were humming in the silence when the signal was given and the engines stopped.

Bees, on a barely warm April day?

'Something rather odd,' Major Lacey said.

They watched him clamber awkwardly down from his carrier. He was older than them, newly transferred from an ordnance depot and untested in battle. The hardened veterans had little time for him – despite their youth they were all trained commandos who had already lost three leaders since the Normandy landing – and there was muttering that if Lacey copped it, their next skipper would be straight from an entertainment unit or the catering corps. But for once, on this opinion of the major's, there was no dissent. They all knew it. There *was* something odd about the place. Nothing could be this peaceful.

The silence grew, became threatening, and the sound of the bees seemed more dominant.

'Bees?' Lacey wondered.

'They're not sodding bees,' said Sergeant-Major Owen Jenkin, who had once played rugby for Wales at Cardiff Arms Park.

And Neil knew with a feeling of foreboding that the sound he could hear was not the sound of a tractor cutting hay. It was heavier machinery than that.

They took their guns and began to move through the trees.

The fragrant smell became another kind of odour, difficult to identify. Strangely pervasive, it engulfed and seemed to assault them as they progressed to the far side of the orchard. Here the land was suddenly bare, stripped of vegetation as ruthlessly as a vast quarry, or an open-cut mine. At first glance it might have been an army camp. Or a makeshift factory complex, except that it was enclosed with jagged wire and overlooked by watchtowers. There were rows of wooden huts. And some people.

At least they looked like people. They neither turned to run away, nor came forward in welcome. Emaciated, vacantly staring, they seemed afflicted by a strange incomprehension, as if they were palsied or insane. Like figures in an alien landscape, without a reason to be there, showing no sign of emotion, no hope or expectation. *Almost*, Neil thought, *no sign of real life*.

As the troops drew closer, he and the others began to feel total disbelief. Most people were clad only in rags, and some were naked. They had thin, rickety legs – flimsy and unstable. Those without shirts revealed arms so skeletal it seemed impossible they could support even their frail hands and fingers.

It was a place of filth and death.

Some lay on the ground, in their own excrement, without the strength to pluck off the lice that swarmed all over them. There was such an air of demented hopelessness and misery that the soldiers could not speak at first; it was a horror greater than any they could have imagined, at least until they saw the pits beyond – a series of huge craters – and in every one of these were piles of angular limbs, gaping mouths and the staring eyes of the dead. Not a few dead, or a few hundred, but thousands. Thirty thousand, it would be confirmed later, waiting to be concealed by earth, hidden and interred in the crude mass graves. And God alone knew how many thousands more had already long since been burnt or buried.

The grisly sight of these stacks of bodies, these naked skeletons with skin that had once been human beings, flung casually on top of each other in this grotesque display of death, was more terrible than anything they could have imagined. The humming sound, they now realised, came from the swarms of scavenging blowflies, while predatory birds swooped and tore at the carcasses for traces of rotting flesh. The stench, which was now inescapable, enveloped them like some noxious and repugnant poison.

Major Lacey vomited noisily.

The distant tractor had stopped, and Neil could now see it was not a tractor but a massive bulldozer, the blade pushing rubbish into yet another and even deeper crater. The rubbish was a pile of bones, shaven skulls and bloodless faces, some twitching as if they might be still alive. The driver of the machine looked across and saw them. He started to climb down, his hands held high in an urgent signal of surrender. Alongside Neil, Sergeant-Major Jenkin whispered an obscenity in Gaelic. He raised his rifle and shot the driver. No-one made an attempt to stop him, or said a word of reproach.

The gaunt group of men and women, the ones who were not

too feeble to stand, watched this and showed no emotion. They waited as if expecting their own deaths. A photographer who had been attached to the unit since they crossed the Rhine started to take pictures of the piles of dead, and then turned his camera on the survivors. They seemed to hardly notice or care.

'For God's sake,' a soldier said, 'do you have to do that?'

'Who's going to believe any of this if I don't?' the photographer replied.

'Neil?' Jenkin beckoned him aside. 'Can you find out who the hell they are?'

It was one of the few skills the army had taught him, apart from an ability to kill the enemy, but he was unsure whether he could handle this. 'Major Lacey speaks better German than me.'

'Lacey's still spewing his guts out. Though I can't say I blame him. Have you ever, in your bloody life, seen anything like this?'

'Never,' Neil said. 'And I hope to Christ I never will again, until the day I die.'

He walked towards the group, who seemed to shrink from him. He gestured placatingly with his hands, like someone attempting to calm scared animals.

'Who are you?' Neil asked them, in his basic German.

'If they had anything to do with what happened, then shoot the fuckers,' said Richie Harris, one of the transport drivers.

'For God's sake, shut up,' Neil said angrily. He turned again to the listless group, and repeated the question. 'Who are you? What are you doing here?'

They seemed incapable of speech.

'Are you prisoners?'

'Yes,' one of the men answered.

'We helped,' another muttered, as if he was ashamed. 'They

gave us enough food to keep us alive, so we could bury the bodies. But there were too many dead, so they stopped the food.'

'How long since you had anything to eat?'

'I think . . . four days.'

'Five days,' a painfully thin woman corrected him.

'And water?' Neil asked her.

'No water. The guards turned off the only tap many days ago.'

'Why?'

'To make us die quicker,' she replied.

'And these guards? Have they gone?' he asked her.

'No.' She pointed to several brick barracks in the distance.

Neil told this to Jenkin, who dispatched a squad with Tommy guns to surround the barracks. His orders were explicit; kill anyone who attempted to leave. He told others to bring their water bottles, and make sure the inmates all got enough to drink, but not too much at first. Jenkin was nominally in charge, as their Major was traumatised and incapable. He shouted for a signaller to get the news through to battalion headquarters, and urgently contact the Red Cross. They needed a water cart, food, medicines, disinfectant to kill lice, and they desperately needed nurses and doctors, because in the Welsh Sergeant-Major's opinion there was typhus here, and perhaps typhoid fever, too.

'What else can we do?' he asked Neil.

'Food and water. Nothing else till the medics get here. Treat them gently. Help them lie down in the shade. These poor bastards are walking corpses. Some aren't going to last much longer.'

Neil gave his own water bottle to the woman.

'How did you manage?' he asked.

'Our own urine,' she said, 'until yesterday.'

He realised she was probably in her fifties, although so gaunt it was impossible to tell. Her head had been shaved, but tufts of it were beginning to grow again. The tufts were stark white. The skin of her neck and all down her arms were covered with suppurating ulcers.

'Just a mouthful,' he said. 'There'll be more later.'

She sipped and held the water in her mouth, as if treasuring it, before she swallowed. Then she handed back the canteen and smiled.

For an astonishing moment, the smile almost made her beautiful.

'What's your name, Madame?' he asked her.

'Madame?' she answered. 'Thank you for calling me Madame. My name is Sarah Weismann. I have been called so many things these past years, but never Madame. Not for such a long time.'

'You must rest, Mrs Weismann,' Neil said.

'Yes,' she nodded. 'What's your name, English soldier?'

'Neil Latham.'

'Thank you, Neil Latham,' she said, quietly. 'It is good to know that kindness still exists in the world. Some humanity survives.'

'Not over there,' Neil said, indicating the brick buildings from which uniformed SS guards were emerging, surrendering to the squad with Tommy guns.

'No,' she said. 'Not there. Would it shock you to know the women guards were the worst? The most evil and vicious?'

'After today,' Neil told her, 'I don't think anything could ever shock me again.'

~

Ambulances were on their way. A doctor arrived and began to paint crosses on the foreheads of those he thought had any chance of survival, provided they were removed from the rancid and insanitary huts. He advised the soldiers to give them tiny amounts of food and sips of water. Their stomachs could not tolerate more. After starvation for so long, too much food could burst their fragile intestines, and too much water might choke or drown them.

As if in confirmation of his prediction, sixty died during the next hour, and others kept dying constantly throughout the day. It seemed to Neil some had only waited for rescue before giving up the struggle to live. But, extraordinarily, Mrs Weismann endured, and sat covered by a blanket the rescuers provided, watching what happened.

The guards showed no contrition. They were soldiers, they asserted, members of the elite *Waffen-SS*, responsible only to the *Reichsfuhrer*, obeying his orders. They had their papers of authority. The women camp guards, many of whom were unpaid volunteers, also said they were simply doing their duty. Their duty was the business of extermination in accordance with the wishes of their leaders. Jenkin instructed his men to hold their fire – no matter what their feelings – but if any of these bastards, male or female made an attempt to escape, they were to be shot. In the legs first, he said clearly, asking Neil to carefully and accurately interpret this, then a bullet in the guts so they would die slowly and very painfully.

Jenkin was consumed with a cold rage. He told Neil to make other announcements. First and most importantly, there was an urgent need to bury the bodies, because of the spreading threat of typhus. The SS were to complete the task they had forced the starving inmates to do; they would begin immediately to drag the rotting corpses to the mass graves. They were ordered to remove their death's-head badges, their medals, caps, tunics, and all emblems, and throw these into the pits with the dead. When they protested they were prisoners of war, and entitled to be treated as such, and that these people were just Jewish criminals, Jenkin took a Tommy gun and began to shoot in the earth around their feet. Spurts of dust encircled the alarmed guards. They backed away from the fusillade, but found themselves surrounded by more allied troops. Minutes later, stripped of their insignias and all the trappings of power, they were carrying dead bodies to the pits. Other units and officers arrived, but no-one made an attempt to countermand Sergeant-Major Jenkin's order.

All that day the commandant and his *Waffen-SS* force were made to haul the carcasses and human remains into the mass graves. Then floodlights arrived, and they were told to continue. When they protested, claiming they were hungry, the barest ration of food or drink was given to them. The local burgermeister and his town council were sent for, and told to observe what they had allowed to happen in their jurisdiction. They stood in an uncomfortable line, trying to pretend they had known nothing, and swore they had always believed this to be a prison farm. Later on, various district businessmen and dignitaries were drafted in to witness what had been done in their name.

'We're innocent,' they complained heatedly to Neil. 'If only we'd known this . . .' He ignored them, waiting with Mrs Weismann, concerned for her and trying to persuade the doctors to remove her to hospital. But the few doctors available had no time to spend convincing one stubborn woman.

Some of the female guards were soon exhausted and sickened by what they were being made to do. They began to show distress. Many collapsed in tears, and those surviving prisoners strong enough to stand and witness this, cheered the sight. Others, stricken by a deeper anguish, could only gaze at this phenomenon with a quiet satisfaction.

At times it seemed to Neil there would never be sufficient pits or enough earth to cover the dead. The threat of typhus meant all the survivors must be washed and cleansed of lice, which terrified them, for cleansing was synonymous with gas jets and mock shower rooms where people were herded to die. Eventually the SS, stripped of all their arrogance and looking sick and haggard, were taken from the site in trucks to be imprisoned and face trial for war crimes and mass murder. By then, with most of Germany overrun by armies converging on Berlin, it was confirmed that this was no solitary camp, not some terrible aberration run by a sadistic commandant, but that throughout the Reich and its occupied territories there were more than three hundred such extermination centres.

During all this time, Sarah Weismann refused to leave.

'Please,' he begged her.

'When it's over,' she said.

When it was over, the thousands of unnamed dead covered by earth, they began to burn the camp. While they did, Sarah Weismann asked him to accompany her. They went to one of the huts, as the arson squad spread fuel and prepared to direct flamethrowers onto the gasoline.

'Get her out of here,' they warned.

'Ask them to give me one minute,' she said to Neil, and went inside the wooden prison barracks. It stank of filth and disease.

On either side were narrow tiers of wooden shelving, like planks. There were frayed and ragged scraps that had once been blankets, chewed by rats and crawling with insects and lice. They stopped by one of the cramped shelves, and she pointed to a space above their eye level.

'I slept up there,' she said. 'It was always difficult to climb up and down, and in the last weeks we didn't bother. We lived in our own dirt. There was no room to turn over without the risk of falling, and in winter the cold and damp made it impossible to sleep.'

'Dear God.' He shook his head, unable to comprehend it, and she took his hand. Her fingers, no heavier than a child's, clung to him.

'They didn't just want to kill us, you see. They wanted to destroy every Jew's faith in themselves. Our belief in ourselves as human beings. When you're whipped, made to run naked or raped at the whim of some creature; when you're deprived of food until you ache with hunger; when men and women are made to squat and perform their functions in front of each other like beasts, you slowly lose all the will to live. All you want is a speedy and painless death.'

'You didn't,' Neil said, feeling the awful sense of desolation she must have suffered here.

'I wanted to die just as much as the others,' Mrs Weismann said, 'but someone had to stay alive, if only to remember her.'

'Remember who?'

She beckoned him. At the end of the hut, beneath the lowest shelf was a bundle of rags. Before he knelt to remove them, the smell of death warned him. The body must have been lying there for over a week, but it looked preserved, almost human. There was the usual yellow waxen pallor of starvation. The woman – for it was a woman, he thought – looked wizened and aged.

'Who was she?' he asked. 'Friend?'

'No. Family.'

Her mother, he thought, but had no time to say so.

'My daughter,' she said. 'She was seventeen years old.'

He remembered trying to answer, and being unable to speak.

She had taken his hand again, more gently this time. She was dignified, somehow retaining her composure, eyes pleading with him to leave the prison hut and let them burn it, allow her child to be cleanly cremated instead of flung like a helpless figurine into a mass grave full of strangers.

He woke with sweat soaking him, weeping as he saw the flames engulf the wooden prison hut, hearing a voice trying to calm him.

'For God's sake, Neil, what is it? Are you all right?'

He felt the warmth of soft breasts, arms tight around him, as she tried to comfort him. He realised it was Caroline, and they were in bed together for the first time; each supposedly visiting friends in London, but in fact spending the weekend in the picturesque old port of Rye, in a room of the Mermaid Inn. He hastily mopped his eyes as she leaned out to switch on the bedside lamp. It was still night, and nothing moved outside their window on the cobbled streets.

'You were in a state. Shouting something about a fire. What happened?'

'A bad dream,' he said. She was a nice girl; they worked in the local bank together, and found each other attractive – which was why they were here – but this was not something he could talk about. 'A nightmare,' he added, 'something that happened in the war.'

'The war's been over for two years,' she said.

Not this, Neil thought. *This will never be over.* He felt the chill of the sweat that drenched his body, and saw the flames consume the hut, and with it the wasted old woman who was Sarah's daughter.

Chapter 2

The only sound was the rhythm of the diesel engines, for the people on the crowded deck had all been warned to remain silent, and there was a hush over the entire ship. A hush and a tense anticipation. They were so close; success lay somewhere in the darkness beyond the bow, and the thought of it ran through them like an electric current, fusing them in a common excitement; the old men and women who had never thought to see this place; families who had sold everything they owned or borrowed all they could, mortgaging their lives to be here; eager children without qualms, for their parents had promised them that this was indeed the promised land.

Just two more hours and they would be safely through the blockade, and there would be small boats waiting off the coast, outside Gaza, fishing boats and ferries arranged by the Haganah to take them ashore. Difficult to believe there were nearly two thousand people aboard the battered old freighter. Helen thought of the turmoil if the weather had been unkind, and felt glad it was a calm, peaceful night, and the sea all the way from Brindisi in Italy had been like a millpond.

A millpond, she thought, and smiled.

'What's funny?' muttered Michael, beside her on the deck.

'I'm starting to think in English,' she whispered. It was true. More and more lately, her inner thoughts were expressed in the only language she now allowed herself to speak, and some nights ago she had even had a dream in which she, and other people whose faces she could not remember, all spoke English. Someone had once said, when you dreamed in a language, you had begun to adopt it as your natural tongue.

Michael was unimpressed.

'Who needs it any longer? We're going to be Zionists, and so you'd better start to learn Hebrew,' he said, and grinned as he deliberately misquoted the words of the Passover service, 'Learn how to say *Tomorrow, in Jerusalem.*'

Someone near them hissed and told them to be quiet. The people packed around them were nervous; it was little wonder, for so many of them had waited for this moment, had dreamed of it all their lives. Others – like Michael and herself – had snatched the chance as an escape from the relentless months of being held in a series of oppressive Displaced Persons camps, classed as refugees with no rights, no real identity, and no hope of freedom or a passage on any of the ships leaving Europe for other parts of the world.

It had all gone so badly wrong.

Who would have guessed, that night long ago at the border? They had been so full of confidence. After managing to walk upstream through the chilled water, and reaching the causeway – no more than a rocky ledge where the stream tumbled from a cliff above, but which, in the full spring thaw with melting snow would be a raging torrent – after they had crossed it and climbed the mountainside, they realised they had actually done the impossible. Although there was no border post, no landmines or barbed wire to signal the frontier, the terrain itself and the look of the houses told them that they had found their way into Austria.

The euphoria was real, but short-lived. A few hours later the ordeal began. Believing the war was over, they had swiftly discovered it was not. Hoping to meet American or British troops, they had instead met a retreating German infantry patrol, and been caught and questioned. The patrol had no interest in them as human beings, they simply made it manifestly clear that they were going to kill Michael and then intended to rape Helen. Their eager faces, no longer lacklustre with fatigue and defeat, but glistening with sweat and lust assured her of that. And afterwards, she knew, they undoubtedly meant to kill her as well, when they had sufficiently indulged themselves and no longer had further use for her.

If it had not been for the strangest circumstance . . . she shook her head, her mind shying from all memory of it. The past – or at least some parts of it – were best forgotten. What had happened there in Austria – and afterwards – she could not bear to remember or allow herself to think about. Already her life had taught her that certain things had to be effaced from her memory. Or else one could not endure. Better to recall the bleak and joyless refugee camps, the endless queues for bare food rations and ill-fitting clothing, the months that turned to years of indifference and disappointment when they could find no country to take them, and the day when Michael had told her about the freighter that was soon leaving for Palestine.

'From Brindisi,' he'd said.

'Where?'

'It's on the east coast.' They were in a camp in southern Italy, outside Naples. 'Only about a hundred miles from here.'

'It might as well be a thousand.' She had felt angry with him, for bringing this news, for allowing her to feel this hope.

'Ilona,' he started to say, but she interrupted him.

'Helen. My name is Helen. And why do you tell me about ships, when you know we have no money to go to this place, Brindisi, let alone the fare to Palestine?'

'Don't worry about the fare to Palestine.'

'Of course I won't worry. What's the point of worrying, when it's impossible we can pay it?'

'It's arranged,' Michael said.

She stared at him. 'Arranged. How?'

'I went to see the Rabbi, and told him you were sick in the head, depressed and unhappy. So bad that I was troubled you might kill yourself.'

'*What?*'

'He was very concerned. He asked what could we do? Should we get a doctor? Put you in the psychiatric hospital?'

'Michael, how dare you . . .'

'I said no, not a hospital. Talk to the man from the Haganah. Ask when they next have a ship running the blockade to Israel, to find room for us. I said we all know they pay fares to send people there to work on a *kibbutz* – so if they send us, maybe you don't go nuts.'

'You're the one who's nuts,' she retorted, but could not help a glimmer of admiration for his effrontery. 'What did he say?'

'Told me he didn't know anyone from the Haganah, that they're all gangsters. I told him to please not give me the bullshit – his cousin Manfred Schwartz is in the organisation, and he's not a gangster, he's a patriot trying to help make the new Jewish state. And to stop telling lies and get us on a ship.'

'Miki,' she said, forgetting her own rule about Anglicising their names, 'you said that to a Rabbi?'

'We leave in a week,' Michael said.

'From Brindisi?'

'Yes.'

'But how do we get to Brindisi? We've no money.'

'We have money,' Michael said.

'Where did that come from? The Rabbi?'

'Him? Give us money? More chance he'd eat pork.'

'How much money?'

'Enough.'

'Michael, how much?'

'A hundred American dollars. We can go by train to Brindisi, and arrive in Palestine with some money still in our pockets.'

'Where did it come from, this hundred dollars?' Although she knew.

'I stole it,' he said. 'So don't ask more questions, then I don't have to tell you any lies.'

She sat in the dark, hearing the rhythmic diesel and feeling the heat, conscious of the sweat and tension of the people packed on the foredeck. There was hardly any room to move. The ship was badly overcrowded, for after embarking what seemed like a full complement of passengers at Brindisi, it had then stopped in Cyprus and taken on at least another five hundred people. The owners, whoever they were, might be trying to help the burgeoning state of Israel, but they were also doing their best to enrich themselves. God alone knew how many a ship like this should carry, but Helen knew it should be less than half of the number aboard. Some, who could afford it, had paid their own fares; others were sponsored by the Jewish agency, and a few by the Zionist military organisation in Palestine known as the Haganah.

In Hebrew, she knew, the word meant defence. The existence of this secret army was at first tolerated by the British who controlled the territory by mandate, because members of the Haganah had fought with them against the Germans. But as tensions grew and the situation deteriorated, with Britain protecting her own interests in oil and siding with the Arab League – imposing a strict prohibition on further Jewish immigration from Europe – the Haganah had begun to retaliate, attacking British bases, derailing trains and dynamiting bridges. They were less fanatical than the *Irgun Zvai Leumi* or the Stern Gang, but the reprisals did not discriminate. There were mass arrests. Jewish dissidents were ejected from their homes, and the British Treasury confiscated bank accounts.

Irgun extremists blew up the King David Hotel in Jerusalem. In response, the British drove three trucks loaded with dynamite into the city centre, and destroyed an entire street of shops and apartment buildings. Their commanding general issued a calculatedly insulting order, forbidding fraternisation of his troops with any Jews, declaring it would 'punish them in a way this race dislikes more than any other, by striking at their pockets and showing our contempt for them'.

The United Nations General Assembly declared that such provocative anti-Semitism did little to enhance a peaceful solution, and the commander of the occupying force should stick to military matters and stay out of political policy. The Stern Gang reacted predictably to the affront and ambushed a platoon of Fusiliers. On either side, the numbers killed began to run into hundreds.

In their remote and cheerless camp, a former Italian army barracks inland from Naples, this news of the accelerating conflict was common knowledge, digested and argued about daily. It was invariably garnered by Michael, who had a network of informants; delivery men, the guards, even the nurses in the barracks hospital found time to read him items from the Italian newspapers, and occasionally were able to pass on copies of the American army paper, *Stars and Stripes*. He was a familiar figure there, collecting a few lire for his information, using the money to buy cigarettes on the black market, which in turn were like currency and could be traded for extra food.

They will miss him, Helen thought, and realised by now that over a week had passed and they would both have been missed – listed as having departed without permits. The appropriate initials D.W.P. would be duly noted beside their names, and no doubt the authorities would express relief that two more of their problems had vanished without a trace, and with any luck would not return. But their fellow refugees would certainly miss her buoyant brother, and regret his abrupt departure. Even at his age, Michael was a natural leader; he was often the one chosen to head their troubled delegations because he had energy and the assurance and courage to ask for extra blankets and to voice complaints about the conditions that were sub-standard in so many of the camps.

She felt his shoulder against hers, heard the steady sound of his breath, and realised he was fast asleep. She felt a wave of affection.

He'd stolen the money to get them aboard this ship.

He'd confronted a Rabbi, giving them this chance.

It was not, never had been, her first choice to come here to this turbulent new nation. But she would not tell him that. Could never tell him. So many times since they had crossed the Hungarian border he had kept them alive, never mind how. It was rarely by legal means, but that was the kind of world they had inherited. She very much doubted if she would have survived, had it not been for her brother. He wanted to find a new life in Palestine; she would not disappoint him by trying to reject this aspiration.

She slipped an arm around him, to stop him from being jolted as the ship seemed to hit some unexpected turbulence, then the beam of searchlights came on, blinding her, and a harsh metallic voice shouted at them from somewhere beyond the freighter's bow.

'Stop engines.'

For a moment nothing happened. Except for the beat of the diesels. It seemed as if everyone held their breath.

'STOP YOUR FUCKING ENGINES.'

People stood up on deck. They started to scream. The diesels slowed, then gradually stopped until there was only the tidal swell slapping against the hull of their ship, and the first pandemonium faded to the frightened cries of children asking what was happening.

The magnified voice seemed to eliminate all distance between the vessels, as it ordered the Italian Captain to turn about. Behind the blazing searchlights they could see the outline of the British frigate, and way beyond that, the faint hint of coastline and the first flush of dawn across the land.

'Shit,' said Michael, who had woken in a daze, 'over there is Palestine.'

'Start your engines again. Turn and head for Cyprus.' The accent was British public school, and Royal Navy. 'Start the bloody engines, you Italian prick.'

A moment later there was the sound of gunfire, and a shell exploded on the port side of the freighter. As hundreds of voices started to scream in terror, another shell landed equally close on the starboard side.

'Do as you're told. Head for Cyprus, you dago.' It was the same voice, but with a snarl in it. 'Turn, or our next shot will sink your ship and kill the lot of you.'

There was one moment of indecision, when it seemed as if everything in the world had stopped. Even the flow of the tide, and the frightened gasps of the children. Then the diesel engines grumbled and picked up rhythm. Helen and Michael stood on deck, hampered by the crowd and unable to move; the hundreds of people around them were held frozen like frightened animals in the fierce glare of the lights, until the unwieldy freighter turned and headed north-west across the Mediterranean, towards Limassol in Cyprus. Another naval vessel moved out of the dark, showing its deck lights now, as it moved astern to ride escort.

'Ilona,' Michael was staring towards the waking dawn light. 'That really is Palestine.'

'Yes,' she said. 'We nearly got there.'

The man from the American embassy was neatly dressed in a grey suit and wearing what appeared to be a college tie. A miniature flag with stars and stripes stood on his desk, as if to establish beyond doubt the country he represented. He was polite and compassionate, which Helen knew was a bad sign. Michael would realise that, too. It was to be one more futile interview, with yet another contrite official.

'If I had my way,' he attempted a smile as he said this and her heart sank, 'if I had my way in this matter, you'd be on a ship to the dear old US of A with the very next batch of refugees out of here. But we keep running up against this same problem.'

'What problem?' Michael asked, trying to remain calm and control his resentment, although she knew this was difficult. 'Why should there be a problem? You say you'd like to send us to your country, and we want to go there. So how can there be a problem?'

'I'm told that has already been explained to you.'

'Not properly.'

The American's scarcely suppressed sigh, his shrug, seemed to suggest they were being childishly obtuse. He was a well-groomed man in his thirties. His desk was as orderly as his appearance. Manila folders were placed on it in tidy alignment, the day's files awaiting his attention. The one spread open in front of him, growing thicker with each succeeding year, was theirs.

'We have long waiting lists, a great many more people seeking asylum than we can accommodate. So Congress has decided to enforce stricter guidelines. You and your sister fail on all counts.'

'We fail, but you're not willing to tell us why,' Michael said. 'To you, we're just numbers. Nuisances.' His despair expressed itself in growing hostility, and the official tried not to show annoyance.

'My assistant, Miss Barker, has tried to explain the situation to you. She tells me you're not prepared to listen, or be cooperative.'

'That isn't true.' Helen knew she must intercede, before this man lost patience and terminated their file. That would be the end of it. 'Your assistant does very little, except treat us like children. Well, we may be young, but we haven't been children for a long time. She can't seem to realise that. Perhaps for people who weren't there, it's not possible to understand.'

'Miss Ferencz . . .' he tried to interrupt, but she was determined.

'Let me speak, please. And listen to me. Try to realise what it's been like. We were turned out of our home, forced to leave our village, they took our parents to one of their death camps. We've never been able to find out where. Even after that, we managed to live through the Nazi occupation; we helped the partisans fight, and we escaped from the communists when they tried to force us to their ways. Did your blonde assistant ever tell you that, or did you have more interesting things to talk about with each other?' She saw the man's face flush. It was well known in the camp that they were lovers. 'Did she say that we almost drowned in a freezing river, escaping from the Russians? And that we crossed into Austria a week before the war ended, and were caught by the Nazis?'

'Believe me,' he said, 'this is all in your records. I'm aware of the hardships you've experienced, but it makes no difference. The United States will accept Displaced Persons, but there are restrictions.'

'No Jews,' Michael said.

'That's not strictly correct,' the American said carefully.

'Everyone knows it,' Michael retorted.

'Then everyone has been misled. These camps are prone to rumour, and information of this kind is often distorted.'

'No Jews,' Michael insisted again, and the man behind the desk began to lose his composure.

'You're confusing two issues,' he said forcefully. 'Congress has passed a bill to allow the admission of almost a quarter of a million displaced people. But the bill excludes Jews, *and others* – it excludes anyone who was not in a camp or had been granted official refugee status by the year 1946. This has given rise to the preposterous speculation that Jewish people are unwelcome. Which is quite untrue.'

He sounded as if he was reciting a doctrine he had learned by heart. They made no response, and for the first time he seemed to be embarrassed. He looked down at their file. Helen suspected it was a ploy to avoid their gaze, and anticipated what he would read there.

'We did apply for refugee status. It's in our papers. We had already filled in application forms for entry to America.'

'That's noted in here,' he agreed. 'You were turned down.'

'And now you're turning us down again? But still not giving us a reason why.'

'The reason you were turned down the first time is simple. It was 1947, the Cold War. Anyone who came from Eastern Europe had to be investigated. The last thing the American people wanted to import was a bunch of communists.'

'We're not communists,' she said.

'It appears not,' he said, 'but these inquiries take time. And you didn't have the patience to wait.'

'We had the chance to board a ship trying to run the blockade to Israel. As all we'd got from the American mission was months of delay, we had to make a choice.'

'The wrong one,' he commented, and Helen looked away, not wanting to let him see that she agreed, that secretly she knew it had been a foolish mistake.

Yet they had been so close to escape. It was still a vivid scar in her mind, the overcrowded freighter packed with frightened people, the British frigate with spotlights dazzling them, the loud hailer directing their captain to turn about or his human cargo would be killed. She could still hear the panic and screaming as the shells landed on either side – if they were really meant as warning shots they were intimidatingly close – and the cold British voice again, ordering the ship to turn away or this time it would be sunk.

The captain had had no option. The vessel had returned to Cyprus. In a Nicosia court they were charged with being illegal immigrants, suspected associates of Haganah terrorists, in possession of forged papers. No-one seemed able to agree on what should be done, and there appeared no hurry to reach any conclusion on their future. After six months they had managed to escape, aided by anti-British Cypriots, and with their help had stowed away on a tramp steamer, without even knowing where it was going.

It was with a feeling of despair and futility that they wound up in Brindisi again, and from there to yet another camp. It had been that way ever since. One camp after another. Without the necessary papers or sufficient money to bribe their way out, they remained stateless and members of the culture which was now Europe's largest problem: Displaced Persons. It was sometimes hard to recollect that it was more than two years since that ship had been forced back within sight of a promise of freedom.

'Were you here when the war ended?' Michael asked him, and for a moment it seemed the American would ignore the question.

'No, I was in Washington DC,' he said eventually.

'Then you wouldn't have any idea what it was like. We'd been told everything would change after the fighting was over. But nothing did. We were told you'd beat Germany, then march through the rest of Europe to free Poland and Hungary, and all the places Hitler had conquered. But you didn't do that. The Russians wouldn't let you. So people like us couldn't go home. There was no food, no-one to help us. Too many of your soldiers and administrators were too busy helping themselves – making a fortune on the black market. We were always being given papers to fill in and told to wait our turn, but there were thousands waiting. People said it would be a year, then longer. Perhaps two more years. So after being treated like shit for so long, you can't blame us for taking a chance on Palestine . . .'

'Miki, stop it,' Helen said firmly in Hungarian. 'He doesn't give a damn. His job is only to get rid of us, so let's not waste our time.' She glimpsed a fleeting reaction from the man behind the desk, and wondered if he spoke their language. She no longer cared.

'Just a moment,' the American said as they rose. 'You asked why you were turned down again. At least I can clarify that for you. It's not personal. Not discriminatory. The Congressional bill restricts the intake of refugees to skilled tradesmen and farmers. You have no skills or experience in anything.'

'Except thieving and staying alive.' Michael spoke bitterly in Hungarian, and this time she was sure the man understood. But he ignored the remark.

'That's why this application has been rejected. It's nothing to do with being Jewish. Nothing whatever.' Neither of them replied. It seemed to upset him, as if he was determined to convince them. 'Please, just listen to me. The countries who finance the International Refugee Organisation all feel the same. They only want industrial workers; labour for building roads, for railways and mines, people for the garment industry, even domestics. They don't want the very young, the sick or the old; they don't want teachers, doctors or intellectuals. In most countries those are precluded categories.'

'We hardly seem to belong to a category, do we,' Helen said sadly. 'We're the wrong race, wrong age, wrong in every possible way. Damaged goods that no country wants.'

'I wouldn't say that.' He was clearly uncomfortable, far more so with her dejection than Michael's anger.

'Oh, I would,' she replied. 'What are the words written on your famous Statue of Liberty? *"Give me your tired, your poor, your huddled masses yearning to breathe free."* Isn't that what it says?'

'Yes,' he answered, astonished.

'I studied it. Because one day I hoped to see the statue and read those words. But it seems as if we fail the test to breathe your freedom – on all counts.'

'I'm truly sorry,' the man behind the desk said.

'We don't want your sympathy,' Michael retorted. 'We'll find somewhere, some better place where we're allowed to live.'

'I hope so.'

He watched them leave.

'Goddammit,' he said after the door shut, gazing resentfully at the presidential photo of Harry Truman on the office wall. 'Why don't you and your lousy Congress do some of your own stinking dirty-work?'

Chapter 3

The rain fell interminably, and the whole countryside seemed to be in danger of drowning. Vast pools of water lay on the ground like lakes, while jeeps and trucks, with headlights switched on in the midday gloom, splashed past. Forlorn figures – a fortunate few of them huddled into raincoats and wellingtons – trudged between the buildings, mouthing curses as the vehicles drenched them.

What a bugger of a place, Neil thought, not for the first time, as he watched the rivulets streaming down his window pane. The rain had been torrential now for weeks, and his hut with a tiny bedroom and adjacent office was damp and beginning to smell of mould. The ground outside was a quagmire. Dark grey clouds crouched ominously over the surrounding hills, assuring the prediction of a further deluge. It was probably as well that Caroline had written to say her holidays had been postponed, for she would expect blue Italian skies, and any chance of that seemed unlikely. Though if she were here now the wet and melancholy atmosphere would not matter in the least; they would lock the door, climb into bed and have a rampant few days before leaving for a tour of Venice and Bologna. Cheer him up no end, it would.

He smiled at the thought, casting his mind back to their first time, the snug comfort of the Mermaid Inn, under an eiderdown with Caroline. There had been many similar nights since then. Strictly speaking, it was more often in hay barns, the backs of cars, or in the woods than between the sheets at the Mermaid because of the expense – but none the less erotic for all that. Gazing out the weeping window he thought with some nostalgia of her long legs wrapped tightly around him, and the way she climaxed with such exuberance. It could never be said Neil missed working in the bank counting other people's money, but he did miss Caro, although with his leave and her holidays they had preserved their relationship. Except this time a holiday had been postponed, and her letter had neglected to say why.

There was a distraction, a sudden disturbance outside. He saw a young couple, their clothes ill-fitting and ragged, jump back in alarm as a truck skidded dangerously and showered them with mud. The girl slipped and fell. The boy seemed attentive and concerned; he helped her to rise, then turned to yell angrily at the driver in what Neil recognised as highly colourful Hungarian profanity. He was about to call them and suggest they come into his hut where at least it was dry, but they had already turned and walked off into the gloom.

He returned to his desk and the pile of work that awaited him, abandoning the drab view. But today work was difficult. It was not only the wretched weather that made this refugee camp so different to his previous postings in Munich and Rome. The Milan Centre, situated north of the city's industrial wasteland, was a grim and depressing place inhabited by hundreds who had been homeless for years, an increasingly dispirited lost legion for whom the International Refugee Organisation had failed to find asylum. An air of apathy and pessimism was ingrained in this place. Neil's posting here was to be his last in Europe, after which a new job and a completely new life beckoned. That time was close, barely a month remained. The way he felt about those who ran this camp, it could not come quickly enough.

This all began with Sarah Weismann, he thought, *and in a way it was true.*

If they had lost touch after that first meeting, he would probably still be in the bank, might even be meeting Caro later to make love in the woods, or driving down to Hastings for fish and chips, and after dark to the golf club where their favourite nesting spot was the soft sandy bunker at the tenth.

But there had never been a chance they would not remain in touch, he and Sarah Weismann; the bond between them was stronger than that; it had been ever since the moment when he took her frail, wasted hand and watched the concentration camp hut burn, and her daughter's body inside, burning with it. He had waited while she said her prayers and mourned aloud in what he realised was Hebrew, then made her go to the field infirmary the medics had set up, persuading a doctor to treat her as a priority, while he used his influence with a nurse to give her extra vitamin pills. Later she was moved to the Royal Army Hospital, where only those with a chance to survive were taken.

Knowing she was indifferent about survival, he had asked Major Lacey for extra time to spend with her. They needed interpreters at the hospital, and he wished to volunteer. The Major, recovered from his collapse at Belsen, was less than agreeable. You're a commando, not a bloody male nurse, he told Neil, who reminded him the war was over and commandos were useless, a waste of time, whereas he might make a real contribution

54

at the hospital. Finally he went over Lacey's head to the Brigade Colonel, and became such a nuisance he was gladly given leave of absence.

All his days were devoted to making Sarah want to live. He encouraged her to talk about her daughter. Nothing was too painful to be discussed; he had asked several doctors about this, and one, a bluff and sensible general practitioner in civilian life, had suggested the only way to ensure sanity was to confront the madness – to articulate it – if she could find someone who could bear to listen.

I'll listen, Neil had said, and he did.

After she had told him everything about her daughter – the beatings to force her to volunteer as one of the commandant's rota of compliant lovers, the brutal mass rapes by the officers and guards that followed her refusal, the anguish of seeing her child growing visibly older in appearance each day, and hopelessly sick in her mind – after that, she spoke of the rest of her family. Her sister, who had escaped before the war to Holland, but was reported as being rounded up in Rotterdam and not heard of since. One cousin, who had been perceptive enough to leave Berlin after *kristallnacht,* when the SA storm troopers and the SS unleashed their terror, smashing Jewish windows and reducing city streets to rivers of glass. This cousin had managed to cross Belgium and reach England, where she hopefully still existed.

She spoke of friends who were dead, some by suicide, unable to face what they knew was coming. A niece who was no doubt alive, for she had survived by becoming an informer for the Gestapo. Oh yes, she told Neil when he expressed shock, there were some who bought their lives with the death sentences of others. She talked at length of her husband, who had been a dentist until he was forbidden to practise, and how two men from the local police who had been his patients came one night and accused him of hoarding gold that should have been used for filling teeth, and when her husband, confused and very frightened, protested that he did not know what they were talking about, they took him down to the *Polizeiamt* and tortured him. She had never been officially informed what happened next, but he had not returned, and through the strange network of disclosure that existed, the grapevine of hearsay, she finally found out the truth. Unable to tell them what he didn't know, he had been bludgeoned and kicked to death.

There were days when Neil thought he could no longer stand listening to any more horror, and as if realising this, she would talk of happier times, of her earlier married life and comfortable apartment adjacent to the Tiergarten, near the Unter den Linden, with its large rooms and high ceilings, and the grand piano her husband had bought her as a surprise on their tenth anniversary – which could not be a surprise at all, because the piano was too wide to fit into the elevator – and their windows had to be removed so it could be winched up by crane. She'd laughed, recounting the party that evening, and how she'd had to pretend to be suitably delighted when the piano was unveiled. Another day, in another mood, she told him of a former friend who had betrayed her, and made use of the racial laws to evict her from this same apartment.

In time, her meagre frame filled out. The frail features became almost normal, her fine bone structure revealing a delicacy it had been impossible to imagine. When her hair finally grew, he found her a new dress, borrowed a jeep and took her to the village. The owner of the only women's *salon*, nervously equivocal the moment he realised her background, claimed to have clients for the remainder of the day. Neil demanded to see his appointments book which disproved this, and told him to wash and fashion his friend's hair in whatever style she requested, and to make her look like a princess. He explained that his unit was conducting investigations into the local populace, especially those who knew about the camp and had thus knowingly connived at murder. Being aware that systematic killing was taking place and doing nothing was complicity, he told the apprehensive hairdresser, and said he would sit and wait until Madame Weismann pronounced she was satisfied, after which they would decide if the bloody barber deserved payment. On days like this, he was filled with rage that such people would avoid punishment and become part of the new Germany, enriched and nurtured by the Americans.

His fellow commandos could hardly be unaware of this strange liaison. Over a few drinks, they sometimes made oblique references to her as his old kraut auntie, which Neil felt able to deal with, until one night a corporal suggested he had an abnormal sexual attraction for this antique oddity. The corporal had tried to duck, then ended up in agony, unsure whether to clutch his painful groin or stem the flow of blood from his nose. The next day his nose was such a swollen landmark on his face that he was promptly christened Pinocchio. The platoon, for the rest of their tour of duty, recognised that Neil had embarked on some kind of private crusade and even the mildest teasing stopped.

The unit had eventually moved, but he used influence to remain at the hospital until Sarah was fit enough to be discharged. He borrowed a jeep and drove her across Hanover to

West Berlin. Her former apartment building by the Tiergarten was destroyed like so much of the city, but in time she found a suitable room in which to live. *It is small but clean, and has a bathroom on the same floor*, she wrote to Neil a few months later, and assured him she was lucky. In Berlin, any modest shelter was almost a luxury, and while there was talk of reparations for the loss of her home and her treatment in Belsen, she felt it would take a long time. They corresponded regularly. In later letters she told him the government had at last provided her with a tiny pension – she called it 'guilt money' – on which she could manage, and was glad Neil had found a suitable job in a bank, and who was this Caroline he had mentioned, and was there a photograph?

Visiting her in Germany afterwards, he had brought a picture of Caroline. She studied it carefully, and smiled approval.

'Nice looking,' she said in German. 'Very pretty, and a happy face. You and she would make beautiful babies.'

'Sarah,' he laughed in protest, 'we're not even thinking of marriage, let alone beautiful babies.'

'Who mentioned marriage? I'm sure that you could make babies with this girl – if you don't take good precautions.'

'You're a wicked woman,' he said with affection, assuring her they took precautions. And that it wasn't actually love, at least he didn't think so, but it was a love affair – his first real one. It seemed natural to be able to discuss this, although it was not a matter he would talk of with anyone else. Even his own family. Particularly his own family.

During these years, they continued to write to each other. Then, startlingly, on one of her visits to London to stay with her cousin who had survived the war, Sarah told him she was emigrating. She had applied and been accepted. It came as a complete shock to Neil.

'Emigrating? Where?'

'Australia.'

'It's so far,' he said, dismayed.

'Far from Germany, yes. Far from all those people who keep explaining to me how ashamed they feel. I don't want the burden of their shame.'

'But the fare – surely it's expensive for such a long way?'

'It's free. A migrant scheme,' she told him. 'At first they had doubts. They only want fit people who can work. Maybe I should apply to a Jewish charity? I told them I don't want charity – Jewish or Christian. I just want to be independent.' She laughed at his expression; he thought she suddenly seemed ten years younger with her excitement. 'So they gave me interviews, thorough medical examinations – and I passed. Fit and well! Imagine that! I leave from Bremerhaven in a few months' time – as soon as a ship is available.'

It was all arranged. He felt stunned, but tried not to show it.

'I may never see you again.'

'On the other hand,' she said, 'you might.' He remembered her studying his face with a quizzical look as he pondered this reply.

'How?'

'Are you happy working in the bank?'

He hesitated, then shook his head. He had expressed his discontent often enough in letters. 'You know I'm not.'

'You should leave it.'

'I keep telling myself that. And my parents keep telling me it's a good, safe job, and not to take risks with my life.'

'Is that how you want to live your life? Not taking risks?'

He didn't answer for a moment. The truth was, he had begun to feel trapped in a pattern that was becoming ominously stereotyped. Each morning, after an early breakfast at the farm with his parents, driving to work in the tiny Austin Six bought with his discharge pay; five and a half days a week behind the counter of the bank, greeting customers, carefully remembering their names, paying out or crediting their accounts, plus the obligatory chat about the weather.

'Beautiful summer we're having, sir.'

'Yes, but I expect we'll pay for it later.'

One always paid later, in England, for fair weather.

Of course, there was Caroline, but even that – the regular love-making, the weekly ritual of Saturday night at the cinema – even with Caro, for all the sensual delights, there was a sense of obligation, a feeling of future commitment. People were starting to assume they would soon tie the knot; his mother had begun to talk about glory chests and 'the day'. If he was to be completely truthful . . .

'Neil?'

He realised Sarah had been talking, and he had not listened.

'Sorry, I missed that.'

'You were dreaming.'

'I was thinking about risks,' he said.

'And I was telling you where to take them,' she smiled. 'I've been going to Australia House here in London, to read the newspapers and collect brochures. They're advertising for interpreters.'

'Not me,' he protested. She ignored this.

'To work for the United Nations Refugee Organisation in

Europe. You must be English-speaking with two other languages. I said I know a young man who speaks perfect German, and is also proficient in Italian.'

'Learning Italian,' he corrected her.

'A fast learner,' Sarah said. 'With a real gift for languages – which I imagine will be totally wasted at Barclays in Bexhill.'

The same thought had occurred to him, more than once. But he was still uncertain.

'You really are going there? To the other side of the world?'

'Yes, Neil.'

'Why?'

'Because it is the other side of the world. This side has too many memories. So before I'm old, I'd like to see the other side.'

He could recollect the conversation clearly. They had lunched at a Lyons Corner House while he tried to think what to do, and in the end had agreed to go with her to Australia House in The Strand, and afterwards he could make decisions. But he needed more time to think about it. It was apparent to him that he was not really adventurous. His only real adventure had been his time in the army. At the age of twenty-four, he did not have Sarah's capacity for taking chances with the future.

They caught a bus that took them past Charing Cross Station and the Savoy. At the last stop before Fleet Street they got off, crossed the road to the Aldwych and walked to a large building. Doric columns framed the entrance. There were brochures in the windows, with inviting images of landscapes, sandy beaches and a magical harbour.

'Shall we go in?' Sarah asked, and Neil felt as if his entire life had been directed towards this moment. It was hard to remember that four years ago she had been shaven and emaciated, a skeletal relic waiting for death in a concentration camp.

He had followed her inside, where she told a commissionaire, uniformed and wearing an impressive number of campaign ribbons, that she had brought her interpreter friend to see Mr Sinclair. The commissionaire smiled at her as if he knew her well and asked them to wait. He made a phone call, then directed them across the marble foyer and up a wide ornamental staircase. Sarah tapped on a panelled oak door, and from somewhere within a voice had invited her to enter.

His father led the way as they walked past the spring lambs, through the hop field, and paused, leaning on the stile with little to say to each other.

'So you're givin' it up? The bank?'

'Yes.'

'No reason? Just packin' in a good job? Chucking it, a job that would've been steady for the rest of your life?'

'I'm sorry,' he said inadequately.

'I never reckoned on you takin' over here,' his old man said, 'never saw you as a farmer. But tossin' in the bank. You were doing well, you said; told us they were even talkin' about promotion.'

'Yes, they were.'

'I jest don't understand you, Neil. Never have, son.'

'I know, Dad.' There was no anger; the fault was on both sides. They liked each other, but found it difficult to communicate.

'So what are you goin' to do, then?'

'Work in Europe at first. For a year or so.'

'What sorta work?'

'Interpreting for the International Refugee Organisation.'

'Jesus Christ, I thought you would've had a gutful of refugees and sodding Europe, in the war. Don't sound like much of a job.'

'It's what I want to do. After that – maybe see some more of the world.' He knew it was a lame reply, and saw his father shrug.

'Well, I s'pose it's up to you. Your choice, old son. But how does Caroline feel? I know your mum will be really choked – she'll reckon you're crackers.'

I've already been told that, Neil thought, but decided not to pursue it. His mother had expressed her disappointment forcibly: she had hoped for a wedding and warned him that if he expected Caroline to wait while he went off on this foolishness, he was being conceited and stupid. Neil was closer to his father, and wished he could find some simple way to explain. But he could hardly tell this kindly man – his dad – that this was all to do with a recurring nightmare, with a Jewish lady of great dignity, and the flames that had consumed her daughter in a wooden hut that smelled of death and shit.

The rain had eased slightly, and he made himself a cup of the bilious coffee the Milan Centre seemed to favour. The milk had gone sour, and there was no tea. The store which had exclusive rights to supply the camp had promised to send him tea bags, but no doubt the rapacious Swiss couple who ran it were instead in the back streets of Milan, busily trading on the black market. During his time with the Refugee Organisation, Neil had met some fine people, dedicated men and women, but there were others ready to use any form of human misery to their advantage, and, in the words of an Irish friend, 'would take the pennies from the eyes of a dead man'. There were some – too many – here in this camp. People in positions of authority. It was unfortunate that he had to work with them. But not for many weeks longer. If all went well, by the end of the month he would be on his way to Australia. He had been offered an unexpectedly prestigious job there, and had gladly accepted it.

He tried to drink the noxious mixture, shuddered and put it aside. His desk was littered with forms and handwritten notes to be typed, details gathered from the interviews he had conducted with the day's hopefuls, most of them German or Italian speaking, although he had picked up a knowledge of other languages including Bulgarian and some Serbian. Beginning purely as an interpreter, his promotion had been rapid. He now questioned applicants, making his own assessments and rating their capabilities, then passing his judgements to a committee that would generally rubber-stamp his decisions on who was suitable. Today's list, among them Slavs, families from the subsumed Baltic States, Austrians and Italians, had all been tense, all anxious to create a good impression, most of them managing only to convey their quiet and frantic desperation.

It sometimes seemed to Neil as if half of Europe were eager to be somewhere else. Nearly six years since the surrender, with so many still stranded in refugee camps, exhausted by the war and facing the grim reality of its aftermath – the knowledge that they were yesterday's news, that the world had moved on to another conflict, this time in Korea – who could blame the survivors for their anxiety? Eight million people displaced at the war's end;

two million still, and with only a few governments now willing to take them. Britain had done more than her share, considering her battered economy; France had given a Gallic shrug, too concerned with internal conflicts; America had relented, but the waiting list was endless. Australia wanted migrants and had vacant jobs to be filled, but for many it was a last choice, not only because of the distance, but also from a European belief that it was an outpost, a pale reflection of England at the bottom of the world. More than a few English people had these perceptions, too.

It's a colony, ain't it, voiced an ex-serviceman applying for a ten-pound passage at a centre where Neil had first worked in London.

It's not a colony, he was told.

'Course it bleeding is, he insisted. Belongs to us, it does, to Britain. One of ours.

Another was surprised about the size of its cities. She had always thought the country was like a big farm, full of sheep and cattle.

Someone claimed it was like Croydon in South London – Croydon being held up as his mirror of suburbia. He had a nephew who had written to tell him – it was just like Croydon, with palm trees.

Neil wondered what it was really like. He had helped process the passage of so many others – how would he find life when he reached there? He thought of Sarah's surprisingly few letters in the time since her arrival. And how, after her initial enthusiasm when she landed, he had found the last one disturbing.

She wrote that she was working in the hospital, a job that suited her, as she had once been a nurse. Her living quarters were not at the hospital, but a short distance away by bus at a government hostel; the accommodation was modest as the name implied, but comfortable, and so she would stay there as rooms were hard to rent in that area. New ships continued to arrive with migrants, and there were now people of many nationalities. The summer had been hot – and strange – coming as it did at Christmas time. Instead of the cold and snow at home, it had been what the local people called 'a hundred in the shade', which was how they measured temperature instead of using centigrade as Europeans did. There were a great many things that were different.

It was an old letter now, brought months ago by sea, following him from one posting to another, and for a long time preserved in his wallet. He had read and re-read it with a curious feeling of concern. Her frequently dashed-off notes, while still living in Berlin, were always amusing, animated and full of comment. This, in contrast, had seemed oddly stilted. It was more like a letter written carefully to a stranger. He wondered why, and it began to trouble him.

The wait for the telephone call seemed endless. Because of the time difference it had to be made at noon, which would be evening in Australia and hopefully Sarah would be at home. He had managed by sheer determination to get a number from the immigration department in Sydney, an exercise which had elements of a bureaucratic farce. His first cable giving her name and requesting a phone number had brought a suspicious response. Why did he want such information, and what precisely was his business with the subject?

The *subject*, Neil cabled in reply, was a personal friend, and he wished to ring her up and find out how she was. It took several more frustrating attempts to convince the public servants in Sydney of this, even having to remind them that since he was contracted to both the International Refugee Organisation and the Australian government, and had his own entry papers to the country, his *bona fides* had been thoroughly checked. But if they wished to know more about him, why not try looking up their own department files.

By this time he had spent the best part of a week's salary on cables. Finally he had a number to ring, but no idea how far from the telephone her quarters might be. Therefore it needed to be booked in advance, person-to-person, and since his own office had no telephone, it could only be made from the busy administrative centre. He was uncomfortably aware of the curiosity of the staff as he enunciated the name, Mrs Sarah Weismann – and then had to spell it for the operator. After which he sat waiting, trying to affect indifference and ignore their overt interest.

Stewart Mitchell, the Head of Mission of the Australian Bureau, kept appearing from his room with documents to be filed, frowning and glancing pointedly at his watch. The implied rebuke was clearly to indicate the day was passing, the government's time was being wasted, all for a personal matter which could hardly be of any real importance. A public servant in his late thirties, Mitchell was a man with sharp eyes and an acquisitive manner. He and Neil disliked each other intensely.

Mitchell resented the younger man's flair with languages, and the standing it had brought him in less than two years with the IRO.

'Difficult to get through to Sydney,' he said, 'especially from Italy. Might take days.'

'I'll make up the time,' Neil replied. 'If you're worried about that.'

'A cable might've been far simpler.'

'I could hardly talk to her by cable.'

'Very droll,' Mitchell said. 'Who is she anyway?'

'A friend,' Neil said, and heard the telephone ring.

One of the clerks answered it, and she beckoned him. He took the phone with a nod of thanks, then saw Mitchell was lingering. He turned his back on him, and spoke.

'Hello, Sarah.'

'Are you Mr Latham? Mr Latham?' The operator seemed to be repeating herself, until he realised it was the echo of distance.

'Yes,' he said.

'You booked a person-to-person call to a Mrs S. Weismann at 769 0030. I'll spell that name . . . that name,' came the echo.

'There's no need,' Neil said. 'Is she there to take the call?'

'It's a foreign name so I'll spell it,' the operator insisted. 'W for William . . . William, E for Edward . . . Edward, I for Ingrid . . . Ingrid.'

'Please,' he said, but she went on regardless.

'M for Mary . . . Mary, A for Alan . . . Alan, N for Nell . . . Nell . . .'

'For God's sake,' Neil said, 'is she there?'

The time-lag echo was intensifying as the line deteriorated, but she seemed determined to finish spelling the name.

'And N for Nell . . . Nell. That's Weismann, Mrs Weismann,' and the echo repeated yet again . . . 'Weismann . . .' Her accent made the pronunciation sound strange. 'Nice weather over there, is it?'

'Not especially,' Neil said, startled by the sudden informality.

'Pity. Been really lovely here,' the operator said. 'Blue skies for weeks. Stand by, please.'

It's like something out of Alice in Wonderland, he thought, then heard Sarah faintly assuring the telephonist she was indeed who she claimed to be – and yes – was ready to accept the call. Finally there she was on the line, her voice resonating across the thousands of miles of space.

'Hello, Neil . . . Neil . . .'

'Sarah?'

'I've been so worried, waiting here,' were her first words. 'I knew it had to be you, but just can't imagine why . . . imagine why . . .' It was difficult to make out what she was saying with the iteration. 'Neil . . . is something wrong?'

'No, not with me. I'm fine.'

'Then why are you ringing?'

'I was worried about *you*.'

'Why?' He heard her saying again *why* – and wondered if she was repeating the word, or was it only the echo?

'Just a feeling I had. Are you all right?'

'Yes.'

'You sure?'

'Of course. This is a terrible line. I keep hearing myself saying things twice.'

'I can hear you saying them twice, too. And me saying them twice. Are you happy?'

There was a pause. He thought they had been cut off.

'Sarah?'

'I'm here.' *Here* the echo repeated, but did not convince him.

Something was wrong, but there was little he could do, acutely aware of the audience in the office; the pretty clerk he had taken to dinner covertly watching while she pretended to be busy; Mitchell not even attempting that charade, but standing gazing at him and openly listening. It made him feel exposed and self-conscious.

'Are you sure everything's all right?' he asked, and heard his own voice feed the question back at him.

'Yes,' she said. 'Neil . . . I hope . . . your plans haven't changed, have they? I will see you soon?' Soon seemed like a triple echo.

'Very soon.'

She said something in reply, but sudden static drowned it.

'Sarah?' He thought he'd heard the words 'Thank God', but wasn't sure. 'What did you say?'

'God bless. Goodbye.' Her voice was faint, but the click of the broken connection was clearly audible.

'Goodbye,' he said puzzled, into the atmospheric void.

Sarah stood by the telephone, furtively wiping her eyes and hoping no-one had noticed. After her response of 'Thank God', which he seemed not to have had heard, she had found herself on the verge of tears. It was why she had terminated the call and hung up so abruptly.

'Are you upset about something?' the woman in the office asked, not unkindly.

Sarah shook her head, not trusting herself to speak.

'Not bad news? Enough to scare you, long distance calls like that from overseas. Bad as telegrams in the war. They never brought no good news, did they? Hope there's nothing wrong.'

'No,' she managed to say, and left there, hurrying back to her room. When she reached its sanctuary and locked her door, there was no longer a need for pretence. She lay on her narrow bed. The tears came in a rush, cascading down her cheeks as if they would never stop.

He deeply regretted the phone call; unable to say why, he was left with the feeling it had been a mistake. Sarah had sounded tense and strange. The echo distorting their voices, the lack of privacy, none of it had helped. The whole thing had achieved nothing, except to confirm a perception that all was not well.

He slept badly that night, and for the first time in more than a year the nightmare returned. He dreamed of the orchard, the cattle grazing between the trees, the spring blossoms, and heard the sound they had thought were bees. He saw the gaunt and dying people, the piles of already dead, and felt the heat of the burning hut consumed by shooting flames – and the shouting and banging on the door as he woke lathered in sweat.

'Neil, for Christ's sake, are you okay?' a voice shouted, and he realised it was Freddy da Silva, the Canadian IRO officer who was his neighbour in the adjoining hut. He switched on the light, stumbled out of bed and opened the door.

'Shit, man, you were yelling your head off. What happened?'

'A bad dream,' Neil said.

'Some dream. I held back a while, thinking maybe you had an orgy going in here, only it got kinda loud.'

'Sorry, Freddy, no orgy. Just a dream.'

'Do you have 'em often?' the Canadian asked.

'No. Must have been too much rich food from the canteen.'

'Oh, man – that really is a dream.'

He left, laughing, and Neil went back to bed and slept fitfully.

The morning brought a pale sun, and the sour taste of a hangover, although he had not had a drink. It also brought the unwelcome sight of Stewart Mitchell waiting to see him, when Neil returned to his office after a hurried breakfast.

'Good morning,' he said, and ignored the other's inevitable glance at his watch. On the surface, the Australian Head of Mission had the mentality of a factory timekeeper; he was parsimonious about a few overdue minutes, without giving credit for extra hours worked at night and on weekends. Beneath that veneer was something quite different.

On one hand a martinet when it came to hours and office procedure, on the other an avaricious fraud who ran the Australian section here like his own personal fiefdom.

'About your phone call yesterday,' Mitchell began, 'it's not something I wish to encourage.'

'It's not something that will happen again,' Neil said. 'I'll be leaving soon, as you know.'

'Yes.' Mitchell tried to conceal his satisfaction. 'By the way, here's the cost of it, to be deducted from your pay.'

Neil took the proffered invoice. He stared at the total. It was for thirty-five thousand lire, which, even at Italy's current inflated rate of exchange, was an excessive amount. He looked up to see the other's eyes fixed on him, waiting for a protest, and decided not to make one. He had a feeling he knew what was coming.

'Thank you,' he said.

'On the high side, I thought. Still, you know the Eyeties and their ways of adding up a bill by now.'

'The Italians didn't add the surcharge,' Neil said.

'Quite right. But that's normal practice. It's an organisational rule to add a premium on private calls, to discourage the staff from making them. We can't have every damn office girl wanting to ring up Mum, when she feels homesick. Of course, if your call was part of the job, we could pay for it. I mean, who is she, this Sarah Weismann . . .?'

'I told you, just a friend. And it was nothing to do with the job; it was private and personal.'

'Listen, mate, what I'm saying is . . . I'm agreeable to siphon it off, if you are.'

Neil gazed at him. There was a feeling of tension between them, then he firmly shook his head. Mitchell frowned at the rejection.

'Suit yourself. But it seems a pity we can't absorb it, and save you the damage. All you need to do is concoct a logical reason for the call, and then provide some background on the woman so we can give her a file. Not that it'd be used, but just for appearances' sake. Cover our arses. If you do that, the government can pick up the tab.'

Neil knew it was done all the time. Phone calls home were routine. Visits to girlfriends in Rome, weekends at luxury hotels in Venice, these were just fringe benefits that found a way to be classed as expenses, and were absorbed by the budget. But there was a great deal more, a far darker side to what went on here. He hoped Mitchell and the others didn't realise the full extent of his knowledge.

Stewart Mitchell had a philosophy he was fond of expounding; they were rescuing abandoned human beings in this arsehole of the world and deserved a few benefits, which the Australian taxpayers – back home enjoying the boom years of good wages and full employment – could well afford.

'Thanks all the same, Stewart.'

'Right, in that case I'll dock you for it. But it strikes me that you're being unnecessarily noble, Neil. Bloody ridiculously so. After all, what's a few thousand lire to the department?'

What indeed, Neil thought, after Mitchell had gone. But there was no way so near to departure that he would compromise himself for what would cost a few days' pay, or give details of Sarah that could be incorporated into one of their files. Not a hope in hell.

He knew why the offer had been made. Neil, when he first arrived, had been invited to join the select club of Mitchell's 'mates' who participated in the rackets that existed here, and had startled and upset them by declining. He was unsure if it was on moral grounds or self-preservation, but once offered membership of the magic circle and electing to remain outside it, he knew he was a concern to them, a possible danger, and it was one of the reasons the offer of payment for the phone call had been made. Even persuading him to agree to such a small deception would be a relief to them all; if he had accepted, it would reassure them he was unlikely to consider trying to blow the whistle on their lucrative lifestyle.

Mitchell and his cronies would be very glad to see the last of him. Which, Neil reflected, was thoroughly reciprocated. He could hardly wait to get out of here, and was uneasily aware of how much information he possessed, and the harm it could cause them. It was not something he had set out to gather, but the cheating and corruption was so blatant it could hardly go unnoticed. And when he had realised the full extent of it, the depth of deceit, it had made him feel very nervous. He knew he was vulnerable. You were supposed to be on the team. By refusing to participate, not playing ball, he was making himself the only outsider, and it felt . . .

He glanced through the window and noticed a young couple approaching his office, the same couple he had seen once or twice before, remembering the girl slipping, the truck splattering them with mud and the boy's shouted profanity. They stopped nearby, the girl busily talking, gesturing persuasively, the boy seeming morose and unresponsive. They remained there arguing with each other, while his thoughts strayed.

How did it feel? It felt, now that he was within weeks of leaving, and en route to a good new job in Australia . . . uncomfortable. Being more honest with himself, it felt dangerous. It had not really occurred to him before, but the so-called magic circle feared him. Mitchell was unlikely to resort to personal violence, but some of the others – he tried not to think about it, but the nagging concern would not go away. Bluey McGill, once an army medical orderly who was in charge of the camp dispensary, was reportedly selling supplies of sulphanilamide and penicillin to a group that had links with the Mafia in Milan. Russ Moroney who ran the catering side, was equally up to his neck in graft, a hard man who wouldn't hesitate to act, if he felt that his future was endangered.

Neil could prove none of these things, but he knew this was a corrupt place, the worst refugee camp he'd been in. There'd been some rough ones, some where people were abused or ill-treated, or if they had money, could bribe their way to a new future, but this place sickened him; it was fraudulent and iniquitous, and the staff were mercenaries, whose only ambition was to exploit the DPs and set themselves up financially for life. He sometimes wondered if those who ran the International Refugee Organisation realised that, as time passed and the quality of the personnel in charge deteriorated, the conditions for anyone still trying to find a country to accept them were rapidly eroding.

The couple were still arguing outside. After a moment he rose and opened his door, and they paused to stare at him.

'Why don't you come in?' he said.

They hesitated, then the girl nodded and entered. As the boy reluctantly followed, Neil brought chairs and invited them to sit down. They seemed surprised, as if unfamiliar with such consideration.

'How can I help?'

'You probably can't,' the boy said abrasively.

'Why not?'

'I doubt if we'll fit into the type of people you want. We'll be too young, or the wrong nationality, or just plain unsuitable. You'll manage to think of a reason to reject us. Everyone else has.'

Neil was startled – not by the rudeness, because the people he dealt with were often uncivil – but at his fluent English. The girl spoke sharply, rebuking him in a language he knew was Hungarian.

'Please forgive my brother,' she said. He blinked. Her fluency was even more startling. She sounded as if she might have been born and brought up in Surrey or West London.

'You both speak excellent English. Who taught you?'

'We taught ourselves,' the boy said.

'You did it very well.'

'Glad you think so,' he answered ungraciously. 'In the last year of the war, when we had these visions of going to America or Canada – when we were stupid enough to think they might welcome us there, my sister said we must talk in English. All the time – until we spoke it perfectly, because it would be like a passport to the new world.' He shrugged. It was an angry gesture, Neil could see, fuelled by disappointment and rejection. 'Ilona, who gave up her Hungarian name, is now called Helen, and my name is Michael, not Miklos any more. Which is fine, except that the past few years have taught us it doesn't matter, none of it matters in the slightest, because nobody really gives a shit.'

'How old are you?' Neil asked.

'She's twenty-two, I'm twenty-one,' he said immediately.

Neil saw the girl's gaze turn to her brother, then she smiled.

'Not quite. I'm twenty-one, and Miki – Michael – will be twenty next month.'

'Thank you.' Neil wrote it down. 'Better if we're accurate.'

'Why? Nobody – except my Holy Sister – tells the truth.'

'What's wrong with the truth?'

'It well-and-truly shafts me,' he said, not noticing Neil's smile at his slang. 'No country wants people that young. The Yanks told us, no single males under twenty-one.'

'Australia's different.'

'How?'

'The age limit for single immigrants begins at seventeen.'

'Truly?' It was the girl, looking encouraged.

'Don't get your hopes up high again, Helen.' Her brother was determinedly belligerent. 'You know there'll be other conditions, and we won't qualify.'

'What makes you think that?' Neil asked.

'We learned the facts of life in a hard school,' the boy replied. 'So, the first question is, do you take Jews?'

'Of course.'

'A small quota, I suppose, so you'll look civilised to the rest of the world. And sure as hell, the quota is already filled.'

What do I say to that? Neil wondered. *Admit the embargo on ships, that allows only a limited percentage of Jewish passengers? Or the instructions from Canberra to restrict the recruitment of Jews.* He knew of cases where entry permits had been issued then cancelled, and other instances of discrimination. He had been warned – like everyone else who worked for the department – that these were highly confidential matters, and not to be divulged.

'Never mind quotas,' Neil said. 'Calm down and let's talk. I'll tell you what I can about the immigration policy.'

'We know about White Australia! If you're black, you can't come in.'

'Well, you're not black, are you? So how about trying to brush the chip off your shoulder and let's talk sense,' Neil said. 'I may not like the idea of such a blatant colour bar policy either, but we can't voice objections – not unless we're actually there.'

'Bullshit,' Michael said. 'Voice objections? If we criticised their laws, we'd be put on the first boat and told to piss off.'

'You're probably right, Michael. But people have to stay a while, before they can oppose things or approve of them. In parts of England, if you've only lived there for ten years they say you're still a newcomer. What do they say in your country?'

It was Helen who answered, smiling: 'In the provinces they're the worst. Two generations before they'll say good day.'

Neil laughed. 'In certain nooks and crannies of Scotland, it takes the best part of a century. And only if you wear the right kilt.'

She would have joined in the laughter, but they both realised her brother was unresponsive. Neil felt irritated at his truculence.

'If you don't like the policies, then why are you here?'

'Because Ilona insisted,' he said.

'Helen,' she said softly.

'Because Helen insisted.'

'And why did she insist?' Neil asked, and when there was no answer continued. 'The allocations are full, right? Canada, the States, South Africa, England . . . wherever you wanted to go, there are no places, are there?'

'No.' But he was still obdurate.

'Australia's motto is "populate or perish", so they intend to take as many people as they can. As long as you pass a medical test, and have no criminal record.'

The girl smiled her appreciation at his attempt to pacify her brother.

'I have a desk full of brochures. You can look at them and decide if it appeals. If it does we can start by filling in a form.'

Michael said, 'That's where it usually ends, filling in forms. That's the last we ever hear of the matter.'

Neil produced pamphlets. Helen thanked him and began to glance through them. Michael sat, making no attempt to show interest.

He's had a bad time, Neil thought. Working with refugees had taught him the angriest people were those who had suffered the most. Their aggression was often a retaliation against a society which had tolerated, in some cases approved of, their neglect and ill-treatment.

'If you're Jewish,' he said, and saw them glance at him, both instantly vigilant, 'it must have been very bad for you in Hungary.'

'Yes, it was bad,' Helen said. 'We lost our parents as well as everything else. Our home, friends, everything. Even our childhood. In a time like that, there's no chance of childhood.'

Neil thought of Sarah and her daughter. And the bodies of the children in mass graves. They'd had no chance of childhood, either.

'When the Germans fled, it was wonderful at first. For a few days. Budapest went wild with celebration. We thought it was all over, but then the Russians came to "liberate" us.'

'I can imagine,' Neil said.

'No you can't,' her brother answered curtly.

'What happened to you?' He deliberately turned to the girl.

'We escaped, hoping by now the war had ended, but it hadn't. Even though the rumours of Hitler being dead were true, it still hadn't ended. We were picked up after we crossed the border into Austria, by a Wehrmacht patrol. They tied our hands and legs, and talked of what they were going to do. Perhaps they didn't think we could understand German, or perhaps they wanted us to hear. Miki was to be killed. I was going to be raped, until they tired of me.'

Dear God, Neil thought, *what happens to some human beings when they put on a uniform? Why do they turn into animals, and how can they go home after and behave as if the world is a normal place?*

He realised she was talking again, so softly he had to strain to hear her.

'They were young, these soldiers . . .'

'These pigs,' Michael said.

'Young,' she ignored his interruption, 'barely older than us. They'd run away from the fighting, they had rifles but no ammunition left. Their uniforms were in rags, and they must have known the war was lost, but we were Jews, we were the epidemic their leaders had taught them to fear and hate, and so they were going to do this.'

'Stop it,' Michael whispered.

'Please,' Neil said, seeing the pain of the memory in her eyes, 'don't . . . if it distresses you . . .'

'There were ten of them,' she said. 'I suppose I counted them, trying to block thoughts of being . . . trying to erase it from my mind. I did think of my brother, and how much we'd lived through, and that for no reason they were going to kill him . . . and I wondered how, without bullets. But of course they had their rifles, to use as clubs.'

'Iluska . . .' He took her hands, begging her to stop, speaking in Hungarian.

'We've never talked of it before,' she said to Neil in English. 'We've lived with it since then, but we never speak about it. So it festers inside us.'

'Make her shut up,' Michael said helplessly. 'Why tell him, or anyone? In God's name, why?'

'Because we've kept silent so long, it's like a wound. And I can't bear it any longer.' She held tightly to her brother's hands. 'They decided,' she said, 'it would be more fun if Miki was made to watch. So they untied me, held me down and forced my legs apart. The first one – he was sweating a lot, I can remember that – removed his trousers. He was excited; he had an erection and they all cheered this. They cheered when he . . . he entered me.'

'Bastards.'

'Like schoolboys, I kept thinking. School bullies, I suppose I meant. I was trying to shut from my mind what was happening to me.'

'Filthy bastards,' Michael repeated, savagely unforgiving.

'Then they were all dead bastards,' she said unexpectedly, startling Neil. 'A few moments later, but not soon enough for me, all of them dead.'

'What?' When she seemed unable to answer him, Neil turned to Michael. 'How?'

'They were all killed, and I hope they're rotting somewhere in the deepest hell,' he said with hatred.

'You killed them?'

'How could I? Two SS officers came by in a car. They got out and watched while this first pig finished with my sister. Then they started asking them who they were? What unit? Where had they come from, and what had happened to their officers? Why were their rifles in a pile on the ground, while one of them fucked a Jew?'

'The soldiers had no answers,' Helen said almost inaudibly. 'The SS – I think they were *Obersturmfuehrers* – took out their revolvers and began to shoot them. They killed all ten, one after the other. Some were crying and begging not to die, others tried to run away and were shot in the back. I thought they were going to kill us, but they made us get into the car, and took us to a prison barracks.' She shuddered. 'I still remember those two men, how neat and tidy they were, uniforms clean, badges shining. I remember their eyes, like chips of polished marble. They spoke to us as if they didn't really see us, stating that the elite of the *Waffen SS* were always correct in their duty, so the deserters had been shot, whereas we, as racial filth of the Reich, would be turned over for deportation and sent to Auschwitz.'

Neil felt a dryness in his throat. The silence in the room was acute as he waited for her to continue, but she looked away, expended at last by so much revelation. It was her brother who spoke.

'A cattle train to Auschwitz. After being processed with due German efficiency. Five days on the train,' he added. 'But then the war did end after all – it ended the day before we arrived there.'

'At least that was lucky.'

'Lucky?' Michael considered the word, as if unsure about this. 'I suppose so. Instead of corpses, we became Displaced Persons. For nearly six years. If you call that luck.'

The committee was far from convinced. They were all men in their middle age, and included a politician who had lost his seat, two public servants enjoying a sinecure prior to retirement, and Brigadier Frank Aldridge as the chairman. Aldridge was a wartime officer who clung to his rank in civilian life. But while he occupied the chair – the driving force, and Neil's principal concern – was Stewart Mitchell. As the Head of Mission, if Mitchell disagreed, the others hardly mattered.

'I'd like to recommend them,' Neil said, trying to ignore the Brigadier's dubious grunt as they each studied the application he had drafted. 'I think they've had a hell of a time. They've suffered a lot.'

'Perhaps so. But my reading of people like this is that they're trouble, or they would've been settled by now,' Aldridge said. 'What's more, if suffering was a reason for admission, then our country would be full of misfits and defectives.'

'There's nothing the least bit defective about their ability to survive, sir. That shows initiative. Also, they're hardly misfits when it comes to the English language.'

'What does that mean, precisely?'

'It means they speak it perfectly.'

Neil was aware that Aldridge was strongly anti-Semitic, but he knew the others on the committee often resented the imperious manner, and today he needed their support. Today above all days. But it had to be handled delicately. If Mitchell felt Neil had the slightest personal interest in this ruling, he'd oppose it out of sheer bloody-mindedness. The fate of people in this camp rated low on his list of concerns. He sat saying nothing, watching intently as Neil, conscious of the Brigadier's propensity to dismiss an application and move on, persisted.

'I think the ability to speak the language is important.'

'Well, I'll tell you what I think. I think there are other things a bloody sight more important – like manpower.' Aldridge was clearly declaring it a personal tussle between them. 'Populate or perish is the slogan, which is fairly explicit. Or as an outsider, a non-Australian, perhaps you don't fully understand what it means.'

'Of course I know what it means,' Neil said placidly. If he could get the Brigadier onto his favourite topic – his peevishness that a bloody Pommy was allowed to be involved in the selection of migrants, the others might be irritated by his xenophobia.

'I'll tell you what it means,' the Brigadier said, as if Neil had not replied, 'it means we want tradesmen and labourers, not a bunch of bloody Jew elocution teachers. Eh, Mitch?' He chortled at his own wit, and the others dutifully smiled. 'Jews aren't workers. Might work for themselves, but they're not manpower. And if we do want people who can speak English, there are boatloads of Poms emigrating at ten quid a time. So don't tell me that spikka-da-Inglish matters a bugger.'

'I'm not saying it, Brigadier. It's the Minister of Immigration in Canberra who said it.'

'Eh? What the fuck are you talking about?'

Neil took his time before answering. *Got you, you pompous old bastard*, he thought, *you've walked right into it.* But he remained composed, determined to show no sign of his triumph.

'What did the stupid flaming Minister say this time?' the Brigadier demanded. 'He's always shoving his foot in it.'

'Last week he complained we're selecting too many Europeans who can hardly speak a word of English, and will cost the taxpayer because they'll have to attend language classes. Whereas these two – perhaps elocution is overdoing it – but you were right, Brigadier, they're certainly good enough to *teach* English.'

There was a silence in the room while Aldridge digested this. Neil had the strange notion that Stewart Mitchell was inwardly amused. 'They seem to have impressed Latham, this pair of Yids,' the Brigadier said trenchantly, at last. 'What do you think, eh, Mitch?'

'He certainly does seem impressed.' Mitchell leaned back in his chair, studying Neil.

'But isn't that why I'm here, Stewart? Brigadier? You must both know that's exactly the reason why I'm here?'

'What?'

'To gather impressions.'

'What are you wittering on about?' The Brigadier's aplomb was slipping, and he was becoming decidedly testy.

'That's my job . . . to examine people, and form impressions.' Neil saw the ex-politician smother a smile, and knew he had at least one supporter. 'So if people impress me as being young and intelligent, and the sort of immigrants who'll contribute to the country, shouldn't I fulfil my function and say so?'

'You have a bloody sight too much to say,' Aldridge replied.

'You may feel so, Brigadier. I imagine for you the sword will always be mightier than the word. But it is language by which we communicate. And two young people who can speak fluent English are an asset to the country. I am impressed, as Stewart rightly said, and ask you to trust my judgement.' He smiled with ingenuous cheerfulness. 'Quite apart from us all impressing the immigration Minister.'

'Fair enough,' one public servant said, and the other nodded. Neil felt pleased; it was to them he had been speaking. He knew he had the backing if it did come to a vote.

'They should be on the next ship,' the ex-politician said. Mitchell merely shrugged and nodded acceptance. The Brigadier looked incensed. He reluctantly stamped the application and handed it to Neil with a look of acute dislike. He was not used to being out-manoeuvred, and his gaze promised retribution.

What you've forgotten, you bullying sod, Neil wanted to tell him, *is that this is my last encounter with you. My last such meeting.*

If it had not been for Helen Ferencz and her brother, he would have been in Kent by now on a farewell visit to his family, and hoping to persuade Caroline to join him on the first available ship. He'd had enough of Europe and its post-war misery, more than enough of this camp. With every passing day he felt the onset of danger. He knew too much for Mitchell and his clique's peace of mind. For his own, he wanted to be far away on the other side of the world.

But at least he had done what he intended. He had gone into the meeting determined to obtain a passage for the pair. Australia was their last hope. He doubted if another country would accept them. They were unskilled, possibly unsuitable. But the girl's story had moved him inexplicably; he had experienced horror of his own, had been told desperate and shocking stories, yet he had scarcely been able to stop thinking of her quiet voice reciting the painful events of her joyless life. He had made up his mind, from that first day in his office, to help them escape from the vortex, the pit of despair into which they had been drawn. Europe was full of people being left to rot; but not these two, not if he could help it.

On his own initiative, he had deleted from their records any mention of them trying to enter the Zionist sector of Palestine as illegal immigrants, while it was still under British mandate. He erased all reference to them being held in Cyprus. Or that the authorities there had proposed to deport them back to Hungary.

Helen and Michael had been fortunate enough to learn of it in time, had escaped custody and fled as stowaways on a freighter to Italy. For over three years since then, stateless and illegal, they had been shifted from one refugee camp to another. Most of the time they had survived on forged papers and stolen rations, and although he had not asked the question, undoubtedly on stolen money as well.

Neil had made sure none of this information remained in their file. He realised the seriousness of what he was doing; falsifying official documents was a criminal offence. Forgery would be the least of the charges. But over several meetings, gaining their trust and learning of their long ordeal, he had resolved to take the risk. A new file was carefully fabricated. If the facts had been known to Mitchell, or the Brigadier and his committee, the pair would not be going to Australia.

If anyone knew what he'd done, Neil realised, nor would he.

~

It was unbelievable. Wonderful. It was like a miracle. Helen sang while she packed the two brand new suitcases, with their precious few belongings. The luggage had been given to them by Neil Latham, who said he had a special fund to provide for immigrants, and had also given her enough lire to buy a new skirt and blouse, which she had safely packed away for the journey, as well as some underwear for herself, and shirts and work trousers for Michael.

She wondered if it was true, about the special fund? She had a strange feeling it might have been his own money, but did not want to embarrass him by asking. When she confided this to Michael, he told her not to be a romantic bloody fool; people didn't behave like that, not in the real world.

But he's done so much to help us, she argued.

I know he has, he admitted. The only one who ever bothered. I like him – but you're starting to talk as if he's St Francis of Assisi.

Mr Latham – he'd said to call him Neil – had come to see them yesterday; given them their detailed schedule, the departure time, the tickets for the train from Milan to the border, the identity cards to gain them entry into France, and vouchers for second-class rail seats to Marseilles. There an Australian immigration official would arrange the next stage. They would be taken to a hostel for the night, and the following day would board a ship called the *Castel Florentino*, for Capetown, Perth and Sydney. And after that? She felt light-headed and excited. After that was a brand new world, a place of beaches and long summers with warm sunshine, according to the brochures and pamphlets that she read incessantly.

Even a new name. On Mr Latham's – Neil's – advice they had decided to Anglicise their family name. Ferencz translated quite easily. He felt it would be sensible to begin life in an English-speaking country with an English sounding name, and so their papers were duly amended. Ilona and Miklos Ferencz were now Helen and Michael Francis. He was circumspect about it, but they knew he had made some discreet and careful amendments to their files, and he said that changing their name to Francis was not only useful for their future in Australia, but would act as an additional filter in case any details of their murky past should emerge to haunt them. He smiled when he used these words 'murky past' – so that it was dismissed, left behind them – and no-one had the need to add anything more. He had helped them, and she would never forget him.

The bus would be here any minute to pick them up and take them to the station. There was just time to say a hurried goodbye and express her thanks to him. The others were already gathering at the pick-up point, over twenty of them in all. She told Michael to wait with them, and ran across the camp. His office door was shut, so she knocked. There was no answer. She tried the door and it was locked.

'Can I help?' a voice asked, and it was the Canadian man. His neighbour. Freddy someone-or-other his name was.

'I'm looking for Mr Latham.'

'Neil? Neil's gone.'

'Gone where?'

'I guess to Australia, eventually. But meanwhile, he's gone home to England, to some place in Kent, to say goodbye to his folks and see his girl.'

Helen felt strangely disappointed.

His girl? Of course, he'd be bound to have one. Only she'd seen him yesterday, and he'd never even mentioned leaving.

But on the other hand why should he? She was not important to him. She was just a part of his job, the same job he would be resuming in Australia. He was paid for being nice to people. But still . . .

'When did he go?'

'Early this morning. Plane from Milan to London.'

'Oh, well,' she said. 'I just wanted to say goodbye.'

'If he happens to be in touch, I'll tell him.'

'No need,' Helen said firmly, determined not to feel dejected. She had only come out of simple courtesy to thank him for what he had done. 'It really wasn't important.'

She heard the vehicle tooting, and a shrill whistle that could only be Miki. She turned to go.

'Bon voyage,' the Canadian said.

'Thank you.'

'And good luck.'

I think you're going to need it, he reflected, as he watched her walk away, a thin, rather pretty girl in a shabby dress, trying not to look disappointed.

Chapter 4

Sarah had never felt so alien, so distanced from people, so isolated by misery and depression. This was different to the camp; the camp had been a continual nightmare which she had always expected would end with her death. This was the beginning of the new life she had chosen in a new country, and within weeks she began to realise she had made a grave mistake. The government scheme under which she had been given a passage here required her to work for two years in any job at a situation selected by the authorities. She had been foolish enough in one of her interviews – when she had been so eager to be accepted – to reveal she had once been a nursing sister and, as if this was relevant, she had been assigned as a cleaner to a local hospital. It was an ex-servicemen's hospital, and there were wards with men still not recovered from years of imprisonment and starvation in Burma and Singapore; there were others, shell-shocked or scarred by burns, who she thought might never leave here.

The work did not upset her. It was tedious and unpleasant, scrubbing floors, doing laundry, cleaning the lavatories and communal shower rooms where the worst odour was the carbolic disinfectant. The hours were long, the pay not generous, but that was acceptable, it was part of the bargain, two years' labour in return for her sea voyage. Not a very comfortable voyage, so many women crowded into a cabin, and dreadfully hot below decks crossing the equator and the Indian Ocean. Nor was her accommodation what she expected, but she refused to be dismayed. It was none of those things that troubled her so deeply.

No, it was the attitude that hurt most, the shock of being made to feel so unwelcome, the barbed disparagement that was like a slap in the face. Whatever reception she had envisaged, it had not been this; categorised as someone unrelated and foreign – a 'reffo' was the local parlance – being stared at, people curious, snickering, or what was worse, visibly hostile or else indifferent.

The hostility was offensive and disabling when it did occur. She tried to ignore it. In many ways, strangely, the indifference was harder to bear. She found it bewildering and cruel, and because of it, began to keep to herself. Being a woman who had always enjoyed company, her self-elected loneliness made her melancholy.

There were other things. Small incidents, but hurtful. Being mocked at times when she spoke; she had always assumed her English was acceptable; accented but certainly not harsh or Teutonic. Yet once, when she asked directions in the street, a hard-faced woman had stared at her, then told her to bugger off, to go back to Hitler, and the remark was so wounding, so malignant, that she burst into tears and hurried away, taking the train back to the migrant barracks, abandoning plans for her free Sunday to explore the city and the harbour, feeling distressed and unsafe until she reached the row of corrugated iron huts, in one of which was a plywood cubicle known as her personal quarters.

Trying to console herself, to rebuild her morale, she thought that at least she had her own place. After a concentration camp, this former army barracks was bearable. Not what she'd hoped for, but at least she had a small compartment to herself. The word compartment sounded better than cubicle. Flimsy though they might be, there were walls that gave her some sort of privacy. A roof to keep out the rain, even if it was galvanised iron, hot as an oven in the sun and thunderous when storms came. She had a shelf on which to put her clothes, a hook to hang up her dresses. And a bed.

The lavatories and showers were hardly private, shared with the other women and their young children, but at least they were clean. There was a large communal hut called the dining room where food was served, and here men and women lined up at huge tureens of stew, containing vast amounts of meat, more meat than she had ever seen, although it was tough and often tasteless, and called mutton.

Most of the newcomers hated the food. A group of Italians were delighted when told there was spaghetti on the menu, and stared with disbelief at the tinned spaghetti on toast which was served to them. One took his plate to the window and hurled it outside. Many of the wives were shocked when their husbands were sent away to other areas, even other states, obliged to go to work wherever directed. Complaints were constant. Nothing was the least bit like the bright inviting brochures had promised.

The district Sarah passed through daily on her way to work was drab. A rash of new houses in the working-class western suburbs were being built fast and cheaply; there were already endless streets of identical bungalows with asbestos cement walls and red-tiled roofs. Small gardens with neat flower beds, lawns tightly mown and listless in the summer heat. A succession of high paling fences, uncompromising bulwarks that surrounded each square of land. Sarah wondered if it had ever been attractive, here in this bleak and featureless urban locale before the bulldozers came, and kerbs and gutters were installed, and tar roads laid down. There were now, in the grid-like neighbourhood, no trees.

Attempting to find solace, to relieve her belief that this attempt to change her life had been a dreadful blunder, she wrote to Neil after his telephone call.

My dearest Neil,

How extravagant and kind of you to do such a thing, and how wonderful to hear your voice. I didn't even mind the echo, and hearing everything twice! I hope you enjoyed Italy, and found time to go to Como and take the steamer on the lake. I went there once with my husband, and remember the blue of the sky and the stately homes along the shore. A long time ago, in another life. This year, do you realise, I'll be forty-six, though I'm sure when you first saw me you thought me far more ancient than that. You were two days away from your twenty-first birthday, I well recall. I look forward to knowing you'll be here to celebrate your next one, and will make you a cake with twenty-eight candles. Twenty-eight indeed! 'Time flies on restless pinions,' Schiller wrote, as they taught us in school, but none of us believed it then.

Sydney is beautiful, the harbour a sight to behold. They were spared the war, of course, except for one attack by midget

Japanese submarines that caused a night of panic. I've heard that some people cheaply sold their waterfront mansions and moved to the mountains! They say that things were bad – tough is the local expression – during the war. Clothes and petrol were rationed, cigarettes difficult to get, and beer was in short supply. You poor things, I sometimes want to say, it does sound 'tough', but think it best not to voice such sentiments.

I'm so looking forward to your arrival, and hearing more news of the interesting job you mentioned. I'll send this to Milan in the hope it reaches you, but with any luck you are already en route and will soon be here . . .

The letter finally reached him in Naples. It had followed him around, forwarded from the Milan Centre to his home at Wittersham, and from there in his mother's neat handwriting to the Albergo, a cheap transit hotel in a quiet street behind the *Piazza del Mare*. He was stuck there, impatiently waiting for a ship because a dispute had closed the port. The delay was a frustration that might have been bearable if Caroline had come with him, but Caro was in England and their affair was over, amicable enough but irrevocable.

During his final weeks in Kent with the family, it had been made clear why she had not come to Italy for her holidays. She explained that Australia felt like rather a long way, and also there was another chap. A nice one, he'd hoped sincerely, and been assured the chap was nice and they might soon be making it permanent.

He ordered a beer at the pavement cafe opposite the hotel and read Sarah's letter again. Her English had improved markedly, and the tone was far more cheerful, yet something still puzzled and concerned him. There was so little real news about herself; no names of any acquaintances or friends, no real details of her job or how she spent her spare time.

He wished he could send her a cable to say he was delayed, but since the dispute had escalated in the past few days that was impossible. Not only were the post and telegraph offices now shut, but the docks were silent, the gates locked, all the ships lifeless at anchor. The whole of Italy was paralysed by a general strike.

It might be weeks, even months, before he got away.

Sarah was on her hands and knees, scrubbing the floor of the shower room in the surgical wing, when the summons came. She was washing the concrete slabs with hot water and Jeyes Fluid, a repellent-smelling mixture that made her eyes sting, trying not to breathe the fumes, when the sound of her name on the hospital loudspeaker startled her to such an extent that she knocked over the bottle of disinfectant. It broke into pieces, and the corrosive aroma was like acid. She tried to collect the fragments, but the vapour was strong and made her feel nauseous. Meanwhile, the voice on the speaker repeated the message, this time with a hint of impatience.

'Missus Wise-mun, please. Missus Sarah Wise-mun, go at once to the Superintendent's office.'

'I can't,' she said pointlessly, for there was no-one there to register her predicament. She had to find a dustpan and broom, and clean up the splinters of glass before someone unwittingly came in and stood on them. Ten minutes later, thoroughly hot and flustered, she reached the main hall and knocked on the frosted glass door of the Superintendent's office. She was aware that her hair was dishevelled, and her work clothes were damp and reeked of the pervasive carbolic.

It isn't Germany, she tried to tell herself; *it's not the camp, and the idea of being frightened like this is simply ridiculous. For God's sake, pull yourself together.* But despite trying to bolster her confidence with commonsense, she felt almost paralysed with dread.

'Come in,' a voice called, and she opened the door. She had never been in here before. Her daily superior was one of the civilian nurses, whereas the Superintendent was in charge of the hospital's entire female staff. It was what made the summons so alarming. On her desk was a nameplate which identified her as EDNA RONSON. She was a large lady who looked at Sarah critically.

'We've been paging you. Are you Mrs Wise-man?'

A neatly dressed young man in his twenties sat in the visitor's chair. His suit was European in style; she was not sure why, but she had a feeling he might be German.

'Do you speak English, Mrs Wise-man?' the Superintendent asked, in a tone suggesting that her valuable time was being wasted.

'Yes, Mrs Ronson,' she said, still flustered by the summons.

'*Miss* Ronson.'

'I beg your pardon. I apologise for the delay, but there was a broken bottle in the shower room . . .'

'Never mind.' She sniffed. 'What's that dreadful smell?'

'Disinfectant. You see I dropped the bottle, and then I had to find a broom to sweep up the glass in case someone trod on it . . . cut their feet. I'm afraid it's rather strong,' she trailed off apologetically.

'Extremely.' Miss Ronson gestured towards the young man. 'This is Mr . . . er . . .'

'Hartmann,' he said, rising. 'Christoph Hartmann.' He came forward to take her hand, and bow over it. Miss Ronson regarded this display of old world European courtesy with some curiosity.

'Mr Hartmann wants to talk to you. It'd be more convenient if you did so outside, in the hospital grounds.'

Sarah looked at him and felt a sudden interest. Almost a feeling of excitement. 'But I know you, don't I?'

'You knew my family, Mrs Weismann. Shall we do as proposed, and talk outside?'

They sat on one of the wooden benches in the garden, where convalescing patients read newspapers or walked in the sun, and where a Yugoslav gardener pruned rose bushes.

'Rather an intimidating woman, your Miss Ronson,' he spoke in German.

'Not my Miss Ronson, thank you, Herr Hartmann,' she replied, and looked carefully at him. 'I'm sure I know you from . . .' She shrugged. 'From I don't know where? Have I met you before?'

'No, we never met. At least, I don't think so, unless it was when I was a child. From an early age I was away at boarding school, and after that the naval college. But I'm told I resemble my father.'

'Did I know him? Because the name is unfamiliar.'

'His name . . . our name in those days was Krausen. After the war, I changed mine by deed poll.'

'*Von* Krausen?'

'Yes,' he said. 'My father was Christian Von Krausen.'

'Dear Gott,' Sarah instinctively said, and began to shudder. 'What happened to him?'

'He died – in an air raid.'

'When?'

'November of nineteen forty-four, only six months before the war ended.'

'And your mother? Stephanie?' It was difficult to say her name without bitterness. 'What about her?'

'Also dead. They were both killed in the same raid. Buried in the rubble of . . . of your apartment near the Tiergarten. The one they stole from you.'

It was so totally unexpected, all she could do was stare at him. In the silence between them, she became aware of their immediate surroundings; a patient in a hospital gown limping past, a nurse helping an elderly man to his feet, the regular click of the gardener's pruning shears as he came closer. Sarah switched into English.

'Why are you here?'

'I'm in Australia with the German diplomatic service. For two years now I have worked for our consulate in Canberra. A junior attache. Next year, I may be transferred to our embassy in Washington.'

'Mr Hartmann, I wasn't asking about your career prospects.'

'I'm sorry,' he said, so stiffly formal that she sensed he was intensely nervous.

'I meant why are you *here* today – at this hospital – seeking me out like this? I'm sorry to hear about your parents, but what has it – or you – to do with me, such a long time afterwards?'

'You must have hated us,' Christoph Hartmann said.

'It's the past,' Sarah answered.

'We have to confront the past, Frau Weismann.'

'Not me, Mr Hartmann. Not me. The past to me is yesterday, or last week. Not years ago, the night when my husband disappeared; nor the day when your parents had me declared racially impure and unfit to own the apartment we had bought and lived in all our married lives. Evicted as an illegal occupant.' She saw him flinch, but felt no compassion. She was possessed by a deep anger, although she knew this young man had been a child then, and not responsible for what had been done to her. 'As Aryans and prominent party members, your parents then laid claim to it, and were granted the lease of the property. And I daresay you grew up there?'

'Yes,' he said, 'but I grew up there without ever knowing.'

'How was that, Mr Hartmann? How could one not know?'

'I was only fourteen years old, a cadet at naval college. The war had not even begun. My father came to collect me for the summer holidays, and he said we'd moved. A new home, he explained – near the Brandenburg Gate, so close to the Unt den Linden that you could smell the scent of the lime trees all along the boulevard. And from the big windows of the new apartment, he told me, you could see the Tiergarten, miles of parkland with beautiful trees that came alive in the spring. Strangely enough, I liked that view best in the depth of winter, after the leaves had all gone and the branches were stripped bare.'

'So did I,' she said unexpectedly.

'I asked Papa and Mutti about the apartment. Why had we moved to such a smart district? What sort of people used to live there? They said the former owners were dead, and they'd bought the lease.'

'Did you believe them?'

'I did then. There seemed no reason not to. After all, my father was a successful dental surgeon; why wouldn't I believe he could afford a large *Wohnstube* with crystal chandeliers, and so much elegant antique furniture?'

'And a grand piano,' Sarah said quietly.

'Yes, a grand piano. A Bechstein.'

'That's right.' She watched him carefully. He hesitated, then explained. 'It was the piano that first started me wondering.'

'Why?'

'My parents weren't in the least musical. Nor our friends. So why was the centrepiece of the living room an expensive piano that was used only to hold vases of flowers?'

'Is that all?' She felt a sharp sense of loss. 'A flower stand. Did no-one play it?'

'No. It was polished daily so the wood gleamed like a mirror, but it was never played.'

'A pity. Such an awful waste,' she said, wishing this young man with his disturbing memories would go away. He seemed oblivious of it, determined to explain to her.

'I went back to the naval college. Whenever I was home on leave, I felt that something was strange. I once asked my mother who had owned the piano. She seemed nervous, and said she didn't know who. Papa's lawyers, she told me, had handled it all. I didn't bother asking my father; instead, I asked the janitor.'

'Eisler.'

'Yes. Horst Eisler. He was reluctant to say anything, but he liked a drink, and he liked money. He told me your name. He would only say that you and your daughter had been forced to leave – but he wouldn't say how, and he swore he had no idea where you'd gone.'

'He knew,' Sarah said. 'We went to friends who were courageous enough to hide us. For almost three years we lived in their cellar, and during this time Eisler brought us food, along with the news of how Germany was winning the war. Just like his Fuhrer had promised, he told us. France was occupied, England bombed and crippled across the channel, our troops close to Moscow. Herr Eisler made sure we were well informed about the successful progress of the Reich. As you said, he liked money. When mine ran out, the Gestapo came. He brought them. We were arrested, my daughter Trudi and I – and our brave friends with us – and that really is all you have to know, Herr Hartmann, because the others are dead, and I would like you to go away and leave me now. Or you might learn things you will regret.'

'I already know things I regret, Mrs Weismann.'

'What things?'

'That my father, the eminent dental surgeon, was once your husband's pupil and protege. Doktor Weismann helped him advance, recommended him to important people, sent him patients. I know my mother and you were at school together, best friends who later were bridesmaids for each other, but this was long before the Nazis, and Hitler was a joke, a silly beer hall orator, an uneducated lout with a few thugs in brown shirts as his followers.'

There was an inordinately long silence.

'How did you find out Stefanie and I were school friends?'

'It wasn't difficult. People remembered you. Everyone said you were a great beauty, and very popular.'

'They said that? How strange they found me popular. And

they told you that Franz and your father . . .' For a moment she could not continue; the shock was too great. 'Yes, he was his pupil. Christian Von Krausen was an exceptional student. And for a long time we thought he was a friend.'

He seemed dismayed at the distress he had caused her.

'Please, Mrs Weismann, I didn't come here to upset you.'

'Then why in God's name did you come?'

'I've been looking for you, ever since my parents died. I'd come back from two years at sea, and at last they gave us leave. It happened only days before I reached Berlin. All the people in the block were killed, except Eisler. They dug him out of the basement, but he was dying. He told me enough of the truth to make me go and see my father's lawyer. His name was Kempe.'

'Heinz Kempe,' she said.

'Yes. An elderly man, very formal. It was unreal. He greeted me as if there was no war, or else it was a war which we were going to win. He had an office in the Ruhl building in Kaiser Wilhelmstrasse. Almost everything was destroyed nearby, there was nothing but rubble in the neighbourhood, yet his building still stood there, all three floors of it untouched, and his office was crowded with papers and law books, like it must have looked for forty years or more.

'He said my father had instructed him to demand requisition of your apartment; that father had always liked it and envied you living there, and as someone would surely claim it, why not him? Mr Kempe seemed to think a lawyer had to obey his client's instructions – and the truth is, I'm afraid, he seemed to find no fault with such a process.'

'There were a lot of lawyers like Heinz Kempe,' Sarah said.

'I asked him about you. He knew you'd been taken to a camp,

and felt sure you were dead by now. He said it was a pity. I thought that an unfortunate choice of words.'

She said nothing.

'He was pleased I'd called, because he could finalise probate. There was, it seemed, a large amount of money due; my parents had accumulated great wealth, and since I was the only child I inherited the estate. Apart from property, I had numbered accounts in several Swiss banks and even money in the United States. A few weeks after probate was granted, his building was destroyed in one of the last raids of the war. He was apparently at his desk when it happened. Did you know?'

'That he was killed? Yes, I knew.' She hesitated a moment. 'After . . . after I was discharged from Belsen I went to search for him. I needed a deposition that the apartment had been confiscated, to help me make a claim for restitution.'

'And did you make the claim?'

'No-one could find any papers. No-one really tried very hard. Unlike you, Mr Hartmann, who somehow traced me to this hospital. So perhaps you'll tell me how you found me, and explain why.'

'I found you by accident.'

'What accident?' She was trying to contain her impatience with him, aware that this was her lunch time and she had overstayed the allotted half hour.

'Anyone who applies to emigrate, as you know, has a check on their background and political affiliations. Each person has a file.'

'Of course,' Sarah murmured, 'a file.'

'Our legation keeps a list of Germans brought here under the government scheme. That's where I saw your name. I wasn't sure at first, but according to the information, you were the right age, you were a Berliner, you'd survived Bergen-Belsen – so it had to be you. I made inquiries through the Australian immigration department, and they helped me find you.'

'Did they speculate about why you wanted to do this? My life has taught me, Mr Hartmann, that anonymity is a great deal safer than being noticed. And if one has to be on a file, it's best that file is left unopened.'

'I explained that it was purely personal. That I was the son of an old friend.'

'I see,' she said, after an awkward silence. 'Well, you've told me how you came here. Now tell me why you went to all this trouble.'

For the first time he seemed unsure of himself.

'Can you meet me after you finish work?'

'I could, Mr Hartmann – if I so wished. But I want you to stop playing games, and explain yourself.'

'Will you indulge me?' he asked. 'Please?'

'Why the devil should I?'

'I'm trying to make up for what my parents did to you.'

'That's the past. I told you, I prefer not to revisit it.'

'But I must, Frau Weismann.'

'Why?'

'Because of how they behaved. I can hardly believe anyone – let alone my own family – would be so despicable. So squalid. I spent years feeling ashamed, wishing you were alive so I could beg your forgiveness and make amends. Why do you think I changed my name? Because Von Krausen now meant something so corrupt, I couldn't bear it. But there seemed no way to repay what they'd done, not if you were dead. Why do you think I've searched so hard for you, since I found out you might have actually survived?'

'I thought I was asking the questions, Mr Hartmann. Why did you need to search for me?'

'Very well,' he shrugged, 'if you won't indulge me, here you are.' He handed her an envelope.

'What is it?'

'The deeds of an apartment. It has a view of the harbour, in a district of Sydney called Potts Point. It's yours.'

'How can it be mine?'

'All you need to do is come with me to the lawyer. We sign the deed, which makes it legally your property. It's all paid for.'

'Paid by you? Are you crazy?'

'Not the least bit.'

'You must be. An apartment for me?'

'For you, Mrs Weismann – the only way I can try to redress the unforgivable thing my parents did in Berlin. If you don't like it, or it upsets you, then sell it. Make the choice; it belongs to you. I bought it in your name.'

It seemed insane, but Neil began to wonder if the near miss with the car had been an attempt to kill him. It happened as he left the Chiesa di Monteoliveto, the bombed church which was being restored, where the Renaissance monuments and panels that had been saved were open for public inspection. He had spent over an hour there, enjoying the bas-reliefs and the sculptured tombs by Rossellino.

It was one of many churches he had prowled through, for time was beginning to hang heavily and he was bored. The strike which had closed most of Italy was in its fourth week, and both sides appeared inflexible. After nearly two years of sifting emigrants for Australia, he was at last on his way there, only to be stranded in a Mediterranean seaport.

He knew no-one here in Naples. He had walked a lot, and been on a tour to Pompeii. On the bus he had met a tourist couple from Epsom in Surrey, and two nights ago they had dined together and drunk rather a lot of wine. After dinner, they had gone upstairs and shared a bottle of brandy, and he had sat on the floor in their hotel room which was considerably grander than his, and the wife, Christine, had sat on the carpet beside him. She was blonde and pretty, and in her mid-twenties, smiling a lot, her bright gaze inviting and beckoning him, and when her husband had closed his eyes to go to sleep on the sofa, she'd leaned over and quietly kissed Neil, then after several more kisses, had taken his hand and guided it beneath her dress.

She was warm and very moist, and appeared not to care that they were only a metre away from her husband, as she slipped off her pants then fumbled with Neil's buttons and undid his trousers. He slid out of them while she hoisted her dress – both feeling a high excitement, aroused by the danger of the husband's proximity – and after fondling each other they made love in a silent and frenzied intensity.

Afterwards, when they were breathless, expended, triumphant at the completion of their orgasm achieved without the slightest sound, the husband had sat up wide awake.

'Finished, Chrissie?' he asked.

'All finished, love,' she said.

'And how was it – on a scale of one to ten?'

'About eight,' she said. 'Not at all bad. Rather nice, in fact.'

'Sod that,' he replied. 'We don't want *nice*. I won't tolerate anyone being *nice*. This is simply about getting you a fuck, not falling for some virtual bloody stranger.'

'What the hell . . .' Neil was stunned. He saw the man smiling at his wife. And her smiling back.

'Sorry, darling,' Christine turned to Neil. 'Just one of those things. He's both ways, you see. Absolutely torrid with the gents, but really not very interested in me any more. I'm quite sure he fancies you like mad.'

'Potty about him,' her husband on the sofa said. 'Watched his bum going up and down, while you two were at it. Positively riveting, darling.' He'd said this to Neil, who grabbed his trousers and fled.

The car was parked down the street towards the bay. The engine must have been running, for as Neil began to cross the road it seemed to leap forward, gathering speed, and as it drew nearer it swerved directly at him. He had a moment of alarm, then reacted instinctively – jumping back onto the broken pavement, bumping and knocking down an elderly couple – and while he was helping them to their feet, trying to apologise to them, the car had skidded around the corner with tyres shrieking and was gone. In a brief glimpse, he saw the vehicle was a blue Fiat; the driver appeared to be Italian, not drunk, not particularly young, a man in an open-necked shirt, his eyes fixed directly on Neil, as if aiming at him like a target.

When he got back to the Albergo, he went into the bar and ordered a drink. Sitting there, he tried to reconstruct the moment, to create an image of the driver in his mind. A Neapolitan, clearly.

But that told him nothing. It was the eyes . . . the direct gaze. The more he thought about them, the more certain he was it had been deliberate. And yet who – and why? It was then he happened to turn towards the entrance to the foyer, and saw a figure standing there. Not until the man had come inside, did he recognise it was Stewart Mitchell.

'Mate,' Mitchell put out a limp hand, and gave an amiable and sympathetic smile. 'I heard about the strike. What a bummer.'

'Yes, hardly my idea of fun.' Neil was trying to regain his composure after the shock of seeing him here.

'It's getting worse, they reckon.'

'God, I hope not. What are you doing in Naples?'

'Drove down from Rome. Hired a convertible Alfa-Romeo. Bloody lovely it was, especially with a sexy Eyetie sheila beside me – her skirt up and the hood down.'

'Someone tried to run me over,' Neil said.

'Eh? Someone did what, sport?'

'Tried to bloody kill me,' Neil said.

'Good God. Seriously?'

'Seriously.'

'Then for Christ's sake, call up the politzia – or perhaps you've done it already?'

'No, Stewart, I haven't done it.'

'Why the hell not?'

The waiter brought Neil's drink. He asked if the Signore's friend would care for anything. Mitchell said the Signore's friend would like a beer, and to make sure it was a cold one. When the waiter had gone to fetch it, he asked again why Neil had not gone to the police.

'Well, for a start,' Neil said, 'I only got a glimpse of the car. No chance to see the number.'

'What about the driver?'

'Local, by his looks. In his thirties, I'd say.'

'Would you know him again?'

'I don't know. I might. He aimed directly at me.'

'Then don't frig around. Go to the cops.'

'They're on strike, too,' Neil reminded him.

'So they are. Still, someone must be left on duty,' Mitchell said. 'Some token Plod on shift. Has to be a bit of law and order, even in flaming Italy. I mean, fair go – a member of the IRO and what's more, almost an Aussie – we can't have bloody dagoes going round Napoli trying to run you over.'

Neil had the strangest impression that Mitchell's words, while jocular, were meant as a derisive taunt. 'There is another problem,' he kept his voice carefully casual, 'if I report it, and by chance the police catch someone, it means a charge. Which would mean a trial – God only knows when. And I'd have to wait here for it, as the only witness.'

'Now there, mate, you may have a point,' Mitchell agreed. 'It's the last bloody thing you'd want, to be stuck here in this lousy dump waiting for a court case.' He watched the waiter set down the beer, tasted it and shrugged. 'For one thing, the bloody beer's like possum's piss. Personally, I can't wait to get home, to get hold of a decent schooner of Toohey's New. Remember to ask for it, when you get there; best brew you'll ever taste, specially after that warm bitter you Poms poison yourselves with. So you won't report it?'

'I don't think so.'

'Maybe it was an accident. Bloke lost control of his steering.'

'I doubt very much if it was an accident.'

'Then why you? Got any enemies?'

'Not here,' Neil said, finishing his drink. He gazed at the other man. 'At least I didn't think so. Until today.'

Mitchell didn't even blink. Just stared back at him.

'You know what I think, Neil?'

'What, Stewart?'

'Maybe it wasn't really an attempt to kill you at all. Just a sort of warning.'

'From anyone we know?'

'A warning,' he continued, ignoring the remark, 'to show you how easy it would be. Might be one of your late colleagues. Some bad buggers in our section at that Milan Centre – I think we both knew it.'

'Who was in charge? Doesn't corruption begin at the top?'

Again Mitchell ignored what had been said, although his eyes grew chilly. 'They didn't like you, mate. I can assure you of that. When you're making a few easy quid, it's one in, all in. Or else the others feel threatened. They reckon as an outsider – a Pommy bastard, not really one of us – you might be a dobber. They got real shitty when you said no thanks. Looking a gift horse and all that crap – know what I mean? Then, after you left, they started worrying. Bluey McGill's a hard man, and he has some mean friends. Russ Moroney's done time.'

'What about you? Just happen to be here in Naples, on the spot so soon afterwards. That's what I call convenient.'

'It wouldn't have been me, mate.' Mitchell grinned at him. 'I don't need to hire the driver of a Fiat to scare the shit out of you.'

'But you're here unexpectedly – and although I didn't tell you, you seem to know it was a Fiat.'

'Calculated guess, Neil. After all, we're in Italy, and every second car's a Fiat. Why not let me buy you a drink?'

'No thanks.'

'Okay. Since we're agreed that making charges would keep you stuck here for months – and that if you were silly enough to try it, Bluey's mates would see it never got in front of a magistrate – as we're in agreement on those points, I can tell you they had it fixed to put in the frighteners. It *was* a warning. If that driver had wanted to run you over, you'd be in the morgue now. And whether you believe me or not, I came to try to stop it before anything worse happened.'

'Of course I don't believe you.'

'Suit yourself.'

'You're a bigger bastard than any of them.'

'Just shut up and listen. It wasn't on your account I drove all this way. I'm not here for your benefit, sport.'

'I can certainly believe that.'

'I came to tell them to back off, but I was too late. I had to drive here because the strike's shut down the phones. You can't get through to anyone. I'm here because the last thing I want is violence – an inquiry that might lead back to the Milan Centre. Cops, questions, the bloody Brigadier waffling on. You still don't believe me? Well, try believing this. I'm not opposed to violence – when necessary. But when there's another way, something far easier and more effective, why not make use of it?'

Neil felt growing unease.

'I don't follow you,' he said. 'Is this some kind of threat?'

'You could say that. I tried to tell the others you won't spill the beans. You can't. Not when you've been tampering with people's files. Felt sorry for those two, did you? Or were you shafting the girl, and she conned you into it? Either way, it doesn't matter a bugger to me.'

'What the hell are you talking about?'

It was futile, but he had to make the effort.

'You know exactly what I'm talking about. And who. Ilona and Miklos Francis, formerly Ferencz.' Mitchell said. 'You fooled that committee – bunch of amateurs – but you never fooled me, mate, not for a second. The Yanks had a file with all their details. Very different to the file you showed us. A few important bits missing in your version – like Palestine. Attempted illegal entry. We have a strict quota for Jews, and I doubt if we'd welcome Zionists or gaolbirds. After their ship was turned back, they copped gaol in Cyprus – until they escaped from custody. Lively young couple, eh? Are these really the sort of people we want in our fine sunburnt country?'

'They did nothing criminal.'

'Try telling that to a judge. I could have that pair sent back, any time I like.'

'For Christ's sake, leave them alone,' Neil said.

Mitchell laughed. He signalled the waiter for another beer.

'I'll leave them alone,' he said, 'as long as it suits me. It depends on you. You've landed some soft job, we hear, when you get to Australia. Liaison officer in some do-good committee dealing with migrants' problems. My mates don't like the sound of it. They reckon it might be best if you jacked it in – resigned.'

'Tell your mates they can go to hell.'

'I knew you'd say that. I did warn them you're one of those stubborn bastards.'

'The job is nothing to do with you or them. There's no reason why we should ever meet again.'

'Let's hope not,' Mitchell said. 'Because if you ever turn out to be a problem, trouble wouldn't stop with little Miss Francis and her brother . . . you'd also be in the deepest shit.'

'Look, threats are pointless.' Neil tried to be diplomatic, but anger and dislike made him reckless. 'I think Milan's a disgrace. I think you're a nasty, evil prick. But I don't intend to be a problem to anyone. I've got better things to do with my life.'

'Good. Because let's be really clear about this, you'd come to a very sticky end. Forgery, conniving at the entry of undesirables while in a position of authority – can't you just hear the judge up there on his bench? *Undermining the immigration process, abusing your trust, criminal behaviour deserving of the most severe penalty*. You'd go inside for three years minimum. And that means any accusations you might try to make against us would be a waste of time. Tainted evidence from a convicted crim.'

He stared at Neil, his eyes were hard, his voice as sharp as a razor.

'Or put it this way – since you're going to Godz-own country to become one of us. It'd be like a barbecue, with you on a spit as helpless as a sucking pig. And I'd only have to light a match.' His smile made Neil want to shiver. 'Make sure you never forget that,' Stewart Mitchell said.

Chapter 5

The tram laboured up the William Street hill, bell clanging as it passed through the crossing in Darlinghurst Road towards the section stop. It was a different type to the trams in which she usually travelled; this one was modern and had corridors and more comfortable seats that were protected from the weather. In the parts of Sydney that she knew, Sarah had only experienced the antique and bone-shaking conveyances that were known as 'toast rack' trams.

She imagined they were called this because of the rows of wooden benches that were always packed solid with people in the peak hours, draughty transports with access on either side but no real doors to close, so that summer or winter you were exposed to the heat or cold, or even worse, the driving winds. They were hazardous for the conductors who had to swing along the platform outside, burdened with their bags containing the tickets and money, while young newspaper boys jumped on and off, taking risks to sell the afternoon headlines.

But this tram was quite different, just as Mr Hartmann had said the district they were going to was different. As they disembarked, she realised it was more than that; it was like stepping into another country. First of all she was aware of wonderful aromas, the smell of garlic, and the soft odour of yeast from a bakery. Where they stood on the busy corner there were lots of small shops; the bakery, a grocer's, an open-fronted fruiterer's with a large Greek man being cheerful with his customers, and next door a real European-style delicatessen, with sliced meats, hanging salamis, familiar cheeses on display, trays of olives, and surely that was *brockwurst*.

'*Brockwurst*,' Mr Hartmann said, as if reading her mind.

Sarah told herself she really must stop thinking of him as Mr Hartmann. He had asked her to call him Christoph, then explained that in this country people always shortened names and everyone called him Chris, so why not make it Chris? She was unsure how she felt about this, whether she wanted to keep it formal despite his surprising kindness – or whether the deep hurt his parents had caused her all those years ago was too painful to accede to what he so badly wanted, which was both forgiveness and friendship – so in the meantime, she temporised by calling him nothing at all.

'This is quite unlike the rest of Sydney,' she said.

'It's known as Kings Cross. But I understand everyone just refers to it as "the Cross".'

She looked around her. The place felt vigorous and alive; it was crowded with men and women who seemed more casually dressed than elsewhere. She saw girls wearing slacks and bright makeup, an artist stood working at an easel without harassment, there were even men shopping with their purchases in string bags, a sight that was more reminiscent of Berlin in the old days than here.

The bell clanged, and the tram went away from them down

an incline called Bayswater Road towards the eastern suburbs. Sarah kept gazing about. Across the street there was a butcher, W.A. Grubb & Co. Near it a snack bar, identified by a painted sign on the windows as the Hasty-Tasty. There was a shop that specialised in rare brands of tea and coffee, and alongside it was a Parfumerie. There were flower stalls, tobacco kiosks and newspaper stands. It was like Europe. She smiled, and Christoph Hartmann watched her and wished she would smile like that more often.

'Like it?'

'It's wonderful,' she said. 'A surprise.'

'Cosmopolitan.'

'Yes. Is the apartment near here?'

'Quite near. About half a mile away.'

She felt a slight disappointment, and hoped it was not obvious. She had wished it might be right here, somewhere in the heart of this vibrant bohemian village. But he read her expression.

'This is always on your doorstep, when you want it. A few minutes by bus. It's lively, the Cross, and good for shopping. But at night it's also a red-light district, and has clubs that stay open as late as the police allow. The place hardly ever stops. Where we're going is a nicer neighbourhood to live. At least I hope you think so.'

'I'm sure I will,' she said, and felt a sudden debt of gratitude towards this rather correct young man, who had sought her out with such tenacity, and was now anxious she would like the apartment he had generously given her. He would not even allow her to think of it as charity. When she had said – at his lawyer's where they signed all the papers – that it was benevolence of a kind she had never known or expected, he swiftly corrected her. It was, he said, a tiny gesture that would not even repay half the damage his parents had done her. She should remember his family had deprived her of her real home. To be allowed to spend some of the money he had inherited trying to repay her for this, was his privilege. Would she please understand that?

It was difficult not to respond to his sincerity.

'Which way . . . Chris?'

She could tell the use of his name pleased him; he smiled in return, and it relaxed and warmed his face.

'Towards the harbour. We can take the bus, or walk if you'd prefer.'

'Let's walk.'

She wanted to see it all. They went past coffee shops; there seemed to be an abundance of them. The Arabian, the Willow Tree Cafe, the spacious Californian. Inside the latter was a great deal of smoke and laughter; it looked companionable with groups of mainly young people engaged in noisy debate; at some tables couples sipped their coffee and made plans, while others sat alone reading newspapers or books. Beside the window a young girl was busy writing, glancing up as they passed, then returning to what was clearly more important to her in the pages of her notepad.

Among her impressions was a profusion of narrow doorways, clearly entrances to a variety of curious places. HOTEL ELEVEN, she saw one doorway inscribed, and thought it looked enticingly shady and illicit. Next to it, by a numerate oddity, was CLUB FORTY-FOUR. They passed the open foyer of a cinema, and further on a neon sign blinked RESIDENTIAL HOTEL – ROOMS TO LET. At the bottom of a narrow flight of stairs, a peroxided girl in a short skirt watched the street through the smoke haze of her cigarette. Her eyes assessed Chris as they walked past.

'She's out early, looking for customers,' Sarah said.

'I believe it changed during the war,' he said. 'It was popular with the American soldiers who came here on leave. Of course, it has a flamboyant history, this area. It's hard to believe, but in the early days of the colony this was nothing but open fields, a farm owned by a Judge. Eleven acres was granted to him, and he built himself a mansion. I bought some books for you, in case you want to find out more about the region . . .'

He really is too correct, too serious, she thought. *Not at all like Steffi when we were his age* – and the remembrance of this brought instant recall of Stephanie's wickedly delicious humour, their shared laughter, and the sharp pain of disbelief when she realised her friend Steffie had betrayed her. Of all the things that had happened, even in the concentration camp, it was very nearly the worst. But Steffi was dead – and miraculously she was alive – and this young man, too formal by far, was just as alone in the world as she was. On an impulse she took his arm, and he turned and smiled at her. He carefully adjusted his stride so they were in step.

'We'll cut through here. Orwell Street. That was the name of the Judge's mansion, Orwell House.'

'Fine,' she said. And after a moment, 'Chris . . .'

'Yes?'

'You're not using my name, because you don't know what to call me. I'd be very pleased if you'd call me Sarah.'

'Sarah,' he said. 'I'd like to, if I may. Thank you.'

'Don't thank me – just remember to say Sarah.'

He nodded, and smiled again, which was what she had hoped.

If he was Steffi's son, he had to be less serious. They came to a corner. Facing each other were two quite large art-deco buildings.

'What are they?' she asked.

'That one is called the Minerva. It's your local playhouse.'

'How splendid,' she said, 'to have a local playhouse. I'll go if I can afford it.'

'Perhaps sometime when I'm able to get away from Canberra, we could go together?'

'I'd like that.' She indicated the building opposite. 'And what's this, since you're such an authority on Kings Cross?'

'The Roosevelt. A nightclub,' he said. 'Not so respectable.'

'Well, then, I shan't be going there,' she assured him solemnly, and was rewarded with another smile.

They reached the next intersection, and Macleay Street was spread out before them. Even from here Sarah caught a brief glimpse of the harbour, but her attention was taken by the elegant street, so like a European boulevard; a canopy of plane trees, clusters of small shops, cafes and striking buildings; among these a decaying but still grand villa surrounded by wrought iron railings that enclosed a magnificent garden. When they passed she saw it was called the Cairo.

Further down the street there seemed to be one massive apartment block after another, the largest of them a high tower with a distinct Spanish influence that was redolent of Hollywood. As they drew near to it her heart sank. *Please God*, she thought, *not this*. It was doubtless expensive – that was apparent by the parade of smart cars parked outside – and from what little she had read in the newspapers it was one of the *chic* apartment blocks built in the thirties. Surely, she thought, Christoph Hartmann could not have envisaged her in a labyrinth like that!

To her relief they went past. Near the corner, where Macleay Street ended and Wylde Street began, he stopped. There was a squat three-storey building, solid brick and sandstone, with tiny balconies on each floor. Modest and undistinguished. You could almost pass by and not notice it. As if he felt this, he was apologetic.

'It's nicer inside,' he said, 'and the view is quite pleasant.'

Christoph had a bunch of keys. He selected one and opened the front door of the building, then gave the keys to Sarah. He told her it was apartment number three, which occupied the entire third floor. They went up two flights of stairs, and came to a tiny vestibule at the top. Sarah found the key and they went in. It was larger than she had expected; a compact entry hall led to adjoining living and dining rooms; after that was an extensive corridor with a kitchen off it, three bedrooms, a main bathroom and a second shower and lavatory.

There were also front and side balconies. The latter looked across Garden Island, where there were naval dockyards, but the view was far more extensive than that, including a sweeping vista all the way from the Harbour Bridge to the bulky outline of South Head. It was a bewitching sight, with freighters on their way to the wharves and warehouses, and ferries from the northside plying to Circular Quay. The whole pageant of the harbour was spread out before her.

When he first said an apartment, she had envisaged one or two rooms, a utility flat, perhaps in one of the inner western suburbs. She would have been content with that. But this – not only was it in a favoured district, but it was every bit as pleasant as her Berlin home, even as large, while having the advantage of this breathtaking outlook. After the places in which she had lived for almost ten years, this was beyond her wildest dreams. By the time she had walked in each of the rooms again, inspecting the apartment for a second, then a third time, she was awash with helpless tears of joy.

That night after Chris had gone, she sat on the side balcony watching the moonlit harbour. It was still difficult to accept this miracle had happened to her. Expectation had been absent from her life for so long, that this sudden good fortune was accompanied by a fear of some event that might occur to snatch it away. She felt uneasy with happiness, and tried to chide herself for being foolish.

The apartment had been sold fully furnished. He hoped she would like the furniture, but if not they would sell items and replace them with others more to her taste. He had a feeling she might like most of it, for although there was no grand piano, much of what was there reminded him of the Tiergarten apartment. Did she agree?

She not only agreed, but suspected he had selected and bought some special pieces; a sofa, a set of dining chairs, and an old oak dining table were uncannily similar to her own furniture the last time she had seen it. The more she thought about this, the more certain she felt he had carefully chosen them to make her feel completely at home here. If so, he had succeeded. The fear of losing this blessed gift at last began to fade. She did feel at home. She belonged.

Sarah Weismann marvelled at her luck, at the remarkable affinity she had with two such young men – each of whom had helped her survive since the day she had stood, head shaven, dehydrated and starving, waiting for death. Neil would soon be here, please God, although from all accounts he was delayed in Naples by a general strike, and she had heard nothing since a hasty letter many weeks ago. Now, astonishingly, here was Christoph Hartmann, whose mother had been Steffi Gressmann, her closest childhood friend who had married and become Stephanie Von Krausen. Whatever Steffi had done to her, whether through greed or malice, Sarah had good reason to be grateful to her son.

From the secluded balcony she watched a ship arrive, brought in by the pilot boat and a bustling tug, while the brightly lit ferry boats scurried back and forth to Circular Quay. The night was so still that when the larger ferries came past she could faintly hear music played by a trio on board – she had heard them once when she took a ferry ride: three musicians with violin, piano accordion and double bass, playing to the passengers, collecting whatever few pence their audience cared to give, the sentimental sound of their music drifting across the water. It was unbelievably beautiful, and she felt thankful that she was here – in this harbour city able to look down on such a sight. For the first time in ages, she was filled with an immense gratitude that she was alive.

Dawn came, and the first glimmer of sunlight began to change the colour of the sea as their ship, the *Castel Florentino*, came through the giant headlands that stood as a gateway to the harbour. Ahead of them was a vista the like of which Helen had never imagined; glittering water encircled by sloping land, the light revealing terraced hillsides of homes that stood proud and aloof around the harbour that had once – more than a hundred and sixty years ago – seen the arrival of convict vessels. Land had been reclaimed here, a few great mansions of the early settlement remained, but other traces of the penal colony had vanished. Helen felt an excitement that had nothing to do with the historic past, for she knew little of it; hers was the elation of being here at last, on the threshold of a new life and whatever it might bring, to be finally free of the long and wasted years they had spent in so many of Europe's desperate refugee camps.

She was out on deck by fortunate coincidence. Unable to stand another moment in the squalid hull where they slept in such cramped proximity – hundreds of men crowded into double bunks at one end of the ship and women and their children in dormitories at the other – she had fled the noxious smell of packed humanity to seek a breath of fresh air, arriving just in time to see the sun's first rays touch the rising tide, and create in her this feeling of exhilaration.

It had been a loathsome journey. The *Castel Florentino* was not a passenger ship; she was an unwieldy freighter, cheaply and hastily converted to take almost a thousand people at the lowest possible rates, for there was now an ever-increasing flood of men and women being recruited in Europe for many of the country's post-war building projects. Australia had taken its decision to populate or perish, but there were not enough ships to fully accomplish this policy. Their vessel was destined for the breaker's yard until it had been found and refitted like a cattle boat. It was registered in Liberia, a country that had no ocean and no standards of seaworthiness, or else it would not have been allowed to leave any port.

Helen didn't care. They had jobs; it had been arranged and the news given to them when they reached Marseilles. They would repay the cost of their passage by two years' employment with a construction company that was building houses in a district called Cooma, for some large new hydro-electric project. Michael was to work as a builder's labourer, while she would be a clerk in the office, and also serve as an interpreter.

She decided that it had a grand sound to it – Cooma – and had learned it was in the Australian alps, and it was possible they might even be able to ski, the way they had when they were small children on the hills above their village in winter. Her only slight concern was Miki, who had promptly declared he did not like the idea of being a builder's labourer. *Never mind*, she thought. He'd complain at first, then accept what lay ahead. It was freedom and a new start, or at least it would be after they had worked their obligatory two years.

For her it was also a relief from being at the mercy of some of the men who ran the refugee camps, and she shuddered at the memory of what certain people – respectable citizens selected for their probity – had asked her to do. There were so many women both desperate and willing, that the men who ran the camps were quite overt about their expectations; they would grant whatever was required; in return all the women need do was get into bed. No discussion, no affection; just take off their clothes and be available. She had kept rejecting these crude advances, watching others get their papers; sometimes in her torment wondering why she could not do what they asked, empty her mind and let them do as they wished for an hour or two, if only to be free.

But they were not all like that. She thought, as she often did, of the man who had done so much for them. Neil Latham. It was solely because of him she was standing here, watching as the freighter passed a tranquil bay with many yachts at anchor, and approached a headland on which there were tall buildings. If only he had bothered to tell her he was leaving, and given her a chance to thank him. Not that it mattered any longer. By now, he would barely remember her.

Sarah had been awake since the first glimmer of dawn. She made coffee, and took it out to the balcony as the sun lit the water, and she watched an old cargo ship proceeding slowly down the harbour. An official-looking launch came out to meet it, and tied up alongside as some uniformed men went aboard, and she realised these were customs officers. There were a great many people on the decks, a surprising number, for it hardly appeared suitable to be a passenger vessel. With its general shabbiness, peeling paint and obvious signs of rust, it looked as if it should be headed for the scrapyard. She could read the name *Castel Florentino* on the stern, and wished she had binoculars to see what some of those on board looked like, and thought that when she could afford it, she would try to buy a pair. And then she remembered; she could afford it.

Sarah took out the letter that she had found last night, when she went to bolt the front door. The envelope had been pushed beneath it, which meant he must have returned for this purpose sometime during the evening. She took it from the pocket of her dressing gown, and read it over again.

My dear Sarah,

One small thing I forgot to tell you. Or perhaps I thought it safer to write this and leave it for you, so you could have time to consider it and not be upset with me.

I know you are committed to work at the hospital until your contract with the government is over, and therefore if you wish to

*live in your apartment and not return to the assigned quarters you
will have many more expenses. In the Bank of New South Wales
at Kings Cross, I have deposited an amount of money in your
name to help with accounts for rates and electricity, as well as the
extra travel costs you will have, and even for small things like
flowers, and wine – which are things you have been without for
too long. The branch is in Darlinghurst Road, and it is arranged
with the manager that you should go there, introduce yourself, and
sign the required forms to operate the account. There is no point in
frowning, as I expect you might be doing. It is already your
account and has no longer anything at all to do with me.*

*If you feel angry about this – if you consider it charity or feel
that I should have told you, I can only repeat that you must please
allow me to make amends for what your friend, my mother, did.
It is the only way I can regain some self-respect.*

*There is a thousand pounds in the account, and if you choose
to be offended and not accept it, then it will remain there, and in
time it will diminish and be wasted by bank charges. Do you wish
to see the Bank of New South Wales profit in such a manner?
Please, dear Sarah, go and sign your name, and use the money as
you need. If not, I shall be sad, you will be poor, and the bank will
benefit. Think of my mother – of how she was before she became
your enemy. Would she have been in favour of the bank squirreling
your money away?*

Sincerely,

Chris

Squirreling, she thought. *Fancy that.* Suddenly the phrase made
her laugh. Dear correct and proper Christoph Hartmann was
revealing a sense of humour.

He's absolutely right, Sarah decided. *The Steffi I knew would be livid at the thought of a bank 'squirreling' her money away.* She resolved that she would go today, take what the Australians called a 'sickie', and visit the Kings Cross branch to sign the documents. And after that . . . well, after that she would buy herself some flowers and have coffee at the Arabian.

She looked out at the morning. Macleay Street was waking up. A milkman was delivering to the flats opposite. A truckload of sailors went past, to the naval dockyard where two corvettes were anchored. The sun was beginning to warm her; it was going to be a lovely day. The first day of the rest of her life.

She had a fine apartment, a menial job as a cleaner in Concord Hospital for another four months, and a thousand pounds in the bank. She was rich beyond all her expectations.

PART TWO

1951–1953

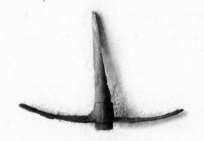

Chapter 6

Immigration formalities were mercifully swift, a welcome contrast to the excessive zeal of the customs officers. The inspection procedure had seemed endless, with their belongings searched and sharp warnings that the import of illegal substances, indecent books, or anything agricultural like seeds or plants would be severely punished by fine or imprisonment. The same threatening phrase was barked at each person or family group, but as the majority did not speak English, it became a tedious and futile exercise in bureaucratic bullying.

Finally they were sorted into various groups. Most were going to migrant reception centres, while waiting to be assigned work. The largest number, going by train to Bathurst, were disembarked first. After them came others bound for the camp at Greta, then the relatively small contingent already contracted for Cooma straggled down the gangway. It was mid-morning, becoming hot, and they were conscious of persistent flies. Their first excitement, already diminished by the lack of welcome, became puzzled confusion when they saw a convoy of open lorries waiting for them on the dockside.

'You mob, the Lawrenson workers for Cooma, over this way,'

a man in charge shouted, as they looked at the flat-top trucks in dismay. 'C'mon. What did you expect, chauffeurs and Rolls-Royces?'

No-one had much more than a suitcase of personal belongings, except for a middle-aged Polish woman visibly perspiring in a long fur coat, and trying to find a porter to carry two cabin trunks for her. The Grand Duchess, Michael had named her at the start of their voyage only a few days out from Marseilles, and the title had stuck.

'A porter.' She hailed a passing dock worker imperiously.

'Eh?' He stopped and stared at her in astonishment. 'Are you talkin' to me?'

'Of course to you. I require a porter.' She spoke slowly and loudly, enunciating with great care as if it might help him understand.

'Bloody reffo,' he said incredulously. 'People turn up in this bloody place and think it's bloody Christmas.'

'There must be porters.' The Duchess was at her grandest.

'You'll be lucky.' He strolled off to tell his mates about this eccentric apparition.

There were a group of migrant workers building an extension to the dockyard terminal. They wore shorts and sleeveless singlets, and were tanned and leathered by the sun. The rhythmic hammering and the rasp of saws cutting timber gradually ceased as they became conscious of the new arrivals.

There was a moment of silence, then the shouts began.

'You poor silly bastards,' came a voice.

'Go back,' called out another, 'before it's too late.'

'Yes, go back.' Now there was a chorus of voices supporting him. 'It's a shitty place, this. You'll be sorry you came here.'

'You will,' others taunted, and to sensitive ears the teasing had a harsh edge to it. 'None of us are welcome. They hate reffos.'

'It's two years of hell.'

'Ignore them,' Helen said, seeing Michael stop to listen.

'Just what we needed, after the way those bastards from the customs treated us. Makes us really feel good to arrive.'

'Take no notice. They sound like Yugoslavs.'

'They do. Serbs or Croats. Or Slovenes. Crazy people. You can tell that by the way their heads come to a point,' Michael said, and she laughed.

'You won't laugh, girl, when you find out what it's like here,' the man who had first spoken called across at her. 'Wait and see. It'll soon wipe that laugh off your sexy little face.'

Michael turned and shouted at him. 'Shut up, you miserable Croatian bastard. Get fucked and shut up.'

This produced a startled silence among the construction crew. A bunch of wharf labourers laughed. The Grand Duchess, sitting on one of her cabin trunks, looked puzzled at the effect he had created.

'Whatever did that young man say?' she asked, but no-one bothered to answer her.

A truck driver grinned at Michael. 'You better settle down, sport, and get on me truck,' he said amiably, 'or you'll set a new record – only five minutes in the country and you turn on a blue.'

'What's a blue?' Michael asked.

'A fight.'

'A blue, eh?' He stored it away, along with the other slang he had accumulated. 'I wouldn't mind turning on a blue. If he gives my sister any more crap, I'll beat the shit out of him.'

'You probably could, too,' the driver grinned, looking at him. Helen could see he was impressed, for Michael had grown taller and filled out; he was muscular and sometimes aggressive, not at all like the boy who mocked the Germans in Budapest, and had climbed out onto the roof with her at nights, watching the city burn and searchlights vainly chase the bombers. A long time ago, measured by what had happened to their lives since. Sometimes she missed that wilful fourteen-year-old. On his next birthday he would be twenty-one, and the intervening years had made him cynical and tough.

'Your sister, eh?' the driver said. 'Well, the pair of you hop aboard, up front near the cabin. It's less bumpy there.'

'Where are we going?' Helen asked, as they climbed on the truck.

'Search me, girl, I'm only the driver. They'd never tell us anything really important like that,' he laughed. He had an engaging face. 'We get an order to switch on our engines, and I just follow the truck ahead. That's what we do, all follow each other, and hope the bloke in charge knows where he's going.'

'Sounds like chaos.'

'You said it. Hey, you really know the lingo, you two. Speak real good, not like half the New Australians.'

It was the first time they had heard the expression.

'New Australians? Is that what we're called?'

'You'll be called lots of things, but that's what the government wants us to call yer. Anyway, it shouldn't be a long ride. Mostly they send the workers by bus or train, but since your boss has bought up some clapped-out Yankee surplus, I'd make a guess at Mascot.'

'Mascot?' The word puzzled her, because she knew it meant an object to bring luck, but here it must have another meaning.

'It's a suburb. Where the airport is. Lawrenson's have got themselves a few old bombers – scrap-metal jobs from the Yanks as cheap as chips – and been fitting 'em up as transports.'

'Are we going in an aeroplane?'

They looked at each other with alarm. They had never been in the air, but had seen enough planes crash and explode after being shot down not to welcome the prospect.

'Search me,' the driver said again, and Michael marked the phrase down to remember, as the man went to help the Grand Duchess.

The Polish woman sat beside her cabin trunks, exhausted by the heat in her fur coat, and looking rather fearful.

'What's the problem, my old duck?' the driver asked her.

'I don't think I should have come here,' she said forlornly. 'It doesn't seem quite suitable.'

The propellers spun on the twin-engine Dakota, and the wings rattled. All the seats and the bulkhead panels seemed to vibrate. The noise was deafening. Michael had never been so frightened, not in the bedlam of shellfire in Budapest, nor when the *Wehrmacht* corporal nearly shot him; not even when they escaped across the border to be caught and terrorised by the patrol of deserters, or on the train journey that was to end at Auschwitz. Scared, yes, but not like this. It was just impossible this piece of junk would lift off the ground with so many people packed on board, and he wondered what it would be like – oblivion or whatever it was that happened afterwards.

He wished he knew some prayers, but ever since their parents had been taken away, they had both abandoned prayer as a solace which did not work – and it seemed a bit late now to make a pact with Jehovah.

'You're hurting my hand,' Helen told him, and he realised he was holding it tightly.

'This thing can't possibly fly,' he said through gritted teeth.

'Don't be ridiculous.' It was the Grand Duchess, sitting on the other side of Helen, who leaned across her and gazed at Michael. 'Are you going to tell me a darling young man like you is frightened?'

'I . . . well . . . yes, just a bit,' he managed to say.

'Don't you realise this aeroplane has carried troops, probably thousands of them, all through the war?'

'Which means it's old and worn out.'

'Nonsense.'

'It sounds old and worn out. Why is it nonsense?'

'Because up there in front is the pilot, and his crew. They know the plane. Do you really think they would be on board, ready to fly us if they felt it was dangerous?'

'I . . . never thought of it like that . . .'

'Of course you didn't,' the Grand Duchess said.

'Have you ever been in an aeroplane before?' Helen asked her. She wished she could remember the woman's name; her real name. She could hardly call her *Your Grace*.

'Oh yes. Many times.'

'When?' Michael forgot his usual ridicule, ready to listen.

'When my husband was alive, he worked in the Polish foreign service – and we flew to many places from Warsaw. To Rome, Madrid, Moscow, and in the years before Hitler, to Berlin and Hamburg.'

The vibration intensified; Michael could no longer hear

above the crescendo of engine noise, although the Duchess was still talking as if her words were not being drowned. He had a sensation of moving, and the motors seemed to settle to a steadier volume. She smiled and pointed down. The ground was falling away below them.

'You see, my darling young man? We're in the air.'

'Oh, Jesus Christ,' Michael muttered.

'See how those buildings become smaller all the time?'

'I don't think I want to look.'

'Of course you do. You must look. It's a special experience, your first flight.' She nodded approval as he looked down, still feeling mild alarm as the houses became diminutive, and the cars on the roads were now like slow-moving toys. 'It wasn't so difficult, was it?'

'I'll tell you after we land safely. If we do.'

'We will,' she assured him. 'I start work tomorrow.'

'In Cooma?'

'No, at a construction camp in a place called Tumut Ponds.'

'What sort of work?' Helen asked.

'I'm a cook,' the Grand Duchess said. 'I am hired to cook for about two hundred men who build a dam there.'

The plane was old and slow; the journey seemed interminable. Amid static, the pilot informed them they were flying south, first over a popular beach called Cronulla, and after that the green of the National Park. At Bulli, where there was white sand and the foam of breaking waves, they turned inland, away from the sea.

For a time there were signs of lush pasture, ridges with forests of pines, and hillsides with cattle, but soon the land became a flat plain, the grass was burnt and brown, and only scattered flocks of sheep grazed. In these stretches of empty land there were few trees still alive – most had no foliage, only white branches that reached skywards like the fingers of corpses. The pilot on his crackling speaker explained the trees had been ring-barked; he said the farmers used to believe it made the land more fertile because it saved the water the trees consumed. This had now been disproved, but it was too late for the dead trees.

They passed over occasional iron roofs that marked remote homesteads. Now and then they saw country towns; tiny clusters of buildings and a few dusty streets that appeared beleaguered by the vast landscape. *The country is so immense, it feels forbidding*, Helen thought, and remembered from the maps Neil had given her that this was only a tiny scrap of the continent; the flight they were making was less than halfway to Melbourne, and both cities were a mere coastal fringe, a fraction of the distance to Perth or Darwin. She could hardly imagine flying across Australia to either of these places; it would surely take weeks.

As for Sydney, all they had seen of it was the drive from the docks to the airport. When she'd expressed regret that their time there had been so brief, the friendly truck driver had told them it was to save money. Lawrenson's, the firm building houses in the Snowy Mountains – the company they were contracted to – was razor sharp on saving money, he said. She and her brother would soon find that out. If they'd spent a night in Sydney it would have meant city prices for accommodation and transport. Old Sir Cedric Lawrenson was a bigwig in this town, chairman of lots of charities, but when it came to paying, he was a mean bugger, as tight as a fish's arsehole, he'd said, begging her pardon. She had smiled, aware that Michael was mentally storing this phrase to his growing glossary of the vernacular.

Helen dozed for a while. The monotonous beat of the engines, the heat of the aircraft, made her feel sleepy, despite the discomfort. When she woke the Grand Duchess was telling Michael her name.

'Katryna Dyboski.'

'Say that again.'

'Dyboski,' she said slowly and phonetically. 'I know you call me Grand Duchess, but unfortunately I am only Mrs Dyboski.'

'But you look like a Duchess,' he said, and touched her hand. 'And I want to say thank you for seeing me through my first flight.'

'Wait, Michael,' she said. 'We are still in the air. Wait until the wheels touch the ground – and then you may kiss my hand.'

'Mrs Dyboski, aren't you hot in that fur coat?' Helen asked.

'Boiling,' she said, 'but if I wear it, then nobody can steal it.'

'You think there are thieves in this country?'

'There are thieves in every country. Why would here be any different? It is the only thing I still own that my husband bought me.'

'But what's in the two cabin trunks?'

'Some clothes, a few books. But mostly my cooking utensils, the pots and pans, my chopping boards and my knives . . .'

'You brought knives into the country?' Michael gazed at her.

'Of course.'

'No-one stopped you?'

'No-one said a word. I wouldn't have listened if they had.'

'But we were searched. Wasn't your luggage searched?'

'Certainly not,' she said. 'When they suggested it, I told them they were being ridiculous, and I had absolutely nothing to declare.'

Michael recalled the inquisition the rest of them had endured. 'Just as well Grand Duchesses don't get treated like ordinary people by the customs gestapo,' he said, and suddenly smiled, captivating her.

She laughed. 'He has to watch that charm,' she said to Helen, 'or it will get him in trouble with many ladies.'

'It already has,' Helen said. 'Where did you learn to cook?'

'In a base hospital, in the last war. The 1918 war. It was supposed to be the last war, so people always said.'

'Our parents used to tell us that,' Helen remembered.

'I was your age, an assistant to the chef. It's where I met my husband, after he was wounded. He was in the cavalry, an officer, very dashing and handsome.' She was silent for a moment, her mind harking back thirty years. 'We fell in love, and had a beautiful life together. But we Poles are so stupid, so stubborn. I said to him – this Hitler is insane and dangerous. We have good friends in England. Why don't we go, while there is still time?'

'He wouldn't?'

'He was in the Polish army reserve. He said it would be like desertion. For God's sake, did he think he was a real soldier? How long did his army last, after he was called up and the panzers and the *Luftwaffe* attacked? He was dead in a week, and the only resistance that survived in Warsaw was in the sewers and the ghetto. Not his Polish army, dressed up like chocolate soldiers, fighting like they fought the Cossacks and the Uhlans twenty years before. With the same courage, but with such hopeless antique weapons.' Her eyes were wet and Helen slipped her a handkerchief. 'Silly, sad chocolate soldier,' she said. 'We could have been living in Surrey, retired and growing old together. Instead, he's in an unmarked grave, and I'm to become a cook in Tumut Ponds.'

In Port Said, Neil bought postcards and fought off the hordes of tenacious Egyptians who tried to sell him their variety of offerings; tinsel charm bracelets of the Sphinx, scarves of dubious silk or papyrus paintings of Queen Nefertiti. He sent a card to his parents and another to Caroline – who had announced her engagement, according to a letter from his mother – which hinted at his folly and commented on the lovely photo of her that accompanied the notice in the *Kent Messenger*. She was to marry the son of the local hardware merchant, who would some day inherit the business, and as his mother's note pinned to the cutting stated, had clearly done rather well for herself. The unmistakable inference was that Neil was unlikely to do the same, headed as he was for Australia and disaster.

He wrote a few lines of congratulation on the card, wishing her the best. She was one of his fondest memories, Caroline, and there were still times when he speculated what his life would have been like on the staff of Barclays in Bexhill, married to Caro. Provided, of course, that she hadn't met her hardware chap and fallen for him. It would, no doubt, have been a happy event pleasing both their families, but while he and Caroline would have settled down to married bliss, he had an uneasy feeling bliss might have eventually become more sedate. Buying a house, taking one of the bank's employee mortgages, would have bound him to the job for twenty years or more. In that time there'd be children; they'd join local community groups, the tennis club, make dutiful weekend visits to her parents and his. It was the predictability of it, the prospect of years of an ordered and steadfast life, that was daunting, and made the unknown so appealing.

Barely three more weeks, Neil thought, and felt a growing anticipation. He had helped dispatch so many people there that in a curious way it was like going home. He had never seen this home, but knew it well from furnishing advice to others, about what to say, where to live, details like the cost of living, people's attitudes – all this he had done to send hopeful applicants on their way and now at last he was virtually one himself, armed with the same brochures he had given others, another new immigrant among the two million the country planned to attract, in their need for skilled and unskilled labour.

There was a slight difference, but few on board knew of it. Because of his experience with the IRO and the job that awaited him as liaison officer in the newly formed Migrant Advisory Unit, he had already learned there was a minor perk attached to this new position.

He went up to the top deck, where he travelled in comparative luxury. Most immigrants were crowded into segregated dormitories below deck, in male or female quarters, while he had a privileged cabin on the port side of the ship. Very important, to be on the port side when heading south. *Posh*, he thought smiling, and a pretty blonde girl in shorts and a sun top immediately smiled back.

He was actually remembering *Port Out, Starboard Home*, the renowned travellers' phrase, meaning occupants of the more expensive cabins avoided the direct glare of the sun – which was why the initials spelled POSH, but he wasn't going to tell the blonde girl that. Not when she obviously assumed he had smiled at her.

'Did you buy any souvenirs?' he asked, after they had begun by exchanging comments on the heat and the importuning *gyppos*.

Some scarves, she told him. Gifts. She had an auntie in Melbourne. A few moments later, they found a seat on the boat deck, and exchanged names. Hers was Lucy Whittaker, and she came from Kilburn in north London, and had paid ten pounds for a passage that she hoped would lead to a new life.

'In Melbourne, with your auntie?'

'Not if I can help it,' Lucy said.

Neil noticed a wedding ring on her left hand, and wondered if her husband was aboard. For married couples, it was a major cause of complaint on all these ships that the sexes were strictly separated. Even families. There were too few cabins, because the vessels had been converted to take the maximum number of passengers, and the luxury of individual privacy did not enter the thinking of civil servants who assigned cheap passages. As a result, furtive couplings constantly took place in secluded areas, in bathrooms, laundries, and for those prompt enough to claim possession, in the lifeboats. Some members of the crew rented use of their quarters on a short-time basis, and shared the proceeds; the ship's chief cook, it was said, would arrive in Sydney a rich man from the flood of bookings to use his larder – conveniently fitted with a lock – where amid sacks of flour, sugar, dried egg and powdered milk, passion was spent in as brief a time as possible, as the charges for this love nest were one pound for fifteen minutes, and bookings were strictly monitored. Any protracted dalliance could cause a queue, and was charged at an excessive half crown per extra minute.

'I'm not married,' Lucy proffered the information, in reply to his glance at her plain gold ring. 'At least, I was, but no longer. I'm not sure why I keep wearing this.' He wondered if she was a war widow, like so many women of her age. 'It was in Germany,' she added, which seemed like the answer to his question.

'Whereabouts in Germany?'

'Bremen. That's where it happened.'

'During the war?'

'No,' she said. 'After. In the occupation force. He'd been in the war, the last year of it. Breezed through without a scratch. That's why Bremen was such a shock.'

'What exactly happened?'

'Well, the usual thing, I suppose.'

Neil was beginning to feel puzzled.

'I see,' he said, not seeing at all.

'He just walked into the bar and that was it. Wham. Bingo!'

'He was killed?'

'Killed? He's not dead.' She looked as puzzled as he had.

'Then what happened in the bar?'

'He walked in and met *her*. His fraulein. The German tart.'

'Oh.'

'Love at first sight. That's what he wrote and told me. Sorry, pet, he said, but this is the real thing at last . . . and by the way, she's three months pregnant. So I divorced the bugger.'

'Ah.'

'What did you imagine?'

'Well . . . I thought you might have been a widow.'

'You mean, like someone blew up the bar, and Brian with it? No such luck.' She had an attractive laugh, a lively face, and her slim body was tanned a golden brown. Neil had to wonder if

Brian had been in full possession of his faculties. 'It's this stupid wedding ring,' she said. 'I should chuck it overboard, but it has its uses. Helps keep the reptiles at bay. Why on earth did you think I was a widow?'

'Because I can't imagine anyone in his right mind leaving you for a German tart.'

She gazed at him. Brown lashes framed her light blue eyes. She smiled and said, 'I think you meant that.'

'I did mean it. What did you mean about reptiles?'

'Blokes,' she said, 'who hear about me being divorced, and fancy their chances. I'm sitting at a table with about six of them.'

'Pervs. That's what my Aussie friends call them.'

'Pervs.' She laughed again. It was delightfully uninhibited.

'I'd hate you to think me a reptile or a perv,' Neil said, 'but would you like a drink?'

'I'd love a drink,' Lucy said.

That night, after supper, there was a dance in the main lounge. The ship did not consider ten-pound passengers merited an orchestra, but one of the stewards was employed to play the piano, and people shuffled around the packed floor. There was no room to dance, barely room to move, so they swayed to the music, and her body felt warm and pliant against his, and afterwards they went out to watch the canal and the desert, so arid and inhospitable by day, but somehow tranquil with shadows and soft sandhills in the moonlight.

Later, it was long after midnight, and the ship was quiet – the normal night owls, the bridge players, boozers and occupants of the lifeboats exhausted by the Arabian heat – when he accompanied her down to the small cabin on E deck which she shared with eight other women. It was much hotter this deep in the ship; the passageway was tiny, the cabins compressed, the walls so flimsy that even whispers felt as if they could be overheard. Someone was snoring in an adjacent cabin, a steady rhythmic rumble, and they smothered their laughter. When they made arrangements to meet the next day, a female voice from nearby called out to kindly shut up. They weren't sure if it was directed at them or at the snoring, but feeling encircled by so many people, he kissed her a chaste goodnight and made his way up to his *posh* cabin and the comfort of the sea breeze.

In the morning Neil sought out the ship's Scottish purser, reminding him how often he had been helpful, interpreting for the Glaswegian – who not only knew no foreign languages, but spoke a brand of English few foreigners could comprehend. He explained that he would like a special favour in return for all this.

Lucy was transferred to the same table by lunch time. The purser tactfully rearranged the seating, so they were placed beside each other. After lunch they went on deck to see the ship leave the canal and turn east into the Indian Ocean. That night when dinner was over, they decided the dance floor was too crowded, had a drink in the bar, then slipped away to the luxury of his single cabin, and went to bed together.

Cooma was bursting with people, and lashed with driving rain. It was their first experience of a mountain town, wide sloping streets and shops with iron roofs projecting across the width of the pavement, providing shelter from the harsh climate. The weather could be extreme and ferocious; they had already discovered that in the course of one long and exhausting day.

After the heat of Sydney, they had landed at Cooma in a violent storm, through which they had flown for almost an hour, buffeted by wind and blinded by thick layers of shifting cloud, as the pilot had to swing to the west and seek height, trying to circumvent the worst of the storm.

'Have faith,' the Grand Duchess had said, and while Helen felt airsick, Michael now seemed to thrive on the danger. The squall and torrential rain battered the old aircraft, which shuddered as they'd splashed down on the narrow bitumen strip.

'Thank God,' Helen had murmured, after the engines had changed from the noisy reverse thrust and they were bumping slowly along. Opening her eyes, she'd stared at the sight of her brother leaning across her seat to gently take the Grand Duchess's hand, and raise it to his lips.

'If I were young again, my darling boy,' said Katryna Dyboski, 'you and I would be making some arrangements about a cosy place to spend the night.'

Buses were waiting, but reaching them from the aircraft was an ordeal, as they had to climb down the swaying steps from the plane into the wild weather, then run across the tarmac to where the vehicles stood in line. Men in oilskins cursed as they roughly handled luggage into the back of the transports. Helen was glad she and Michael had kept their precious suitcases with them. The Grand Duchess watched in alarm, as her cabin trunks were tossed into the rear of the adjacent bus. She now looked anything but a Grand Duchess. The oldest on board, and one of only four women, she had been jostled in the rush to escape the rain. She was mud-splattered. Her fur coat was wringing wet, her once fastidious hair in disarray, and mascara ran down her face in streaks of black, like a caricature of a circus clown.

'To be boiled and frozen in the same day. I knew I shouldn't have come here,' was all she'd said.

Helen tried not to think what the future held for Mrs Dyboski, as a cook for so many men at this place named Tumut Ponds.

Still wet and chilled and looking bedraggled, less than half an hour later they peered out the misted windows as the buses drove through the outskirts of Cooma, past a sturdy building with a flag, then a park with a war memorial, and into Sharp Street.

Despite the weather, the streets were crowded. Helen saw the majority were men, standing in tight groups, insulated from each other as they watched the buses pass, and she knew at once there was tension in the town. She overheard the bus driver talking to the man who had been sent to take charge of them from the Lawrenson Company, which seemed to confirm it.

'Bloody place. It's gonna explode one day,' the driver said. 'The stupid bloody government's overdone it. Wog bastards, dagoes, Balts, Krauts, they're tryin' to make a little bloody Europe here, and it ain't ever gonna work. This is bloody Australia, mate.'

'It was only a fight in the hotel, Jacko.'

'Knives,' the driver responded. 'Them Balts or whatever they were – Czechs, Poles, far as I'm concerned they're all bloody Balts – went after a bunch of Huns with knives. They might hate 'em, I can't say I blame 'em for that, but it ain't our way. Not knives. Our way is fists. Give a man a knuckle sandwich, that's fair enuff. Tells the other bloke who's boss, and keeps the dentists in work.'

The man from Lawrenson's laughed.

'But we need the labour force, mate.'

'Do we? I ain't so sure about this whole Snowy River thing. Hydro-electric, or whatever they call it. You know there's two towns gonna be flooded, don't you?'

'I heard rumours about Adaminaby.'

'They're true. And Jindabyne. Jinda's gonna be drowned.'

'Never!'

'I heard for a fact, it'll be at the bottom of a bloody great lake.'

'Shit! Jindabyne's where my mother-in-law lives.'

'Well, tell her to make sure she stays home the day the sluice gates open.'

They both roared with laughter.

There were tents waiting for them on a patch of ground at the far side of the town past Bolara Street, but the storm had blown down half of them, a drain had burst, and the area was a quagmire. Emergency plans had been hastily made. It was the first time anyone had told them they would be living in tents, but worse was to come.

The buses parked at the site. Everyone raced through the rain and packed into the leading vehicle while the Lawrenson representative, introducing himself as Angus Kerr, explained that this was only an overnight stop, and early the next day they would be delivered to their destinations. Some were bound for Island Bend or Three Mile, one for Tumut, and the rest would be taken to a new location, past a village called Berridale. But that was tomorrow; tonight was the problem, due to the weather. The forecast was crook, he told them. No two ways about it, the bureau predicted the rain would become worse before morning. So the only alternative was to sleep in the buses. He was sorry, but it was not the company's fault, more an act of God, and he assured them things would improve tomorrow. He hoped they'd all understood what he had told them.

He saw a great many blank and puzzled faces.

Had they understood him? If not, then put their hands up.

There was silence, until Helen stood and phrased his question in German. A forest of hands were raised. She switched to Italian and more hands went up. Mr Kerr frowned.

'One of the deals in our contract is that everyone has to attend English classes, and learn the language,' he said tersely.

'Shall I tell them that?' Helen asked.

'Don't bother. Inform them it's an emergency. Dammit, even if they can't speak, they're not blind. It's obvious the site's a mess. Just explain tonight's arrangements.' He sounded highly irritated at having made his conciliatory speech to learn it had been understood by only a mere handful.

Helen bore the brunt of the announcement. There was a chorus of disbelief when she said they had to sleep in the buses. People began to shout questions at her –

How could they change clothes? They were cold and damp.

What about blankets?

Were there showers and washing facilities?

Would there be food?

Where were the lavatories?

'What are they saying?' Mr Kerr's temper was becoming decidedly shorter, hearing the angry babble, but unable to comprehend a word of it. He could hardly fail to see the outrage in their faces.

'They want to know about food and blankets.'

'They'll be provided.'

'When? It's already almost dark.'

'A truck should be here soon, from our base at Adaminaby. They may even bring lanterns.'

'How about showers? Washing and other facilities?'

'Look, young lady – this is a temporary transit stop, not the Kosciusko Hotel . . .'

'These are questions they ask me to put to you. They want to know if you have the answers?'

'Of course I have the answers.'

'Then they'd be very pleased to hear them,' Helen said, aware rather too late that she had managed to annoy him.

'Very well. Tell them there are no showers,' Mr Kerr said, sharply. 'Only cold water taps. You'll need your own soap. And of course, there are temporary dunnies. Structurally sound and considered reasonably safe, unless this wind gets up to gale force.'

'Excuse me,' she knew it might further antagonise him, but was confused by his pedantry, 'could you explain this word, *dunny*?'

'And you call yourself an interpreter?' He was a pigeon of a man in his late thirties, and clearly inflated with his own importance.

'I do call myself that, sir,' Helen said with careful courtesy. 'But I've never heard of this word. Is it in the dictionary?'

'Are you trying to be funny, Miss-whoever-you-are?'

'Helen Francis . . . and I cannot see what is wrong about asking for the translation of a word that is new.'

'Dunny? New?' It appeared he didn't know whether to laugh

or mock her. 'Where have you been most of your life, Miss Francis – if that's your real name, which seems unlikely?'

'It's my name now, by my own choice. As for your question, where have I been – I've been in Hungary. Sometimes in Germany, Austria, Cyprus, Italy. In none of these places have I found such a thing as this.'

'Well, then, you must've had a very uncomfortable time,' Mr Kerr said, and smirked as if his own remark amused him greatly.

Michael rose to his feet. He was tall enough to be noticed, even in the overcrowded bus.

'You silly old fart,' he said loudly in English.

'I beg your pardon.' Mr Kerr looked at him, with a startled disbelief.

'You heard me. How dare you treat my sister like that. She's only trying to help you.' He turned to the others and spoke in German, which most of them understood: 'He's telling us they have things called *dunnies* here. It's an Australian word, meaning a shithouse. This man said they're quite safe, unless there's too much wind.'

There was a roar of laughter. Mr Kerr flushed, assuming he was the object of some foreign ridicule – which was not far from the truth. Being unable to fathom the reason for the laughter, nor grasp what had been said to humiliate him, augmented his fury. Michael read the hostility in his expression, and knew he had made a blunder. But the man's behaviour, his contempt towards Helen, had provoked him. He shrugged and put a protective arm around her shoulders.

'Sorry, Iluska,' he murmured. 'But he's a bastard.'

'Yes,' she said. 'A bastard, and also now an enemy, I'd say.'

'Who cares? Tomorrow will see the last of him.'

I hope so, she thought, and while she knew Miki had tried to defend her, she wished he had not been so impulsive.

In the depth of that night, the buses stood like stranded arks in a flood of rain. It had been well after dark before the promised truck had arrived, bringing blankets and hastily prepared sandwiches but no lanterns, and when they had eaten and trudged through the rain to queue at the primitive toilets, after it was apparent there would be no hot tea or coffee, most of them stripped off their sodden clothes and huddled under the single blanket that had been provided, in a vain attempt to get warm. The lights on the buses had to be switched off in order to save the batteries, and the air swiftly became rank with the odour of damp clothing.

'What a terrible place.' Helen heard the Grand Duchess from the seat in front of her. 'I wish I was back in Poland.'

'So do I,' a man's voice said, 'now how about shutting up and let the rest of us get some sleep.'

'At least,' Michael leaned forward to console her, 'it can't get much worse than this.'

'Oh, yes it can,' the Duchess said. 'When you're older, my darling boy, you'll realise that no matter how awful things are, they can always get worse.'

How old must we be to realise that? Helen wondered. She had removed her wet blouse and skirt – her best clothes that she had saved for arrival almost ruined by the mud and rain – but the blanket felt rough and chafed her skin. The rain was relentless, and grew heavier. It beat against the windows and drummed on the roof of the bus, drowning any attempt to talk, and muffling the Duchess's snoring.

As Helen grew tired, she tried to imagine what she had expected of her first night on Australian soil. Certainly not this.

Then, finally, gratefully, she slept.

Chapter 7

'What a dump,' Michael said. 'Talk about the arsehole of the earth.' With a sinking heart she had to agree with him, as the buses pulled out and left them at the camp site in the hills beyond Berridale. Their worst fears had been realised when they turned off the dirt road and saw the sign proclaiming A NEW SIR CEDRIC LAWRENSON PROJECT. It comprised a row of bell tents, two Nissen huts and what appeared to be a mobile shed of some kind. In the distance was a line of primitive outhouses, lined up like sentry boxes. Only two of the buses had stopped here; the others sped past to other work sites at Jindabyne and Island Bend. The Duchess had been taken by utility to remote Tumut Ponds, their last sight of her sitting by her cabin trunks in the back of the truck, looking ludicrous and lost.

Already they missed her.

After they were disembarked, Angus Kerr placed himself beside Helen, and began to read out the list of names assigned to each tent. He had difficulty with many of the pronunciations and aroused sniggers, until he handed the list to her.

'You read it. I'd suggest some of these people would do well to change their names to something we can understand, if they want to get anywhere in this country.'

Helen read the list. There were sixteen tents, with five men allocated to each. When this aroused murmurs of complaint, Mr Kerr hastily announced, through Helen, that any overcrowding would soon be rectified. There were shortages, he explained. So many shortages. Strikes and shortages were the curse of the country. But he promised everything would soon be better.

Michael was billeted with a Yugoslav, two Lithuanians and a German, who everyone knew had served in the *Wehrmacht*. On the ship he had made a point of establishing this, explaining he had been conscripted. Michael had laughed, and said everyone knew there were no volunteers in the German army; the poor bastards had all been forced to fight for the Nazis. The Yugoslav – rumours abounded he had been involved in a Croatian death squad – had told Michael to shut up and remember the war was over. Helen was concerned; she would certainly not have chosen this volatile mix of nationals for the same tent, and hoped there would be no trouble.

Mr Kerr was giving more orders, instructing her to tell them there were sleeping bags and straw *palliasses* in the nearest Nissen hut. The second Nissen hut was the dining room, where hot tea would be served in ten minutes. If they were not on time, he told her to make the message quite clear, it would be cold tea. As they dispersed with their luggage, she realised hers was the only name she had not read out. She was also the only woman in this primitive encampment of eighty men.

'Where are my quarters?' she asked.

'I'll show you,' he said. 'Bring your suitcase.'

She followed him past the tents, along a roughly graded dirt track to the shed, which on closer acquaintance was a prefabricated mobile hut. It was mounted on wooden piers like a caravan, and had been towed to the site. Inside it was fitted out as an office with two desks, one with a sturdy Royal typewriter as well as a telephone. At each end of the structure there were partitioned cubicles, and an open door allowed her a glimpse of a trestle bed.

'That's yours,' Angus Kerr indicated. 'And this is mine.'

He pointed to the opposite end. There was barely six metres of office space between their rooms, and it was apparent the walls were nothing more substantial than thin plywood on timber studding. She frowned, and was disconcerted to find his gaze fixed on her.

'Is there something wrong, Miss Francis?'

'It's hardly the kind of accommodation we were promised.'

'You should be quite cosy in there,' he said, and she thought she saw a glimmer of a self-satisfied smile; it was gone in an instant, leaving his face bland, with her feeling uncomfortable and cautious.

'I was thinking of the tents,' she replied. 'They won't be suitable shelter when it starts to snow.'

'What would you know about conditions here?'

'We were told we'd be working in the mountains. But there would be timber huts, and proper homes for the families.'

'There are no families at this site. And there'll be huts for the men before the winter starts, if your brother and his mob get on with it as the company expects. Now settle in, then I need you to explain the work schedules and some of the main camp rules to them.' He went to the door, paused, then turned and gazed at her. 'And by the way – when you require it – we have our own private dunny at the back of our quarters.'

He went out, leaving her uneasy and disturbed.

Our own private dunny. Our quarters.

She took her suitcase into the tiny cubicle. There was a small window streaked by the rain. The bed, although it was narrow, took up most of the space. On the horsehair mattress lay a blanket and a pillow. The lack of sheets or a pillow case did not concern her; she had not seen such accessories since she was thirteen years old. The proximity of Angus Kerr, who she now realised was to be her supervisor and a man she would have to work alongside daily, was what *did* concern her. It troubled her greatly.

She looked out at the bleak landscape, and wondered what to do about it. It was an unpleasant experience, twenty-four hours after her arrival, to feel threatened and intimidated. She had been through so much, she should not have felt vulnerable like this. Perhaps it had something to do with being a long way from home. Europe, for all its faults, offered familiarity. Here, so soon after debarkation, she was stranded in an alien environment.

Beyond her window there was only a barren hillside of granite rocks that winter would cover with snow. As if the winter was already here, bringing a chill to the air, she shivered.

Sarah was tired. A Ukrainian cleaner had been dismissed, accused of stealing from the patients, and Miss Ronson had not had her replaced. The extra workload, it was announced, would have to be shared by the present staff, as there were no suitable applicants. Sarah knew this was untrue; there were migrant women in most hostels eager to work and earn money. She also realised she was being given a major share of the departed Ukrainian's tasks, and for some reason was being punished by the formidable Edna Ronson.

It could only be because of her good fortune. Although she told no-one the extent of it, she was obliged to inform the department that she had left the migrant reception camp, and provide them with a change of address. The words 'Macleay Street, Potts Point' had raised eyebrows in the office where she reported this, and soon afterwards the hospital superintendent had taken to unprecedented behaviour, arriving unannounced to inspect and often criticise her work. At times, she had been frostily directed to smarten herself and properly clean toilets and basins that were already spotless. She did so without complaint; Sarah had learned the value of passive compliance in a far harsher world than Miss Ronson's hospital, and merely contented herself with counting the remaining weeks before she was free to choose her own life.

But it was exhausting, for in addition to the ten-hour shifts she worked, there was an hour's travel each morning and night. The return journey lay ahead of her now, as she stifled a yawn and surveyed the nurse's bathroom, so shining clean that not even the acerbic Ronson could find fault with it. It tempted Sarah, for she felt grubby and in need of a shower, but this was strictly against the rules. Instead she washed her face and hands, brushed her hair, frowned at her tired face in the mirror and looked forward to a long soak in a hot bath at home, followed by a light supper, then the simple pleasure of climbing into bed to listen to a concert on the radio. Probably falling asleep in the middle of it, she reflected.

She took off her uniform and changed into a street dress. When she left by the staff exit it was already dark. She began to walk towards the nearest bus stop, only vaguely aware of a figure standing outside the lighted front entrance to the hospital, until she began to hear footsteps hurrying in pursuit.

'Sarah,' he called, and she turned incredulously, recognising his voice immediately, but before she could even manage a reply, Neil had covered the distance between them and wrapped her in his arms. Absurdly, her first thought was to apologise that she was filthy from hours of work and in need of a bath.

As if it matters, she decided, hugging him with delight. At last! For weeks she had been wondering when he would arrive. His brief, final letter had been from Italy months ago, waiting for a ship in Naples and worried about a looming strike. There had been no news of him since then.

'When did you get here?'

'Yesterday. I contacted the migrant centre,' he said. 'They told me you'd moved, but didn't seem to know where.'

'I wrote to you with the new address.'

'That one never arrived. Probably still in Naples. So the only way to find you was to come here, but a bossy woman told me I'd have to wait until you finished work.'

'A large bossy woman?'

'Built like a Sherman tank,' he replied, and Sarah laughed happily, her fatigue forgotten.

'Our very own *Gauleiter*, Miss Ronson,' she said.

'So where are you living?'

'A remarkable thing happened. I'll tell you all about it, after I show you my new home. We'll have dinner. Can you stay with me? I have a lovely spare room.'

'Well . . .' Neil said, 'we'd better talk it over with Lucy.'

It was only then, as the slim blonde girl approached, suntanned and strikingly attractive even in the dim streetlight, that Sarah realised he was not alone.

~

Her luxurious hot bath was relinquished. Instead she took a quick shower, then dressed carefully in a blue housecoat, and spent a few moments on her makeup while she considered what to say.

It was quite foolish to feel so unsettled and constrained by a pretty girl who had almost certainly been a shipboard romance. In fact, Lucy Whittaker had soon established that herself, referring to the luxury of Neil's single cabin compared to her shared dungeon without the least trace of embarrassment. And it was sheer middle-aged vanity to expect him to arrive alone; after all, he was a likeable, personable man, and bound to meet a young woman who would become a part of his life. She was sorry to hear about Caroline, whom she had liked at their few meetings, but it was only natural he would find someone else. Lucy was vivacious and engaging, so why did she feel . . . disappointed?

Was she jealous?

Shtuss, she rebuked her mirrored reflection, remembering the Yiddish rebuke for stupidity. You have the brains of a *schlemiel*.

She sternly told herself to get such idiotic thoughts out of her mind. It was just . . . she shook her head.

Just what, she asked the foolish old face in the glass.

Just that Neil Latham was like a son who was also her closest and best friend, and she loved him deeply. She had waited with such patience for his arrival, planning so much that they would do together; ferry trips on the harbour, strolling in the bohemian village which was her own treasured neighbourhood, visiting favourite cafes and coffee shops, riding trams or walking the streets of the city to show him places she had found that would charm him. As well as acquainting each other with details of the past two years, and all that had happened since they last met.

PETER YELDHAM

She had counted on the two of them sharing these simple pleasures, which might not appeal to Lucy Whittaker. If that was the cause of her disquiet, was she being selfish? If so, it was a problem she must resolve. She made herself smile at the ageing face in her mirror, stood up briskly, and went to join her guests.

Sarah lay awake long after they had gone. The luminous hands of her bedside clock showed it was past midnight, and the knowledge she had a bus to catch in barely five hours' time created a stress that threatened to make sleep impossible. She had done her best, but was left with an uneasy feeling that the evening had not been a success.

It was nothing tangible; just an apprehension that had begun when they all stood at the front door, exchanging kisses and promises to visit again soon, and she and Lucy had assured each other how much they'd enjoyed this first meeting. After she shut the door, she could hear the sound of their voices as they descended the stairs – Lucy bright and vivacious as she had been all evening, Neil's voice a deep murmur as he replied – giving her the strange impression they were putting on a performance. Trying to dismiss this aberrant thought, she switched on the front balcony light and went outside to watch them emerge from the building, the pair of them looking up as they saw the third-floor light, waving to her while she waved back. Finally they had walked up Macleay Street, glimpsing a taxi and hailing it, giving her one last wave as they climbed into the cab before it drove away.

Sarah had turned off the light, and locked the balcony door. There was no cleaning up left to do, the kitchen was immaculate for Lucy had insisted on washing up, and Neil had helped dry the dishes. Afterwards they had sat in the living room and had coffee. She had tried very hard – perhaps too hard – to behave as naturally as she would have if Neil had been alone.

She had carefully avoided any discussion of the past in either Germany or England, which would have excluded Lucy, and listened to their account of Suez and Ceylon and other highlights of their trip, and how they had taken leading roles in the Neptune frolic when the ship crossed the equator, which sounded a great deal more lively and entertaining than her own voyage had been.

When Neil asked about her experiences in Australia, she was frank about her early months and the lack of welcome which had distressed her. She even – although she had intended only to confide this to Neil himself – told them both how she acquired the apartment, and about the extraordinary arrival in her life of Christoph Hartmann, which meant revealing what had happened in Berlin with his mother, her once best friend Steffi.

'But what an awful thing for her to do,' Lucy had said, and she'd agreed, yes, it was awful.

'And how marvellous of her son. He sounds remarkable.'

Sarah agreed, Chris was remarkable. She wished they had been able to meet but he had recently been transferred to Washington.

Talking of Steffi's betrayal was difficult and painful to discuss, especially in front of a stranger, but that was the decision she had taken. Not to think of Lucy as a stranger, but as someone Neil had wanted her to meet at this first reunion, because she was clearly important to him. Which was why she felt such concern at her belief the evening had been a failure, and why she lay sleepless until 3 a.m., waking tired and disappointed to face the day's long journey to work with a blinding headache.

The utility truck hooted. Helen went to the window of the administration hut, opened it to wave a signal she was on her way, then hurried to collect an old army greatcoat she had bought at a local sale. She was about to leave when the door opened and Angus Kerr entered.

'Leaving? I hope you've finished those lists.'

'They're on your desk,' Helen said.

'You'd better wait until I check them.'

'It's my day off, Mr Kerr. I've made arrangements, and my brother and a friend are waiting for me.'

'It's not "Mr Kerr". How many times have I asked you to call me Angus? People might be more formal where you come from, but in this country we like to be easy-going.'

Easy-going? She felt like challenging him, but decided against it. Safer to disregard the remark, and say only what was necessary.

'I've typed the lists and checked them, and you won't find any mistakes,' she told him. The truck hooted impatiently for her again. 'I'm sorry, but that's my transport and I'm late.'

She went to brush past him. For a moment it seemed he was going to block her way, then he stood aside. But as she passed him, his hand slid across her buttocks, clutched her and gripped tightly for an instant. She gasped and froze, feeling a moment of fear, a memory of the smirking ring of young soldiers like a vivid scar in her mind, then she wrenched from his grip, whirled and faced him.

'Don't do that, Mr Kerr. Don't ever try to do that again.'

'Do what? What's got you so het-up? You people, you New Australians, are a funny mob.'

'Funny? There was nothing funny about what you did.'

'I don't mean *funny*. See, that's the trouble – you think you know the language, but you don't get the real meaning. Funny in this case means strange, it means *peculiar*. For Christ's sake, there's nothing terrible about a pat on the bum, Helen. Just a way of getting to know you. Being friendly. After all, the two of us working together, living close to each other, we oughta be friends. If we were, I'll tell you something right now. It'd make life a whole lot easier.'

'You keep your filthy hands to yourself, or I'll put in a complaint.'

'You will, eh? Who to? Any complaints of that sort have to be channelled through me. You want to make a complaint to me?'

He laughed. She stared at him, with acute dislike. He could hardly be unaware of her feelings, but he went on in the same manner.

'Bypass me and go to the company's regional manager if you want. Herbie McFie, up in the main office at Jindabyne. You don't think old Herbie's gonna care about some silly office sheila objecting to a pat on the arse, do you? I know for a fact, he's had his share of whatever's on offer in that department. A regular buttock bruiser is our Herbert. Listen, it happens all the time here – it's meant to be a compliment, you stupid Hungarian cow.'

She wanted to lash out and hit him, but that would be stupid. She stifled a retort, turned and left the hut.

Michael was waiting impatiently by the truck, and the driver already had the engine running. They were going into Cooma to have a meal in a cafe, and had arranged to meet the Grand Duchess who was getting a lift from the Tumut Ponds camp. The meeting place was the Royal Hotel in the main street, and they would be late.

'What kept you?'

'Nothing,' she said.

He looked at her carefully.

'That rotten bugger giving trouble?'

'No. I had to check some typing.'

She knew Michael doubted her, but she tried never to speak of the disagreeable atmosphere in the office, and Kerr's unsettling effect on her. The way he constantly looked for excuses to make her feel inadequate, scanning her typing for mistakes, doing his utmost to find urgent work he required late in the day so her hours were far longer than she was paid for. Nor would she mention his habit of continually sneaking glances at her, so that whenever she looked in his direction their eyes met and she felt his scrutiny. Above all, she did not intend to confide what had just happened, or the event two days ago when she was half dressed after taking a shower, and he had pushed open the door and walked into her room without knocking. He had gone through the pretence of an apology, but she knew it had been deliberate, and a few moments earlier he would have achieved his objective and found her standing there naked.

She had to remain silent, knowing Michael's impulsive nature and how it would enrage him – but there was another reason for her silence. Most were minor incidents, apart from the latest molestation. They were almost trivial occurrences, and there was nothing she could prove. A man she worked with looked at her. All right, *stared* at her. He tried to find fault with her work. He had failed to knock on her door, encountered her barely clothed and apologised. There was a word to describe such an assortment of trifling complaints and a person who insisted on bringing them to public attention.

She had found it in the dictionary; a disorder, the Oxford said, called *paranoia* – hence the accuser was considered *paranoid*. She had no wish to be thought suffering from this, although the incidents were not trifling, they were an accumulation of disturbing events that were like constant threats, and she could still feel the heat of outrage and the disgust of his hand touching – it was more than that, groping – her bottom. Not only outrage and disgust, she realised, but a chilling moment of fear.

'What is it?' Michael demanded, aware of her introspection.

'Nothing,' she insisted.

It truly was nothing, she tried to tell herself. Not important enough to be discussed, and apart from Miki, who could she discuss it with? Yet it occupied her mind, troubling her, keeping her awake at nights. Today's abuse, the crass and blatant sexual approach, would not easily be forgotten. But nor would it be spoken of again. With his influence, he could so easily make her appear a troublemaker – or even paranoid!

'If it's that bastard Kerr, I'll kill him,' Michael said.

And that, she thought, *is why I can never tell you. Why I could never dare risk it.*

Cooma was more crowded than their first brief sight of it, the stormy day of their arrival over six weeks ago. The Duchess was there waiting for them outside the hotel, wrapped in her familiar fur coat. She hugged them both, and after declaring it was wonderful to see them, stated in her imperious way that she didn't know whether to laugh or cry. Something crazy had happened.

Crazy?

Good or bad craziness? Michael grinned, knowing her propensity for creating drama.

Just crazy, she repeated. She had gone inside the hotel to the main bar, to sit and wait for them, and a barman had ordered her out.

But why, they asked?

No women allowed in there, she told them.

They looked at her with disbelief.

'Absolutely true,' the Grand Duchess said. 'I thought it was a joke, but he insisted. Then he brought the owner, who said it was a rule in all hotels. No women allowed to drink in the bar.'

'Why not?'

'I got the impression it might upset the men.'

Helen laughed, then realised Katryna was serious.

'How could it upset them?'

'Stop them swearing or fighting, I suppose. He wouldn't say any more. Just told me that was the law and we're not permitted. There's a separate women's parlour at the back of the hotel with a side entrance, for us if we want.'

What kind of a country had they come to, the Grand Duchess wished to know, where men and women had to go into separate rooms to have a drink?

Sarah walked leisurely along Macleay Street. Saturday was her favourite morning; apart from being her day off, the street was always full of familiar faces. Mr Leonides was in his shop, carefully arranging fruit in his window like an artist. He waved to her to wait, selected a carnation and hurried out to give it to her.

'It should be a rose,' he said, 'but they're out of season. In Nicosia it would be a rose.'

She thanked him, asking him to keep her some cherries as she had special guests for dinner, and went past Macleay Regis. The elderly man with his bow tie and panama hat was walking his poodles.

'Good morning, Mrs Weismann,' he said, raising his hat. 'Say good morning, boys,' he told the poodles, who dutifully wagged their tails and tried to lick her ankles.

'Good morning, Mr Miller, good morning boys,' she said. It was a Saturday ritual, and this was a special Saturday. Neil and Lucy were coming to dinner again, and this time she would prepare them a wonderful meal, buy a bottle of the best wine, and spend the next hour shopping and deciding on the menu.

Coq au Vin, she thought, and knew Mr Leonides had the small onions and the button mushrooms she needed, and she would see what the delicatessen had to offer in fresh chickens. And then to follow, a platter of cheese and fruit. Brandy with the coffee to finish. It was exciting actually planning a dinner party, the first real one she had given in the apartment, for when Chris Hartmann came to Sydney he had insisted on treating her to a restaurant, and she discounted the evening with Neil and Lucy four nights ago, because it had taken her by surprise and she had improvised a meal. *Yes,* she thought, *Coq au Vin,* and it could simmer gently all the afternoon.

She walked to Darlinghurst Road, pausing to talk to people

she had come to know from her weekend shopping trips, buying a newspaper from her favourite kiosk, and flowers from the friendly girl who ran a stall outside the California.

When Neil had telephoned from their hotel last night, she had suggested dinner again, and he had instantly agreed. They had settled on seven o'clock. She was changed and ready when the doorbell rang. She hurried to open it with a practised welcoming smile, then realised he was alone.

'Where's Lucy?'

'Can I tell you about it over a drink?'

He kissed her and came inside, immediately conscious of the signs of preparation; the delicious aroma from the kitchen, the drinks tray waiting, fresh flowers in vases, the dining table set for three.

'I should have explained last night. Before you went to all this trouble.'

'It was no trouble. But where is she?'

'In Melbourne by now,' Neil said. 'She has an aunt there.'

'She mentioned a relative. Is she visiting her?'

'No, going to live with her.'

'Oh.' Sarah gave him his drink, and poured her own. They went and sat in the living room. 'I had the impression the other night, she wasn't very fond of her aunt.'

'I had that impression, too. But there was a letter for her the next day.' He sipped his drink and smiled wryly. 'It turns out Lucy's auntie is rather rich. It also seems there are no other relatives, and from what I can make out promises were made in the letter. I suppose hints, really, about the future. Lucy has been trying, ever since, to decide what to do.'

'And she's decided to go?'

'Yes.'

'And how do you feel about that?'

'I'm not sure,' Neil said. 'Relieved, I think.'

'Really?'

'It was wonderful on board ship. A great deal less wonderful the other night, when I brought her to meet you, and I could see how hard you were trying to like her . . .'

'What?' Sarah said, involuntarily. 'Neil, I'm not the judge of whoever you choose to live with. Don't make me be that.'

'I wouldn't dream of it,' he said. 'But you and I are friends, we have been ever since Belsen, and I hope we will be all our lives. You got along fine with Caro. You had reservations about Lucy.'

'Oh, God, was I that transparent? I feel it's my fault.'

'Of course it's not your fault.'

'Then whose is it?'

'Mine, for being gullible. Lucy just wanted a fling. And a more comfortable cabin. She's had affairs galore since her husband went off with his fraulein.'

'How do you know?'

'She told me.'

'When?'

'When she was packing for Melbourne.'

'Oh.'

'She said she was fond of me, and it would've been nice, and might even have lasted a few years – but auntie was hugely rich, which meant a lifetime of luxury. She doubted if I could provide her with anything equivalent to that.'

'What an absolute bitch,' Sarah said, indignant on his behalf.

Neil laughed. 'No, just a realist. And I was fooling myself. It was a shipboard romance, nothing more.'

'And you're truly relieved?'

'I'm certainly not in mourning.'

Sarah suddenly felt happy, almost light-headed.

'Let's have another drink,' she said. 'Let's have several. I've made a lovely meal, and we have an excellent bottle of local wine. And a French brandy afterwards.'

'You'll get me smashed.'

'Do you good. You can collapse in my spare room. It's been waiting for you long enough.'

Chapter 8

Neil looked down at the park. It was lunch time, and crowds of city office workers sat eating sandwiches on benches in the sunshine, tossing crusts to pigeons who swooped to squabble over the offerings. Couples picnicked together. Solitary figures lay on the grass, absorbing the sun's warmth before returning to their offices, while lovers embraced, oblivious to them all. Above a stand of Moreton Bay fig trees the sky was a canopy of azure blue, reminding him of southern Italy, but with a deeper texture of its own. The lucidity of the light was dazzling.

Henry Falconer came to join him.

'Good view.'

'Wonderful,' Neil said.

The colours were sharp-edged and vivid. The park was bright with ornamental flower beds. He could see clusters of chrysanthemums and spectacular displays of soft-hued dahlias. There were oleanders in full bloom, rows of glowing red hibiscus, and the autumnal tints of red and orange liquidambers. As if that was not enough to delight the eye, girls in colourful sleeveless dresses strolled in groups – from this distance like a moving, decorative tapestry.

'A picture to paint, isn't it?' Falconer said. 'Best time of the year for me, autumn. In winter most of the flower beds will be empty, the deciduous trees shorn bare of their leaves, and those pretty creatures in their bright dresses will be rugged up in scarves and coats against the wind.'

'I had noticed the bright dresses,' Neil said, and the other smiled. 'But it's hard to imagine it being cold here.'

'Wait till the westerlies blow. Or come back and tell me it's not chilly if we ever send you down to the Snowy Hydro Scheme. Perisher Valley, for instance, is not lightly named.'

His secretary brought in sandwiches and coffee.

'I thought we'd have lunch up here. You can admire the view, and we can talk. Thanks, Celia,' he said, and the secretary nodded, smiled at Neil and left them alone.

It was his first private meeting with the head of this newly formed Immigrant Advisory Unit. He had been welcomed after his arrival, shown his office and told that Falconer was due to leave for Canberra to battle with the bureaucrats of the immigration department, so it was a good opportunity for him to relax for two weeks, get to know the city, and find himself somewhere to live. Accommodation was not easy at present he was told; there was a serious housing shortage and anything in the classified columns of the newspapers was generally besieged by those desperate for a place to live, and snapped up the same day. It was one of the reasons for the massive immigration programme; more housing was an urgent need in every town and city. Neil was glad of the time to explore, but able to say he luckily had a friend with an apartment in Macleay Street, who insisted he accept her spare room for the present.

This time, while they shared sandwiches, and Falconer

poured the coffee, Neil told him about Sarah Weismann. From the time of their first meeting over six years ago. Beyond the tranquillity of the orchards, the horror that had shocked the world, the headlines, newsreels and revulsion that had been Bergen–Belsen. And how his life since had been linked with this woman nearly twice his age, closer than a friend, more valued than his own mother.

Henry Falconer was in his early fifties, a public servant with a distinguished career, and a friendly manner. He knew a great deal about Belsen, and a surprising amount about Neil.

'You worked there in the hospital, didn't you?'

'For a few months, while Sarah recovered. I didn't know anyone was aware of that.'

'Typhus,' Falconer said. 'You joined what they called UNNRA's Flying Squads, dusting liberated camps with DDT. Now the war was over typhus was the enemy.'

'We couldn't save enough people in Belsen,' Neil replied. 'The final act of genocide by the Germans was to dynamite the water supply. The prisoners thought they'd turned it off, but it was far more vicious. They blew it up. There was no water, no food, not nearly enough doctors. Thousands died. One day – the worst after we got there – the death toll was three thousand in a morning.'

'But some volunteers helped to turn it around,' Falconer said, after a moment, 'or so I heard. Among them was an English soldier who spoke German.'

Neil was startled. He took a sandwich and said nothing.

'This soldier insisted there was an answer. In England, he said, at London University were a hundred medical students, soon to graduate. He went around arguing with people, begging the army and the air force to get them there. By bombers, transport planes or in trucks, but get them there before everyone died.'

'Who told you this, sir?'

'And they came, these young men, the students. They did what older, senior doctors could not have been able to do. Did it cheerfully, willingly. They stripped and shaved the people. They cleaned out the filth, killed the vermin, disinfected and deloused the survivors. Made them feel like human beings again. It was all recorded in unit standing orders by Sergeant-Major Owen Jenkin. You remember Jenkin?'

'Of course, sir.'

'Don't call me sir. Call me Henry.'

'He played a good game of rugby, Henry. The same Owen Jenkin.'

'Yes, I believe he did. And you helped get those medical students.'

'The Colonel in charge of the hospital arranged that.'

'I heard on good authority you made a real pest of yourself. Went round badgering people until they did something.'

Neil tried to conceal his astonishment.

'Doesn't sound like me, Henry. The Colonel was the one.'

'It was the Colonel who told me,' Falconer said. 'He made the decision and used his rank to get them there, but you were involved. Why do you think I offered you a job? I like people who believe in things and make pests of themselves. I heard you were thinking of coming to Australia, and I hoped the offer would persuade you.'

'It did.'

Henry Falconer smiled and deliberately changed the subject,

as he looked across Hyde Park and pointed to a spire. 'If you haven't seen it yet, that's St James's Church over there. Francis Greenway, our great convict architect, built it, along with the mint and the military barracks, and gave this city a taste of Georgian elegance. In our new rush to re-develop, let's hope they don't tear it all down.'

Neil replied he hoped not. He asked for details of his job.

'It's not going to be easy, I'm afraid,' Falconer said. 'A lot of work, and far less of us to do it than I counted on. Treasury's cut our budget, and I've got a hell of a backlog of investigations for you. Of course, we're a liaison group, not a court, but if newcomers are exploited or their employers take advantage, we'll try to sort it out. Your task is to decide which cases are genuine.'

'Are there many complaints?'

'Heaps. Phone calls, letters, some barely literate, others in their own language. The government and the bureaucracy has this idea people should simply be grateful we've taken them in. I don't agree – so we're going to do the best we can on the lousy budget they've given us, but I'll be fighting for more. In the meantime, I can offer you a secretary who's more a clerk, but she's willing. We'll find the money for translators if you need them. When you travel, it won't be first class. However, I hope we'll manage.'

'I'm sure we will,' Neil said.

'Good,' Falconer said, pleased. 'Now tell me about Milan. About the camp there.'

The sudden question, deceptively casual, took him completely by surprise. He had a startled moment to wonder if the relaxed conversation, the friendly manner had all been a prelude to this.

'It was one of the briefings I got in our national capital,' the other told him, noting Neil's disquiet. 'I tried to talk about budgets. That was why I went. Instead I ended up in a session with some Commonwealth Police and certain people from ASIO. They gave me chapter and verse, and the upshot was, I was requested to ask you – purely off-the-record and on a voluntary basis – about the Australian bureau. In fact, about the entire Milan Centre.'

'What about it?' Neil vacillated.

'What you thought of it?'

'Not much. A dump. Lousy weather, incessant rain . . .'

'Forget the weather. Tell me if the rumours were true.'

'What rumours?'

Henry Falconer studied Neil. His gaze seemed to suggest this evasion did not deserve a response.

'I don't think I heard any rumours,' Neil said eventually.

'Then you couldn't have been listening. They heard them ten thousand miles away, here in Australia.'

'About what, in particular?'

'Corruption. Black marketing. Crime.'

'There was crime in most refugee camps. People left to rot there, becoming desperate and disillusioned . . .'

'I'm not talking about that, Neil. I said I was given chapter and verse. I mean systemic, organised corruption. Not petty crime. And not by Displaced Persons. By the people who ran the place. In particular those who were part of the Australian mission there. Public servants and others seconded to the International Refugee Organisation. We believe medical supplies were being sold on the streets for big profits. Cocaine and other drugs were imported with the aid of the Mafia, and there was also a network of prostitution.'

'If that's true, surely it's a police matter?'

'We need evidence. You were there; the impression was you might've been able to help.'

'I wasn't there long.' He was aware how lame it sounded.

'Long enough,' Falconer said. 'You knew Stewart Mitchell?'

'Of course. Head of Mission. My boss, virtually. Most of his key staff were Australians, a few from New Zealand.'

'Did you know a man named McGill?'

'Bluey? Yes, I knew him.'

'Moroney? Russell Moroney?'

'Of course. Look, I had almost nothing in common with any of them, so apart from work I kept to myself. My best friend there was a Canadian . . .'

'Just answer my question.' Falconer's voice was decidedly cooler. 'Are you saying you never saw anything illegal, or heard of corruption among the Australian staff there?'

'There's always gossip . . .'

He realised Falconer was looking at him hopefully.

'Gossip? What gossip?'

Dear God, he thought, *if only I could tell him the extent of it. They deserve to be in prison; they were criminals, using privileged positions to defraud and victimise.* But he had no illusions about what would happen if he did. Mitchell would make good his threat, and there'd be no future for him here, let alone any hope for Helen Francis and her brother. They would certainly be deported and Neil himself would face charges. Worst of all, in the end it would be as Stewart Mitchell had smugly predicted in Naples; Neil's evidence would convict no-one. Not from a prison cell.

'What gossip?' Falconer repeated the question.

'Nothing of substance. There was some talk they milked their expense accounts for weekends in Rome or Venice, but it's only hearsay. I think it's true they ran a loose ship; perhaps an audit would reveal something.'

'But you can't?'

Neil shrugged. He felt very uncomfortable, acutely aware of the other man's direct appraisal.

'Milked expense accounts?' Falconer was almost scornful. 'And that's all you can tell me?'

'What am I expected to tell you?'

'Apparently very little. I'll inform the people in Canberra they were mistaken about you.'

'I'm afraid they were. I'm sorry.'

'Yes, it's a pity. Well, I think that's all for the moment. We've finished. You can go.'

Neil rose. He expressed his thanks for the lunch, and said he looked forward to beginning work. Henry Falconer was decidedly more formal. He replied – without much conviction – that he hoped they would make a good team. His reserve was palpable.

As Neil left the office he glanced out the window. Clouds were drifting across the sky, obscuring the sun. Shadows lay over the park, and the day had begun to change.

'What is it?' Sarah asked.

'Nothing.'

'It can't be nothing. You look like a wet weekend.'

'A what?'

'It's one of my Australian expressions. You look like one.'

'It's something I'll work out,' Neil said.

'Is it the job?'

'Not exactly.'

'The boss? This Mr Falconer?'

'No, he's quite decent.'

'You like him?'

'Yes,' Neil said, after a moment's thought, 'I do.'

'Good. Lucky to have a boss you like. You realise soon I will be saying goodbye to my *Gauleiter*, Miss-Sherman-Tank-Ronson?'

Neil laughed. Sarah nodded approvingly.

'That's the first time you laugh tonight. When I finish my hospital job, we'll have a party. A celebration that my two years are over and I'm free. The end of my career of scrubbing toilets.'

'I should hope so.'

She gazed at him thoughtfully. 'Are you going to tell me what's wrong?'

'If I tell anyone, Sarah, it'll be you. But not tonight.'

In the depth of winter the snow fell and lay on the tents, and at least twice each night the occupants had to wake and push at the canvas to remove it, or else the weight of snow turning to ice would have buried them. Michael led the agitation for more bedclothes, declaring they would get ill and be unable to work, and eventually they were each given an extra blanket. But it was not enough, for their palliasses lay on the freezing ground, and the chill rose through the straw and hessian to afflict them. Even builders' sarking – the aluminium-lined tar paper which they pilfered from the job and used as groundsheets – could not properly insulate them against the cold.

Bundles of old broadsheet newspapers were in demand; they packed them into the palliasses and folded them between the blankets to help retain their body warmth. In a normal winter it might have helped, but from all accounts this year was hardly normal. As for waking in the night and needing to go to the lavatory, that was torture because the latrines were a hundred yards away, and the air was like ice. Returning chilled to their beds, it was almost impossible to get warm again.

What seemed like a long time ago, in Marseilles, they had been told this was a land of tropic heat and constant sunshine, and had been shown pictures of crowded sandy beaches, with vivacious girls in shorts or swimming costumes, so they had left behind their heavy boots and thick woollen clothes, and now thought of them longingly.

They had never expected such relentless arctic cold.

Angus Kerr received regular bulletins about the situation from Sir Cedric Lawrenson, the one-time builder's labourer who had become a millionaire and now presided over a construction empire. In these messages, Sir Cedric assured his workers he sympathised with their hardship in this most bitter winter; they would doubtless know he understood what the conditions were like, for he had worked his way up from the kind of jobs they were doing – the inference being, if they laboured hard enough for him, perhaps they would achieve the same success he had. His messages – which Kerr read out to Helen, and she typed onto a stencil – were then mimeographed and distributed to everyone in the camp. She had to type translations in German, and also in Serbian for the many Serbs and Croats who had lately arrived.

Sir Cedric asserted that it was always his intention they would be housed in secure wooden huts, each with their own room where they would be warm and comfortable, and there would be electric light instead of the barely adequate kerosene pressure lamps. He blamed the delay on the bureaucrats who ran the Department of Public Works, and on government bungling. He made use of the bulletins to stress his own beliefs, that there were far too many strikes and a lack of a real work ethic among Australians, and he hoped his European workers would not succumb to the malaise of tea breaks – which the Australians called 'smokos' – nor copy the way the locals downed tools the moment their shift ended – not to mention their incessant demands for more money.

He was a fair man – Kerr dictated and Helen typed – and he paid a fair wage. If he was to pay the exorbitant amounts some of their communist unions were trying to demand, then the firm was liable to be bankrupt and no-one would have a job. But for those who worked well, and received a good report from their regional bosses, there would be more work and better contracts if they wished to stay with the company after their fixed two-year contracts ended.

'Some bloody chance,' Michael said, and the disparate group who shared the tent were for once in agreement, 'we're hooked for the rest of our two years, but not a day longer with this mean old bastard.'

The stories of Lawrenson were legend. It was said he was once a migrant himself, who had bought his title, but no-one was sure if this was true. He was often in the newspapers, photographed opening new factories, or being seen on ceremonial occasions with politicians, while his wife was a well-known society hostess and fundraiser for charities. It was a different story for his employees. There, charity was in short supply.

Forever running into problems of liquidity, with his bankers wary of the inflating overdrafts on which his raft of companies seemed to float, the workers often found their pay was not forthcoming and were told to buy what they needed on credit at the local stores. Sometimes weeks would pass before they were recompensed. Once the excuse was government interference, though what this might have been was never fully made clear; another time there was a bank clerks' dispute, while on occasions the weather was too bad for the company aircraft to land and bring the pay, or the plane was being serviced and unable to fly. Their wages were rarely paid on time; if they were lucky there would only be a delay of a day or two.

Rebellious at this treatment, several of the Lawrenson groups had threatened a strike, but were promptly warned not to contemplate such action; it would infringe their work contract and they could be deported. This was bluff, but accustomed to years of insecurity no-one had been willing to make a stand, fearing the risk of a forced return to refugee camps in Europe.

In early August, Sir Cedric and some of his senior executives paid them a brief visit. A collection of cars arrived, and Lawrenson, accompanied by a group of men clad in warm winter coats, fur-lined boots and hats, inspected the site. Angus Kerr escorted them, ordering Helen to join him in case an interpreter was required. For most of the short tour, Kerr set out to busily ingratiate himself with Sir Cedric, eagerly relating how well the men were working under his personal direction, and how they understood the firm's difficulty in providing huts – but, after all, the majority were used to icy conditions in Eastern Europe – and had personally asked him to inform Sir Cedric and his directors that this winter was comparatively mild.

Helen listened with growing disbelief, barely able to restrain herself from an interjection. Kerr's sycophancy was rampant, and he appeared oblivious to her disquiet. Finally the party paused by a group of Czechs who were excavating rocks from the hillside.

'Where are these people from?' Sir Cedric asked, and Kerr, uncertain of the exact origin of most of his work force, because they were all Balts or wogs to him, glanced at Helen for an answer.

'From what was once Bohemia in Czechoslovakia,' she said.

'I expect they're relieved to be safely here in Australia?'

As she hesitated over a reply, unsure if this were true, Angus Kerr took the opportunity to obsequiously agree with him.

'More than relieved. They're delighted to be in this country, Sir Cedric. Delighted. Most can hardly speak English, but Miss Francis should be able to confirm how much they enjoy it here, sir.'

'If you'd be so kind,' the magnate requested her.

Helen asked them the question. Did they like the country, and were they pleased and relieved to be here?

For a moment no-one replied; she was fluent only in Slovak and thought they might not have understood her. But then one laughed, without a trace of humour. Another deliberately spat on the ground in front of him. Finally, a tall young Czech in his twenties gave vent to a heated torrent of words. He spoke so rapidly, she had to concentrate intently to follow what he was saying.

He told her it was a bastard of a place, and this was a bastard of a job. Long hours, rotten pay, lousy living conditions and filthy food. He'd worked for Lawrenson's for nearly eighteen months, and was looking forward to the day – quite soon now – when he could tell them to shove the stinking job right up their collective arses. And would she please be kind and brave enough to interpret exactly what he had said, for the benefit of this bloated prick of a plutocrat and his bunch of shady minions.

Helen tried to remain calm, while wanting to laugh. It was so evident his reply had been a tirade that Angus Kerr was now bright red with embarrassment; Sir Cedric Lawrenson and his party were taken aback by the loud violence with which he had spoken – while the rest of the Czech workers nodded agreement with an amused satisfaction.

'It's right, everything he say. It's true.' One of them spoke English with a thick accent. 'You tell him, lady. Tell him truth.'

Sir Cedric and his coterie all heard this, and looked at her.

Well, now I have to say something, she thought, and took a deep breath. The young Czech, the cause of her predicament, waited for her to translate, watching her intently.

'I don't expect it will come as a surprise, Sir Cedric,' Helen said, 'that he's not the least bit *delighted* to be here.' She deliberately emphasised the same word Angus Kerr had used, and relished doing so. 'I could hardly say otherwise, since his manner spoke for itself.'

'That's enough, Miss Francis,' Kerr tried to interrupt hastily. 'Please be quiet.'

'You be quiet, Mr Kerr. I give the orders here,' Sir Cedric said sharply, and she saw the manager's flush deepen, and his facial muscles contract with suppressed fury. Lawrenson took no further notice of him, and turned back to her. 'Since he obviously shouted at me, young lady, I'd prefer to know the extent of the complaint.'

She hesitated. 'Are you sure, sir?'

'Of course I'm sure. Whatever he may have said.'

'Yes, sir.'

She knew it would be foolish to repeat the full text of insults, but wondered just what she could say to this building baron and his coterie of subordinates. They had arrived in their limousines, expecting instant obeisance, strolling through the camp with total indifference to the conditions in their thick warm clothing; even the brevity of their visit was a show of arrogance in itself.

To hell with it, she thought. *He asked me; I'll tell him.*

'Well?' Sir Cedric gazed at her, impatiently.

'You want it as spoken?'

'I want to know exactly what he said, so please don't waste any more of my time, young woman. I insist on knowing.'

'Very well. He said this is a bastard of a place – and a bastard of a job – long hours, low pay, the awful food and living conditions, and he can't wait for the day when he can tell you to shove the Snowy scheme up your arse. He did say collective arses, but it's my impression he meant yours in particular.'

'*What!*' It was Kerr's voice, little more than a sharp whisper.

She could feel them all staring at her; Kerr himself gaping in disbelieving and dismayed shock; Sir Cedric's eyes fixed unblinkingly on her. She wondered if she had said too much already, but if so, there was no way now to stop.

'He also spoke of bloated plutocrats, and made several other comments on you and your minions as he called them. But they were rather rude remarks, so I'll exclude repeating them.'

'Good Christ,' a member of the managerial group sputtered.

'He's mad,' said another.

'He's fired,' Sir Cedric Lawrenson said.

There was a unanimous murmur of agreement. One of the party accompanying Lawrenson gestured at Helen to convey it.

'Translate that. Just tell him he's dismissed.'

'No.' She was startled by her own audacity. She saw their immediate reaction of angry astonishment but it was already too late to retract. 'You can't do that, Sir Cedric.'

'I can do what the hell I want,' Lawrenson snapped. 'This is my private company.

'Yes, sir, it is . . . and I'm sure you can. You're the boss. But to discharge this man would be unjust and unfair.'

'Unfair? Did you say *unfair*? After what he called me?'

'He didn't say it to you . . .'

'*I beg your pardon?*'

'He didn't. He spoke to me; it was you who made me repeat his words. If he's to be dismissed because of what I was obliged to tell you at your request – *what you demanded I tell you* – then I have no choice but to support him if he takes the matter to the union . . .'

'The union,' Sir Cedric said heatedly, 'I won't tolerate a damned female migrant provoking me with talk of bloody unions . . .'

'I'm sorry if it upsets you, but they have lawyers, who might want to make a case of this. Or else there's the newspapers.' Helen was icy calm now, knowing she had crossed the line and her job was already forfeit: 'After all, there must be a story in people like us, people who came here because we were told it's a land of free speech, losing our jobs by being foolish enough to believe it.'

'That'll do, Helen.' Kerr could contain himself no longer. His voice was shrill with outrage. 'You're dismissed as well. Sir Cedric, kindly allow me to handle this. I'll have her on a train and out of here by tonight . . .'

'Will you be quiet, man!'

'But Sir Cedric . . .'

'For God's sake, just shut up and go away. And the rest of you gentlemen, will you please return to the cars. You other people, since you are being paid – get back to work.'

The tall young Czech seemed to know what had been said. He nodded and for a moment his gaze lingered on Helen, then he walked up the hillside and resumed excavating. His workmates followed his example. Kerr hesitated, clearly wanting to lodge a protest that might restore his prestige, but deciding it would be unwise. He turned on his heel and left. The executives made their way down towards the waiting cars. Moments later Helen and Lawrenson were entirely alone.

'Are you threatening me?'

'No, sir.'

'It sounded remarkably like it. Unions and newspapers.'

'May I ask you a question?'

'I expect so. You don't appear to be the sort of person who takes no for an answer. Ask it.'

'What is an interpreter to do, if someone like you demands an exact translation? Am I to lie to you?'

'Certainly not. Have you never heard of tact?'

'So I should tell you what you wish to hear, even if it happens to be mostly untrue?'

Sir Cedric Lawrenson stared at her. He looked as if he was about to argue, then seemed to think better of it.

'What nationality are you?'

'Hungarian,' she said.

He shook his head, and sighed.

'I should have known.'

'Do you have a prejudice against us, Sir Cedric?'

'A prejudice? I'll tell you a story, young lady. A world famous scientist was once asked if he thought aliens from other galaxies might exist. He said yes, of course they exist. They already live among us – and are called Hungarians.'

Helen smiled. He chuckled, looking unexpectedly benign.

'I'm one myself,' Sir Cedric Lawrenson said.

At the end of August, three weeks later, came a directive to shift from their primitive hillside camp to new quarters at Adaminaby. The news of the transfer was received with jubilation since it was still bitterly cold, and there was heavy snow and ice on the high ground. To their relief, the tents were to be left behind – left standing for some other poor buggers, Sandor Jaroslav, the outspoken young Czech who had caused the confrontation, told Helen – for they all knew that more snow, chill winds and winter temperatures were predicted until late September. And old Lawrenson was never a man to let a few tents go idle and unoccupied, no matter what the conditions.

Helen said she was sure Sandor would manage to find something to complain about at Adaminaby, and why not try to practise keeping his mouth zipped, because one of these days it would be bound to get him into real trouble. Sandor had grinned, and said she was in a bad mood because she'd been the only girl in camp, and now they were going to be alongside a real town where there were lots of girls – all ages and very pretty from what he had heard – so she'd have some competition. How did she feel about that?

She smiled, squeezed between Sandor and Michael in the lead truck, as the convoy transported them down the jagged mountain road. In the distance were a line of emus foraging for grass below the snow line. It was a welcome sight; the only animals they had seen in the past months were an occasional forlorn kangaroo, a few dingoes that kept their distance and often howled at night, and constant bush rats, scavenging for food, burrowing in the tents to plunder scraps of newspaper and the sarking to build nests. It was a relief to think they might be seeing the last of the rats.

In sheer high spirits, massed voices were raised in a chorus of national songs, and if the words were in different languages and the tune inclined to stray off key at times, the feeling was one of elation. While she shared the euphoria, the news of this move to better conditions had not come as a complete surprise to Helen. She had expected something of the kind ever since her encounter with Lawrenson, but hugged the knowledge to herself. Besides, she doubted if anyone would believe her. Not Michael, and probably not Sandor Jaroslav, even if she was spending a lot of time in his company and becoming fond of him.

It surprised her, this growing feeling, because Sandor was something of a paradox. For a start, he could speak English and had understood all that had taken place. She found this out moments after Sir Cedric Lawrenson had gone to join the rest of his party, and she was about to return to the administration office where Angus Kerr would doubtless be waiting to rebuke her, when he had scrambled down from the site they were excavating to intercept her.

'Thank you,' he said, smiling at her astonishment while telling her she was not only nice looking, but also had much courage to talk back to the bloated plutocrat – beautiful and brave, he insisted – speaking fluently but with a strong accent.

'Why didn't you tell him yourself, in English?' she'd asked.

'If I try to talk like that to him, they say shut up and throw me out. So I tell you, to see what you'd say – or if you'd say it. And then, Mine God, their faces . . . when you speak to them like you did . . . it was marvellous to watch!'

'Not for me, *sport*,' she said acidly, using one of her brother's favourite terms. 'I could've lost my job.'

'Then we would have found better jobs together,' he grinned, and while trying to be annoyed at his presumption, she realised he was rather attractive.

Later she found out he had been a medical student when Hitler marched into Prague, and had escaped and taken nearly a year to make his way to France, where he had learned the language so he could continue his studies. But by then France was conquered and he was interned as an alien. After three years as a labourer on a prison farm, he had managed to make his way back to Prague, fought in the south with the resistance against the Germans, then escaped again into Austria as the Soviets took over his country.

'Like us,' Helen said.

But not quite like them.

She learned – unlike Michael and her – that he had been accepted by the British and given employment in a field hospital, part of the army of occupation in West Germany, earning his keep as an orderly while he studied medicine, and had even completed his third year exams before the army unit was returned to Britain. That was when the allied hospital was shut down, and his life changed. The Germans made it abundantly clear they had no need of a Czech medical student who would be a drain on their resources until he graduated. They had a ruined country to rebuild, and their own people to foster. So he had applied to emigrate to Australia.

'And now you hate it?' she prompted him.

'Who said that?'

'It's the impression you give.'

'Hate's a big word. I hated the Nazis, and all the people who looked the other way – the ones who pretend they see nothing. Not only Germans. Plenty Latvians and Croatians were fascists. The Swiss – they accept money in their banks; the Pope, he says prayers and the rest of the time stays quiet and safe in the Vatican. Most of all, I hate what was done to Lidice, which was near my home in Bohemia. You know about Lidice?'

Only rumours, she said, heard long afterwards. Nobody knew for years. Did they really kill everyone who lived there?

More than that, he said. Much more than that.

'But why?'

He had been silent for a time, not wanting to answer. Then he told her it was in retaliation for Reichsfuhrer Heydrich, Hitler's friend and deputy, appointed as the so-called Protector of Czechoslovakia. He had been assassinated in Prague but the Gestapo declared the plot was hatched in the little mining village of Lidice. So they came to Lidice, deciding that an example would be made.

'They begin by shooting all the men,' he said. 'First the coal miners, more than six hundred of them. Then the old men, and after that they shoot the schoolboys. The women and young girls they take to concentration camps, where they died, and the babies removed to God knows where, and never seen alive again. Then the village is demolished, bit by bit, all the buildings, the streets broken and buried by tractors, so that not a single trace remains. The name is removed from all maps, all documents, to show the world it no longer exists.'

'How can people do such things?' she wondered.

'Easily,' he'd said.

Part of the attraction that drew them together was their ability to talk so freely. He was able to confide in her, to be more explicit about his feelings for Australia. He certainly did not hate it, but he was disappointed. If he could afford it, save enough money, he'd leave and go back to Europe.

'What's in Europe?' Helen asked.

'Two more years of medical study. A chance of a degree.'

'What's wrong with here?'

'Here I have to start all over again.'

He told her about it. When he applied, they had encouraged him. Said he would be welcome. Doctors were in demand; just two more years and he would graduate. But when he arrived, then it was all of a sudden a different story.

'What I'd learned, the exams I'd passed, meant nothing. They had no status. Even if I was already fully qualified, a doctor, it would not be legal for me to practise.'

'Why not?'

'Rules. The Australian Medical Society does not accept any European degrees.'

'But why not?'

'They say they have different standards. I think they don't want no more competition here. Instead of study, first I must work two years to repay my fare. So I ask to be an orderly in a hospital. You think that's reasonable? I think it is. But they say no. Builder's labourer, they decide, that's what I should be, for Lawrenson. I don't hate Australia, Helena. I hate the rules, and the lies they tell me, and making me swing a pick when I should be learning to use a scalpel.'

'It seems a waste,' she said.

'English doctors are allowed. Wog doctors, not good enough. That's more than waste. It's stupidity, it's . . . I don't know the word . . .'

'Prejudice?'

'Yes, perhaps . . .'

'Discrimination?'

'That's the word. Many fine surgeons, physicians – they don't let them work. They must qualify again. Not even in country towns which need doctors, not even there can they practise.' He shrugged cynically. 'Perhaps their patients would not like them. Perhaps they don't trust them to be proper doctors, like Australians.'

'That's silly.'

'Is it? You ever go into Cooma?'

'Only once.'

'I used to go. Now I don't bother. You ask to buy something in a shop, they don't answer, and only serve you after everyone else. The same in a hotel, if you wish to have a drink. You get ignored, people stare at you, so you learn not to go to the Royal or the Grand. You go to a hotel called The Wog's Pub, but you won't meet no Australians there, because they refuse to drink in such a place. As for the policemen, if they see you in a group, just talking, passing the time of day, making gossip, they tell you to move on.'

'Sandor . . .' She tried to reason with him, but at times he was impossible. In a strange way their disagreements fuelled the growing attraction between them. 'It can't really be like that.'

'I swear it is. The only ones who smile at us, even speak to us sometimes, are the girls. They like us because we don't get drunk at the dances, as Australian men often do – going outside to have beer, or wine which they call "plonk" – leaving the girls sitting in the dance hall like . . . I don't know what . . .'

'Wallflowers.'

'Hah! Yes. And if they dance with us, these wallflowers, that makes the men angry. If New Australians marry a local girl, people here say it must be because he gets her pregnant. Why else would she get hitched to a bloody foreigner?'

'You have to realise,' Helen said, 'that everything here has changed so much. Only a year ago Cooma was a small country town, now it's filled with people. There's a housing shortage, far too many cars and trucks for the size of the streets, and the whole place is overcrowded. Be fair and give them a chance to get used to us.'

'You be fair,' Sandor said. 'I'll be fair if ever they treat us as normal. But they won't. They don't like us; they don't want us here. We're garlic eaters, reffos, Balts, Eyeties, squareheads and dagos. Never mind whereabouts we come from. Or that we have traditions and heritage, and thousands of years of history. With all the wars, we still have great cities and monuments that are the envy of the world. Do they know it? Would they care? Of course not. If we don't eat steak and chips, and talk like them, we're strangers. Foreign bastards.'

'If you feel like that, then you'll always be a foreign bastard. I refuse to be a stranger,' Helen stated unequivocally. 'I'm going to belong here.'

'Then good luck,' said Sandor Jaroslav. 'Marry some fool who won't respect you. Buy a house with a clothes line in the backyard that twirls around. Write to me in Prague and tell me about it.'

'You'd go back there? To the communists?'

'Tomorrow if I could. If it meant a medical career.'

'You're a crazy man, Sandor.'

'Not crazy enough to throw away a stethoscope and spend the rest of my life digging ditches in Australia.'

Late September brought a lustrous spring. If the earth and trees did not rejuvenate with the volatility of seasons in the northern hemisphere, they brought new pleasures. The startling brilliance of wattle trees, like a bright canvas of yellow and gold after the bleak winter, was followed by jasmine and wisteria twisting into bloom on bungalow verandahs, and orange and red Chinese lanterns illuminating the hillsides with their unique floral foliage. In the gardens of Adaminaby, bulbs propagated; freesias and daffodils, hyacinth and jonquils, emerged, blossomed, and transformed the town. Colour was abundant; it cheered the heart. Soon iris and strelitzia, the bird of paradise flower, flourished to celebrate the approach of summer and the longer, warmer days.

Apart from the distinctly better conditions – billeted now in solid wooden barracks, each with a partitioned hut that included a window and their own private door – Adaminaby was a lively contrast to the isolation of the heights beyond Berridale. An old township built on a hillside above a wide valley, it had been established in the 1830s as a cattle station, and with the discovery of gold on the Eucumbene River had become a staging camp for miners who flocked to Kiandra. After a few years, when the gold ran out, it settled into being a typical country town, existing on the price of wool and a thriving sawmill, enlivened on Saturdays by graziers and stockmen from the Monaro who had made it their rendezvous for a few beers and a bit of a chinwag. Now it was a place on the verge of extinction.

The first projection of the Snowy Mountain Scheme had planned a wide lake below Adaminaby, which would transform it into an inland holiday resort, and popular predictions were that by the year 1960 it would be a waterfront megalopolis. Instead of that, a new decision had suddenly been taken to extend the dam, and the future city of Adaminaby, rather than becoming a summer playground and a prosperous winter wonderland, was consigned to be drowned by the vast Eucumbene Dam, and would cease to exist.

While some residents made arrangements for their houses to be raised from their foundations and freighted to higher ground where a new town was being planned, most refused to believe any government could allow their historic township to be flooded and destroyed. It was, after all, a place of some importance. It not only boasted numerous stores, hotels, the still thriving sawmill, a picture palace and a community hall where dances were held each Saturday night, but it also contained the local racecourse and the biggest showground in the district. They could hardly let all that disappear below a dam, the optimists insisted.

The barracks into which the Lawrenson work force moved had been constructed by Italian carpenters who had now been shifted to build a new camp at Tumut. The people of Adaminaby said they would really miss the Italians, for they had beautiful voices and sang songs from opera while they worked, and were happy people – even if they were dagos. What sort of mob are you, they asked?

A little bit of everything Helen replied, while enjoying their astonishment at her lack of a foreign accent. Garlic eaters, Huns, Balts, bloody Hungarians, Polacks – we're a real mongrel mob, a mixture of peculiar nationalities, we are.

The locals did not quite know what to make of this answer, but Helen was pretty and lively, and they decided they liked her. They weren't so sure about her brother, Michael, or the feller who seemed to be her boyfriend, a wog named Sandor, but they came to the conclusion they did like Helen.

Chapter 9

The community hall was lit with fairy lights. On the rostrum, which served as a stage for amateur dramatics, a dais on school speech days, or a platform for politicians at election time, the musicians were tuning their instruments in preparation for the Christmas Eve dance. It was a tradition, and even if their town was threatened with destruction, and might soon be engulfed below a vast lake which pessimists already predicted would be four times as large as Sydney Harbour, at least this year there would be a dance. The biggest, the best dance ever.

The local Anglican Minister, the Reverend Robert Leigh, had voiced his disapproval, and persuaded the Methodists and the Catholic Church in Cooma to form a united front on this issue. He devoted his next full sermon to his belief that the night before Christmas was for attendance at church, and more good would come of divine prayer for the salvation of the district than godless revelry. In former years he had been able to overlook this, because it was an insignificant event by comparison with the large congregation that filled his church. This year was different – the town was threatened – and he enjoined his flock to turn their backs on frivolity, and not listen to Satan. His flock, after duly considering the sermon, decided the dance must prevail. There might never be another.

It was an act of defiance, the minister declared. He and his theological colleagues were disgusted. Despite his denunciation, or perhaps incited by it, plans grew. It would be not only the largest and most dynamic dance the town had known, there was going to be something special, something exhilarating about this Christmas Eve. Everyone declared there would be nothing to equal it; in years to come they would look back fondly and remember this night. To prepare for it, they had sent a plea to Melbourne for the trumpeter Eddie Marks, who had grown up in the district, and now played in jazz groups with radio stars like Horrie Dargie. They asked Eddie to come home in case it was the last dance, the last music heard in the hall – which might soon be no more than a submerged relic, drowned and encrusted in barnacles – the very same hall where in short trousers, aged ten, he had played a trumpet solo of Bunny Berrigan's *I Can't Get Started*, and not only mesmerised them all but had won an eisteddfod.

Throughout the afternoon, crowds of people began to converge on the town. Word of mouth had already ensured it would be a gala event, and the *Cooma Gazette* had reported a special fund had been raised to hire additional marquees; there would be loudspeakers, beauty contests, a tombola, raffles – and by kind permission of the council and the police, a bar would be set up. The Reverend Leigh objected vehemently to this, but the local Sergeant was an Irish Catholic and could not stand the Anglican Minister. The matter had been settled, and the Sergeant's only concession was that drinks would be served until one minute prior to midnight, but as this was a strictly family occasion, any drunks would be arrested and would spend Christmas Day in a cell – no lawyers, no bail, no option.

Tickets were two pounds for single men, a pound for married couples, two shillings for unaccompanied ladies, and all children free on condition they didn't get in the way.

By nightfall the town was packed. Buses and trucks ferried in teams of men from Island Bend, Perisher, Seven Mile, Tumut Ponds, and Jindabyne; road gangs, tractor and bulldozer drivers, electrical teams, even the senior engineers and their families turned up, as well as the Norwegians who were building the first power station at Guthega. Women were vastly outnumbered; most were locals, but along with the construction workers from Cooma came many nurses, wives and office staff. The community hall had no hope of accommodating so many visitors, but fortunately the weather was fine, the loudspeakers worked, the bar was set up under the stars, and the carnival crowd spilled into the marquees and the town streets.

Inside the hall the conventional circle of chairs – where at regular dances many girls sat waiting, tapping their feet to the music, hoping not to look abandoned while waiting for boyfriends – had been moved to make extra dancing space. The men lucky enough to have partners stood waiting, while the orchestra cleared its throat – blowing chords, playing scales and plucking strings. The rostrum was barely able to fit all the musicians. Not only had Eddie arrived with his trumpet, but he had brought his quintet – saxophonist, guitar player, clarinettist and drummer. They were augmented by the local band who had refused to be left out, and consisted of a piano, violin, xylophone and an elderly lady who played the accordion.

Sandor found it hilarious, and declared it could not possibly work musically; it would be a fiasco, a hideous cacophony, with none of the instruments blending, but nevertheless he asked Helen if he could take her to the ball. She teased him by appearing to ponder this, then accepted him as she had intended to all along, although warning him she had promised so many dances she could only guarantee him the first.

And the last, he insisted.

And the last, she agreed.

The music was a surprise. From the first pure notes of the trumpet, Eddie Marks and his brass section slid into the strains of his own composition *Moonlight* and the local quartet, confounding Sandor's prediction, blended perfectly with them. Eddie put down his trumpet, moved to the microphone and started to sing:

Moonlight, brightly shining like a blaze of noon . . .
A mystic hillside by an old lagoon,
That I remember from afar . . .
How the strings of a guitar
Made lovers' music to a star . . .

They began to dance. Despite the mass of people, they found ample space, Sandor moving easily and proving to be a skilful dancer. Helen who had hardly ever danced in her life managed to follow his steps, while loving the mellow euphonic sound of the orchestra.

She felt happy, stimulated by the warm summer night, the vibrant atmosphere and feeling of such accord with the local people. It was something she had privately encountered since their move to Adaminaby – but it was rare en masse like this. It created an ambience of growing acceptance, an air of goodwill that was less to do with the eve of Christmas and approach of the New Year holiday than with people becoming accustomed to each other, beginning, however slowly, to tolerate new nationalities and other ways.

She hoped it would last. For her, there was the realisation it was almost the end of a year in the country, and their first Australian summer. While a great deal of the time since their arrival had been difficult, some downright unpleasant, she was starting to adjust, to feel she could settle and learn to like it here. So much had changed, and she could pinpoint the moment when it did. The day she thought she had thrown away her job, interpreting for Sandor, being scared, then challenging and confronting Sir Cedric Lawrenson.

A Hungarian. It had made her laugh, the sheer absurdity of it. He had not been offended by her laughter, fully aware it was friendly. He had even told her his former name. Tibor Esterhazey. He had decided there was more chance in an Anglo-Saxon society if he changed it. He was one of the smart Hungarians who had foreseen the future and fled Europe, arriving on a freighter in Australia in 1938, with just enough money to start a small backyard-repair business. From there, employing a bricklayer and a carpenter, sub-contracting plasterers and plumbers, taking risks and borrowing money, he was on the verge of bankruptcy when the end of the war created a sudden demand for new houses, and brought him a windfall beyond his wildest dreams.

She would never dare voice it, but sometimes she wondered if Lawrenson had moved them from the rigour of the tent camp outside Berridale to this more pleasant location, because of that day and their meeting. It was probably conceited of her to even think so, but at least it had made one huge difference in her life. Angus Kerr was no longer accommodated in the same building, sharing living quarters so uncomfortably adjacent to her. While she still had to cope daily with working alongside him in the same office, there was a subtle change in his attitude. Sometimes, she had the feeling Sir Cedric Lawrenson might have said something; if not, then Mr Kerr was apparently adroit at reading the new mood of confidence she emanated.

Life was changing. Helen now felt whatever the future might hold for her, it would evolve here. She felt an affinity with the country, one she would hardly have believed possible almost twelve months ago. Thinking of this, she looked across the hall and caught a glimpse of Michael, dancing with Deirdre Miller. She liked Deirdre, a lively and attractive local girl with lustrous red hair, who worked behind the counter of her family's produce store. Michael had met her on a blind date soon after they moved to Adaminaby.

Helen hoped her brother felt the same about this place as she did, but knowing him, she had her doubts. She gave herself up to the warm sensation of her body moving in unison with Sandor's.

And ever after in the glow . . .
We lingered there in shadows low,
Danced like dreamers in the light,
We danced to magic in the night.

'You're supposed to keep in time to the music,' Deirdre said. 'But you're always half a beat ahead – which is why we're out of step, and that's the reason you keep treading on my bloody toes.'

'Let's just stand still,' Michael said, 'and snuggle tight against each other? Then I could feel your tits, and you could have a grope of whatever you like best about me.'

'God, you're awful, Michael. You're really disgusting, some of the things you say.'

'Well, I'm a bloody migrant,' he said, grinning. 'What else can you expect from an ignorant drongo who was born in Hungary?'

'Get fucked,' Deirdre whispered in his ear.

'Ohh,' Michael said loudly, 'can you possibly mean what I think you mean?'

'Shut up,' she said.

'No, I'd rather get fucked,' he replied, as an elderly couple who were dancing past looked at him strangely, then at each other as if they must have misheard. When they had gone, he murmured: 'Why don't we give up this unequal struggle? Let's go back to my hut and have a struggle there – with our clothes off. It'd be much cooler, too.'

'Later,' she smiled. 'Don't forget, you've promised to dance with your Grand Duchess. Keep in step. Try not to tread on *her* toes.'

'I wouldn't dream of it. But if she treads on *mine* she might break them.'

Deirdre laughed and nudged him as the song ended. 'Go on, she's waiting over there, pretending to enjoy herself. Be nice to her.'

'Of course I will. I hope you'll be nice to me later.'

'I promise.'

'Don't let any of these rotten reffos sweet-talk you,' Michael warned her with a grin. 'All they want is one thing, the dirty buggers. And be careful of the Italians. They'll pinch your bum, those bloody Eyeties, while they sing operatic arias in your ear.'

'I know all about the Italians and their ways, thank you.'

'You can explain that remark later, in bed.'

'Wave to Mrs Dyboski. And keep time to the music.'

'I'll try,' Michael said, obediently waving to the Grand Duchess. 'You keep yourself pure for me, and don't go off with any garlic-munchers.'

She squeezed his hand, and watched him step his way through the dancers to join Katryna Dyboski. *Trust him*, she thought fondly, *to head straight across the hall, as if he owns the place.* Michael would never tiptoe around the outskirts, it was not his way. She had known him for over two months, through a chance meeting when some girlfriends had organised a night out with a few spare fellers. She had been going to bed with him regularly, since their third date.

He was a refreshing change to the boys she had grown up with here in the Monaro, where her family had lived and run an agricultural store for three generations. She liked his cheeky irreverent manner, and he could arouse her to orgasms more intense than she had experienced in any of her brief encounters in town, or her one short affair with the son of a local grazier. He was also very sweet, she realised, as he saw him reach the bulky figure of the Polish woman, take her hand and raise it to his lips – ignoring stares and smirks, as if they were in middle Europe, and not the Adaminaby Community Hall. She smiled at this, then a man in his best Continental suit with sleeked-down hair approached and bowed to her, requesting, mostly in sign language, the pleasure of a dance.

~

'You look very glamorous, Duchess,' Michael told her, trying to keep time to the music, finding to his surprise that she moved lightly and easily, almost floating as she danced with him.

'Flattery,' Katryna Dyboski said. 'I'm very fond of flattery. Especially from you, my gorgeous darling boy. That's a rather pretty girl you were dancing with. Is she your friend, Deirdre?'

'That's Deirdre.'

'She looks nice. And also quite sexy.'

'She's very nice,' he said, 'and also sexy.' They laughed.

'And are you serious about her?'

'Your Grace, I'm sorry, but I think I just stepped on your toe.'

'It was nothing. Light as a feather. Tell me about Deirdre.'

'Her great-grandpa started the produce store in town. Her father and the family all work there. Deirdre serves behind the counter.'

'And how do they feel about you, this family?'

'Can't you imagine?'

'Perhaps. But you tell me.'

He was silent for a moment.

'When people live in a place for a long time they disapprove of change. You can imagine how they hate the Snowy Scheme, which is going to flood their town. Also they're not at all fond of migrants, and they get very cranky if any of the family brings one home.'

'Did she bring you home?'

'Yes. Sunday lunch, the first week after we met.'

'And were they cranky?'

'She has three brothers. They didn't say a word to me, right through the meal. Just ate their food and stared at me, like I was some nasty object the cat dragged in, while Deirdre talked, or tried to, and her mother asked me if it was safe to drink the water where I came from, and her dad said Hitler was a bit of a loony, but he might've had the right idea on some things, like the Jews. What did I reckon?'

'My dear . . .'

'I said I reckoned that was a hard one to answer, since I was a Jew and my parents had been killed in a gas oven, but if he felt like that, I should leave. He asked why, and I said it was because I didn't like to sit at the same table with him. Not if he was in favour of gas ovens.'

'Did you leave?'

'I started to, but the three brothers got up. Big buggers, all of them. They said I'd insulted their father, and probably been up to dirty tricks with their sister, so before I left they'd beat the shit out of me. But they'd do it outside, so the family wouldn't have to watch.'

In the hall the music stopped, and the dancers were applauding the band as they left the rostrum to take a rest. The Duchess seemed to barely realise this; she was staring at Michael.

'What happens – with these brothers?'

'Come on, I'll find you a drink.'

He took her arm and they left the dance floor. A man he knew slightly, one of a bunch of recently arrived Polish workers, walked past with an empty glass in his hand. He nodded at Michael, then glanced with a brief, puzzled frown at the Duchess. She did not notice this, intent only on Michael and concerned with what he had been telling her. The man went off towards the bar.

'Michael, please, tell me. You fight the three brothers?'

'We went outside. I said one at a time. They laughed, and

began to hit me. First it was their fists, then they used their boots. Next thing I remember I'm on the ground, everything's hurting and that's when I heard the sound of a shot.'

'A shot! Who shoots?'

'Deirdre shoots. She had a shotgun. She fired in the air, and told her brothers to back off. Only she didn't say "back". They weren't sure if she meant it, so she fired again, really close, and this time they ran. She got me into their truck, drove me back to camp, took off my clothes, bathed my bruises, and stayed the night.'

'And in the morning, how were the bruises?' The Duchess's eyes sparkled mischievously.

'Almost better. Responded to the treatment,' he said. She hugged him affectionately, as Deirdre appeared beside them.

'My dear girl,' the Duchess said, 'he just tells me about the day of the fight, and the shotgun, and his bruises.'

'Oh, did he,' she smiled. 'I know you're Mrs Dyboski, and he calls you Grand Duchess. Can I call you Katryna?'

'Of course you can.'

'It's nice to meet you at last.'

'For me, too. But the fight . . . it makes trouble for you?'

'Nothing I can't handle.'

'Surely a big row with the three brothers and the parents?'

'No. Not a row at all. Just angry looks, and a stony silence.'

'No shouting?'

Deirdre shook her head. Katryna Dyboski looked surprised and rather bewildered.

'In Poland we'd shout. Till it's settled. In this country they don't say nothing?'

'Not in our house. There's a lot of families like ours. My

parents would rather avoid a fuss, sweep things under the carpet, that's their way. When I got home the next day . . .' she paused, 'I suppose he told you I stayed the night . . .?'

'To look after his bruises, he said.'

'That's right.' They both laughed. 'When I got back, Dad was on the front verandah. He looked as if he wanted to raise the roof. He got as far as frowning, then Mum gave a warning cough, and he shut up. He's never mentioned it since, nor have my brothers. They know I'm seeing Michael, but we don't discuss it, and I certainly don't bring him home any more, which is a shame, because if they really took the trouble to know him I think they'd like him.'

'They would. It's sad when people choose to hate each other just because they're different. It's what makes us feel unwelcome here.'

'Do you know many Australian families?'

'None.'

'Not even one, in nearly a year?'

Katryna shook her head. 'It's hard to meet people, and even if you do, nobody invites you to their homes.'

Deirdre was silent for a moment. Michael stood watching them both, saying nothing.

'We're not very good with new people who come to this country,' she finally said. 'I don't know why. But from what I hear, it's always been like this.'

'Parochial,' Michael said.

'What's that mean?' Deirdre was the one who asked, but both the women looked puzzled.

'My clever sister told me it means narrow. Narrow views, narrow-minded. With a small, restricted outlook on the world.'

'Is that what you think we are?' Deirdre sounded offended.

'Calm down,' Michael grinned. 'Your dad, yes. He's a prize example – and your brothers. Not you.'

'Of course not you,' the Duchess said. 'Sometimes, for a lovely young man, he talks foolish. Go and get beer for us all, Michael, and Deirdre and me will yack about you behind your back.'

'Yack,' Michael laughed.

'What's the matter with yack? Isn't it an Australian word?' she appealed to Deirdre.

'Certainly is,' Deirdre assured her.

'So, my darling boy, you go and bring beer. We'll yack.'

Michael smiled and nodded. It was a mellow evening, a full moon shining across the valley, and he felt at ease. In that particular moment he was as relaxed and as happy as he could recall at any time since he and Helen had encountered the duplicity of their neighbours and friends as children, seen their parents deprived of their pharmacy and been spat on as they were driven from their village. Since that day contentment had been rare in his life – until now.

He would remember this instant long afterwards; the gaiety in the large wooden community hall, standing between the old Duchess of whom he had grown so fond, and Deirdre, who radiated degrees of passion and a wonderful cheerfulness, and who was such an exhilarating addition to his life. He remained there, wanting to relish the moment, feeling her fingers entwine with his, as his blood stirred with her warmth. It was a stimulating reminder, a promise they would spend the night together, even if she did have to go dutifully home to her family for Christmas dinner. He would have his own quiet meal tomorrow with Helen.

He had reserved a table at a cafe in Cooma, hoping only that there would be no request for Sandor to join them. He was not sure what it was about the Czech that disturbed him, but the thought of Sandor's attachment to his sister cast a shadow on the summer night.

He was about to get the drinks when he suddenly saw the Duchess's face was chalk white and she swayed as if she were ill.

'What is it?' he asked.

She stared at him without recognition, like a stranger. As if she could not speak – had been maimed by a stroke.

'Katryna, for Christ's sake, what's the matter?'

Deirdre took her by the arm. 'Are you sick? We'll find you a place to rest. I'll ask if there's a doctor . . .'

The Duchess's eyes were rigidly fixed on something beyond them, past Michael's shoulder. He turned and saw the Pole returning from the bar with a drink in his hand. There was nothing unusual about the man; he was slim, in his early thirties, his dark hair slicked back, and he had a pock-marked face. Nothing at all distinctive about him – except that he was looking with a curious shock of recognition at Katryna – then, as he saw Michael studying him, their gazes locked.

But only briefly. The man gave what appeared to be a rather perplexed shrug at the interest displayed in him, then abruptly turned and walked away. He made a pathway through the clusters of people waiting to resume dancing, and was quickly lost in the crowd.

The young duty doctor in the casualty ward at Cooma Hospital was overworked, and not very sympathetic. He had made a

213

cursory examination of the patient, and there was a queue waiting.

'I wish I had time,' he said, 'to find out what troubles her so much. But I haven't. She seems to have had a severe shock, but she won't tell me why. Can you assist in this matter? Otherwise I'll have to discharge her. Do you have the slightest idea why she's in such a hysterical state?'

'I don't think she's hysterical,' Michael answered. 'I think she saw something that made her afraid.'

'Like what?' the doctor asked. He was twenty-four years old, and had been promised a residency at St Luke's in Sydney. Instead, by some erratic and bizarre mischance he had found himself assigned to Cooma. It was not a locality he would have chosen. His father was a judge, his uncle a professor of surgery at the prestigious Royal North Shore Hospital who refused to use his influence, in case it was construed as nepotism. The youthful doctor was not amicably disposed towards most migrants, particularly those who arrived in the casualty ward late on Christmas Eve in a state of terror that nobody seemed properly able to explain.

Michael knew there was no way he would tell this *schoolboy* what he thought. But he felt sure he did know what had caused this – if not why. It had been the man at the dance. She had seen the face of a man in the crowd, and moments later was shivering with fear and whispering in Polish – a language he did not understand – while she vomited helplessly outside the community hall. Deirdre had nursed her while he went hurriedly to find Helen, asking if she could grasp what was being said, then made a call to the district ambulance, and insisted on accompanying Katryna to the casualty ward of the Cooma hospital.

'I don't know what she saw,' he replied to the doctor, who frowned and seemed irritated by the answer.

'You just assume it was something that made her afraid? If you don't actually know, such an opinion is hardly much help to us, is it? Quite the contrary.'

Michael refrained from a retort. Telling the doctor would achieve nothing. But he did know. A Pole named Jan Elsner was the man who had walked past. Elsner had arrived with a recent influx of East Europeans, and worked as a carpenter on the new site, where they were building houses for Belgian construction workers and their families. His was the face the Duchess had seen. When she recovered, Michael needed to find out why this had caused her such terror.

'All right,' the resident said reluctantly, after examining her again. 'She does seem in distress. We'll keep her in overnight. But I hope you do realise it's Christmas Day tomorrow.'

Yes, I've heard of Christmas Day, he wanted to respond, *even us ignorant reffos have celebrated that in whatever peculiar place we came from*. Instead he replied as politely as he could: 'I know you're short-staffed, Doctor, and I'm grateful. Thank you.'

The doctor told one of the nurses to hospitalise his patient in an emergency bed – if she could find a spare one – until the morning when she would have to be discharged or transferred to the main ward. He walked off to join a probationer who had brought him a plate of sandwiches and a cup of tea.

It was exactly midnight on the clock in casualty.

'Merry Christmas,' Michael said, but nobody appeared to have heard him.

~

'Merry Christmas,' Deirdre gasped, as she felt herself on the brink of losing control, and wrapped her legs tightly around him. Her naked body felt as if it was on fire. She began to tremble as his hands lifted her buttocks and she arched against him. Sunlight spilled through the thin curtains, and outside, cicadas shrilled a distant chorus. Inside the tiny cubicle where he lived, they came together in clamorous delight, unable to restrain their rapture, oblivious of its effect on the occupants of neighbouring billets, divided by less than soundproof walls. They held each other fiercely until their throbbing bodies began to subside, and he kissed her long and tenderly.

'Wow!' she said. 'Golly Moses and Holy Mackerel!'

'What a wonderful way to spend Christmas. Are you sure your religion allows this sort of thing on such a day?' Michael asked.

'Shut up,' she laughed. 'I wish we could cancel Christmas and stay here instead.'

'What time do they expect you home?'

'Not too late. I ought to help Mum with the cooking.'

'It's only nine o'clock,' Michael said.

Her large grey eyes were inches away from his as she smiled.

'Is that all it is?'

'That's all.'

'You have to telephone the hospital.'

'Mid-morning, they said.'

'And you have to smuggle me into the shower block, and stand guard to keep all your perving workmates away while I shower.'

'Now?'

His disappointment made her laugh again.

'No. Not for at least two hours.'

'Two hours, eh?'

'Yes. How do you feel about that?'

'Still randy,' Michael replied.

'Lovely,' she said. 'That's what I hoped you'd say.'

The relieving duty nurse was later to report there appeared to be absolutely nothing wrong with the patient when she brought in her morning tea. At the time Mrs Katryna Dyboski, who had spent the night in one of the emergency beds in a verandah off the casualty ward, was dozing, and had seemed to respond. The nurse had asked if Mrs Dyboski wanted some biscuits with her tea, and it was her impression that the patient had shaken her head, or else murmured no thank you, but she was not sure of this, as she'd been interrupted by an ambulance arriving with an emergency case, a patient needing to have a knife wound stitched.

The nurse was frightened when she made this rather vague statement. She had been in charge of the casualty ward, and as a matter of routine should have taken the patient's pulse and checked her condition. But as the hospital medical superintendent would later point out, because of Christmas rosters and a staff shortage, the nurse was a probationer who should not have been left without adequate supervision, and the duty sister and resident doctor would be required to answer some questions, in particular about an impromptu and rather wild staff party which had begun sometime after midnight. The revelry had apparently lasted until dawn, with only cursory visits to check the condition of patients admitted during the night, one of whom was Katryna Dyboski.

An inquiry was convened, but ended without censure. The hospital, in its wisdom, pronounced their staff were not responsible, when a hastily ordered autopsy revealed that Mrs Dyboski, born in Krakow, Poland, in 1898, had suffered a massive coronary during the night, and had died instantly. A relieved medical superintendent declared that was the end of the matter.

Angus Kerr was in a foul mood. The directive from Sir Cedric Lawrenson, in which he had insisted work should proceed throughout what was normally a holiday period until New Year, was bad enough. But as if this annoyance was not sufficient, the situation had been made intolerable because so many men were reporting sick, whereas in truth they were nursing hangovers. And little wonder! Christmas and Boxing days had been riotous displays of drunken disorder. It seemed as though, missing the familiar festivity of their own countries, the lack of snow, the sight of holly and the sound of carol singers, the Lawrenson workers had turned to alcohol to alleviate their homesickness. The wet canteen had been totally packed, and the unruly behaviour had continued ever since. Beer flowed constantly; there was also a growing mountain of empty wine bottles, along with brands of vodka, slivovitz, and other outlandish drinks they had introduced to the country, together with their strange and different customs.

These opinions he imagined he kept to himself, but in the company of friends – real Australian friends – Angus Kerr admitted he did not like migrants. Couldn't stand the bastards. He thought them complicated and difficult. They smelled of garlic, and half of them couldn't speak a proper sentence to save themselves. If the country had to have immigrants, the sensible thing would have been to bring in only British migrants. Some of them could be bastards, too, Kerr said, but at least you could understand what the hell they were whingeing about. Well, most of 'em. Not ones from up north like Manchester, or some of the Scots. Or the bloody Welsh or Irish, come to that. But they were better than the dagoes and Balts and the rest.

If the hangovers were an inconvenience, there was worse. A group embroiled in a fight in Cooma had been detained in town awaiting a magistrate. And now a carpenter was missing. His foreman had reported it, complaining he was three men short; one drunk, one in Cooma gaol, and the latest had walked off the job – or so it seemed.

'What's his name?' he demanded of Helen, since the wretched foreman was a migrant himself, and had made the report in some indecipherable language that only she could understand.

'Elsner,' she said, 'Jan Elsner.'

'What sort of name is that?'

'Polish.'

'Well, where the hell's his file?'

She crossed to her desk to bring it. In his vexation he reflected it was unlike her not to have the man's record to hand; she would know he was certain to want it. Which – since he spent a considerable amount of his time reflecting on Helen and how to make progress and ingratiate himself in that direction – made him begin to be aware something was troubling her.

She brought the file, and handed it to him. It was slim, and for a moment he held it without bothering to turn the pages.

'What's the story on him?'

'No story,' Helen said immediately – and he noticed this. As if aware of his interest she added: 'At least none I know of. Just that he hasn't reported for work.'

'Polish, you said. Where was he born?'

'Krakow – according to his file.'

'Never heard of it.'

She shrugged, as though indifferent, but he was again aware of some disquiet that troubled her. He resisted the idea of questioning her on this, and opened the dossier instead.

It was like many others; the contents were almost standard. It contained a Displaced Persons identity card with a photograph, and a more recent one on acceptance as an immigrant. There was a medical report, date of birth, country of origin, family particulars – both his parents were dead and he had no surviving relatives – as well as comments from the selection officials who had interviewed him. As he came from behind the iron curtain, there was also a comprehensive report on his political affiliations.

'No communist allegiance known,' he read, and this time watched Helen to see her reaction.

But there was no reaction whatever. To an increasingly curious Angus Kerr, this was the equivalent of a response in itself. She was so determinedly non-committal, it could only mean she knew the man, or at least knew something about him.

He thought about this as he gave every appearance of reading the file, acutely conscious of her standing alongside, waiting. It was like a game – one that was played with intense pleasure if the quarry was a slim, attractive girl who had so far scorned his advances. He would play this game even if it led nowhere; it would divert his mind from the aggravation of workers who got drunk, workers incarcerated in gaol, or this damned Polish carpenter who was missing. As Helen was so clearly worried by his interest in the man's non-appearance, he was therefore very interested in the man.

'What is it, little one? What's wrong?'

She undressed slowly, and Sandor lay in her bed and watched her as she unclipped the brassiere and removed her panties.

'Nothing,' she said, and slipped into her bed alongside him.

'Iluska,' he had taken to using the name in moments of intimacy, 'what do you think . . . am I some kind of an idiot?'

'That's a funny question at a time like this.' She did her best to smile, reaching for him. Her mouth met his, and his hands began to caress her breasts. For too brief a time, her desire supplanted the fears that had been alarming her.

Most times after making love she would feel sleepily content, but tonight the tenseness would not go away. Sandor could sense it.

'Something is wrong,' he persisted.

'I hope not. But I'm beginning to think it is.'

'Then tell me what's the matter?'

'He's still missing. That man.'

'Which man?' He gazed at her. 'You mean the Polish one?'

'Jan Elsner. Yes.'

'But when we talked about it yesterday, you agreed he's probably drunk, or in gaol.'

'He isn't in gaol.'

'How do you know?'

'Mr Kerr telephoned the Cooma police to find out.'

'Angry Angus?' It was Kerr's nickname around the camp. 'Why

bother? Such a lot of trouble, because one man misses work.'

'It is a lot of trouble. And I'm not sure why. But one thing I do know, this seems to have become some kind of fixation for him.'

'Fixation? What's that?' Sandor asked.

'Obsession. All he thinks about. He's established it's at least four days now since anyone in the camp has seen Elsner.'

'Who says four days?'

'The men who work with him. The ones who live in the same block of huts. As well as his foreman who's complaining.'

'Then it's simple. He's run away. That's the only answer.'

'I don't think so.'

'It has to be. Not drunk or in gaol, what else is the answer?'

'I don't know,' she said, but felt more and more afraid.

'Listen to me. The night of the dance, he guesses your friend Mrs Dyboski recognises him, and he's shocked to see her – like she is to see him. He becomes frightened the Duchess knows something from his past. Soon word will spread about him. So he runs. Escapes to somewhere safe, where no-one will know him. What do they call it here? What does your brother tell you is the Australian words?'

'Shoots through?'

'That's right. That's what they say. He shoots through, and he's in Sydney or Melbourne.'

'None of his clothes are missing. Not his suitcase, not even his toothbrush. Kerr keeps telling me how carefully he's checked it all.'

'But why does he keep telling you this?'

'That's what's bothering me. In the past few days he seems to have spoken about nothing else. Just Elsner. Keeps on, as if . . . he has to tell me. Seems to enjoy it. As though . . . no, that's stupid.'

'As though what?'

'No, it's silly. I'm imagining things. It's been such an awful time.' Her eyes felt moist. She found a handkerchief and wiped them. 'Katryna dying so suddenly, and the funeral in that small, lonely graveyard. I kept thinking all through that dreary service, how much she would have hated it. How sad she came across the world, to die in a place she hardly knew, and be buried by a priest she'd never met.'

'Come here,' he said gently, and wrapped her in his arms. The warmth of their naked bodies began to comfort her.

'Elsner ran away,' Sandor said softly, persuasively. 'Never mind what bloody Angry Angus says, about suitcases and toothbrushes. If you're scared, Ilona, you run like hell. Run for safe places. You don't stop to pack clothes or clean teeth.'

Long after he was peacefully asleep she remained awake, her thoughts in turmoil. If you're scared you run away, you don't stop, Sandor believed, and had almost convinced her.

But the man calling himself Jan Elsner did stop. He didn't run away after he and the Grand Duchess had seen each other at the dance. When she and Michael went to Cooma Hospital on Christmas Day to identify the body, they saw Elsner leaving. The Pole had not been aware of them, but her brother had recognised him. When he asked the nurse on duty, she'd told them he was a compatriot who had come to inquire about the patient, and she had given him the sad news. Which meant Elsner knew Katryna was dead, and that he was safe. Whatever knowledge of his past that she possessed had died with her.

Remembering Michael's anger when they realised this, she knew exactly why she was so afraid.

It began to rain during the night, and by dawn the hillside roads to Kiandra were dangerous with sliding mud. The convoy of bulldozers and trucks bringing the heavy machinery had to slow down, but they reached the site safely. When they did, the engineer in charge passed the word along that unless the rain became heavier, they would start to shift the rock and clear the area as soon as the demolition squad got their act together and blew up the mountainside.

The bulldozer drivers and earth-moving operators knew there was no chance the work would stop, even if the rain became torrential, as the giant concrete mixers were already here, and the schedule was rigid. The concrete had to be poured in time for a special visit by the Minister of Works and a bunch of politicians in a week's time. There was growing agitation in some of the newspapers that the cost of this hydro-electric scheme was too high, and pressure was being mounted to have it curtailed. When the bigwigs arrived for a ritual inspection, they had to see progress. Enough concrete must have been poured by then to convince all concerned that in a few months' time this desolate spot – which had once been a thriving goldfield and was now nearer to a ghost town – would be the site of a power station.

The drivers sat in the cabins of their huge machines, smoking, waiting impatiently for the last of the gelignite charges to be set. They were being paid on time and results, and were making four times what other workers in the rest of the country were earning. It was hard graft, with few amenities, apart from the occasional taxi arriving at their camps with Sydney prostitutes, up by train for a week or two's visit. The prostitutes often started at one end of a hut, and worked their way through the occupants of the cubicles. Sometimes, if one fancied a particular bloke, she might move in with him for no extra charge, until she grew homesick for the bright lights, or her presence became known and she was ejected.

The tough men who drove the big dozers liked the prostitutes. It was uncomplicated. There were also tarts in some of the nightclubs in Cooma, but they avoided these places. There was precious little point enduring the long hours and tough conditions, if you were going to end up squandering it in a Cooma clip joint. After a year or two of hardship at the money they were earning, they could all afford to buy homes and new cars, or the sort of expensive lifestyle that would make this exile worthwhile. But not if they blew it all in town on local tarts. Bloody silly, that would be.

'Should be a beauty,' one said. 'Big fireworks display.'

Up on the slope, near an outcrop of rocks, there was a sudden shout and some excited activity. It spread to others in the demolition squad, who started to run towards the scene.

'What do you reckon's happened?' a driver speculated.

'A stop-work meeting. Or else they ain't got a match to light the fuse,' said the inevitable comedian.

The explosive experts were Norwegian. They came from all over the hillside, and clustered around the group of rocks into which, earlier, they had drilled and set their charges. They stared at what had been uncovered by the rain that gushed down the slope like a river.

Half buried in a shallow grave was the body of a man. Even smeared with the layers of mud carried by the rain, they could plainly see the knife wounds that had almost severed his throat.

Chapter 10

The first police came from Cooma two hours later, a uniformed constable and a detective, responding to a radio message sent to their base by the Norwegian demolition squad. The murder site was secured, and the charges that were set and ready to blow were temporarily disarmed. To the consternation of the engineers who had a deadline to meet for their political visitors, work was halted until the authorities had made their necessary investigations.

The local medical officer arrived by jeep, and an ambulance later transferred the body to the morgue, which was a tiny building adjacent to the Cooma Hospital. The cause of death was the severance of the carotid artery, and to the best of his ability, the doctor estimated the man had been dead for five days. Since it was the thirtieth of December, this gave a newsworthy impetus to the case in normally slack summer holiday period, because the report meant the victim had very likely been killed on Christmas Day.

Radio bulletins and press headlines carried the story of the MIGRANT MURDER as it was instantly labelled. It was given added colour because of the location; near the town of Kiandra, which a century earlier had been a flourishing goldfield with a population of many thousands, until the gold ran out. It had then become a primitive ski resort – one of the first such resorts, so local legend had it, to exist anywhere in the world.

In his quarters at the Adaminaby camp, Angus Kerr heard the story on the news that night, and his interest was immediate when it was announced the victim was as yet unidentified. The following morning he took a jeep and drove into Cooma, to the local police station, where he introduced himself and asked to speak to the officer investigating the case. He had, he said, some idea of who the victim might be. A Polish carpenter had been missing for at least five days, and while the body had been found at Kiandra, about twenty miles away, the description he had heard on the radio seemed to fit.

He was asked to wait. A burly detective came to join him, and introduced himself as Sergeant Bill Walsh.

'What's the name of your missing bloke?' he asked.

'Jan Elsner,' Kerr told him, and the Sergeant asked him to spell it and carefully wrote it down.

'Can you identify him for us?'

'Not personally,' Kerr said, mentally thanking God he didn't know the Pole by sight, and would therefore not have to endure the trauma of a decomposing body. 'But I reckon the clerk in my office, Helen Francis, could possibly help. Francis is the name she's adopted, but don't let that throw you. She's actually Hungarian.'

'Speak any English? It's hell when they don't.'

'No problem. She speaks it perfectly.'

'That's a relief. And she could identify him?'

'I can't say for sure,' Kerr became cautious. 'She might've known him. I get the impression she did.'

'How do you mean, sir – you get the impression? Did she know him or not?'

'She said not.'

'You think she wasn't telling the truth?'

'It's just a feeling I have about the way she behaved.'

'Behaved? And what way was that?'

Kerr suppressed a sigh. The country detective was as stolid as he was abundant in shape.

'I've been trying to make inquiries why the man hasn't been at work, and I came to an opinion that she knew him, although she didn't admit it. That's all. No matter what she said, I formed that belief.'

'Shacked up with him, you mean?'

'No, I don't mean that. Elsner's only a new arrival, so I doubt it. Matter of fact, I dunno much about her private life. I'm just trying to help in this matter.'

'And we're grateful,' Sergeant Walsh said.

'If it turns out she can't identify him, there are plenty of his workmates who could. But they're on a shift at Island Bend, and out of contact until tonight. I'd say Miss Francis is your best bet.'

Neil came out with a cup of coffee and joined Sarah at the balcony table where she liked to sit when it was sunny. He kissed the crown of her silvery head, and she looked up and smiled. Relaxed and tanned from days at the beach, he was wearing a cotton shirt and shorts and making the most of his summer holidays. He was thoroughly at home here at last – after insisting he paid rent at the market rate for an apartment with a harbour view, which was the closest they'd ever come to a quarrel, she remembered. He had stipulated that his fair share was ten pounds a week.

'Too much,' she'd said, 'I won't accept it.'

'I can afford it – and you must accept. Or I'll get myself a room up the road, and probably pay more. And we'll meet once a week for dinner, and both feel lonely.'

'Five pounds,' she had insisted. They had finally settled on six.

She smiled at the memory of it. That had been months ago, and they had existed companionably here in Macleay Street ever since. She sometimes thought she had never been so content, living in this gracious apartment, sharing her delightful bohemian village with the young man who had restored her wish to live. Life, in its aberrant way, had a great many twists and turns to it.

'Are you going to the beach today?' she asked him.

'Yes. I'll catch a tram to Bondi later. I want to make the most of the last of the holidays.'

'Back to work next week?'

'On Monday.' His voice was without expression, but Sarah heard the regret in it. Something about that job troubled him. And it bothered her, because she wondered why.

Neil could sense her concern. She wasn't to know that since the first meeting, when Falconer had questioned him about Milan, his evasive answers had remained an impediment between them. From that day for the past eight months they had worked in a detached formality, colleagues but not friends.

'Anything in the newspaper?'

'Not much.' She handed it to him. 'Some poor migrant is murdered, down at the Snowy Mountains, where they are building these dams and power stations.'

Neil looked at the headline. The story was on page two, with a picture of Kiandra, covered in winter snow, an empty landscape with a caption saying ten thousand people had once lived here. Also there was a smudged photograph of the victim, badly reproduced.

'Unknown migrant murdered,' he read aloud, and shrugged. 'I doubt if he'll be unknown for long. If he worked there, someone must be able to identify him.'

She felt sick. The man was naked on a slab, coated in mud, and although the big detective had covered the lower part of the body out of consideration for her, all Helen's shocked gaze could focus on was the gaping wound in his throat.

'Do you know him?' Sergeant Walsh asked.

'Not personally. I did see him once, but not to speak to.'

'Is it this man Elsner?'

'Yes. I believe so. Jan Elsner. I brought this with me.'

She gave him the file, and he looked at the first page, with the required immigration details and the two photographs.

'That's strange,' he said. 'Mr Kerr gave us the name of the bloke who was missing, but said he couldn't identify him. And that perhaps you could. Why didn't he bring in this file, with the photos?'

'You'd have to ask Mr Kerr that,' Helen replied carefully. It came as a shock to her, the realisation that Angus Kerr had contrived this; to have her brought here to confront and identify the murdered man. It confirmed the feeling she'd had that he suspected something. She became aware the detective was looking at her curiously.

'He said he felt sure you knew the man, but that you denied it. Is that right, Miss Francis?'

'Not strictly, no.'

'Would you like to explain?'

'He certainly never asked me if I knew him.'

'You didn't volunteer the information you'd seen the man?'

'Why would I? Just once I saw him. I spend a lot of my time interpreting, so I know most of our workers, at least by sight.'

'Did you ever interpret for this Elsner?'

'No. I've never spoken to him. I thought I told you that.'

'Don't get upset, Miss Francis.'

'I'm sorry, but I am upset. Do we have to stay in this place – with the body – while I answer your questions?'

'No, of course not,' Sergeant Walsh said, and opened the door for her. They went outside. He locked it behind him. 'Feel better?'

'Yes.' She took a breath of fresh air. 'Thank you.'

'Okay, let's talk about your boss, Mr Kerr. Why would he say such a thing?'

'I don't know,' she said. The detective looked at her with an expression that seemed to doubt this, but he did not comment. After a moment she continued: 'He's a difficult man. We're not friendly.'

'Any special reason why?'

'Lots of reasons why. I don't think he likes foreigners . . . or should I say New Australians? And also . . . he made advances once, and I told him not to.'

'I see,' Walsh nodded.

'And there may be something else,' she said with sudden heat, 'perhaps Mr Kerr doesn't like to look at dead bodies, and he thinks just because I'm a Hungarian and grew up in the middle of a war, that I'm used to it.'

'Okay,' Walsh said. 'Relax, Miss Francis.'

'I'm sorry if I get angry, but it's unfair. You said all he has to do is bring this file. Which is absolutely correct. The pictures in it would have told you.'

'Yes. Never mind . . .'

'But I do mind, Sergeant.'

'What I mean is, now we've identified him, it shouldn't be too difficult to nail his killer. So at least you've helped our investigation.'

He glimpsed what almost seemed to be a look of dismay, and wondered what he had said to make her react in such a manner.

'I'll organise you a lift back to Adaminaby.'

'Thanks.'

They left the hospital and walked back through the town. It was unusually quiet. Tomorrow, New Year's Eve, the place would be alive, the pubs bursting with drunks, and the streets more than likely violent. Walsh thought he could do without it.

'I should ask this, since you'd know better than anyone how things are out there. You might've heard rumours. Have you any idea of who might have had a reason to kill him?'

'No,' Helen said, 'not the slightest.'

Sergeant Walsh merely nodded, giving no indication that for the first time he felt she was lying.

Angus Kerr saw the police vehicle arrive back at camp, and he watched from the window as Helen got out. When the car drove away, he sat at his desk and waited for her to return to the office, but the door remained shut and there was no sign of her. Having prepared himself for a scene, in which he would airily profess it had been the detective's idea she should identify the victim, he was disconcerted by this. He had been relishing an encounter, from which he hoped he might learn more about why Elsner's disappearance had so disturbed her. For he was convinced there was something to be learned. And this notion – which had begun as a distraction, a game to discomfort her – had assumed a far different status now that it was established as murder.

But where was she? He rose and this time gazed openly out the window. After all, it was only midday – within their normal office hours – and he was entitled to rebuke her if she didn't return to work. Which was when he saw her distant figure hurrying to meet one of the returning labourers, among a group on their way to the canteen for their lunch break. He could clearly see her take one of them aside, and speak to him urgently.

He knew at once it was her brother.

And another piece of the jigsaw in his mind fell into place.

'It's him. Jan Elsner. There's no doubt.' She hoped at least for some show of surprise, but he merely looked at her and nodded.

'Haven't you anything to say?' she asked.

'What do you want me to say? He was an evil bastard and I'm really glad he's dead.'

'Michael . . .'

'I am. Someone cut his throat, which is exactly the right way to kill a pig like that. So apart from hoping that he died slowly and shit scared, what's it to do with us?'

'How did you know his throat was cut?'

'Lots of people know.'

'No, they don't.' She felt ill with apprehension, and shocked by the malevolence of his reaction. 'I didn't know. So who told you?'

'It must have been on the radio, or in the newspaper.'

'It wasn't. The detective said they didn't release the cause of death. The only statement issued was that a migrant had been found murdered at Kiandra, killed on Christmas Day. No other details.'

'Well, someone told me.'

'Are you sure, Michael?'

'Of course I'm sure,' he said angrily. 'Jesus Christ, Ilona, why all the bloody questions? What the hell is this?'

'Can you remember who told you?' she asked quietly.

'No, I can't.'

'Will you try?'

'Why? What's it matter?'

It matters to me, she thought – but had no time to say so.

'He's dead, and he won't be missed,' Michael said. 'Not by me, and if you're honest, not by you. Now stop acting as if I did it. Because if it was Christmas Day, I was with you.'

'Not all day. Till mid-afternoon. What about after that?'

'I was with Deirdre, and she spent the night.'

'But she couldn't get away from her family till late, she told me. It was nearly nine o'clock before she met you. So where were you all that time?'

He gazed at her so long that she thought he might not answer.

'Alone,' he said finally. 'Call me a liar if you want. We only get half an hour for lunch and I'm starving, so we'll talk about this another time.'

Without giving her a chance to reply, he walked away. When she reached the administration office, Angus Kerr was hanging up the telephone, and he looked unusually smug about something.

'The police will be back tomorrow. Apparently they're not satisfied.'

She sat at her desk feeling desolate, a pile of letters waiting there for her to type. Trying to quell her fears, she began work.

Late that afternoon Detective Constable Harry Renshaw, who was the sole officer the Criminal Investigation Branch was willing to assign to the case, arrived in Cooma by train. The Inspector in charge of the Monaro force was not well pleased. He had hoped to get the entire matter off his back by handing it over to the CIB, but had been told by the Deputy Commissioner there was a bloody crime wave in Sydney – with vice madams waging gang war over who controlled the street girls – and fortunes being made out of cocaine, illegal gambling and sly grog. Also it was New Year, and half his staff were on holiday. So one copper was all his elite squad could spare for an insignificant migrant murder in the sticks.

The Inspector sent Bill Walsh to meet the train. He told him to get the city cop a hotel room – nothing too deluxe or fancy because he was only a bloody detective constable – and on that point Bill should remember he was actually the senior officer, responsible for solving this pain-in-the-arse case. And it shouldn't take long. Migrants fought each other for only two reasons; religious or racial differences, or far more likely, jealousy over a woman. Find out which, and it would be a walkover, a lay-down misere. Then they could get back to the important business of traffic control and keeping order in the town.

Thanks a heap, thought Bill Walsh, and went to meet the train.

'Reckon he's right about the motive?' Harry Renshaw asked.

'I dunno,' Walsh said. 'The important thing with my boss is being allowed to think he's right. We all try our best in that regard.'

They were standing by the exposed shallow grave at Kiandra the following morning. Despite it being New Year's Day, the location should have been busy with the growl of bulldozers and cement trucks, but instead was devoid of activity and uncharacteristically silent. The big machines stood in line across the ridge, idle and abandoned. Walsh knew that their drivers waited impatiently down at Three Mile Camp, fed up with losing so much time and money, and more than likely getting pissed in the wet canteen. There was also pressure from the Snowy Mountain Authority to get the work under way again without any more delay; an inquiry into the killing of one man should not be allowed to impede progress. He told the city detective about it, while they walked down the hillside.

'They're kicking up a stink. They want the hill blasted, and the diggers back. I've taken photos and collected soil samples, but the rain washed out any hope of footprints or much else.'

'I'd say let them back. Nothing more we can do here.'

They reached the police truck parked below on the access road. While Walsh used his radio to pass this news to Cooma, Harry Renshaw studied the isolated terrain. Hard to realise this had once been part of a thriving town, with shops and banks. Difficult to visualise coaches with armed escorts that left every day, carrying gold bullion and the lucky men who'd once found it. Now busy main street had been devoured by termites; nothing remained except a tiny settlement on the far side of the mountain with a post office and a few houses.

'Whoever killed him knew about this place,' Renshaw said, when Walsh joined him. 'If it hadn't been for the rain this would all be under concrete by now, and the body with it.'

'Yes. The killer picked his spot. Even picked his time – late Christmas Day when no-one was working here. He was unlucky with the weather, or else there'd be no corpse and no case. It'd go down as another migrant worker who vanished.'

'Do many do that? Vanish?'

'Sure. Can't blame them. Some of these camps are the dregs. Isolated – not much in the way of amenities. People are often fed a load of bullshit before they emigrate. Most of them expect better, and now and then one shoots through, looking for the bright lights.'

'Ever catch 'em?'

'Not often,' Walsh shrugged. 'Hardly worth trying. We put out a missing persons, but they organise it pretty well. Friends take 'em in. People who run backyard businesses; they work there for cash, change their names, buy a driving licence. It's not difficult these days.'

'And Elsner would've been down as one of those?'

'I reckon so.'

'This interpreter who identified the body. Helen someone?'

'Francis. Helen Francis.'

'Tell me about her.'

'Well, she's young, early twenties. Fiery little piece when she gets upset. Not bad looking, actually.'

'How about the joker who runs the local Lawrenson camp? What's the story on him?'

'Angus Kerr? He's a creep. It's clear he's had a go at her, and she told him to get lost. I'd say he gives her a tough time.'

'The information on her brother? Did that come from him?'

'Yes. He got on the blower to me, after we gave her transport back to camp. He's got some notion the brother and sister could both be involved.'

'What do you think?'

'We obviously need to interview the brother. I told Kerr to have him available for questioning when we get there.'

'But what's your opinion? Could she be involved?'

Walsh hesitated. He scratched his head, then shrugged.

'Difficult to say. I like her, and I think her boss is a cockroach, but that shouldn't come into it. I don't know why . . . but I get a strong feeling she knows more than she's telling us.'

'Well, we can soon find that out, can't we?'

'How?'

'We have to question people. And we need her with us. After all, she's our interpreter.'

Walsh smiled. He wished he'd thought of it. But then he was only a country copper.

From the window beside her desk, Helen saw the utility truck with its police insignia approach along the blue-metal road through the camp. It stopped and Sergeant Walsh's burly figure climbed out. With him was a younger, slimmer man. She looked away, resuming her typing of the work schedule, as they came into the office, and the new man was introduced.

'Mr Kerr, Detective Renshaw, from the Sydney CIB. And this is Miss Francis.'

The young detective came to her desk, surprising her by offering his hand. Unlike Europe, women and men rarely exchanged handshakes in this country.

'Miss Francis? I'm Harry Renshaw.'

She rose and shook hands with him. He turned to Kerr.

'We'll need Miss Francis to accompany us, and interpret.'

'Let me know when you require her, and I'll send her along.'

'We need her full time, Mr Kerr,' he said. 'Right, Sergeant?'

'That's right,' Walsh said.

'But what about her work here?'

'That's your problem. I understood from the local Inspector that you were keen to help us in these inquiries.'

'Well, of course. As I told Sir Cedric Lawrenson, when he rang up to discuss the matter, I want to cooperate as best I can.'

'Good.'

'But surely you don't need her in all cases. A few of the men speak reasonable English. And if you're going to question the person I suggested, he'll present no problem.'

He said it in a manner meant to convey some careful message. Helen turned and looked at him. She glimpsed an exchange of glances between the detectives, but before she could speak the phone rang.

'Can I ask who you meant by that . . .?' she began, but got no further before Angus Kerr pointed at the telephone.

'Answer it, please.'

'Who did you suggest be questioned?'

'*Will you answer the telephone?*' he snapped.

She wanted to shout at him, and demand an answer. The phone kept shrilling. She went to it, and lifted the receiver.

'It's for you,' she said to the sergeant, and they all stood in an uncomfortable silence, while he listened to what was being said, and gave monosyllabic answers.

'Thanks,' he said finally. 'Yes, we will. Right away.'

He hung up and turned to Helen.

'We'll be back. Everyone has to be questioned, Miss Francis, no exceptions to that. Every single person. I hope you understand?'

'I think so,' she said.

'We'll start as soon as we can. But first of all, Mr Renshaw and I have to go to Cooma, to talk to someone.'

She watched them go out, the young Sydney detective looking puzzled, and the sergeant confiding something to him. They got into the police utility truck, and drove off.

To Cooma, to talk to someone, she thought. *Now what?*

She sat at her desk, without a glance at Kerr. There was no need to persist in trying to find out who he'd meant: she knew. They were going to interrogate Michael. If only she could warn him before they returned. Which brought her back to their abrupt departure.

Cooma? What was so important that they had left in such a hurry?

The casualty ward was crowded, but the nurse took them into a visitor's room in the main hospital, where they could talk in private.

'He came here on Christmas morning to ask about a patient,'

she said. 'I was on duty. I've been home on leave, and I only saw the paper this morning, but I recognised his picture straight away.'

'Who was the patient?' Walsh asked her.

'Her name was Mrs Dyboski. Mrs Katryna Dyboski. A Polish lady. She was admitted to casualty on Christmas Eve.'

'And Jan Elsner came to ask about her?'

'Yes. I told him she'd died of a heart attack, sometime during the night.'

'Not a very pleasant task, having to tell a fellow countryman that. It seems they were both Polish.'

'No, not very pleasant,' the nurse said, and paused. 'Except . . . I don't think he was very upset. I'm not sure if I should say this, but I had a peculiar feeling he was . . . no, it seems wrong to even say it . . .'

'He was what?' *Walsh was good at this*, Renshaw thought. *Relaxed and patience personified.*

'Pleased.'

'Pleased?'

'Yes. It's something I've been thinking about since then, and I honestly don't feel he was sad about it. Not like the others.'

'What others?'

'The one who came to identify her body. He'd brought her to casualty the night before.' She smiled, as if this was a more pleasant recollection. 'He called her the Grand Duchess. You could tell he was fond of her. He was really upset, and so was his sister.'

Harry Renshaw had been leaning back, staying deliberately detached, leaving the questioning to the local detective. Now he sat bolt upright.

'What were their names?' he asked.

'I can't remember,' she said. 'I could find out.'

'Before you do, did he and his sister arrive together?'

'Yes.'

'Did they know Mr Elsner had been here?'

'They saw him. He was leaving.'

'Did he see them?'

She thought about this, and shook her head.

'No, because the boy – Michael, that's right, his name was Michael – pointed and said something like "that's him".'

'That's him. Are you sure?'

'No, I can't be positive, but I think that's what he said.'

'To his sister?'

'Yes.'

'As if she mightn't have recognised him?'

'I suppose so. But she seemed to know who he meant.'

'Do you recall what she said?'

'Not really. I remember that the boy – Michael – asked me what Mr Elsner was doing here. I told them he'd come to inquire about Mrs Dyboski.'

'Were they surprised?'

'Yes, they were. Not only surprised. They spoke to each other – in a language I didn't understand . . .'

'Probably Hungarian,' Walsh said.

'I don't know what it was, but it sounded angry. At least Michael sounded angry, and then she said something to him . . . as if she was telling him to stop. I feel sure it was that, because he looked at me and said "Sorry". Then the sister in charge arrived, and he went to identify Mrs Dyboski's body.'

'Just him? Not his sister?'

'No, he said he'd do it. Made her sit down and wait, right where you're sitting. He seemed protective towards her.' Again the nurse smiled, and Walsh thought, *she really liked the boy*. 'I talked to her while she was waiting. I asked if they were going to friends for Christmas dinner, but she said they didn't know anyone and were going to eat in a local cafe. It didn't sound like much fun to me, but I suppose it's tough for migrants when they first come here, isn't it?'

'Yes,' Walsh said.

'I'll go and find out their names for you.'

'We think we know them,' Renshaw said.

For the first time the nurse seemed concerned.

'They're not in any trouble, are they?'

'We hope not. But we have to ask these questions.'

'He was just upset,' she said. 'Michael, I mean. That's why he had the argument, with the duty doctor . . .'

'Argument?'

'It was nothing, really. The doctor's a bit . . . well, stuck-up's the only word. He couldn't get any sense out of Mrs Dyboski. It was Christmas Eve and he didn't really want to admit her.'

'Why not?'

'The paper-work, if you really want to know. But he said she was just hysterical. Michael insisted she wasn't – that she had seen something that had made her afraid. Something or someone, I got the feeling he meant. Then that night she had a heart attack and died. So it seemed to me he might've been right.'

The detectives looked at each other.

'Where do we find this doctor?' Sergeant Walsh asked her.

~

Sandor saw the trail of dust behind the fast-moving vehicle, and as it turned off the road and came through the camp he realised it was a police utility truck. It pulled up outside the administration hut, and two men got out. From a distance he saw them enter the office, and moments later emerge again with Helen accompanying them.

'Jesus Christ,' he said, and began to run.

But the truck did a U-turn and drove back past him. He glimpsed Helen's face, and thought she saw him. He ran to the open door of the office, where Kerr was standing watching him.

'What the hell's going on?' he asked.

'None of your fucking business,' Angus Kerr said, with open dislike. He had never forgotten nor forgiven the Czech for the fiasco and humiliation he had suffered, the day of Sir Cedric's visit.

'Why is Helen with the police?'

'I told you it was none of your business. You're a sticky-beak, mate, a nosey bugger.'

'Nosey? Sticky-beak?' Sandor looked puzzled.

'You're a great one for shoving your oar in.'

'What oar?' He was bewildered by the expression.

'Oh, piss off, you bloody Balt,' Kerr said.

'I'm not Baltic . . . I'm Slovak.'

'You're all the same to me, mate. Just useless reffo bastards. Says on your file you studied medicine. You got Buckley's chance of ever being a doctor here.'

Sandor clenched his fists. Kerr's face tightened. He took a step back, but unknown to him was in no danger of attack. It was a method Sandor had been taught by one of his tutors, an old professor, to control tension. *In moments of anger or acute stress, clench your fists, and count slowly to five. Then release them and walk away.*

He counted silently to ten, before turning and walking off.

They were courteous. The canteen manager was there waiting with the keys, and Sergeant Walsh thanked him. He said they'd need the premises for the rest of the afternoon until opening time, as they were interviewing people about the body that had been found, and Miss Francis was going to help them whenever they needed an interpreter.

The manager said Mr Kerr had given the green light, so the place was theirs. Opening time was five o'clock, but if they wanted a drink on duty there was beer in the fridge. He gave them the keys and left. Walsh asked Helen if she would like something cool to drink. Something soft.

'No thanks,' she said.

'We're going to ask you some questions,' Renshaw explained. 'Then we'll bring your brother here, and ask him questions. You'll stay while we do this, but you won't speak while he answers, or try to prompt him in any way. Do you understand?'

'I understand you seem to be making an accusation, but I'm not quite sure what it is.'

'We're not sure if it's even an accusation, Miss Francis,' it was Walsh this time, 'but there are certain things you've concealed from us, and we need to know why.'

'So let's start with Elsner,' Renshaw said. 'Was that his real name?'

'I don't know . . .' she began, and then stopped. She saw them both intently studying her. Waiting for what they seemed to expect would be the first lie.

It wasn't going to work, she suddenly realised that. *Bluffing and avoiding the truth would be a stupid mistake. Because then they'd question Michael and he'd tell his own lies, which would compound the situation, or if perhaps he should surprise them with the truth it would make her fabricated story clearly counterfeit. It could even cause her to be arrested. What was it called? Avoiding – no, perverting the course of justice. In the end, whatever they might say would not be believed. And it was bound to come out finally, one way or another, about the creature who had called himself Jan Elsner.*

'It wasn't his name,' she said quietly. 'His real name was Josef Vlasoff. He was born in Krakow, Poland – which is about the only statement on his immigration file which is accurate.'

'How do you know this?'

Renshaw's voice was as quiet as hers had been. It was what she was most aware of, this extraordinary sense of hushed stillness in the large canteen room that was normally so noisy; just their voices, softly asking questions, and her giving answers.

'Mrs Dyboski recognised him, at the Christmas Eve dance.'

'Was that what caused her collapse?'

'Yes. She was crying and physically sick, afterwards.'

'How did she come to recognise him?' It was Walsh this time, surprising her that a man his size could speak so gently. As she hesitated, he said: 'Would it be because they were both born in Krakow?'

She felt a great sense of relief that she was telling the truth. You could easily underestimate a man like Sergeant Walsh.

'That's how she knew.'

'Just take us through it, Miss Francis.' It was Renshaw again. 'She recognised him, then what?'

'Michael could see she was ill. He also saw she was staring at Elsner-Vlasoff, and he was looking at her. I didn't see this . . . I was with my dance partner. Michael and a friend took her outside, where she vomited and said something in Polish that they didn't understand. He came to get me, then went to call an ambulance. When we were alone, she told me the man's real name was Josef Vlasoff, and she'd known him all his life. As a child, then a schoolboy. She and her late husband had had a house in Krakow, and they'd spent summers there.

'One year Vlasoff and a school friend had vandalised her garden. She'd told his parents, and they'd begged her not to report it to the police. He'd been in trouble before, and he was running wild. So she agreed, on condition he came to repair the garden . . .' She hesitated, surprised at feeling suddenly unsure of her vocabulary. 'Is that correct, or is restore the right word?'

'Fix the garden,' Walsh suggested.

'Fix.' She nodded her thanks. 'But he didn't fix the garden, this schoolboy. He poisoned all the plants, and ran away. This time his parents called the police, and he was brought before a magistrate and sentenced to six months. Because of his youth, his sentence was suspended and he was put on probation.'

She became aware that Renshaw had brought a bottle of lemon drink and poured three glasses. She sipped hers gratefully.

'Four years later, the Germans invaded. Katryna's husband was killed. Warsaw was in ruins, dangerous to remain there, so she came home to Krakow. He was no longer a schoolboy. No longer vandalising gardens. He was one of those Poles who had joined the SS. They made a habit, the Nazis, of recruiting in the territories they conquered, and Josef Vlasoff was a very eager recruit.

'Ambitious, keen to progress. He became an official in a concentration camp.

'He used to visit Mrs Dyboski every week, insisting she make him coffee – which she could only buy with difficulty on the black market – and he would tell her of his progress, his path to success as an *Obersturmfuehrer* in the SS. She didn't want to listen, but was forced to sit there and pretend; he seemed to gain pleasure from that. Then, after a year or so, when he was tired of the game, he arrested her. Crimes of black marketeering, and plotting against the State. He made sure she was sent to the concentration camp where he worked.'

'Bastard.' Walsh said it so softly she knew she was not meant to hear, so she did not acknowledge it.

'The camp was terrible. It was called Treblinka. Vlasoff was an executioner, he enjoyed killing people, but he made certain he kept the Grand Duchess alive. He wanted her to suffer. And she did suffer, but she survived. Then the Russians overran the camp, and the SS disappeared. Some of them got away, they fled to Italy where an organisation gave them new papers and helped them escape . . . to places like Brazil, South Africa, the United States . . . and Australia.'

It was completely silent for a moment, as they absorbed it. *Places like Australia.* The concentration camps were a world they and most other people had not even dreamed existed, until they saw the horrifying newsreel pictures. Everyone knew some Nazis had slipped through the net, but this was the first time either man had encountered a suggestion of it happening here. Helen looked at them, wondering if they believed her.

'That's what Katryna Dyboski told me. Then the ambulance came, and Michael went with her. I never saw her alive again.'

Michael sat in the same chair facing the detectives. She stood apart, by the window where she could see the sun beginning to go behind the mountain ridge. It would soon be time to vacate this place and allow it to become a wet canteen again. Normality would return with crowds of thirsty men jostling for schooners of cold beer.

'When you saw this man leaving the hospital, you knew exactly who he was?' Renshaw asked.

'Yes, I knew,' Michael replied.

'Your sister had already told you what Mrs Dyboski said?'

'Yes.'

'How did you feel?'

'Angry. Upset.'

'I meant how did you feel about Josef Vlasoff?'

'I just wanted an opportunity to kill him,' Michael said. 'I would have done it there and then, if I could have.'

Chapter 11

The phone rang in the empty apartment. They heard it as they reached the landing. Neil had his arms full of shopping after he and Sarah had walked to Kings Cross, lingered over coffee at the Arabian and then strolled back along Macleay Street, calling at her favourite shops and stopping to chat there. He agreed with her that the neighbourhood was like a village; it had a warmth, despite its raffish years as a wartime playground for American troops. Some of this atmosphere remained, with the nightclubs and strip joints, but the Cross had its own distinct flavour; lively and energetic as well as deviant, shabby alleys that ran between elegant streets of apartment blocks, the few surviving old mansions and nineteenth-century houses turned into studios and art galleries, and the bulk of its population a cosmopolitan variety of people unique in this city.

Neil often felt grateful towards Christoph Hartmann, not just for his great generosity to Sarah, but also for his clever choice of a district that so completely suited her. Suited them both, for he loved living here. Sometimes he speculated on how long it would last.

Sarah found her key, and reached the telephone almost when it seemed as if the caller might give up.

'Hello,' she said, catching her breath. 'Yes, he is.'

She held out the phone, as Neil put down the parcels. To his surprise it was Henry Falconer.

'Happy New Year, Henry.'

'And to you.' Falconer sounded oddly perfunctory. 'Sorry to interrupt your holiday, Neil, but something's come up. Have you been reading the newspapers?'

'Occasionally,' Neil said. Most of his time had been divided between the beach and the test match at the Sydney Cricket Ground.

'There was a migrant murdered at Kiandra . . .'

'Yes, I read that.' Neil began to wonder why he was ringing about this; it was hardly their domain. He felt a moment of slight uneasiness. 'The news on the radio this morning said they'd identified him. Someone called Elsner.'

'It turns out his name isn't Elsner. But that won't be on the radio or in the papers. I got a call late last night, and another this morning from Canberra. Trouble brewing, I think.'

'What kind of trouble?'

'It appears as if he might've come illegally through the bureau in Milan.'

Oh shit, he thought. *Trouble might be the least of it.*

'Are you there?'

'Yes, I'm here, Henry.'

'I thought we might've been cut off.'

No you didn't, Neil thought. *You know bloody well you've just ruined my New Year.*

'Did you hear what I said?'

'Yes. Who was the man, apart from being an illegal?'

'We'll talk about that when you get here.'

'Today?'

'I'm afraid so. I'm in the office now. It's time for us to have a proper discussion about what went on at the Milan Centre. And I really think we should have it as soon as possible – before we're called to any meetings.'

'What kind of meetings?'

'With the Commonwealth police – or ASIO.'

He's trying to scare me, Neil decided, *and he's succeeding.*

'I'll be there in half an hour.'

'Get a cab. I'll expect you in twenty minutes.'

This time they questioned him at the Cooma police station, in the interview room, and Helen was not present.

'You keep asking me the same questions,' he complained.

'And we'll ask them over and over again,' Harry Renshaw promised him, 'because you said you wanted to kill him, and I can't blame you for that. I doubt if most people would blame you for it. But there are laws, and we think you've broken one of the big ones.'

'Thou shalt not kill,' Michael said scornfully. 'A hell of a lot of people broke that one where we spent the war. All the bad guys were trying to kill the good guys, and doing a real good job. Everyone was trying to kill everyone else.'

He knew he was becoming rattled, and starting to talk wildly. It was probably what they wanted, so he'd admit to anything when they were ready to charge him.

'How old were you in the war, Michael?' It was the big cop, Walsh. Playing nice and nasty, like people said the Gestapo did, only he couldn't imagine any of the Gestapo being able to pose as nice.

'I was fourteen when it ended.'

'So now you're what – twenty-one?'

'Yeah. Old enough to hang.'

'Why did you say that?'

'First thing that came into my head. Because I'm tired, and I hardly know what the hell I'm saying.'

'You think we should hang you, Michael?' It was Renshaw.

'In Budapest, the Nazis never asked. They just got a rope.'

'But we're a civilised country. We question people, and if we think there's a case to answer, then we put you on trial. And if you can't afford it, we even give you someone to defend you.' He smiled, then said suddenly, 'You hate Nazis, don't you?'

'Yes, I hate them. I would like to have killed that bastard. I'm glad someone did. But it wasn't me.'

'So let's go back to Christmas Day.'

'Fair go,' Michael said. 'How many more times?'

'Sergeant Walsh has written down your previous answers, and he'll check them against what you say now.'

'And against the answers your sister gave,' Walsh said.

So there were no nice and nasty detectives any more. They were both Gestapo now, Michael realised.

'Listen,' he said, 'you can't keep me here indefinitely. If I'm not under arrest, then you have to let me go. Am I under arrest?'

'Of course not. You're just helping us with our inquiries.' Harry Renshaw smiled again, and Michael felt a sudden helpless rage.

'I think you're a prick, Constable Renshaw.'

'Just say whatever you feel, kid. Let it all spew out.'

'Stinking walloper. You're a shit. You'd be at home in a black uniform with a swastika.'

'Puke it up. Don't hold back. I'm not so struck on you, either. People seem to like you, and I can't work out why.'

'Let's begin the questions again,' Walsh said. He seemed to be uncomfortable with what was happening.

'Right. Back we go to Christmas Day,' Renshaw said brightly. 'After you saw him leave the hospital, then what?'

'I calmed my sister down. She wanted to go and report him.'

'To the local police?'

'Yes.'

'You didn't think that was a good idea?'

'I wasn't sure what to do. I wanted to think about it.'

'And then?'

'We had so-called Christmas dinner.'

'Enjoy it?'

'No, it was horrible. A greasy meal in a lousy cafe.'

'And all the time you were thinking what to do.'

'No, I was trying to cheer up my sister who kept crying.'

'You're fond of Helen, aren't you?'

'For God's sake, she's my sister,' he said angrily, 'the only relative I have in the bloody world. Of course I'm fond of her.'

'What time did you leave this lousy cafe?'

'Three o'clock.'

'Went back to camp?'

'Yes. We hitched a ride.'

'Then?'

'I went to my room.'

'Leaving this sister you're so fond of to cry alone?'

'Look, get off my back, will you! She wanted to be alone. And I was meeting Deirdre Miller. I told you that.'

Walsh looked up from his notes. He and Renshaw exchanged a glance, then scrutinised Michael.

'You told us last time. Not at first. Why didn't you mention Deirdre when we first questioned you?'

'I didn't want to have you breathing down her neck.'

'Have you managed to remember what time you met her?'

'No,' Michael said. 'Not exactly.'

'Deirdre's a local girl,' Walsh said. 'Known her long?'

'A few months.'

'Met her family?'

'Once.' He had an impression Walsh gave a fleeting smile. 'Once was enough.'

'Hard man, her father.'

'He's a mongrel,' Michael said. 'So are her brothers.'

'You meet her often?'

'Quite often.'

'But are you quite sure you met *Christmas night*?'

'Ask her,' he said.

'Don't worry,' Renshaw said. 'We will. And don't imagine you're going anywhere,' he added as Michael rose hopefully, 'we haven't finished with you yet.'

Deirdre was waiting in the Inspector's vacated office. She knew Walsh, who introduced her. Renshaw saw a strikingly attractive girl, with a cascade of red hair, and a trim but decidedly curvaceous figure. She seemed nervous.

'Thanks for coming in, Deirdre.' Walsh asked her to sit.

'I'll stand if it's all the same.'

Nervous or determined, Renshaw was not certain which.

'Who drove you?'

'My dad.'

'Do you want him in here while we talk?'

'No thanks,' she said firmly. 'Anyway he's gone to the pub. He said he needed a few drinks, hearing me say I spent Christmas night with a Yid. That's my father's expression, not mine.'

'You have no prejudices?' Renshaw made it a casual question.

'No. Do you?'

'I hope not,' Renshaw said.

'From what I hear, you've been giving him a hard time.'

'Who said that?'

'It seems to be a general opinion.'

'We'd be upset to hear you talked to Helen Francis. I believe you were told not to.'

'Deirdre,' Bill Walsh intervened, finding the other detective's continual aggression starting to irritate him, 'just for the record, you've said you spent Christmas night with Michael. Correct?'

'Yes.'

'It confirms what he told us. By the way, he didn't tell us at first. He didn't want to cause you trouble.'

'He's like that,' Deirdre said. 'Thoughtful.'

'So all we need to know is – what time did you meet?'

'About five.'

'Five o'clock?'

She thought about it, then nodded, seemingly oblivious to their dismay. 'Yeah, five – or it could've been a few minutes past. Maybe ten past, at the latest.'

Renshaw gazed at her.

'Are you certain?'

'Positive. Why, what's the problem?'

'Could anyone confirm that?'

'My family, if you're calling me a liar.'

'Nobody's calling you a liar . . .'

'Well, you seem to be. Go across to the pub and ask my father if you have any doubts. We had a hell of a row about it. A bloody screaming match. He said I was ruining Christmas.'

'For going so early?'

'For going at all. I got an earful of his anti-Jewish garbage.'

'What happened?'

'I told him to get stuffed.'

'We're the ones who are stuffed,' Renshaw said bitterly, a few moments later. Walsh had seen Deirdre out, and returned to join him in the Inspector's office. 'There's no way he could have killed Vlasoff and taken him out to Kiandra, even if she got there at five-thirty or six o'clock. Unless your doctor got the day wrong.'

'You saw the forensic report. And it's the only day that site was empty.'

'I know. I just hate losing our only suspect. But he couldn't have done it. Not manage to find a truck, drive out there, cart the body up the hill and dig the grave, then get back to meet this girl. How long would that take? Four hours?'

'At least. Impossible in the time he had until she arrived.'

'Then we're rooted.'

~

Deirdre crossed the street. She pushed open the door of the saloon bar at the Royal Hotel, put her head in, and beckoned. One of the school of drinkers grouped around her father saw her, and nudged him. He came to the door to meet her.

'I was jest gettin' started on a few grogs.'

'That's all right,' she said. 'Have a few more, Dad. I'll do some window shopping.'

'Hang on – what happened?'

'I did what I told you I'd do. Saw the cops and said my bit.'

'Yer a bloody fool, girl. Y'could get into real shit for this.'

'Not if you and the family back me up. Like you swore you would do – if I promise not to see him again.'

'But will you keep yer promise?'

'If you stick to your side of the bargain.'

'Right,' her father said. He shut the door in her face, and went back to his drink.

They came back into the room. Michael sat waiting.

'You can go,' Sergeant Walsh said.

He wondered if he'd misheard. He looked at them carefully, saw their confusion and then realised the cop from the city was angry.

'Go? No more questions?'

'No,' Renshaw said. 'You could've saved yourself – and us – a bloody lot of trouble, if you'd told us she arrived soon after five.'

Soon after five o'clock? He tried to conceal his disbelief while his mind grappled with it.

'Deirdre said that?'

'Who else? Go on, clear off. But don't expect a ride home.'

Renshaw was not bothering to conceal his fury at the wasted time, just when he thought this was all wrapped up. He had hoped to be on the night train out of here and heading back to civilisation.

'You spoke to her on the phone?'

'Phone? We don't take evidence over the telephone. She was in the next room.'

Sergeant Walsh was looking at him thoughtfully.

'Her dad drove her into town. What is it, Michael? Something worrying you?'

Her dad drove her in. But Deirdre had lied to give him an alibi. Old man Miller would never be a part of that, nor would the rest of that lousy family, so what kind of bargain had they struck?

Both detectives were watching him, puzzled.

'You want to tell us something?'

'Depends.'

'On what?'

'If I do, will you agree not to use it against Deirdre Miller?'

Renshaw said, 'We don't make those kinds of deals.'

'Right, then I'll go and hitch a ride back to camp.'

He saw Walsh and Renshaw look at each other. Some message seemed to pass between them, and Renshaw gave a reluctant shrug.

'As the senior officer,' Walsh said, 'if you make a voluntary statement, I'll recommend we don't take any action against Deirdre Miller. That's the best I can do.'

Michael hesitated.

'She told you a lie. Trying to help me. It was at least nine o'clock before she got away from the family, and we met.'

'And you were home soon after three?'

'About then.'

Renshaw seemed considerably cheered.

'So you had six hours,' he said, 'and according to the medical evidence, Vlasoff was killed in the late afternoon or early part of that night. You had six hours to do it.'

'If I had done it, would I be telling you this?'

'How did you spend that time?' Walsh asked him.

'Lying on my bunk. Thinking a lot about the poor old Grand Duchess dying like that, how the sight of one man caused such a shock that it gave her a heart attack, thinking of the things my sister told me about Josef Vlasoff and what he'd done. I admit I wanted to kill him. Only, I began to realise that was stupid and dangerous – and too quick. I wanted him to suffer. Much better if he was exposed and tried as a war criminal.'

'You expect us to believe this?' Renshaw was openly scornful.

'Not you,' Michael said, 'I wouldn't expect you to believe anything.' He turned to Walsh. 'I wondered how to go about it, and knew the best thing was to talk to Helen. But I started to worry that we might be in danger. Katryna was dead, but Vlasoff might guess she'd told us something before the ambulance came. It seemed safer to report what I knew to the police. So – I think it was about seven o'clock – I used the public phone in the recreation hut and rang up.'

'Which police station?'

'This one.'

'Who did you speak to?'

'He said he was the duty constable. I told him I had a serious matter to report, about a migrant. That he was a former member of the SS in Poland.'

'What happened?'

'He laughed. Asked if I was drunk, or was this some kind of Christmas joke. Only he called it Chrissie. "Was this a Chrissie joke, or was I pissed?"'

'Do you know his name?'

'No, I asked to speak to someone in charge. He said he was in charge, left alone to handle all the crime in town, and to come in after the holiday and tell the Inspector all about it. I tried to explain . . . but it was a waste of time . . . so I hung up.'

'You didn't come in and report it to the Inspector?'

'After that call? No thanks. It was useless trying to talk to cops who thought it was a joke. Nobody would believe it. And if he had papers good enough to get into this country, how could we prove Elsner was really Josef Vlasoff? So the only answer, if he turned up, was to kill him. Which I swear I would have done, but he never turned up. Not alive.'

There was a silence in the room.

They both studied him.

'You could have told us this before,' Walsh said.

'I'm only telling you now, because of Deirdre. So she doesn't get into trouble. You wouldn't have believed me before, and I doubt if you do now. Well, I can hardly blame you. What proof have I got?'

Walsh went out, and returned with the bulky duty book. They both watched as he flicked through pages, scanned an entry and raised his eyebrows slightly. He read aloud:

'December 25th, 6.49 p.m. Anonymous phone call. Migrant who spoke good English. Claimed the Lawrenson construction camp at Adaminaby is infiltrated by the SS. I suspect he was infiltrated by a few grogs, but told him to come in and tell us all about it after the holiday. He hung up without a reply.'

'Shit,' Michael said, astonished, 'he wrote it down!'

'We write everything down in the duty log, even if we think it's a drunk or a Chrissie joke. Just as well for you that we do.'

Neil looked through the copy of Elsner's file, which had been sent from Cooma on the overnight train. Among the documents it contained was the customary medical report, and a letter notifying the recipient of his acceptance in the Australian immigration program, signed by Stewart Mitchell and endorsed by Brigadier Frank Aldridge, dated August 1951, at the Milan Centre. The names were like a sour taste in his mouth, bringing disagreeable recollection of the months he had spent there, the corruption that was so rampant, and the memory of the threats made by Mitchell in Naples that had kept Neil silent.

Until now. Because in the file there was also a United Nations identity card, the kind issued to Displaced Persons, in the name of Jan Elsner. He had seen a great many of them in Europe during his time with the IRO. Henry Falconer sat watching him examine it. Neil knew prevarication was no longer possible.

'This is a fake,' he said, and felt a sense of relief stating it so unequivocally. The stained and dog-eared card in front of him put the Milan group into a category beyond the pale. There could no longer be a question of his own safety or further evasion, no matter what the future might bring.

'How can you tell?'

'The date on the card doesn't match the validating signature. Signed Daniel L. Steggles, Area Welfare Officer, Southern Command. I knew Dan Steggles. He left Italy a year before this date.'

'Very careless forgery. Or didn't the forgers care?'

'They didn't have time to care. They were churning out things like this every day, in factories, set up in back rooms like sweatshops. I never actually saw one, but we knew they existed. Making false papers for the SS and clients with money for new identities; collaborators, war criminals, frightened customers trying to escape to North or South America, who'd pay any price to get into a Displaced Persons camp, because that was the best way to get onto an immigration quota.'

'So how did this pass inspection at the Milan camp?'

'That's a good question, Henry.'

'Can you answer it?'

Neil was silent for a moment. How did one explain you could exist among so much dishonesty, yet be unable to produce evidence? It was only now, looking at this shabby identity card, that some of the extreme iniquity he had suspected was confirmed.

'It might have been forged there. And sold to Vlasoff along with these other documents.'

'Forged and sold by anyone we know?'

Neil barely hesitated. *Happy New Year and goodbye to my new life,* he thought.

'Probably McGill. He was the main black-marketeer, and this seems like him. But it could only have been with the connivance of Stewart Mitchell.'

'And what about our intrepid war hero, Brigadier Aldridge?'

Neil gave a smile that was expected, but he felt no amusement.

'The Brigadier will swear he took no actual part in what went on. He just got a share for looking the other way.'

'Sounds like a real nest of vipers.'

'Yes, it was. Still is, I imagine.'

'Did you know Vlasoff?'

'No. My guess is he was brought to Milan from another camp. When I was stuck in Naples I found out Mitchell had links to a refugee centre there, and another in Bavaria.'

'Christ Almighty!'

'Which means they could move people around. Milk them of their money, convince them it was for their own safety. It fits. They're experts in the art of extortion.'

'In God's name, how could you have kept quiet about this?'

'Very easily, Henry. If you're being blackmailed, it's not so difficult. When your own future and that of other people is at risk, you'd be surprised how easy it is to keep quiet.'

The men in the construction camp knew. Or thought they did. He could tell it from the way they behaved. Nobody said as much out loud, but they knew. Well, it could hardly be otherwise, with the police questioning him, then taking him into town as if he was under arrest. And the grapevine of gossip, which was all they had here in the way of entertainment, apart from the wet canteen and the dances on Saturday nights, the grapevine said he'd got away with it. That the detectives couldn't prove anything.

It's what people were all thinking, Michael realised. That the cops had to let him go for lack of evidence. He could see it in people's faces; he was conscious of the way they suddenly stopped talking when he was near, or how their eyes slid away to evade his gaze. For a day or two he tried to behave as if unconcerned, then it began to anger him. When he spoke to people they replied in monosyllables, or avoided him altogether. The one time when he went to the canteen for a drink, the hum of conversation turned to silence, then resumed guardedly, without the customary exuberance. Unable to bear the atmosphere, he drained his schooner of beer and walked out, hearing the outbreak of speculation behind him.

He could not believe what was happening; all his life Michael had been gregarious and popular; his cheeky humour had endeared him to people; it was a new and unpleasant experience to feel like a pariah.

He tried to see Deirdre, but she was not behind the counter at the store. He walked out to the farm, but her father and brothers were lined outside the house there like a protective phalanx. The old man looked at him the way he would regard a stray dingo, and said she wasn't home. Gone on holiday.

'When will she be back?' he asked.

In answer, while the others stood silent and unwelcoming, one of the brothers fetched the shotgun. The father, with slow deliberate precision, loaded two cartridges. He raised it, aimed over Michael's head, and fired both barrels into the branch of a ghost gum. The body of a crow plummeted down, ripped to shreds.

Michael stood his ground.

'I have to talk to her.'

'Shove off,' one brother said.

Another took the shotgun, ejected the cartridges and reloaded.

'Only to tell her I didn't need an alibi. I didn't do it.'

'You're on private property,' her father said, 'so the law's on my side. You got less than thirty seconds to fuck off.'

Deirdre's letter came the following day. It had no stamp, and Michael found it beneath his door when he returned from work.

Dear Michael,

I'm sorry for the problems you've had, but I hope the police won't bother you any more. I feel it's best if we don't see each other again, as it upsets my family. Please try to understand,

Deirdre

Late that afternoon he waited outside the family's produce store, an old wooden barn of a building that dated back to the 1870s. He stood in the shadows across the street, ready to intercept her, but she emerged with her father and two of her brothers surrounding her, and they got into a waiting Chevrolet sedan. He thought she turned, as if searching for a sight of him, but before he could step forward to be seen they had driven away.

Neil dressed carefully. The radio predicted a hot January day, so he wore his lightweight suit, one that an Indian tailor had made for him during a frantic twenty-four hours in Colombo, where the ship had made a brief call. The Indian had taken his measurements and extolled the virtues of the cloth with the skill of a born trader, then handed him to a Sinhalese cutter for a fitting, after which the family seamstresses had worked furiously all night, sewing against the vessel's departure time. He carefully picked a tie to match, while wondering how many people would be on the opposite side of the desk, interrogating him.

'That's a nice suit. You look very smart,' Sarah said. 'Is this a special meeting?'

'You mean am I meeting someone special?'

'I wouldn't dream of asking such a personal question,' Sarah smiled. 'But are you?'

He shook his head, and kissed her goodbye.

'Sorry to disappoint you, Sarah, but it's just a meeting with some public servants. Probably a very dull day.'

I wish to God it could be, he thought, and ran for the bus.

In fact there were two men.

'Mr Adams and Mr Barlow,' Henry Falconer introduced them, and they all shook hands.

Mr A and Mr B, Neil thought. *I wonder if those are their real names?* He also wondered, because no-one said, whether they were from ASIO, the CIB or the Commonwealth Police Force.

They had with them what appeared to be a portable typewriter. Mr Adams lifted it onto the desk, and opened the case.

'It's one of the latest tape recorders,' he said. 'Not wire recorders any more. Spools of tape that replay with far better quality.'

'Clever,' Mr Barlow said with a wide smile. 'You never know what these inventors will come up with next.'

'So when everyone's ready,' Adams said, 'perhaps we'll ask a few questions and let Mr Latham talk, and when we've finished the first spool, we could all stop for a cup of tea.'

'Or coffee,' Barlow said.

It's so bloody cosy, Neil thought. *Mr A and Mr B must have a routine worked out.* Like Mr Gallagher and Mr Sheen, in the old vaudeville act. They'd take it in turns to prompt him, let him tell the tape everything he knew, enough to incriminate Stewart Mitchell and his unholy faction at the Milan Centre. The nest of vipers would be cleaned out, which was right; it was as it should be – they'd harmed enough people and deserved punishment. Justice would prevail. But in the process he would be mortally damaged.

These men would be extradited home. It would be arranged as soon as legally possible, Henry Falconer had said, because of the urgency and the importance of the case. So when catastrophe came, it would be sooner rather than later. They would be charged with some heinous crimes. In retaliation, Mitchell would accuse the accuser; he would have detailed data of the way Neil had manipulated a file, had forged sections of it to allow a brother and sister to enter the country illegally. Wherever they were – Helen and Michael Francis – whatever part of Australia, they had no idea of the jeopardy they faced; and as for Neil himself . . . he tried not to think about that. They could hardly let him off with a rap on the knuckles.

'Right,' Mr Adams said, 'the tape's on. All's well. This is an interview with Mr Neil Latham, a former officer of the International Refugee Organisation, and stationed last year at the Displaced Persons camp in Italy known as the Milan Centre.'

Helen sat at her desk, ignoring a pile of work sheets waiting to be typed as she worried about Michael. It was a week since the police had declared themselves satisfied, but the attitude in Adaminaby and the camp remained suspicious, at times downright hostile. He was finding it difficult to accept.

They had discussed it here in this office the previous night, after Angus Kerr had left for the wet canteen, and Sandor had not yet arrived to collect her. It was one of the few opportunities they'd had to talk alone, and she'd learned the extent of his distress.

'The bloody cops make it obvious I'm the main suspect. But when they turn me loose, do they say I'm innocent? Like hell they do.'

'Calm down,' she tried to tell him.

'I'll calm down when people stop treating me like a murderer. What do I have to do? Take an advertisement in the *Cooma Gazette*?'

'Ignore them,' she said, 'it'll soon be forgotten.'

But they both knew the rumours in the camp would persist, unless there was an arrest. As the CIB detective had now returned to Sydney, and it was being said that the local police considered it another awkward migrant problem, a solution or an arrest seemed unlikely.

'Even Deirdre thinks I did it. I wrote saying I was grateful she lied to help me, but there was no need, because the police believed me. The letter came back, ripped in half.'

'Deirdre wouldn't do that,' Helen said.

'Who knows? At first even you had doubts,' he accused her.

'I was scared. You can be impulsive, Michael. If only you'd said – at the start – about making that phone call.'

But he hadn't, because the constable in charge had mocked and made a joke of it, and he'd never dreamed the man would dutifully write it down. And since then, she'd learned he really had been told Vlasoff's throat had been cut, by one of the Norwegian demolition squad. They'd been warned by Sergeant Walsh not to say anything, but the man had indicated the cause of death to Michael by running a finger across his throat. And not knowing this, she had suspected her own brother.

She sighed and put a form into her typewriter. Now was not the time to think about this; better resume work or there'd be a rebuke. She heard Angus Kerr clear his throat, as though this was imminent. But instead, he rose from his desk and stopped behind her.

'I'm going down to the new housing site,' he said. 'I need those work sheets by lunch time.'

'Right,' she said, and waited for the sound of the door, but he did not leave.

'I realise we've been working hard since New Year, but I'll put you down for some overtime. You've earned it. Another five pounds in your pay packet this week, how do you feel about that?'

There was an odd tenseness about his voice. Before she could reply to this surprising conciliation, she felt him touch the back of her neck. She froze, but already his hand had slipped inside her loose summer dress, stroking the bare flesh between her shoulder-blades.

'Don't do that, Mr Kerr,' she said, gritting her teeth.

'You must know how I feel about you, after so long,' he said hoarsely. 'If I get cranky sometimes, it's because I want you so badly. I can't stand working close to you and looking at you all the time – imagining what it'd be like, the two of us in the cot together. You must think of that sometimes.'

'*No.*' She wanted to shout, but tried to stay calm. 'Never.'

Before she could move he gripped her shoulder, and thrust his other hand down the front of her dress, seeking her breasts. She tried to wriggle free, but he held her tightly, his body pressed against her, the heat of his breath on her neck. She jerked her elbow fiercely, and heard a grunt as she made contact with his stomach. Involuntarily he stepped back, giving her the chance to rise, grab an inkwell from her desk and throw the contents at him.

It was only half full, but thoroughly effective, as it splashed down his face and stained his shirt.

'You mad bloody bitch,' he said furiously. 'I was only having a feel. I told you once, how much easier it'd be if we were friends.'

'And I told you I'd make a complaint – and I will.'

'Balls . . . who'll believe you? And why the hell shouldn't I get a bit of what that bastard Jaroslov gets? I know he's rooting you. Plus a few others queued up, I wouldn't be surprised. You little tart, with your bare legs and your tits driving a man crazy.'

She thought he was going to attack her again; he seemed on the verge of losing all control. It would not be a sly attempt to paw her this time, it would be a vicious struggle with a man in a frenzy. For one terrible moment the supervisor's face became in distant memory the sweating face of the young *Wehrmacht* deserter.

Helen realised Angus Kerr was sweating, too. She felt on the desk behind her and found a pen. She clenched it like a dagger, letting him see the lethal nib, making him aware she would aim at his eyes.

It seemed a long time, but it was only moments before caution overcame craving, and some semblance of sanity returned. He shook his head as if at some foolishness – clearly on her part, not his.

'I want that typing finished when I come back.'

The door slammed behind him. She saw him stride to the jeep parked on the access road, rev the motor with unnecessary force and drive off. Heading for his quarters, to wash and change his shirt.

She sat down, feeling drained. She realised her threat to make a complaint was a bluff. He would know it; he had even warned her long ago that McFie, the regional manager, would be of no help. She'd heard it said McFie's female staff were picked only for their looks and acquiescence – and that in Ol' Herbie's office, typing and shorthand were the qualifications least required. It was a comment that never failed to raise laughter in this primarily male domain.

She contemplated calling the police, but there was no evidence. Her word against his, and no law seemed to exist to prevent this kind of situation. She knew office flirtations were rife – there was even an expression *office wife* in common usage – but this was an assault, both verbal and physical. If challenged, Kerr would dismiss it as a *pass* – one of the phrases left behind by the departed Americans. Provided the pass didn't go too far and was unwitnessed, it seemed to be accepted practice. She thought Kerr had gone a lot too far, but had no way of proving it.

At least I can speak the language, and it helps me look after myself, she thought. She knew of some horrific cases, where girls had been ill-treated. One seventeen-year-old who spoke no English – sent to work as a children's nurse – had been raped repeatedly by the husband while the wife stayed silent, and had even called the girl a liar when she had run away to seek help.

Helen wanted to believe it was a good concept, this proposal to bring hundreds of thousands of refugees from Europe, in addition to sponsored British migrants on the ten-pound fares and others who could pay the full passage. But there were always people who took advantage. She remembered the stories circulating about some of the migration officers in the huge Milan camp, and thought for a fleeting moment of Neil Latham. The only one who had ever helped them. For the first time in many months, she wondered what had become of him.

Then she turned back to more personal problems. She began to reflect again about Michael, and what to do.

The spindles on the machine revolved, and the magnetic tape flowed relentlessly, capturing his voice and the facts he was revealing. The device was mesmerising, even on this second day; for they had called a halt late in the afternoon and returned again this morning; it was strange to hear the spools of tape played back and recognise his voice reciting so many details that had startled them.

There was not much left to say. He had provided information on the black-market operations, the drug sales, cash deals for priority embarkation on ships – even the favours sought from, and often granted by, the more attractive wives – so that they and their families could be accepted.

'Good God,' said Mr Barlow, appalled, but this comment was made during a changeover to a new tape.

'Happened all the time,' Neil said, to his own surprise taking a perverse pleasure in shocking Mr A and Mr B. 'Many young girls also found an easy way to be classed as deserving refugees. All it took was a few weeks' bed-and-breakfast with the Brigadier. He liked them as young and lusty as possible, did the Brig.'

'The dirty old bastard,' Mr Adams said.

'And not always one at a time, either.'

'I think we'd better have that on the record, please.'

Mr Adams, the new tape fitted, switched on the power again.

'Tape number five,' he said into the microphone. 'Day two of Mr Neil Latham's statement on the Milan Centre.'

Neil duly obliged with the disclosure of Brigadier Aldridge's sexual proclivities. And for good measure added that Bluey McGill, ex-wharfie, Mafia associate and noted hard man of the group, was a homosexual with a disposition for youthful Italian boys, and on several occasions had bribed his way out of a gaol sentence for paedophilia.

Since he had committed himself and knew the consequences, he elected to leave nothing out. Finally there was only one thing left to tell them.

'That's virtually it,' Neil said. 'I hope enough can be substantiated by your investigators to put these people away for a long time. What I'm going to say now has no supporting evidence, but it's true. There's an illegal organisation called the ODESSA – which is clever because the name sounds Russian, but it derives from its German initials: *"Organisation der SS Angehorige"*. It operates an escape route for the former SS and fugitive war criminals.'

'We've heard various rumours of *Odessa*. If it really exists.'

'It exists. With vast funds, and a network of highly influential connections: politicians, industrialists, prominent people in safe havens abroad. They provide jobs, new identities, shelter.'

'That's a European problem. Where's the connection?' Mr Adams asked impatiently. 'This is hardly part of our investigation.'

'I believe there is a connection. I doubt if it can be proved, but

I think Stewart Mitchell and his clique put SS officers through the *Odessa* system. They'd be paid huge amounts, and with their contacts would have been perfectly placed to be useful to the organisation. It occurred to me when I saw Vlasoff's papers, particularly the identity card. I'm sure he was processed this way.'

They were all thoughtful for a moment, contemplating this and its possible repercussions, as he continued.

'It means Mitchell has powerful friends. Don't underestimate him, or this group's influence. Many of its strongest sympathisers are pro-German cardinals inside the Vatican. It's hardly a secret in Rome that they've provided not only money, but sanctuary.'

He heard one of the men in the room draw a sharp breath, though whether it was Mr A or Mr B he could not tell. But when the recorder was switched off, it was Henry Falconer who spoke tersely.

'I hope we can eliminate those last comments,' he said. 'They seemed inappropriate and hardly relevant.'

Later, when the men had gone and Neil and Falconer were alone, the discord between them was tangible.

'I'm an unquestioning Catholic, but that's beside the point. I dislike unproven gossip. As far as the Vatican is concerned, there's been far too much of it. The remark was unnecessary.'

'It was made to illustrate the leverage these men have.'

'I found it offensive.'

'Then I'm sorry.'

Neil said nothing more. His work in refugee camps had taught him that some topics were better left alone. And even before that, long ago in his unit, killing their way across Germany, they had learned that the atrocities of war were not always committed by the other side.

In different circumstances he might have argued with Falconer that the Vatican was a city state, and like any other, had many shades of political opinion and dynastic opposites. It had a body of sentiment that saw the true enemy as Russia and communism, and nothing the Germans had done would alter their belief. But for all those receptive to Hitler's regime, there were others equally opposed, some who had risked their lives to rescue the casualties.

An Irish priest, Monsignor O'Flaherty, had saved thousands from death; Jews, Allied escapees, partisans and dissident Italians. A towering hero figure in Rome and known as 'The Scarlet Pimpernel of the Vatican', he was something of a vexed problem in the austere corridors, where the gospel of rigid conformism frowned on heroes.

But an argument was the last thing Neil needed now. He was in Falconer's hands, dependent on him for help when the accusations came, as he knew they would. Attack would be the Milan group's only defence – and they would attack his credibility with all the malice of which they were capable. *Which was considerable*, he thought, and suddenly realised a question had been asked, and Falconer was clearly awaiting an answer.

'I beg your pardon, Henry,' he said, 'can you repeat that? I was reflecting on my future. Without much optimism.'

'We'll do the best we can, of course. Perhaps you should make a written statement, and give us the names of those two people whose papers you . . . er . . . doctored?'

'I'll give you a statement, but not their names,' Neil said.

'That may not be sufficient.'

'It's the best I can do, Henry. Try to understand that.'

'I'll try,' Falconer shrugged, 'although I can't pretend to be thrilled about the situation.'

'Nor can I,' Neil said. 'What were you asking me?'

'About Vlasoff. Would the *Odessa* really be bothered with someone of his status? He was just a Polish SS guard.'

'They'd bother with anyone who had sufficient commitment to the cause. Their prime purpose, after all, is to keep the flame burning, to place the *Kameraden* in as many countries as possible. Some in important positions, others in menial jobs – all to bide their time. To wait for *Der Tag*. The status has never mattered. Only the outcome.'

'It sounds insane.'

'It is – to you and me. But so was Belsen.'

'Yes,' Falconer said, with a thoughtful glance that seemed to remind him Neil had been there.

'Perhaps Vlasoff had more status than we realise. I can't tell, because I've only been shown his immigration papers. I haven't seen the police report.'

'No. I'm well aware you haven't.'

Falconer sat at his desk. He was frowning, pensive. Neil wondered what was coming. He fully expected he'd be suspended. If Mr A and Mr B had what they needed, then their source was no longer of value. He could be given his cards, as they used to say back home. Dispensed with. His passport would be sequestered, then later would come the official charges.

'Look,' Falconer said, 'I'm obliged to impose restrictions on what you're allowed to see, until all this is sorted out. But it seems bloody stupid, because after all you're the one best equipped to evaluate this material.' He unlocked his desk and produced the slim police file sent from Cooma. 'Don't take it out of here. We'll talk about it tomorrow. Let me know what you think.'

'Thanks, Henry,' Neil said.

The other gave an abrupt nod, and collected his briefcase. He paused at the door.

'I wonder if there are more like Vlasoff in the country?'

'Highly likely – but I doubt if we'll ever know.'

'Unless . . .' Falconer began to reply, then clearly decided against continuing.

'Unless someone from Milan blows the whistle? Is that what you were going to say, Henry? Unless someone does a deal, names names, and is allowed to walk away?'

'I'm sure we wouldn't condone that,' Henry Falconer said.

I'm bloody certain you would, Neil thought.

He waited until he was alone in the office, then opened the file. He saw a name that seemed surprisingly familiar. Michael Francis? He turned the pages, and came to another name. STATEMENT TO DETECTIVE-SERGEANT WALSH AND DETECTIVE CONSTABLE RENSHAW BY HELEN FRANCIS.

And suddenly, although it was a year and a half ago, he could see her as if it were yesterday. A pretty but skinny girl in a shabby dress, with her stubborn and difficult brother.

Helen Francis.

He sat and absorbed himself in the file.

Chapter 12

Helen hesitated outside. She saw a farmer carry out a sack of fertiliser, and one of the men from the produce store followed him, with heavy hessian bags of stock feed balanced expertly on each shoulder. By the look of him, and judging by his age, this would be one of her brothers. As far as she was aware, none of the family knew her by sight, but unsure if what she planned was possible, she loitered by the saddlery shop next door, admiring a display of polished harness in the window. There were old photographs of the days when horsepower meant wagons being hauled to inaccessible places in the high country. An Aboriginal stockman came out with a new surcingle, and fitted it to the saddle of his horse tethered along the street. He nodded to Helen, and had an easy smile.

'Looks like she's gonna be another hot one,' he said, with a glance at the cloudless sky.

'We need rain.' Helen knew the standard local response.

'Sure do,' the stockman said, and mounted, touched his finger to his hat in farewell, and rode off with a casual grace.

She braced herself and entered Miller's Agricultural Supplies. A large cavernous place, it was filled from floor to its high iron roof with sacks of grain and produce, as well as fencing tools, pumps, and farm machinery. Deirdre was at the till. She saw Helen immediately, and barely managing to suppress her surprise glanced towards a desk, where a man in his fifties sat checking a pile of invoices. He had on a pair of steel-rimmed glasses that looked too small for his face, as if they were borrowed for his scrutiny of the day's accounts. It was a lean, hard face, Helen decided, the sort of man who would be amused by scaring off an unwanted boyfriend with a shotgun, and might equally make her feel unwelcome. She had come here on an impulse, with no pretext worked out to explain her visit.

'What do you want?' Deirdre was uncharacteristically abrupt and rather nervous, as Helen joined her by the till. No-one else had noticed her entry.

'It's a free country, Deirdre,' Helen replied quietly.

'Not round here, it isn't.'

Mr Miller took off the spectacles, and looked across the store in her direction.

'Help you, Miss?'

Before she could answer, the telephone beside him rang. He lifted the receiver, spoke to the exchange, and a call was put through. Helen could see another brother on a gantry above, pausing in his task of stacking bags of feed, ready to descend and offer assistance.

'Did you get his letter?' she asked hurriedly.

'What letter?'

'He wrote. It was torn up and sent back.'

'Never.'

'It was. Please, at least talk to him.'

'Impossible,' Deirdre muttered. 'How?'

'Five o'clock, after his shift, he'll be waiting behind the storage shed.'

'I can't.'

'Try.'

Deirdre's brother was on his way down the stairs. Her father was hanging up the telephone.

'Toothache . . . dentist,' she muttered, hoping they could not hear. 'Thanks very much,' she said loudly, and gingerly held her jaw as she began to leave, while wondering if it was overdoing things.

'I'd ring up first and make an appointment. He's a very busy dentist,' Deirdre called after her. 'Say I sent you.'

Good girl, Helen thought, and felt certain she would do her best to be there. She just had time to hear the brother say that if the sheila had a toothache, they should've sold her one of those veterinary poultices they'd been trying to shift for ages.

His braying laughter followed her down the street.

Neil shut the file. It was extraordinary, almost like hearing her voice again in Milan and listening to her story, while her brother railed against the hand fate had dealt them. Growing up in war and terror, his youth spent in a battle to stay alive, it was little wonder he had openly disbelieved that Neil would help them.

It was an irony that here on the police report were the very names he had refused to disclose, although perhaps not one that Henry Falconer would appreciate.

Michael Francis had been the prime suspect for several days, questioned extensively and finally cleared. Helen, as he had read the transcript, was as articulate as he remembered her.

'The camp was terrible. It was called Treblinka . . . Vlasoff was an executioner, he enjoyed killing people . . .'

The echo of words stored from the incoherent babbling of poor dead Katryna Dyboski, whom for some reason they called the Grand Duchess. Mrs Dyboski had not come through Milan in his time; the only names he knew in this dossier were those of Helen and Michael.

'An executioner who enjoyed killing people.'

The words seemed to haunt him. This Polish recruit, the former schoolboy delinquent turned authorised assassin, had been able to make his way across Europe to Milan, where Mitchell and the others had found it lucrative enough to introduce him to the escape section of the *Odessa*. Neil was convinced of that now. The way he had entered the country so easily seemed to confirm it. But while the secret organisation might claim to be motivated by ideals, Stewart Mitchell had none. He was a total mercenary. So Vlasoff must have come with money; he would not otherwise have been spared a second glance.

'An executioner who enjoyed killing people.'

A wealthy one, it seemed. Well, there were innumerable ways for a concentration camp guard to make money, he knew that, but large amounts could only accrue to those who held positions of authority. Not the commonplace killers, the foot soldiers of Himmler's dreaded *Einsatzgruppen*, the special action groups, who did as they were told. Everyone in that gothic world did as they were told. Everything was strictly regulated. After the mass annihilations, the clothing of the dead had to be collected, the rings and jewellery to be found on or inside the bodies, the teeth to be extracted, all of it strictly supervised. Stealing was *verboten*. This was a recycling process for the coffers of the Reich war machine. So if Vlasoff had the kind of money that bought him security and a new life, where did it come from? What was special or the least bit important about Josef Vlasoff?

And then Neil remembered something he had been told long ago, about the Treblinka camp. Here, together with Auschwitz, the majority of Poland's three million Jews had been slaughtered. But that was common knowledge. What he recalled was a different story, told to him by a *Waffen SS* officer who was vainly seeking clemency – about three truckloads of infants, mere toddlers really, brought from another town in another country – and how a special squad had been selected to eliminate them.

These were not Jewish children. And for this reason, the *Einsatzgruppen* had been unusually reluctant to murder them. But in the end a deal had been agreed: any who refused were sent to the Russian Front; those who volunteered for the task were handsomely rewarded.

Neil sat for a long time thinking of what he had once been told, the dreadful story of the extermination of these children. He had a feeling this was the answer, and wondered if he should discuss it with Henry Falconer. If the information did not tell the police who killed Vlasoff, it might tell them why. Knowing the motive might reveal who was responsible.

Provided, he thought, *that anyone should be punished for the death of Josef Vlasoff.*

Around three that afternoon, Deirdre Miller clapped a hand to her mouth, looked beseechingly towards her father, then ran hurriedly out the back entrance of the produce store, and into the corrugated iron lavatory in the yard. When she emerged some time later, her eyes were streaming and she had to sit down, because she was dizzy.

'Christ, you're not pregnant, I hope,' her father said. 'I'll shoot that bloody reffo's dick off, if you are.'

It was a remark that confirmed to Deirdre she had made the right decision.

'I'm not pregnant,' she said, 'it must be something I ate.'

She made another rush to the dunny, and they all tried not to listen to the sound of her retching. A farmer who'd arrived with an order for grain looked decidedly queasy and said he'd come back later.

'For gawd's sake, get her home,' her father said when Deirdre emerged again. 'She can frighten the chooks, instead of scaring off the customers.'

'I can't help being sick,' Deirdre lamented, secretly thrilled with her performance. It was amazing the effect you could achieve with a few fingers down the throat. She even swayed as if she might collapse, and her brother helped support her to the delivery truck.

'Strewth, I hope to hell yer don't spew in the vehicle,' he said, as they drove off.

'I'll try not to,' Deirdre whispered, stifling a desire to giggle.

Ten minutes later he drove down the dirt track and pulled up outside their solitary farmhouse.

'Tell Mum to git yer some broth. Might settle yer gut.'

Deirdre nodded her head as if a reply was too much for her, not bothering to remind him their mother was at the pictures with her friend, Mrs Magnussen, and would not be back until after the main feature. She waved listlessly as he drove away, noticed he didn't bother to respond – which was typical – and waited until the truck reached the road and turned in the direction of town.

She ran inside the house, found a suitcase and began to pack.

All afternoon the clouds had been gathering, and by five-thirty there was driving rain. Soaked and chilled by it, Michael was angry and discouraged. Helen had been so certain Deirdre would be here.

'Be there at five o'clock,' she'd murmured, when he met her outside the office, with that foxy chiseller, Kerr, watching from the doorway and trying to overhear what was being said.

Now it was half past five, torrential bloody rain, and not a sign of her. So, Helen for once had been wrong. Helen had also been in an odd mood, very tense while Kerr stood looking at them, and he could have sworn that she was trembling.

'I think lunch hour is over,' the supervisor had said.

She had just acted as if he had not spoken, as if he wasn't even there, and Kerr had glared, but without saying another word had gone back inside the office.

It was very strange.

He was about to ask what was going on – was the slimy bastard up to his dirty tricks making trouble for her – but she had seemed to anticipate this, had given a quick smile, tapped his arm and said to be on his way, and that as soon as his shift was finished to get himself tidied up and go to meet Deirdre.

So here he was, tidied up like a drowned rat, the rain stinging his eyes, his shoes and socks water-logged, with no decent shelter and knowing for certain she was not coming. He tensed as he heard voices, then the clang of a heavy iron door as they shut and locked the rear entrance to the store.

'Make sure the back gate's locked.' Her father's grating voice was startlingly close, and Michael ducked below the shelter of metal fencing that enclosed the yard.

He heard a grumble from one of her brothers, then the sound of a bolt shot home, and the click of a padlock. They were so close, only feet apart, all the man had to do was look over the fence to see him. And if he did, Michael intended to hit him as hard as possible. Pay back a few of those kicks in the ribs, the day he was an invited guest in their house. But the footsteps moved away.

'Jest as bloody well,' said her father. 'What silly bugger left that open? Probably bloody Deirdre. C'mon, don't frig around in this rain. Let's get home 'fore we sink up to the axle in the fucking mud.'

He stayed there until he heard the truck doors slam, and the sound of the engine driving away. Had Deirdre left the gate unlocked? Whatever had happened, there was no point in waiting here any longer. Head down in the rain, he walked back to camp. If he could get there before Helen left the office, he'd like a chance to tell her what he thought of her bright idea. He also wanted to quiz her about Kerr. Something was wrong there.

But when he reached the camp, it was almost dark. There were no lights showing in the administration office. He went through the rows of huts until he reached the one in which his room was located. He unlocked and pushed open the door.

'About time,' Deirdre said. She was lying in his bed, her red hair enlivening the pillow. 'I packed some clothes, but I didn't think I'd need a nightie.'

She slid back the sheet to show that she was naked.

'Get dried and hop in,' she said. 'You need a warm-up. And I'm raring to give it to you.'

'You might've sent a messenger.' He was snuggled against her glowing body later. 'I think I'll end up getting 'flu.'

'You can't do that, mate,' Deirdre said. 'No time to get crook. You and me have to work out what the hell we're gonna do.'

'Reckon they'll know by now?'

'They'll know, all right. The minute they got home and found I wasn't there, they'd have twigged. My mob might be a bunch of bastards, but they're not stupid.'

'Could've fooled me,' Michael said.

'Well, what *are* we going to do?'

'Let's think about it later.' He kissed her lovingly, and felt her response as her body thrust to meet him.

'Jesus Christ, Deed,' he said, 'you're bloody fantastic.'

'Now say something nice to me,' she said, slowly rubbing herself against his body, taunting him.

'I don't think I could live without you.'

'That's nice. But do you think we should keep on doing this, or should we talk first?'

'Let's keep on doing it – all night.'

Deirdre laughed. 'Get you, mate! All night, eh? Don't forget we have to work out what happens tomorrow.'

'Bugger tomorrow,' Michael whispered, starting to excite her until they both completely lost control, and came together in mutual delight, happily exhausted. Later on they dozed, then woke and made love again.

Around midnight, a truck drove towards the camp. Angus Kerr was woken abruptly and violently when his door was kicked open. He stared at a flashlight shining in his eyes and felt a shotgun pressed hard against his face. Unable to see who had threatened him, Kerr was only too willing and eager to give the information required.

'Hut twenty-four, door number six,' he said, and saw the four shadowed figures leave. Not daring to switch on his light, he sat in the dark and contemplated what the serious injury or possible demise of Michael Francis might mean for any future chance with his sister.

It was totally silent. Lights were out in all the huts; even the wet canteen was in darkness. They took their time, wanting to be quite sure, not knowing the layout of the camp. Pausing by the steps outside the hut, they used the flashlight to check it was the right number, then entered without a sound. The brothers stopped at room six as their father motioned them to be ready, then put his head against the door and listened.

They had been drinking since seven in the evening, debating what to do. The anger of finding that Deirdre had so easily outsmarted them was no longer the real issue; she had clearly been influenced by the Hungarian refugee, and, as the time passed and the alcohol inflamed their judgement, a sense of rage possessed them. The stupid bloody redhead – their immoral and perverse sister – had been bamboozled by this reprobate, this foreign mongrel.

And so they had come with staves, hardwood clubs snatched from the farm shed, and her father with the loaded shotgun. Their plan, if it could be called such, was to grab their silly bitch of a sister, throw her in the back of the truck with one to guard her, while the rest battered the hell out of the reffo. The shotgun would keep any of his friends at bay. By the morning they fully expected Deirdre would have recovered her senses, and life in the family could return to normal.

Their father nodded. One brother carefully turned the handle of the door. It was unlocked. He gleefully signalled the others, and pushed it wide open. They switched on the torch, and poured into the tiny room. The sharp beam of light traversed the rumpled but empty bed, then revealed Michael – nude except for a pair of underpants – completely unarmed, except for a fire extinguisher.

The device was comparatively new, and he saw their puzzled expressions. Before they had time to realise his intention, he squirted a stream of foam into their faces and they came to a blinding halt, all at once rendered sightless, disoriented, and helpless, stumbling over each other and shouting furiously. While they clawed at their stinging eyes, Michael opened the window and pushed the fire alarm button. It set off a siren mounted on one of the rooftops, and within moments the sound of voices began to be heard outside, converging on the hut.

He watched them blunder out. What a bunch of hopeless hillbillies, was his only thought as he reached down beneath the bed and clasped a hand that held his. Deirdre, looking like a calendar picture of Rita Hayworth, in a pair of panties and nothing else, her dishevelled red hair and firm breasts enough to render him helplessly carnal, slid from below the steel frame.

'Golly,' she said, 'how did you guess the bastards were here?'

'They were sure to come. But not until as late as possible, to catch us asleep.'

He didn't like to tell her it was also intuitive, a survival instinct developed from eluding the rabid animals who had hunted them in the ghetto. Instead, with her family gone and the alarm over, he took her back to bed and proceeded to excite her until they were both utterly expended.

In the morning they resolutely kept their hands away from each other, while they tried to work out what was to be done. They realised it would have been her father, of course, who had torn up the letter from Michael and sent it back. But her family would all have known – even her mum – and therefore she owed them nothing any longer. Her promise not to see Michael – in her vain attempt to give him an alibi – was one she had intended to honour. Not that she wanted to, but as they had all agreed to support her story she felt she really had no other choice.

But not now. To learn through those brief and hurried words from Helen in the produce store that there was a letter she had never received, was a revelation that made her realise her whole family had stayed silent and deceived her. It was that which had provoked such anger and brought about her impulsive decision.

'I don't want to see them again,' Deirdre said. 'If you and I aren't going to be able to work something out, then I'll find a job and a room in Cooma, and to hell with them.'

'Do you mind if I say something?' Michael asked.

'Say anything you like,' she said.

sdf。

'Whatever happens, you're staying with me. At least I hope you are.'

'I hope so, too,' she replied. 'Because I'm mad about you.'

'Likewise,' Michael said, 'but we have to stop making love for a while, and make plans instead. Well, for an hour or two.'

'For an hour or two,' she agreed, and kissed him with such intensity that it almost changed their resolve.

'Behave your bloody self,' Michael said.

'Why?'

'Because every time you do that, I get tremendously randy. And we need to be calm – which means not getting the slightest bit randy – at least not until we've sorted out a few things. Please?'

'Right,' she said, and moved a few inches away from him.

Henry Falconer stood by his office window, gazing down at his favourite view of the park and wondering what he could do about saving Neil from prison. *Not a great deal*, he thought regretfully, if they decide to progress this case. He had been in various meetings all morning, and the prospects were not looking good.

It would be a great pity.

The information on those spools of tape was already being transcribed, and would be used by Adams and Barlow, but not precisely in the way Neil expected. That was what the morning's meetings had revealed. The general consensus was that he had given them a series of facts, undoubtedly true, but was it evidence strong enough to stand the test of cross-examination in a court of law?

Not without corroboration, was the response, and that would

involve the subpoena of other witnesses. Some of these would be hostile, some foreign who would have to be brought to Australia, a time-consuming and expensive process. There was the added problem of proof; verifying events which had taken place in a distant country was difficult, and would certainly mean long and costly legal wrangles over jurisdiction.

Henry Falconer had returned to his office, unsure of the final decision they would make, but deeply worried. He was almost certain there would be no prosecutions. Instead, there would be a great deal of horse-trading; names would be revealed and exchanged for clemency. Specifically names identifying anyone with a criminal record, who had unlawfully got into the country. And particularly the names of anyone suspected of war crimes. Adams had confided they hardly expected to net top Nazis – all of whom would be safe in Argentina or Brazil by now – but there had been a swarm of collaborators in the Baltic States. Also in Poland, and right-wing elements in Greece and Yugoslavia. If they could identify and deport them, clean up the Milan mess, and kick out Mitchell and his crew without severance pay or entitlements, then Neil's testimony would have been put to good use. No matter what happened to Neil himself as a result of his disclosures.

It was doubtless pragmatic and would achieve some results, but it was blatantly unfair. Stewart Mitchell, McGill, and the others had much to trade, and were wealthy and smart enough to hire top silks to barter for them. Neil had been given no such option, nor sought it. Falconer himself felt some guilt about this. He should have been warned, and given the opportunity of legal representation.

If it did happen, he would miss Neil. Their under-funded and tiny organisation did more than its share of important work, resolving migrant disputes, helping re-locate people or reunite them with their families. In the vast immigration department, theirs was a section which received little recognition, but to Henry Falconer, helping people adjust and settle in a new land was a vital function, and he had no-one in the unit more skilled at it than Neil Latham.

His ability with languages was a factor, but Falconer knew it was more than this. The close affinity with Sarah Weismann, as well as being an immigrant himself, these things were a part of it, but there was something else. An extra, and rather rare element. He appeared to be able to make progress with even the unhappiest, most awkward immigrants. He seemed to understand what few people realised – that while Australians considered them foreigners, to the newcomers every single thing about this place was foreign.

Different architecture, different kind of people in different clothes; the weather and the seasons of the year diametrically opposite to what they had known. Neil knew all the tiny and what might appear to some as insignificant details – that on arrival, the flies were an unexpected torment, the humid heat enervating, and probably most important of all, the lack of interest in them by their new compatriots that left them bewildered and disappointed.

Neil also realised, because they had often spoken of it as one of their main problems to solve, that the children were badly treated and laughed at in school. They brought strange, strong-smelling food for their lunches, and wore peculiar thick boots and unfamiliar clothes. Unable to freely converse in English, they were considered stupid. Most were teased, and some could hardly bear it. There were many cases of those afraid to go into the playground, or the classroom.

'We must solve this, no matter what it costs to speed up their English lessons,' Neil had said in one of these discussions. 'That's the key to the whole thing. You can never make friends if you can't talk to each other. And when the children assimilate, the parents will follow.'

Yes, he would miss Neil. It was a shame, what was going to almost certainly happen to him. All because of his misplaced sympathy for two young migrants. A pity he wouldn't reveal the names, but he'd been adamant about that.

'What would it achieve, Henry? I don't regret what I did for them. It was just a shame that bastard Mitchell managed to find out.'

Neil had stayed late at the office the previous afternoon, puzzling over the police file on the death of Josef Vlasoff. Last night he had slept restlessly, waking several times, convinced he at last knew why the former concentration camp guard had been killed. His problem was, whether or not to confide in Henry Falconer? To do so might bring the investigation uncomfortably close to Helen Francis and her brother.

He did not want to endanger them. It would merely get them deported, and would not help him. Even more importantly, the matter that most disturbed him was should anyone – whoever it was – be charged with the killing of this mass murderer?

'Did you read the police report? The Vlasoff case?'

Neil realised Falconer was at the door to his office.

'Yes, I put it back in your desk.'

'Any particular thoughts on who it might have been? Or why?'

'Not really,' Neil said.

The first intimation Helen had that something might be wrong, was when Kerr pulled up in the utility truck outside the office. She could hear his walkie-talkie, the familiar robotic sound of a voice at the other end reporting something that sounded urgent.

He came into the office in a temper.

'Where the hell is your bloody brother?' he asked.

The sharp question and abrasive tone of his voice almost brought an angry response, but she hesitated. Aware that there were rumours Deirdre had been seen arriving at the camp with a suitcase, she had not yet been able to confirm this. There was another story circulating, that Mr Miller and his sons had arrived during the night, and there'd been some sort of an incident. It had to do with a fire alarm, which seemed to be more than a rumour, for Helen herself had woken and heard the siren around 1 a.m. It had only lasted a short time, and was apparently a false alarm, but Sandor said there was talk that hut twenty-four had been the scene of a row, and Michael was supposed to have been involved. So she was wary about her reply.

'I'm sorry, but I don't know what you're talking about.'

'Your flaming brother. Or are you hard of hearing? I've just had a complaint from the foreman on the South Street job, that he hasn't turned up for work.'

'Perhaps he's sick,' Helen said, trying to remain composed and appear unconcerned.

'Like hell he's sick. I'll tell you where the urger is – he's off somewhere shagging that redheaded bint,' Kerr said, and it was then that Helen knew she was not going to put up with any more of this crude conduct.

'What is it about you, Mr Kerr? Where were you when they gave out charm rations?'

'What? You tryin' to be funny?'

'Funny? Certainly not. I'm trying to find out why you behave so abominably.'

'Abominable, am I?' Kerr's face was starting to look flushed and agitated. 'I'm not gonna take abuse like that from you. So you shuddup, before you land yourself in trouble. And as far as I'm concerned, your brother is docked a day's pay.'

'That's completely unfair.'

'And any more back-chat and it'll be the same for you.'

'You can't do that, Mr Kerr . . .'

'I can do whatever I bloody like,' he shouted in her face, the stale smell of last night's beer making her recoil. 'You don't give the orders around here, you bitch. I'm not taking crap like that, not from a bloody Hungarian Jew, acting like you're the Virgin Mary here in the office, but we all know you let that Czech root you silly every night.'

'Stop talking like that,' she said.

'Just shuddup. I'll talk to you any way I flaming well like. Miss high-and-bloody-mighty. You're just a filthy little cow.'

She could hardly believe she was hearing it. He was shouting at her. He seemed to have lost all reason.

'I'm going to write to head office,' Helen said, trying to retain some dignity, but resolved not to let his be the last word. 'I've had all I can stand of you.'

She saw his face suffuse, as if the veins on his forehead were about to explode. He took two quick paces forward, his fist swung, and she felt him begin hitting her. Then came a blow that seemed like an explosion in her mind. She dimly heard the crash of the typing chair as she fell against it. It was the last sound she heard before she lost consciousness.

Chapter 13

'How much do you wish to withdraw?' The teller was trying hard to be courteous – so his expression said – but the client was clearly one of these difficult customers.

'I already told you, the whole lot – in cash,' Michael said.

'But why – sir?'

The addition of 'sir' came after a brief hesitation, and with some obvious difficulty.

'Look, just tell me the balance, I'll write out a withdrawal slip for it, then you can close the account.'

'I'll need management authorisation.'

'Hang on,' Michael demanded, 'whose money is this?'

The teller shook his head, as if he would like to suggest it was really the bank's money, but this migrant would never understand such financial niceties. He sighed and looked at the statuesque redhead, who seemed intent on leaning so closely against the troublemaker, with her arm tucked firmly in his. He thought she was a dead ringer for that popular movie star, Rita Hayworth, who had been in the film at the Roxy Theatre on Saturday night. And then he realised he'd seen this girl around the town, and had even met her at a dance once. He'd actually done a twirl around the floor with her; he could hardly forget that blazing red hair.

'Aren't you Deirdre?' He thought it was a bit of luck, knowing her. It'd make the client less belligerent. 'Deirdre Miller?'

'Never mind who I am,' she told him. 'Just cough up and pay him what the bloody place owes him. We'll be out of here, as soon as you put your brain in gear and get a move on.'

She didn't sound a bit like Rita Hayworth, he thought, and looked again at the balance on the ledger card.

'Three hundred and seventy-nine pounds, six shillings and eight pence,' he said. 'Less the bank charges.'

'Plus interest,' Michael said.

'That's right' she said. 'Two and a half per cent, compound interest.' She looked at the teller, remembering she had once danced with him, and he'd done his best to persuade her to go outside. He had slicked-down hair that was shiny with Brylcreem, and slightly hooded eyes which made him look like a lizard. 'We've done our sums, and we reckon the bank owes Mr Francis just on four hundred quid. Three hundred and ninety-eight pounds, seventeen shillings and fourpence. So start to get it organised, and don't mess us about any longer.'

They left there ten minutes later feeling rich, with notes bulging in her handbag and the rest filling Michael's wallet, laughing all the way to the railway station as she related the teller's vain attempt to get her outside for a breath of fresh air behind the dance hall. There was an hour to wait for the Sydney express, and Michael went to use the public telephone to speak to Helen. It was not going to be easy, to break the news he and Deirdre were clearing out until her family cooled down a bit. But they had little choice; her father and brothers would hunt him until they repaid last night, and this time they'd pick a time and a place where there'd be no-one to stop them going as far as they wished. Which might be to finish the job of kicking him, then drop his body down one of the old abandoned mine shafts.

'What are you going to say to her?'

'The truth, I suppose. I always tell her the truth.'

'Listen, I like Helen – but I'm not sure I'd tell her *everything*. I mean – not completely everything – not in this case.'

He laughed.

He knew she meant the three hundred pounds in cash she had taken from the Miller house, prising up the floorboards below the kitchen table, where her father kept some of the takings he didn't declare to the income tax department. Deirdre had left him a brief note to say she thought this was a fair amount, since there was at least another two thousand hidden in various places around the house, but she wouldn't dob him in to the government. It brought the total they had between them to almost seven hundred pounds, which was why they felt rich, and it was also why they had a definite feeling they must get out of the district by the next available train.

Michael knew he would have to tell Helen at least some of the truth, including the likelihood they might not be coming back here. All he could do was promise that whatever happened, he would keep in touch with her.

Helen, he was already well aware, was going to be very upset.

When the phone rang, he expected her to answer it, but it was a male voice. For one dismayed moment he thought it was Kerr.

'Lawrenson construction office.'

'Helen there?' he asked.

'No, she's not. Who's that?' the voice requested. It was not Angus Kerr, but it was an Australian voice.

'Hang on,' Michael said, all his instincts alerted to something being wrong. 'Who are you? Where's Kerr? Why isn't Helen there?'

'Because she's in hospital.'

'How? What's happened? Who are you, for Christ's sake?'

'Jimmy Ferguson,' the voice said, and Michael recognised the name. Jimmy was a local economics student, who sometimes came to help with the accounts on payday.

'Jimmy, it's Michael Francis. Helen's brother. What hospital? What's going on?'

'They took her over to Jindabyne. The bush nurse's place.'

'But what happened?'

'I dunno. She had a fall, I think. She was unconscious.'

'Jesus Christ,' Michael whispered, and felt his heart contract. 'Where's Kerr?'

'He went in the truck. They made up a stretcher in the back. Mr Kerr called me in to look after the place, while he went to Jinda. I think he wanted to see Herb McFie.'

'But why?'

'Dunno, mate.'

'If it was that serious – why didn't they go to Cooma?'

'Couldn't say, Mike.'

'But how could she have had a fall? What was she doing?'

'Haven't a clue, mate.'

'In other words, you know bugger-all.'

'That'd be about right, Michael. Where the hell are you?'

'Never mind that. How long ago did they leave?'

'About half an hour.'

'I better get there.'

'But hang on a minute, mate, where the hell are you? People have been trying to find you.'

'What people?'

'Well, the foreman on your shift, for one. And Kerr was real cranky. Then some bloke – I think it was Mr Miller who owns the produce store – rang up asking where you were.'

'Listen, you agreed you know bugger-all, so let's leave it that way,' Michael said, and hung up.

Deirdre joined him, aware from his response inside the phone box, that something was obviously wrong. He quickly outlined what little he had learned, and explained they would have to change their plans. There was no way they could get the afternoon train.

'I can't go until I've found out what's wrong, and how she is,' he said. 'I'll get a hitch out to Jindabyne. We'll leave my suitcase here in the cloakroom, and take yours with us, so you can book into a hotel or a boarding house. Somewhere to stay till I get back.'

'I can sit and wait at the station,' she said.

'Like hell. It's not your fault Helen had an accident. So why should you sit on a hard railway bench for the next few hours?'

She gave him a smile that lit her face

'You're a nice bloke, did you know that?'

'Am I?'

'Considerate, that's what you are, Miki.'

'Not too bad, in other words, for a flaming migrant.'

'Not too bad at all,' Deirdre agreed.

'So what's it to be? The Royal Hotel? We can afford it.'

'Silly bugger. Pubs are the first place my mob would check. A boarding house is best.'

They found one in Egan Street, around the corner. A modest brick house with a sign, VACANCIES, and a plump, friendly landlady, who glanced at the lack of a ring on Deirdre's finger and smiled at the explanation that her husband would be back later, but if they missed the midnight train they might have to stay until the morning.

'No worries, love,' the landlady said. 'I'll put you in number three. Nice double bed. One pound, two and six, breakfast included.'

Deirdre insisted on paying her in advance, and walked to the corner with him.

'I bet she makes a beaut breakfast. Give Helen my love: I hope to God it's not anything serious.'

'Me, too. Deed, do me a favour and stay off the streets. That red hair, people seem to remember you.'

'Just as long as you don't forget me. Take care,' Deirdre said, and he left with the abiding memory of her standing watching him, and his sense of pride that she was his girl.

It was a strange feeling, Michael, thought, *being in love with someone*. There'd been many girls in his life – as well as a few older women – back in the camps in Europe, some of them as desperate for satisfaction and companionship as he was. For that's all it had been. A relationship, a bit of hurried romance, the tangle of limbs, the tumult of sex and afterwards, some warmth and comfort to alleviate the bleakness of their lives. But it was never loving someone, the way he did now.

Apart from the ever-present intensity of their desire, there were new emotions: affection, shared laughter, and caring for someone else's well-being more than his own. In the beginning she had been just a raunchy and voluptuous redhead, with an amazing capacity to arouse him; but her loyalty had taken him by surprise, as had the pain of facing the thought he might never see her again. Now, he realised, he couldn't imagine the idea of a future without Deirdre.

The hospital in Jindabyne was a small wooden house with a galvanised roof, a home allotted to the bush nurse, Sister Reynolds, who was on call to handle accidents and medical emergencies, as well as administer to families and at times act as midwife. With the sudden growth of the work force from a few hundred to many thousands, and Cooma Hospital a long and arduous trip from the camps at Guthega and Island Bend on winter roads, she had realised more was needed, and set about converting all the spare rooms in her house into wards. Hence the Bush Nurse Centre became known locally as the hospital, and Sister Reynolds, who could at times be brusque, but was always caring and efficient, became something of a local legend and guardian angel.

She met Michael at her front door, as he jumped down from a petrol tanker and waved his thanks to the driver.

'Who're you, and what do you want?' she asked.

'Michael Francis. I think my sister's here,' he said, and the bush nurse looked at him carefully for a moment, then nodded.

'She's here, all right.' Pauline Reynolds wasted few words. She could be crusty, and was known to have told off a doctor or two in her time. 'Says she had a fall, which is nonsense. Follow me.'

He followed her through the house. Almost every room held patients. Helen was in a tiny single room at the back of the house, asleep. Her appearance was a shock; one side of her face blackened by bruises, her right eye closed and swollen, as well as a splint attached to her arm, and heavy strapping around her body just visible through the flimsy nightdress that had been provided.

'Good God Almighty,' he said, shocked.

'Exactly,' Sister Reynolds said trenchantly.

Helen opened her eyes, trying to smile as she saw him. It was more like a grimace.

'Miki.'

He kissed her on the forehead, which seemed as if it might be the only part of her face not to cause her pain. Sister Reynolds noted this, and regarded Michael with a trace more approval.

'What happened?'

'An extremely good question,' the bush nurse said pointedly. 'She's been hit.'

'I fell.' Helen's voice was weak, but stubborn.

'She was hit first, in my medical opinion – which only covers a mere thirty years' experience. Hit very hard a number of times. She fell as a result of these blows. She also bruised her ribs so we've strapped them. I'd say she's broken her arm, but I've got no luxuries like an X-ray machine, so I decided on a splint till the doctor gets here. He's on an accident call at Cabramurra. She was unconscious, and she's still concussed. And very obstinate.'

'Helen, who did it?'

Helen shook her head.

'Someone did,' Michael said softly, and Helen shut her eyes.

'See what I mean,' Pauline Reynolds said.

'Yes,' he said. 'Can I sit and talk to her?'

'You might get some sense out of her.' The large, capable nurse paused at the door. 'There is one other thing I don't understand.'

'What, Sister?'

'With injuries like this, she should've been taken straight to the Cooma hospital. Very flattering, Mister Angus Kerr saying he thought she'd get better treatment here, but it didn't really stack up.'

The door closed behind her, and they were left alone.

'Nice woman – and no fool,' Michael said. 'Was it Kerr?'

She said nothing.

'Or Sandor?'

The one eye out of which Helen could see gazed at him, as she turned her head painfully.

'Sandor?'

'I didn't really think so. Just wanted a reaction and I got one, didn't I? That dirty bloody bastard, Kerr.'

'Please, Michael, don't be stupid.' There was more strength to her voice. 'Please don't make trouble. Why do you think I supported his flimsy story that I fell? Because I didn't want you to find out, and do something crazy.'

'You're a drongo, Angus. If you think I'm going to cover for you, you flaming dill, then think again.'

Herbie McFie had talked to the bush nurse, and learned the extent of the girl's injuries. And had been told, in Sister Reynolds' inimitable manner, that she didn't believe a word of the ludicrous story that the girl had tripped and fallen. Certainly not without some assistance, and if she could get the patient to come to her senses and tell the truth, then it should be a matter for Sergeant Walsh, the local custodian of the law.

McFie, despite his reputation as a womaniser, was a shrewd

operator. If his female staff were chosen for their compliance, at least his office philandering was by mutual consent, and he had never had a situation like this. As regional officer, he had four Lawrenson sites to supervise. He kept his ear to the ground, and had previously heard reports of the way Kerr harassed this girl. And now she was a mass of bruises, possible broken arm and concussed, and Angus Kerr obviously thought both the bush sister and McFie were fools. He had brought her to Jindabyne instead of the district's main hospital at Cooma, and Herbie knew why.

Bloody Kerr had wanted to talk to him, ask him to intercede and get him off the hook. Angus had hit the girl; it was obvious.

'She fell, Herbie.'

'Bullshit.'

'It's true. I admit I was making a pass, but nothing serious. Nothing to go nuts about. The little bitch is a real prick teaser.'

'Oh yeah,' McFie said.

'She is, honest. I wanted to lock the door and have a go at her there and then, but the silly cow got panicky. Went to slap me across the face, missed and fell against the desk. Hell of a crack as her head hit the edge.'

It sounded plausible. Even possible. But McFie was an expert in the ways of office bosses with good-looking secretaries, and Angus Kerr was a consummate liar.

'You're on your own, mate,' McFie said. 'If the girl dobs you in, Pauline will call the cops. If that means Sir Cedric gets to hear of it, I'm not sticking my neck out for a stupid turd like you.'

'I thought we were friends, Herbie?'

'Acquaintances, mate. Distant acquaintances. I'll give you a bit of advice though. If I were you, I'd do two things.'

'What are they?' Kerr asked, still hopeful of support.

'I'd drop into the church, and say a prayer she doesn't utter your name. Then I'd hightail it home, and pull your bloody head in, about as far as it'll go.'

Angus Kerr decided against another call at the bush nurse's hospital. He had an uneasy feeling the Sister did not believe him, and she was not the kind of woman to tangle with. He was livid with McFie who had been worse than useless, and all he could hope now was that Helen would remain silent, and the whole thing would die down.

He'd be very careful in future. Perhaps arrange for her and that troublesome brother to be transferred. They might like a change, perhaps to the camp at Island Bend. Or better still, up at Guthega. There'd be skiing up there in the winter, and he seemed to recall her once say they'd learned to ski as small children, before the war.

They had less than a year left on their contract, and there'd be three or four months of snow, come late May or early June. He'd find some photos to show her of the ski slopes, and even contrive to get her a raise. The brother could go and work as a miner up there, where they made the really big money. It should suit them both. He might even have to include Sandor Jaroslov, because the girl mightn't agree to go without her lover – but that wouldn't be a bad thing; it would get rid of another migrant he couldn't stand – the bloody Czech with his airs and graces, just because he thought he was going to be a doctor.

So if she would just shut up, he'd get away with it. And then he could pick a new girl for the office, someone who'd be a bit willing and hop into bed with him at the drop of a hat, like one of those sexy sheilas that bastard Herbie had in his bloody harem.

The wet canteen was packed, being pay night. Angus Kerr knew he had done the right thing, going there, taking Jimmy Ferguson for a drink, because it showed he had nothing to hide. There had been just a moment, a slight hush when they'd come in, but he had waved to several of the foremen, bought Jimmy a couple of schooners and felt he had handled it really well. If you fronted up like it was a normal night, they'd reckon you had nothing to hide. And it was looking better all the time, because the longer she delayed spilling the beans, the less likely she was to say anything.

He was even asked how she was, and told the story he'd stuck to here in the camp, about the dizzy spell and giving herself a real bash on the corner of the desk as she fell, and everyone knew how painful that could be. Jimmy went home; Kerr had a couple more beers, lined up for his meal with two of the foremen, and decided then to call it a night. He walked home through the rows of huts, well satisfied by events.

When he switched on the light in his quarters, the first thing he glimpsed was Michael sitting waiting for him. A split second later, he realised Michael was not alone. His redheaded girlfriend was with him.

'Get the hell out of here, or I'll call the security guard,' Kerr snapped, emboldened by the fact of the girl being there.

'I don't think you'll call anyone, Mr Kerr,' Michael said, as he held up the supervisor's private telephone, wires trailing from where he had ripped it from the connection in the wall.

'That's a crime, damaging government property.'

'So was breaking the window to get in,' he was told.

Kerr's eyes dilated as the girl took a knife from her handbag.

'I came along so he wouldn't use this,' she said. 'He bought it in Cooma this afternoon, to cut your balls off. I made him promise he wouldn't. He agreed, but only on certain conditions.'

'Anything,' Angus Kerr vowed – his moment of confidence evaporating as he stared at the knife.

'Not *anything*,' Michael said, 'just *one* thing. That you never touch – or abuse – or upset my sister again. Because if you do, I won't stop at your balls, mate. I'll fucking disembowel you.'

Deirdre repressed a shiver. She knew this was a part of what they had worked out, but by God he sounded believable. Enough to convince her. As for Kerr, he looked as if he was about to crap himself.

'There's also this,' Michael said as Deirdre gave him a bundle of hand-written pages. 'In the hospital she told me everything. The names you called her, the punch that nearly killed her – and all the other attempts you made, right back to when we were in tents up above Berridale. You little prick, you've made her life a misery all this time, ever since we got here. I wrote it down, every word, and it goes to old man Lawrenson himself . . . who knows her, as I think you remember.'

'No, please . . .' he pleaded, realising it might mean charges; it would certainly mean being sacked without notice, and the end of a cosy job. 'Please.'

'It'll be typed, and she'll sign it. We'll use it, don't worry, if you give trouble. Just call it blackmail, and never forget we have it.'

Deirdre took the papers. She put them away in her handbag, then opened the curtain and glanced outside. She carefully climbed out the broken window. Angus Kerr felt a wave of relief, as he realised he was going to get away with it. Just empty threats. No contact with Sir Cedric, no retaliation; no police, nothing really. Just a few silly threatening words. Even the knife was a charade. The girl had it in her bag, and perhaps all that talk about a statement was bluff. He wanted to laugh, but it was smarter to stay quiet and look humble . . .

That was when the first punch hit him hard in the solar plexus, taking all his breath away. The second punch came a split second later, a short jab to the same sensitive spot, and he tried to struggle to voice a protest, to shout for help, but there was no hope of speaking when he was gasping for breath.

'This is just a sample, Angus. Just a few thumps to make me feel better. Helen asked me not to do this, but I really think I ought to demonstrate what'll happen next time.'

'No . . .' he tried to shout, but it became a stifled moan, as a punch hit him in the mouth, rocking his head back, then with an open palm Michael backhanded him across the face, a series of stinging slaps that had enough force to make his eyes water. Kerr backed away, until he was against the wall of the room, and could retreat no further. Cornered, and in a paroxysm of frustration and helpless rage, he spat at his assailant, which was a serious mistake.

Michael wiped the spittle away with his sleeve. The sharp lift of his knee caught the supervisor unaware. Kerr had never known such pain and felt as if his entire genitals had been driven somewhere into his intestines. When he doubled up in agony, Michael showed no mercy. He kept hitting him, holding him upright against the wall with one hand, while punching him with the other, hurting him but avoiding any more blows to the face that might mark him.

Outside the shattered window, Deirdre kept watch and flinched at the sound of the battering. She had no idea Michael could be so vicious. In this mood, she felt, he might be able to take on her three brothers at the same time, and the thought of it cheered her immensely.

Inside the room, Angus Kerr was a sodden, whimpering mess. He fell to the ground, trying to beg for mercy.

'Mercy, you evil shit,' Michael said. 'You're not getting any mercy. Those were for my sister. This one's for me.'

He dragged Kerr to his feet, and hit him a final time with all the force he could manage.

'God,' Deirdre said, 'you were ruthless. What a bastard!'

Michael put his arms around her. They were both in the top bunk of their first-class sleeper as the train clattered through the night towards Goulburn.

'My fists are still sore.'

'Imagine what he's feeling like. At least he didn't go to the police. Not as far as we know.'

'He won't go to the police. If he does, he'll be facing charges himself for assault against Helen. And he knows bloody well I meant what I said about sending the statement to old Lawrenson.'

They had spent two days in the Egan Street boarding house, where the friendly landlady had borrowed a typewriter for them, and Deirdre had made copies of the pages. Michael had gone twice to the bush nurse's hospital, where Helen's bruises were turning purple, but the swelling around her eye was diminishing. Her arm was broken, but the doctor had set it, and she was sitting up in bed with a plaster cast and wearing a sling, even managing a smile at the sight of him.

'Sister Reynolds says you're doing fine. I'll bet you'll be out of here in a few days.'

'Not till I look less gruesome.'

'You look great,' he lied, and kissed her.

'No, I don't. I got hold of a mirror this morning. I'm sorry now; it wasn't a very clever idea.'

'Listen,' Michael said, 'in a week or two those bruises will be gone, and so will the swelling. You'll be as good looking as ever.'

She shook her head, but he knew she was pleased. Which meant it was a good time to break the bad news.

'I have to admit a couple of things. First of all, I beat the shit out of Kerr.'

'Michael!'

'I had to. Sorry, you can get as angry as you like, but there was no way he was going to treat you like that and get away with it.'

'I'm not angry,' she said. 'But if he makes a complaint . . .'

'If he does, he can kiss his job goodbye. And he'll be up in court, with everyone knowing about this.'

He showed her the typed statement, and she read it carefully, then looked at him with surprise.

'You wrote it all down, everything I told you? When?'

'After I left here. I wasn't likely to forget a single thing. Deirdre typed two copies, and we want you to sign them.'

She managed her signature, although it was her right arm that was heavy and awkward with the plaster.

'Now,' Michael said, 'I'm afraid this is the next news, and if the other didn't make you angry, this might. We're shooting through, Deirdre and me. I've drawn the money I saved from the bank – she's got some as well – and we're off.'

'Oh, God.'

'I knew you'd say that.'

'You'll be in trouble, breaking your contract. It's against the law. They could put you in gaol.'

'They have to catch me first.'

'Isn't there some other way?'

'Not if I want to stay with Deirdre – and I do.'

'You're in love?'

'Yes,' he said, and she smiled and took his hand.

'I'm glad about that. One smart thing you've done at least.'

'But we have to get away from her family. Neither of us will feel safe till they're way behind us. And besides, half the mob at Lawrenson's still think I killed Vlasoff.'

'If you leave, they'll all think it.'

'If I'm in Sydney, I won't give a damn what they think.'

She sighed and shook her head, but he could tell she wasn't angry. He gently touched her swollen face, then kissed her. This time it was goodbye, and they both knew it.

'I'm going to miss you,' she said.

'We'll stay in touch, Iluska. Nothing must ever change that.'

'Then you write.' He knew she was trying not to cry.

'I promise. Just as soon as we find a place to live. I'll give you our address.'

'It'll be the first time in our lives we've been apart.'

'I know. But there's Sandor, isn't there? You've got him.'

'His contract's nearly up,' Helen said after a moment.

'He might stick around.'

'Yes, he might.'

'And we had to go different ways some time. We're not kids any longer, are we?'

'No,' Helen said, determined to keep her tears at bay, 'we're not kids any longer.'

They woke to the sound of a polite tap on the door, and the voice of the sleeping-car attendant.

'Cup of tea, Madam, Sir?'

He came in with a tray of tea and biscuits, was about to hand one to the occupant of the lower berth, when he realised it was empty and they were cramped into the upper bunk.

'Thank you,' Deirdre said, managing to take the tray while keeping herself covered by the New South Wales railway blanket. 'We both felt the view was better up here. And the air's fresher.'

'Quite right, Madam,' said the attendant, used to these kind of quips from his passengers, and having caught sight of Deirdre's bare thigh despite the railway blanket, thought he'd certainly be in the same bunk with this little ripper, given half a chance. 'We'll be arriving at Central station in about forty minutes.'

They thanked him, sipped their tea, and decided this was the only way to travel. In Cooma, they'd promised themselves a bright and sunny start to their new life, and the idea of twin bunks (one unused) in a first-class sleeper felt like a good way to begin.

They raised the compartment blind, and saw suburban houses flit past in the early light. Then the clutter of backyards, fences that bordered onto the railway tracks, brick tenements huddled together; hardly a glamorous gateway to a city, but full of novelty and wonder to them both; the streets beginning to waken, milkmen making deliveries, newspaper boys on bicycles, a child waving from a window, cars and trams moving and beginning to fill the narrow roads. They were running away to a new life. They still had over six hundred and seventy pounds, which felt like a fortune and was more than either of them had ever possessed, or imagined they might. For Michael, the streets of Budapest and the bleak despair of refugee camps were like a distant memory, and as the train gushed steam and slowed by the old morgue station before entering the gloomy cavern of the city rail terminus, he felt as if he was coming home.

Chapter 14

The first surprise was when the mail truck from Cooma stopped at the hospital, delivering a bouquet of flowers, and Sister Reynolds brought them into the back garden where Helen sat reading in the shade. Black grapes hung in clusters from a trellis above her head, and she could hear the hum of bees gathering pollen. It was a perfect summer day.

Her last day of convalescence. The arm would remain in plaster for some weeks yet, but due to the bush nurse's insistence that she could not return to work until she was both fully recovered and felt able to face the world, she had remained here until the swelling around her eye and all the facial bruising was gone. Now she could look in the mirror without flinching, her appearance restored to normal.

'You have an admirer,' Pauline Reynolds said.

Helen took the cellophane-wrapped flowers, a bright display of zinnias, chrysanthemums and asters.

'They're beautiful,' she said, and realised they were the first flowers she had ever received in her life. There was a sealed card attached, and she looked at it, wondering. The speculation on who might have sent this was almost as great a pleasure as the gift itself.

Who? Michael?

He'd be settled somewhere in Sydney by now. He and his tempestuous redhead. She smiled at the thought of Deirdre, who fired shotguns and took cash from beneath the family floorboards – but she wished their impulsive escape had not been necessary. Already she was missing her brother, and concerned that breaking his contract would eventually mean trouble. *He'd promised to write and give his address. Was this his way of doing it?*

Or perhaps it was Sandor. He'd managed to visit twice, when he'd had a deep and serious discussion with Sister Reynolds about the patient's condition, after which he was forced to admit the bush nurse was more than capable. It was a remark that had made Pauline Reynolds declare all student doctors were equipped with the essential ingredient required for a medical degree, a large quota of self-importance.

'You trying to guess who sent them?' she asked Helen, who nodded and smiled. The two had become friends.

'Who do you think it was?' Helen asked.

'Probably Czechoslovakia's gift to the medical profession.'

'Sandor? In that case I'll guess Michael.' She opened the card and stared at it in amazement. 'We're both wrong.'

'Who is it?'

'Listen!' She read aloud. *'Sincerely sorry to hear of your unlucky accident. Trust you will soon be back with us again. Best wishes, Cedric Lawrenson.'*

Sister Reynolds had a laugh that many local people claimed could frighten crows off the carcass of a dead sheep, or scare foxes out of a chicken yard. It boomed out now, robust and boisterous.

'Sir Cedric!' She could hardly speak for hilarity. 'It'd be the first time he's put his hand in his pocket for years. Imagine it – flowers from old Lawrenson. I bet he claims it as a tax deduction.'

'Don't be mean,' Helen said, joining in the laughter. 'It was a lovely gesture. But I wonder how he knew?'

'That's easy. From Herbie McFie.'

'McFie?'

'When I told that lecherous reprobate you weren't going back to Adaminaby until I passed you fit, even if they had to hire four interpreters to take your place, I'll bet he and Kerr had to concoct a story for head office. Because even though you still refuse to tell me the truth, I know it wasn't an accident. That creature hit you.'

'Pauline, we agreed not to go into details. I had a good reason for not saying anything. Now it's best left that way.' She also thought it best, despite her friendship with the bush nurse, not to mention that Michael had taken his personal retaliation.

'If you insist. Anyway, that's how old Cedric would've heard, and you must have made an impression for him to lash out on flowers. Jolly nice ones, too.'

'Yes, they are,' Helen said.

The second surprise occurred when she went back to work the following day. Bracing herself for the disagreeable prospect of confronting Angus Kerr, she found McFie there instead, with a cheerful middle-aged man whom he introduced as Len Richards, the new Adaminaby construction unit supervisor.

'Len's taking over from Mr Kerr,' McFie said, and asked her if she'd mind strolling out to his car with him, as there was a matter he needed to discuss. Outside the office, he told her that Angus Kerr had been assigned to a new job in charge of a group building sheds up at Island Bend, and she wouldn't be seeing him again.

'With any luck,' McFie said, 'next winter up there will be cold enough to freeze his balls off.'

'Let's hope so.'

He grinned, but Helen was pointedly aloof, determined not to give McFie cause for optimism that she might forgive or forget.

'I gather you told Sir Cedric I had an accident.'

'I thought it best for all concerned, Helen. If you want to make an accusation against Kerr, I certainly won't try to stop you. But in the process a lot could come out, and I reckon it mightn't do your brother much good.'

'What are you trying to tell me, Mr McFie? No charges against Kerr, no report on Michael leaving the job illegally?'

'That's more or less it. I like a quiet life, like to run me own regional office in me own way, and if old Lawrenson gets stirred up, then life stops being quiet. He seems to think pretty highly of you – and if he knew the way Angus treated you all hell would break loose. It's best if we avoid that. So you shut up about Kerr, and I don't think your brother's gonna be put on anyone's wanted list. If someone does find out he shot through, it won't be because of me.'

Helen felt a great sense of relief. She thought it best not to tell McFie that she had never intended to bring charges.

'Seems fair,' she said.

'Good. And by the way – it's great to see you so completely recovered. It would have been a terrible thing for a nice-looking girl like you to have been scarred, or had your looks ruined.'

She knew it was partly his way to cement their understanding, but mostly an overt sexual overture. The man couldn't stop himself, and this was the moment to deal with it.

'If that had happened, Mr McFie, you can be sure Kerr would be in gaol by now, and I think you might have been looking for a new job.' She enjoyed his startled expression. 'Was there anything else we had to talk about? Because if not, I'll go and start work. Just as soon as I write a letter to Sir Cedric, thanking him for his flowers.'

'Flowers?'

'Yes, he sent me flowers. Didn't you know?'

In the days to come, she would remember the startled look on McFie's face with a great deal of pleasure. It was the perfect note on which to give him a brief smile, nod a brisk goodbye, and leave him standing there. Looking, as Michael would doubtless have relished expressing it, like a stunned mullet.

The first week was wonderful; they spent it in a city hotel, but by the end of it their money had gone so fast they became nervous. What seemed like riches in Cooma was a modest amount in Sydney. In their innocence they went looking for a flat, but the prices were alarming, and agents demanded what they called 'key money'.

'What's key money?' Michael asked.

'New Australians, are youse?' The agent looked them over.

'I'm an old Australian,' Deirdre declared, 'and I've never heard of anything called key money.'

'Where're you from?'

'Adaminaby.'

'Bugger me,' the agent said. 'Where's *that*?'

'Down near Kosciusko. Ever heard of Kozzie?'

'From the flaming bush? Well, that explains it. Key money simply means you buy a chance to get a flat.'

'How much?' Michael wanted to know.

The agent assessed them carefully before he replied.

'Depends. A decent flat, about five hundred quid.'

'Five hundred? For the flat?'

'For a key to get into the place. Then each week you pay rent. If you want a harbour view, might cost you seven or eight hundred.'

'Goodbye, sport,' Deirdre said.

'I might have a hole in the wall for a coupla hundred.'

'You must think we're a pair of galahs,' Michael said, leaving the agent scratching his head, and wondering how a reffo had picked up local expressions like that.

They asked the desk clerk at the hotel, who said flats were as scarce as hen's teeth, but advised them that the classifieds in the *Herald* were the only answer. Early next morning they went out to buy a copy, and over breakfast searched the TO LET column. It was depressingly small, compared to the size of one headed WANTED TO RENT. In fact, there were only four advertisements, three supplying phone numbers and one an address. They occupied a phone box for half an hour, trying vainly to get a reply, but all the numbers were continuously engaged. So they went by tram to Rushcutters Bay, to the sole address given in the paper. A long line of people stood waiting forlornly.

'Not a hope,' said the man at the end of it, 'I hear the queue started at six this morning, and they must've taken forty people's names since I got here.'

'But if it's only one flat, what's the point of queuing up, and why do they take so many names?' Deirdre wanted to know.

'For them the more people they see, the more to choose from. For us poor mugs tryin' to get somewhere to live, we jest keep hopin' we'll strike it lucky. No matter how far down the queue.'

'It's crazy,' Michael said.

'It is, mate. But no use tryin' ones who give phone numbers. You can never get through.' He grinned at the look they exchanged. 'Found that out, have you? Not a hope unless you start early.'

'How early?' Deirdre asked.

'Well, you can get a paper at the *Herald* office at two in the morning. Any dill who advertises their number can expect a call about five minutes later.'

'At five past two?' They looked at him with disbelief.

'If they're mug enough to put the number in. And they might keep on gettin' calls for a week.'

'But where do ordinary people live?'

'Where they can. With relatives. Or in boardin' houses. If you got any cash, you can put a deposit on a fibro out at woop-woop. That's if you want to live in the sticks. There's a housin' shortage; had one since the war and it's gettin' worse. Where you been lately?'

They decided not to stay. The chances of success seemed remote, to say the least of it. They walked up Bayswater Road, thought about taking a tram back to the hotel, but instead cut through Roslyn Street, and found Darlinghurst Road and the centre of Kings Cross.

Nothing had prepared them for this; the crush of people, the exotic contrast, the colour in what had seemed to them, until now, a conformist and rather staid city. They stared at the sights. A woman in a purple leotard walking a group of four pampered poodles, cutting a swathe along the footpath with an arrogance at least the equal of her charges; a pavement artist drawing to an admiring group, swift chalk portraits of his audience; an impromptu jazz trio playing on a street corner, while a pale and anaemic young girl danced to the music, but whether she was a part of their group or alone in her own dream world they did not know; above all, the intriguing mix of people, animated and voluble, conversing in a variety of different languages.

Michael heard a passing couple arguing in Hungarian, and felt a strange ache of homesickness. He gazed around him at the kiosks and flower stalls, like a glimpse of remembered places in Europe. He saw the boutique shops, the crowded delicatessens, he sniffed their odours and the strong aroma of coffee, saw club doorways and stairs that led to neons blinking pale in the daylight and advertising ROOMS TO LET.

The California looked lively and interesting, and they were just in time to occupy a spare table for two by the window.

'It's certainly different,' Michael said, and Deirdre told him what little she knew about Kings Cross, mainly from newspapers, and in particular a popular weekly scandal sheet called *Truth*.

'Dad likes *Truth* because it has pictures of naked women in it, and stories about divorces and love nests, and gang wars and murders.'

'Sounds just like him.'

'Kings-bloody-Cross, he used to call it. He reckoned it was the sin capital of Australia, and couldn't wait to read about all the scandal that took place there. The Dirty Half Mile, that's another name for it, because of the gambling and sly grog, the tarts, and nightclubs. *Truth*'s always got lots of stories about the dirty half mile. And there's a witch . . . Rosaleen something . . . the wicked witch of the Cross, who's a painter as well as a witch. Dad said it was all disgusting. Horrible.'

'If he said that,' Michael reflected, 'we might like it here.'

Deirdre smiled. A young waitress came to take their order, and when she had gone Michael pointed to a sign across the street.

'Rooms to let. Why don't we go there, after our coffee, and ask how much?'

It was a brothel. Rooms booked by the hour, a woman in a faded kimono told them. She looked at Deirdre with interest, and asked if anyone had ever told her what a good living a girl could make on her back – especially one who looked a bit like some big fillum star.

They exchanged a glance and began to edge towards the stairs.

'Well, you do. Can't remember her name but you look like 'er. That red hair would get in the punters. Your boyfriend needn't be left out. A good-lookin' strong young feller like 'im, some of the other girls might even take a shine . . . a few of 'em could do with being looked after by a decent ponce . . .'

They fled.

Retreated back to the California, for more coffee and serious consideration about what to do next.

'Any other bright ideas?' Deirdre asked.

'Well, they can't all be brothels.'

'Wanna bet?'

'Are you going to admit your dad was right?'

She looked glum at the thought. They sat in silence, until the same waitress came to the table with a steaming percolator, and asked if they wanted another cup.

'Regulars get a free refill.' She was freckle-faced, with an engaging smile and a mop of unruly blonde hair. 'This is your second visit in half an hour, so that makes you regulars.'

'We'd like to be regulars,' Michael said. 'We're trying to find a place to live, somewhere around here.'

'Only not like the joint across the road,' Deirdre added, and the girl laughed so much she almost spilled the coffee.

'That's a well-known whorehouse,' she said.

'So we found out.'

'You should've asked me.' She finished filling their cups, and studied them both thoughtfully. 'What are you looking for?'

'We started off looking for a flat.'

'You have to be lucky – or rich,' the waitress said.

'We've found that out, too. Now we're looking for a room. And a view if possible,' Deirdre said, a trifle wistfully, 'but that doesn't seem very likely.'

'Would a tatty room with a view of next door's washing be of interest? Lino on the floor, a gas ring for cooking, and a bathroom down the hall?'

'Where is it?'

'About five minutes' walk from here.'

'Whose is it?'

'Mine – only I'm moving out. Got a job in a radio show, and I'm off to share a flat.'

'How much key money?' Michael asked her.

'Key money? For this dump? Fair go,' the waitress said. 'If you want it, the landlady's an old actress friend of mine. Looking for a new tenant. We could take a squizz if you like, when my shift ends.'

The room was in Roslyn Gardens, up three flights of stairs with a hall carpet that was threadbare. The view was the adjacent yard of an old Victorian house and its clothes line, on which swung two pairs of expansive underclothes known as long johns.

'Lovely, eh,' said the waitress, whose name they had learned was Liddy Samson, and who was about to abandon her day job at the California, because she had been cast in a new radio serial called *The Wild Stranger*. It was scheduled to run four times a week for the next twelve months, with an option, Liddy added, which was the important thing – the option – because look at *When a Girl Marries* or *Blue Hills*, or a few other serials that seemed to have been running forever.

'They belong to the doctor next door.' She indicated the undergarments. 'He's a local abortionist who makes a fortune, and also looks after the gunshot wounds of any crooks who get shot.'

She smiled at them both.

'I did warn you,' she said. 'It's a tiny, shitty room, and there's only a single bed, but Andrea who owns the place is nice.'

'I've lived in worse,' said Michael, who had rarely lived in anything better, but he looked at Deirdre for her judgement.

'The bed's very narrow,' Deirdre commented. 'Just as well we like to sleep real close to each other. And the neighbourhood seems interesting. Not many places you can look out the window, and see an abortionist's long johns.'

As if on cue, a handsome, elderly woman appeared. She was tall and stately, and moved with the grace of a ballet dancer.

'This is Andrea Allison,' Liddy said, and the elegant woman bestowed a smile and extended her hand. Michael instinctively knew it wasn't meant to be shaken, and raised it to his lips.

'My dears,' Andrea Allison said, looking at him approvingly, 'it's not the Ritz, or even the Hotel Australia, but it's cheap. Three pounds a week, and if you want to live in the Cross, you can't do much better than that.' She looked out the window, and sighed. 'I'm sorry about the view. I keep sending him letters, asking why he wears such frightful underwear. He claims it helps to keep his impulses enclosed.' She smiled at them both. 'He's a terrible man, but amusing. This place is full of terrible but amusing people.'

Helen enjoyed the hastily scrawled letter that Michael sent her, with his vivid descriptions of their new landlady, the odd and rather alarming doctor who was their next door neighbour, and the exotic district in which they now lived. It seemed so remote from her, this cosmopolitan place called the Cross, with its blend of the aberrant and the urbane. She smiled over the letter and secretly envied them their happiness.

That night, knowing Michael was secure and that he had found a girl he loved, and a place in which he liked to live, she slept soundly for the first time in weeks. That night she no longer fretted over what had troubled her so much during the weeks in hospital; the problem she must soon face. Sleep was a relief; it could wait for another day.

~

The humid February heat had been building up since before dawn, and at breakfast time the radio predicted a scorcher.

'I'll stay home,' Sarah decided. 'I don't like scorchers.'

Neil had no such choice. He was due to settle a dispute at a migrant camp near Liverpool, and spent two hectic hours, after a long, hot train journey, trying to mediate between a vociferous bunch of warring Yugoslavs. A Serbian husband had left his wife and moved in with a Croatian girl half his age; her enraged family had chased him with an axe. The local police had been called in, and found themselves soundly abused by both parties. The entire camp had formed into two bitter factions and, as a last resort, Neil had been invited to intercede and see if he could peacefully settle the matter.

Peaceful, it had not been.

With a canteen full of people shouting at each other, reasoned discussion had been impossible. Fortunately, Neil knew the Serbian and Croatian spoken languages were the same; it was only the written word that differed, with cyrillic script used by the Serbs. He also had a smattering of useful phrases, one of which was '*shut up and listen*'.

He shouted this now, to immediate effect. There was a startled silence. If he had then continued in English, less than half would have understood him, but he was aware most of them knew German. He deliberately spoke it in the way they did, loudly and with vigorous gestures. Thus he kept their attention, asking the abandoned wife if she wished her husband to return to her.

No, she said firmly, she wished to divorce him.

He asked the young girl if she wished to continue living with the woman's husband.

She hesitated, then declared she didn't think so. He had

made promises to buy her a car, and a diamond ring, and now she'd found out he had no money. Also, she had thought she was pregnant, but this had proved to be a false alarm.

The husband shouted abuse at her, and Neil bellowed at him to *shut up and listen*. He warned the Serbian he was about to get himself into serious trouble – with the police, with the camp authorities, and with his few remaining friends. Neither woman wanted him, so he had better go and find himself one who did. Preferably one who was of legal age, and not someone else's wife.

The husband spat at him. Neil let the spittle remain on his cheek for a moment, while everyone went very quiet, watching them. He carefully took a handkerchief and wiped it off, then slapped the man hard across the face. There was a roar of approval from both sides, and a great deal of applause and laughter. The husband glared at Neil, then turned, gazing at them all, realising he was totally isolated, and slowly walked out.

Neil left with promises there'd be no more violence, or any victimisation of the hapless husband. He hoped the truce would last; he gave the wife the name of a free legal service, and endured the long hot journey back to the city. It was one of many such days; some of these adjudications were successful, others ended in stalemate or disaster.

The office was like an oven, the two small fans hopelessly ineffective. There was no trace of breeze, but black storm clouds were rapidly gathering to the south. He sat and tried to write a report of the Yugoslav skirmish. The phone on his desk rang, and Neil picked it up.

'There's a call for Mr Falconer,' the receptionist who doubled as his secretary said. 'He won't be in until late, so you'd better take it.'

'Hello,' Neil said.

'Henry,' a voice answered, giving him no chance to explain he wasn't Henry, 'I thought you should know. Adams and Barlow leave for Milan next week.'

Neil felt as if he had been kicked in the stomach.

'I'll tell him,' he said, hanging up before there was a reply.

Adams and Barlow. Mr A and Mr B were going to Italy, to the Milan Centre. That disposed of his forlorn hope it might be dealt with by getting rid of Mitchell and the others. It was not going to end up in a file. He had been stupid and naive to even contemplate it.

He looked down at the park. The flowers were exhausted and vapid, the shrubs wilting in the heat. The storm clouds had spread, the sky was darkening, and he could hear a sound of distant thunder.

Curly Wilson, so called because he was completely bald, not a hair anywhere, except those growing out of his nose and on his ears, was a friendly man in charge of transport for the Lawrenson group in the Snowy region. In his spare time he had taught Helen to drive, and he promised to arrange for her licence now she was back from hospital. Curly serviced the vehicles, and kept a log of jeeps or trucks borrowed; the times, the names of drivers and mileage readings. He was very methodical, and Helen watched as he checked his records.

'Yep, that's right, Helen. It was a ute. Departed 3.15.'

'I'd better make a note of it, Curly. For our new boss.'

'Here, love.'

He gave her the book, and she looked at the entry. There was no possible mistake. *Utility truck. Returned 7.30 p.m.* And the other details: registration number, the driver's name, total mileage all listed.

She made a note for appearances' sake, and handed it back.

'Any problems, Helen?'

'No. Just Len, wanting details on how things work. Likes to put himself in the picture. Nothing important.'

'He's an improvement, eh, on that rotten urger, Angus.'

'He certainly is,' Helen said, but her thoughts were elsewhere.

'Beaut to have ya back. The place was a shambles. McFie sent me an interpreter who could hardly speak English. Imagine me trying to tell a Yugoslav he's gone and stuffed the carby, and this nong Herbie sent has never even heard of a carburettor. How's the arm?'

'It's fine, Curly,' she said, 'the plaster comes off tomorrow.'

'And in y'self, otherwise? Sure you're all right again?'

He thought she looked pale, and seemed quieter.

'Better for seeing you,' she said, liking him and knowing this reply would please him. Even though she felt sick and empty.

'Good on ya, girl,' he called as she walked away. He finished an oil change on a jeep, and whistled a tune. The place hadn't been the same without Helen for the past few weeks. She was a great girl. Real nice. He wished his own daughter back in Sydney was half as nice.

She sat waiting. Alone.

Len Richards had gone for the day. Sandor arrived wearing his suit and a tie, clearly expecting her to be in her best dress.

'I thought I was taking you to the cafe for a meal. We were going to celebrate the unveiling of your arm, tomorrow.'

His English has improved a lot, she found herself thinking, and wondered why she would notice a thing like that at such a moment.

'Sandor,' she said quietly, without any preamble, 'why did you kill him?'

He just stared at her. Making no attempt to reply, he shakily sat down on the nearest chair, still gazing at her.

'You did kill him. When I was in hospital, especially when I was convalescing, I had so much time to think. Time to lie there and reflect about Christmas Day – and the night before, at the dance – when Katryna saw Josef Vlasoff. Michael came to get me, asking me to find out what she was saying. Remember?'

'Yes,' Sandor said.

'You offered to get her a drink of cold water, and came back with it while I was trying to find out what had happened. Part of that time she was talking – almost raving – in Polish. And you understand Polish, don't you?'

'I understand enough.'

'I should have realised earlier.' She shook her head, sadly. 'Perhaps I didn't want to. Or couldn't face the idea. At first I was so afraid it was Michael, I had no suspicion of anyone else. After the relief of his being innocent . . . other things happened. Being hurt, then he and Deirdre running away – but all the time I suppose I knew, if it wasn't Michael you were really the only one it could have been.'

'Iluska . . .'

'Not Iluska, please. Not any more. Since I came back, you must have known something was different.'

'Yes,' he said finally. 'We were different. You kept me at a great distance.'

'I was hoping you might tell me, but you said nothing. So I had to prove it. I asked Curly Wilson about vehicles used on Christmas Day. I pretended it was a casual check on transport, for the new boss. The vehicle you borrowed was a utility. Time 3.15 p.m. You said you were going into Cooma to visit friends and take presents to them for Christmas. What friends, Sandor?'

'All right,' he said, 'there are no friends.'

'You returned at 7.30 p.m. The mileage recorded in Curly's log is almost exactly the distance to Kiandra and back. Where did you kill him? Here at the camp, in his room?'

'No.'

'Then where?'

'I never meant to kill him anywhere. For God's sake, what does it matter, where?'

'Because I'm asking was it premeditated? Did you drive him out there under some pretext, and kill him at Kiandra?'

'Don't be ridiculous,' he said. 'Didn't you listen to me? I never intended to kill him at all.'

'Then why? And how . . . and most especially *where*?'

After a pause he spoke, but did not answer her directly.

'What you said is true. At the dance, I heard much of what she told you; he was in the SS, a member of the *Einsatzgruppen*, at Treblinka. Dear God, you and I know they were the filth of the earth.'

Sandor put his head in his hands for a moment. She remained quiet, watching him and waiting for him to continue.

'I telephoned the hospital on Christmas morning, and they told me Mrs Dyboski was dead. Then I saw Elsner – Vlasoff – come back to the camp. I swear he was smiling. I saw him go to his room, and I went to the kitchen and stole a knife. When I knocked on his door, he opened it – as if he had no worry in the world. I showed him the knife, told him I knew who he was, and that I was taking him to the police. To arrest him for war crimes. But first we had to go and borrow transport, and I would tell the mechanic why I wanted it. And by tomorrow everyone in the camp would know.

'The place was deserted; it was Christmas, and people were meeting in the canteen for drinks, for celebration of the birth of Jesus, even some for prayer. Your friend Curly wasn't there; he'd left a note saying back in half an hour. I told Vlasoff we'd wait. I made him sit on the ground out of sight.

'He started to laugh, and told me that in Australia they would not care about what he'd done. There were many people here, worse than him. It was easy here, because all they feared was communists. When I took no notice he said he knew I was a Czech, and he'd done his best to rid the world of Czechs.

'He asked me if I had heard of a town called Lidice, which had been incinerated and destroyed so that it no longer existed, and boasted he had contributed to that. Not in Lidice itself, but in Treblinka, where they had brought three truckloads of small children – not Jews, these children, just Czechs – and he and some of his *Kameraden* had been well paid to exterminate them. He actually said the word exterminate, as if he had done the rest of the world some favour.

'So I killed him, there, behind the workshops. I didn't stop to think of the consequences. I cut his throat – the carotid artery – before he could move or make a sound, then I hid the body while I spread oil and dirt to obscure any trace of blood.

'When Curly came back I asked him could I borrow a truck to go to Cooma. He wrote it down in his log, but I had no reason to fear that. I used a blanket so there would be no bloodstains, found a shovel, drove out to Kiandra, dug a grave and buried him. It should have worked; he was meant to disappear. If it hadn't rained, there'd have been no body and no trace of what had happened to him.'

Helen said, 'We talked about his being missing, remember? I told you Kerr was acting strangely and seemed to be suspicious. You tried to convince me that Vlasoff had run away.'

'I didn't like lying to you,' Sandor said. 'But without the rain everyone would have had to believe it. He'd have been buried when they laid all that concrete.'

'And your lie would have become the accepted truth,' she told him, and there was an awkward silence.

'Yes,' he finally responded. 'I know what you're thinking.'

'Do you, Sandor?'

'I swear I had no idea they'd suspect Michael. I thought I'd have to confess, but thank God he was cleared. You don't know the relief that brought me. Many times I wanted to tell you, but always there was this thought – why should I be imprisoned for killing this animal, this monster? Hadn't he persecuted and caused the death of your friend, Katryna? And the tiny children from Lidice. He got paid to kill them. He boasted that he could do this, and they weren't even Jews. As if killing Jews was easy. He told me those who refused this duty were sent to be killed in Russia. But he survived, and was smuggled out of Europe as some kind of hero – for murdering babies. Surely to God he deserved to die.'

'Yes, he deserved to die,' Helen said, 'I could never blame you.

But nor could I ever be at ease with you again, ever make love to you or feel any trace of affection.'

'Why?' he asked.

'Because you let me suffer all that time, when I was frantic about Michael. You let me feel afraid, and said nothing. To kill Josef Vlasoff was not a crime to me, but to remain silent was unforgivable.'

Sandor was pensive for a long time, digesting this.

'I'm sorry,' he said. 'I was in love with you, and afraid I'd lose you if I said anything. And now I have lost you.'

'I'm sorry, too,' Helen said.

'Will you tell the police?'

'The police no longer seem to be bothered. In view of what he was, perhaps the system may not want to catch his killer.'

'But will you tell them?'

'No. You'll be gone in a few weeks. Free to go back to Europe, if you want, or to study medicine here.'

'I wish that was possible. But they won't let me. Not here.'

'They will, if you want it badly enough. Fight them, Sandor. Make a fuss. Or else you'll remain a stranger and a foreign bastard.'

'And if it ever comes out, what I've done . . .'

'How can it? I doubt if we'll meet together like this again, so try to understand. Nobody should be punished for the death of that creature. As far as I'm concerned, you're as safe as if he really was beneath all that concrete. No-one else will ever know. Not Michael, not anyone at all. Just us.'

'I could've told you. It might have all been different.'

'It might've. We'll never know that. Because you didn't feel able to trust me.'

⁓

The cable from Italy was decoded, and a sealed copy was sent to Henry Falconer by special messenger. It was what he had feared, and the moment had come when Neil had to be told. Falconer invited him to lunch at the Black Tulip, ordered the most expensive bottle of wine on the restaurant's list, and broke the news.

Adams and Barlow were still in Milan. Mitchell, McGill, the Brigadier and several others had been interrogated over the course of the past month, and had finally indicated they were willing to name names. In return they would be allowed to plead guilty to some of their lesser crimes – virtual misdemeanours, Falconer said angrily – for which they would receive light or even suspended sentences.

A decision had been taken in Canberra, at the highest level, to accept this. As he had expected, the alternative had been rejected as too costly, requiring an extensive number of witnesses for long periods. There was also dispute on whether crimes committed overseas, even in the service of the Commonwealth, could be tried in Australia. Whenever the trials took place, the question of jurisdiction would be a major argument, and a successful outcome in either country was by no means certain.

'So no real trials.' Henry Falconer took a long sip of his wine as if he might find some solace there. 'Just a legal charade, to get the maximum amount of information at the minimum cost.'

Unfortunately, he went on to explain, Stewart Mitchell had not only learned the source of their intelligence, but he had actually heard Neil's voice on tape, because Adams and Barlow had used the series of recordings to shock them into confessions. Afterwards, Mitchell had dictated a long statement that implicated

Neil Latham in a conspiracy, forging documents, and fraudulently arranging the false immigration papers be provided to two Hungarians, Helen and Michael Francis, who had criminal records under their former name of Ferencz.

Over the second bottle of the restaurant's best wine, Falconer explained that, despite his own best endeavours to have the matter filed and forgotten, it was not going to happen because Mitchell had refused to cooperate with Adams and Barlow unless action was taken against Neil. He defied them to go ahead with their case against him; they would have to start with lengthy extradition proceedings in the Italian courts, and if they ever did manage to get him home, he'd fight them and appeal all the way to the Privy Council. Alternatively, he would comply with what they wanted, but only on his terms; they could make their own decision.

'You mean Mitchell blackmailed them into bringing charges against me?' Neil asked with disbelief.

'I'm afraid so.'

'Good God.'

'He claimed that if he and the others were pleading guilty, you also had a case to answer. Bloody Adams and Barlow sent details back to the mandarins in Canberra, who agreed. It was piss weak of them,' said Falconer, 'and fucking unfair.'

Neil had never heard Henry Falconer swear before. He was normally the model of a bland and outwardly proper public servant. Perhaps it was the second bottle of wine. Neil himself was stone cold sober, and wished he was otherwise. It was shockingly unfair.

He would face criminal charges: forgery, conspiracy – God alone knew what else they would throw at him. Even worse, as

Henry pointed out, the two he had tried to help would be taken into custody, and in due course, almost certainly be deported.

That night he told Sarah the entire story of the two young Hungarians; their escape, the capture by the *Wehrmacht* deserters, the failed attempt to reach Israel, the wasted years in refugee camps, until the day he had first seen them in the Milan Centre. And the decision he had taken there, to try to rescue them.

'It was bloody stupid,' he admitted, 'and conceited to think I could get away with it. But they were a pair of lost kids, and nobody was going to help them. They were angry and bewildered; they didn't fit anywhere; people had stopped caring about what happened to them. They'd have ended up as human debris. I had to try to help them.'

'There's nothing wrong with that,' Sarah said, distressed by the news, although she had long been aware of something troubling him. 'You helped a lot of people. That must be taken into account, surely. I'll offer to go to court, if they insist on charging you, and testify. I'm living proof of how you helped us in Belsen. I'm here, safe and enjoying a decent life, because of you.'

'That was different. This was a rash and dangerous thing to do in that place, among those people. To be honest, I thought I'd covered my tracks. I was nowhere near as smart as I imagined. And now Henry Falconer's had no option but suspend me. I'm to stop assisting migrants in any way and cease handling the urgent cases in the pipeline. Orders from on high.'

He was shaken by the abrupt rapidity of events. It had always been a threat since that distant day in strike-bound Naples, in the bar of the Albergo with Mitchell, but as time passed he had begun to relax and believe it might never surface again. The killing of a Polish delinquent who had become an SS officer had changed all that.

'If they bring a charge, how long before it happens?'

'I don't know. Henry is going to try to delay it if he can. But it's inevitable, I'm afraid. Perhaps a few months, maybe six if we're lucky.'

In his room later, he sat and watched the glimmer of the new moon on the harbour. He knew what he had to do, although it was probably another infringement. Well, to hell with that. At least they must be warned, so they could make their own decision. He sat down, and took a writing pad and his fountain pen.

Dear Helen, he began, then sat staring helplessly at the page, wondering how to break this kind of news.

PART THREE

1953–1954

Chapter 15

The train began to climb again as it reached a forest of candle bark trees, then emerged into bright morning sunlight. There was a wide expanse of hillside, sterile tufted grass splashed with outcrops of rock, dotted with red stringybarks and spotted gums. A flock of sheep grazed, doggedly trying to find nourishment, and a wedge-tailed eagle soared on an updraught towards distant peaks.

The guard came through the carriages to announce they would arrive at Cooma in fifteen minutes. The fly-fishing group woke to gather their rods and camping equipment, bleary-eyed after a sleep, and hungover from their night of non-stop drinking. They were after trout – they had continually informed their unfortunate fellow passengers – and going to have a few grogs by the river and catch a heap of the best game fish in the high country, the fighting mountain rainbows. Neil stretched his cramped limbs, relieved the trip was almost over, silently wishing the endangered rainbows the best of all possible luck.

He had made several vain attempts to write to Helen Francis. Night after night, certain that he had phrased it properly, that he'd finally conveyed the situation with regret as well as urgency – trying to intimate without saying it, that if they wanted to take evasive action then they should seriously start to consider this – only to realise the next morning that what he had written was too cold and clinical. It was impossible to inform her so abruptly of the situation, and the jeopardy she and her brother faced.

Discarded letters filled his wastepaper basket. It was not surprising Sarah noticed; she could hardly fail to be aware of it, or his increasing concern and despondency.

'You can't write this sort of news to people,' she'd said. 'Not you, anyway. You have too much sympathy, and you feel to blame.'

'I am to blame.'

Sarah had shown one of her rare moments of anger.

'Rubbish! You changed their documents to help them. Did they object? No, of course they didn't. Now it's gone wrong and you want to bear all the guilt.'

'I want to warn them.'

'Then do it. But not this way.'

'You mean go and see them?'

'Of course.'

'I've been trying to avoid that.'

'Why?'

'A sort of cowardice,' he'd admitted. 'I'm not sure I want to see them. Her brother's not easy to talk to. He'll certainly blame me. And she's . . .'

'She's what?'

He found it difficult to answer. He remembered her quite vividly, the first meeting in his office in Milan, when she told him about being raped by the German deserter while his comrades watched. Insisted on telling him, despite her brother's plea to remain silent. It had been painful for her, like lancing a wound, and perhaps had been done to gain his sympathy. Whether that was her intention or not, it had worked. He didn't know why; it was something he felt unable to express even to Sarah, but he was strangely diffident about meeting Helen again.

Yet here he was.

In the end, he had decided he owed her a personal explanation. As he was suspended from duty, it left him free to visit the Snowy or anywhere else, and so he had written – instead of the awkward letter – a polite note saying that he would be in the Cooma region very soon, and wished to discuss a matter of some importance with her.

He had absolutely no idea of the effect it would have, or the alarm it would cause her.

When his letter arrived, because personal mail was so rare, Helen immediately assumed it was from Michael. It had been weeks since his note, telling her about Kings Cross and giving their address. She had responded at once, and ever since had waited for a reply, becoming increasingly uneasy at the lack of news. Then, realising this was not Michael's handwriting, she saw on the back of the envelope the name Neil Latham, with a Sydney address. She felt surprise and a sudden excitement.

But when she read the letter it left her feeling chilled. It was very formal, studiously polite. He would soon be visiting Cooma, and *wished to discuss an important matter with her*. Although he did not say so, he must be in the same job. How else would he have known where to reach her? The important matter was obviously about her brother, illegally on the run from his work contract. There would be a hunt for Michael, and perhaps Neil Latham thought she could assist them in their inquiries.

She was unsure what to do. The letter seemed to require an answer, so she wrote back to the address. With equal formality and her best attempt at civility, she asked him to let her know when he might be visiting as she was always busy, but obviously hoped to be available to meet him, whatever matter it may be that he wished to expatiate with her. She chose the word *expatiate* with great care, first checking it in the dictionary, hoping it would convey that she was no longer as he had known her in Milan, a refugee and a pauper desperate to escape Europe and find a new domicile. Now, thoroughly at home here, she felt – as well as her fears for Michael – a resentment that Neil had surfaced from her past to remind her of those days of desolation.

His reply was brief, as if a sense of her irritation had conveyed itself to him. He thanked her for her reply, and said he would be coming to Cooma the following Saturday for the weekend, hoping it would be convenient. He intended to take the late express on Friday night, and if it was on time, which he gathered was rare, it would arrive at about 8 a.m. the next morning.

When the train pulled into Cooma station, she knew him at once. Tall and lean, in casual dungarees and a cotton shirt, he had a small leather suitcase. It was nearly eighteen months since she had seen him, but he seemed unchanged. She had no idea why, but she found that aggravating.

Don't be stupid, she told herself, *if you get angry because he has a job to do, that certainly won't help Miki. It's not his fault that Michael's got himself into bother. I'm sure he's been told to investigate, and it's wrong for me to feel antagonistic – just because he left the camp in Italy and never even bothered to say goodbye.*

'Hello,' Neil said, and she smiled and nodded a welcome as they met and shook hands. A noisy group carrying fishing rods and camping gear got off the train behind him. Several whistled at her, and shouted to Neil, who ignored them. 'This is a surprise. I didn't expect you to meet me.'

'You put the day and time of your arrival,' Helen said, 'so I felt I should be here. Or someone should.'

'Wasn't it inconvenient?' he asked.

'Not especially,' Helen said. She had a feeling of unreality about their meeting, and this whole conversation. 'I borrowed a jeep, and it was a lovely drive in. Just me and the mountains.'

'Just you, and not your brother?'

'I'm afraid not,' she said, wondering why he had said that.

'So will we meet with him later?'

This is surreal, Helen thought.

'You want to meet with Michael?'

'It concerns you both.'

'You mean you don't know?'

'Know what?'

He looked puzzled, and Helen realised he clearly did not know, and she had misread the whole situation. The reason for this visit – whatever it may be – was not what she had been dreading. She felt almost light-headed with relief. Behind them carriage doors clanged shut, the guard's whistle shrilled, and the train steamed out, on the last leg of its journey to Bombala. The noisy fishing group had gone, climbing into a waiting private bus. She hastily changed the subject.

'Where are you staying?' she asked. 'The Regency?'

'No.' He took a card from his pocket and looked at it. 'The Monaro Glenview Inn.'

'Oh God,' Helen said impulsively, 'it's awful.'

'Is it?'

'Truly. Tiny rooms, dreadful food. Everyone who stays there complains. Have you paid in advance?'

'No. But they're expecting me. I made a reservation.'

'We can soon fix that.' She went towards a public telephone box. Before he could offer to pay for the call, she produced pennies and inserted them. 'The Regency's a bit extra, if you don't mind.'

'I don't mind,' he said, still trying to come to terms with the change in her. There seemed no comparison to the painfully unhappy girl in the Milan camp. This one drove a jeep from Adaminaby, had an air of confidence – admittedly after a first moment of confusion – and was now discussing suitable rooms and taking steps to save him from the apparent horrors of the Glenview Inn.

'Right,' she said, hanging up. 'The Regency has a nice corner room onto the upstairs verandah. Breakfast included, three guineas.' She smiled. 'They're rather haughty, being the best hotel in town, so their prices are in guineas.'

'Like doctors and lawyers,' he said, and gave her the other hotel's reservation card. He watched her dial the number. This time the door of the phone box was ajar, so he could hear what was being said.

'Good morning. I'm speaking for Mr Neil Latham, who had a booking this weekend. No, he's in hospital, I'm afraid. Well, nothing too serious, but highly infectious. Scarlet fever. Yes, just as well he found out in time, or everyone might've caught it. I'm sure he'd love to come and stay, when he's out of quarantine.'

She agreed it was a pity, hung up, smiled at his expression, and tore the card in half. Neil started to feel the news he had to break could wait until a more suitable time. They went out to a waiting jeep.

'Would you like to drive?' Helen asked.

'You know the town better. I'm sure it's safer if you drive.'

'Don't be too certain,' she said, 'I only got my licence a month ago.'

'I'll take the chance,' Neil said, and they both smiled.

He felt a strange ambivalence; glad he had come, yet loath to think of the moment when he would have to confess to her what the future held. She looked so assured, relaxed, so utterly different. He wondered if her brother had adapted so readily.

'How's Michael?' he asked her, when they had to stop for a convoy of trucks transporting diggers and heavy machinery along the main street. 'Has he settled down?'

'This happens all the time. Trucks, traffic jams. The locals don't like it.' Then she said casually, deciding this had to be resolved without any further delay, 'Michael's not here.'

'Been transferred?'

'Not exactly.'

'Found another job?'

'Not even that. I thought this was the reason you're here.'

'What do you mean?'

She delayed replying, then thought there was no point in lying. Besides, she remembered him as being understanding.

'He left.'

'When?'

'About seven weeks ago.'

'Another job?'

'I don't know,' Helen admitted.

'Did he advise the employment office?'

'Not Michael. He just took off. Shot through, as he'd say. Which makes him illegal. I thought someone must've reported it, and that's why you were here.' She glanced at him. 'But it's not, is it?'

'No.'

She waited for him to expand on this, but he stayed silent. The trucks went past, and traffic began to move again. Helen pulled up in a side street beside a large and handsome hotel, uniquely Australian with wide upstairs verandahs, a landmark of so many country towns.

'It looks splendid. Thanks for being at the station. And for organising me,' Neil said.

She was puzzled by his strange lack of response. She didn't remember him as someone who evaded issues.

'Look, why are you here?' Again, she was conscious of the way he hesitated. 'You did write and say we had a matter to discuss. What kind of matter?'

'I'll explain later. If we can meet.'

'Whenever you want.'

'Shall I phone you? Do you have to go back to work?'

'No, I have the weekend off.' After a moment she added, 'And a loan of the jeep – if you'd like to see some of the district.'

'Could you wait while I book in and have a quick shower?'

'Of course.'

'Then I'd love to,' Neil said.

They met by accident, Michael and the Doctor. Very nearly collided, as they left their adjoining front doors, the Doctor from his substantial private house, and Michael emerging from the Roslyn Gardens residential on his way to break the news to Deirdre that he had walked off yet another job. He was reluctant to tell her, contemplating the likelihood that they might have another row, in the middle of the crowded California this time, where she had taken over from Liddy as a part-time waitress. They had had a huge row – but in the privacy of their room – after he had only lasted two weeks on the previous job, then collected his meagre pay and told the unfriendly and militant foreman to get stuffed.

The row between Deirdre and him over this had begun with a lot of shouting, and ended with tremendous passion and the rhythm of bedsprings, and it was this he was thinking about – the lovely enjoyment of making up – which was how he almost bumped into the Doctor.

The owner of the long johns didn't look in the least like an abortionist, or a surgeon who repaired shot gangsters. He was a small man, rather formally dressed, almost Victorian with a stiff high collar and a three-piece suit that must have once been expensive, but was now decidedly dated. He wore lace-up boots, and carried a bowler hat. His name, Michael knew from his landlady, was Dr Reginald Forbes-Clark.

'Steady, old son,' the Doctor warned, as they were on the point of collision.

'Sorry,' Michael said, stepping aside, about to go past.

'You're a neighbour. One of Andrea's occupants, I believe?' He held out his hand. 'You and that astonishingly alluring redhead.'

'If you mean Deirdre . . .'

'Marvellous-looking girl. I've noticed the pair of you. She absolutely drips sensuality.'

'Does she?' He was unsure whether this last remark was a compliment or an insult.

'You're a lucky young man,' the Doctor said, which seemed to indicate it was definitely complimentary.

'Thanks,' Michael said. He was about to walk away.

'Looking for a job, or have you found one?'

For a moment Michael hesitated, but Forbes-Clark appeared friendly and interested.

'I've found three since we moved here – and left the third about an hour ago,' he admitted.

'None to your liking? Or was there some other problem?'

'Just dumb jobs. Boring. This was storing and packing goods. I was supposed to join the union, or they were going to hold a stop-work meeting on Monday. I thought, to hell with being a storeman and packer, so I told them to shove it, collected a week's pay and left.'

'And now what?'

'Dunno,' Michael said, starting to resent this inquisition.

'There's plenty of employment.'

'I know that. Easy over on Parramatta Road to pick up a job in five minutes. Washing cars, or brickie's labourer.'

'You want something better?'

'Wouldn't you?'

'There's jobs around here,' Forbes-Clark said. 'Never mind Parramatta Road or the suburbs. You could try something local.'

He stopped beside a dark green Bentley that looked brand new. Michael had never seen one before, but he recognised the insignia on the bonnet, and he could tell it was expensive.

'I'm not qualified for anything much. We could never get any work in Europe. Or learn much, except how to survive. Builder's labourer was the job the government gave me out here.'

'So you've done your two years? Free to please yourself.'

'That's right,' said Michael without hesitation, and watched the Doctor unlock the door of the gleaming Bentley.

'Where's the lovely girl?'

'At the California.'

'You meeting her?'

'Yes. She's waitressing part-time.'

'Hop in and I'll give you a lift there. It's on my way.'

There's one thing about a car like this, Michael thought as they drove along Macleay Street and turned into Darlinghurst Road, with people's eyes admiring the Bentley, *it makes you feel like a prince*.

'I'm early for an appointment,' the Doctor said. 'Why don't we have a drive out to the beach, to show you how the Bentley travels. We might even discuss a job, and see if it interests you.'

Cooma had little in the way of historic buildings to offer, and after a brief look at St Paul's Church, the courthouse and the Victorian cottages in Lambie Street, they left the overcrowded town. Saturday, as Helen explained, always brought in hundreds from the nearby Snowy camps; by mid-afternoon the pubs would be packed, there'd be fights in the streets, racial conflicts between new and old Australians, and by nightfall the cells at the police station would be crowded.

She took the Kosciusko Road, and they stopped at Berridale for lunch at the old inn. Over a salad, with freshly made damper – which Neil had never tasted and pronounced delicious – she told him about their first primitive camp, in the hills above the snow line.

'Tents – in winter?'

'Not me. But all the men. And straw beds . . .'

'Palliasses,' Neil said. 'God, we had them in the army. But not in mountain country, in the freezing cold. Old Lawrenson must be a real penny-pinching bastard.'

'Well, he's Hungarian,' she said mischievously, and watched his reaction.

'You're joking.'

She shook her head. 'He came here before the war. In 1938. His name was Tibor Esterhazey in those days. He started as a builder, but it was a hard time. He didn't succeed until the housing shortage after the war.'

'Is this true?'

'Absolutely.'

'Who told you?'

'He did.'

Neil tried to conceal his astonishment. With anyone else, he might have been sceptical, but it was so patently genuine that all he could do was engross himself in his meal, while he reflected on the metamorphosis of the pallid and dejected girl he had expected to encounter. Helen Francis was not at all as he remembered her.

'Quite a lot's happened to you since we met,' he finally said.

'Yes, Neil. Quite a lot.'

They meant it in very different ways. Helen had no intention of disclosing the misery of those first months, or the ordeal she had endured with Angus Kerr. Her arm was out of plaster and restored to full mobility, so there was no need to speak of her time in hospital. No need to recall the events of Christmas, nor speak of Sandor, who had left a week ago, after a brief and painful attempt to say goodbye to her. Despite her air of assurance, bolstered by the relief of knowing this visit had nothing to do with Michael, she had secrets to keep.

Neil had intended his remark as a compliment, impressed by her and the way she had adapted so successfully. Yet he began to recognise that it also made his task harder. For what he had to tell her, when he could find the right moment to do so, was going to cause havoc in her new life, and ruin so much more than he had realised.

After lunch, they drove through Jindabyne and up the alpine road over Wollondibby Creek. The surface was graded and the jeep handled it easily. Later the road deteriorated and became little more than a cattle trail. Where they finally stopped, high above the Thredbo River, a sign pointed to Dead Horse Gap. Someone had painted a message there: GO BACK. DO NOT PASS GO. DO NOT COLLECT £200.

The afternoon was still warm, and they climbed a ridge from where they could see a magical view. Carpets of wild lupins extended into forests of ash and cypress pine, and beyond that were glimpses of the three granite rocky peaks.

'The chimneys,' Helen said. 'That must be them; they even look like chimney pots.'

'Where's Kosciusko?' Neil wondered.

But it was too far away, lost in drifting cloud that sheltered the high summits.

She knew it was time to talk, to learn the reason he had come here. She could feel his growing tension. They walked a short way along the ridge, until they found adjoining rocks where they could sit.

He began to tell her.

He made no mention of seeing the police file, or reading her testimony of what Mrs Dyboski had told her. That could wait. It was best to keep it simple – and short. The sequence of events, beginning with the phone call on New Year's Eve when Henry Falconer had called him to the office. How the murder of Josef Vlasoff had focused attention on the Milan Centre, because the Pole was processed through there. And the personal pressure brought on him, to reveal what he knew of the corruption that had taken place in that camp.

He told her about Adams and Barlow, *Mr A* and *Mr B* from ASIO, and the spools of tape; how they had been used – really misused by being played direct to Mitchell – after Neil had cooperated and told everything he knew. Enough to put the group behind bars where they belonged, but in the end other, easier choices had been made.

Finally, he told her of the blackmail card Stewart Mitchell had held for so long, and had now played – and how it threatened to destroy both their lives.

'Your life and mine – and Michael's,' he remembered to add.

She had listened without saying a word. It was even difficult to read her expression.

'I'm sorry, Helen.'

'It wasn't your fault,' she said. 'We'd better get back.'

The clouds had thickened and drifted lower, obscuring the view of the granite chimney stacks. The sun had lost its warmth, as it went behind a forest of snow gums. There was barely sufficient time to drive back to Cooma before it was dark.

~

'What sort of a job?'

Deirdre had not bunged on a blue as he thought she might, and had even admitted she didn't think he'd last the week. She could not imagine him as a storeman and packer; she had said so after her amazement at seeing him step out of the Bentley, and enter the California with a farewell wave to Dr Forbes-Clark. But when they reached the security of their room, she was more than suspicious about the offer of a job by the city's leading abortionist.

'Come on, you think I'm a ninny? Anything he offered you would be as crooked as a two-bob watch. So what sort of job is it?'

Michael suggested they could discuss it more easily in bed, and she told him to behave himself. They were going out to meet Liddy and her boyfriend for dinner, and before that she wanted a bath, but first she had to know what sort of trouble he was getting himself into.

'He admires you,' Michael said. 'Alluring, he called you. Said you drip sensuality.'

'Dirty old bastard,' Deirdre said. 'Him and his long johns.'

'It's a great car, that Bentley. A mark six.'

'Stop messing about, and tell me what he offered.'

'A sort of manager. Part-manager, I suppose.'

'Of what?'

'He's bought into a club, gone partners with a bloke called Jimmy Kincaid.'

'Jimmy Kincaid's a notorious racing identity. At least that's what *Truth* calls him. Which means a crook. What sort of club is it?' she asked suspiciously.

'Baccarat.'

'Baccarat? That's illegal.'

'It's got to be illegal, Deirdre. No gambling is legal. Don't worry, we've got police protection.'

'Did he tell you that?'

'He told me lots. He took me for a run in the Bentley, all the way to Watson's Bay, while he put this deal to me. The Doc's invested money in the club, but he doesn't trust Kincaid. That's why he wants me to work there. To sort of keep order in the place, plus keep an eye on Kincaid.'

'That's not a manager,' Deirdre said, 'that's a bouncer.'

'Like hell it is. At eighty quid a week?'

'*How much?*'

'He said fifty, I wanted a hundred. We haggled till he stuck on eighty. I can hire a bouncer for peanuts if I want one.'

'Strewth,' she said, impressed by what was many times the basic wage.

'Also,' Michael said carefully, 'there's something else.'

'Like what?'

'If you'll learn how to deal cards, he said you'll get paid eight pounds a session. Six sessions a week.'

'Holy Moses,' she said. 'Eight sixes are forty-eight quid!'

'He wants really good-looking sheilas. Says they bring in the punters, and the bigger the tits the more careless it makes the blokes with their bets. Only in your case, it'd be your sensuality and red hair, and looking like Rita Hayworth. Plus tits.'

'The dirty old bugger,' she laughed.

'He said if we put you in a low-cut tight-fitting velvet gown, they'd all lose their shirts.'

'As long as it's not their trousers.'

'Come off it. I wouldn't agree to anything like that.'

'Between us we'd make . . .'

'A hundred and twenty-eight a week,' Michael said, 'and a cut of the take if I boost earnings and keep Kincaid's hand out of the till.'

'Seems too good to be true,' Deirdre said, suddenly nervous. 'I mean why you? Why us?'

'He wants someone new to the scene. Someone he can trust.'

'That sounds like bullshit. He's never even met you before.'

'He's been watching us. Checking things.'

'And just decided he can trust us?'

'No. He said if he paid enough, he'd know he could trust us. Also, he found out I haven't done my two years. I said I had, but he'd checked up before he made the offer. So he could dob me in.'

'Shit.'

'Only he won't, because we're friends.'

'Doesn't feel friendly. Feels more like blackmail.'

'No, we're definitely all friends.'

'Are we?'

'Definitely. Because we want his hundred plus a week, tax free. And he needs someone he can control – which is me. And I'll tell you what else, Deedee.' He put his arms around her and felt the heat of their bodies begin to stir. 'If I learn to drive, he's got a cop on the payroll who'll give me a licence, no questions. When he's satisfied I'm doing a good job, he says we can borrow the Bentley and drive down to Palm Beach to his weekend place, for a few days' honeymoon.'

'Honeymoon?'

'Yeah. What do you think?'

'Are you asking me to marry you?'

'Not if you don't like the idea.'

'You great galah,' she said, 'I love the idea. I love you. Tell you what – Liddy can wait, 'cos we should celebrate.'

'How?'

'You know how,' she said, and pushed him on the bed. 'Engaged! Wait till my dad hears. It'll kill him!' She laughed joyously and began to remove his clothes.

Much later they came downstairs. After their rapturous love making, some of Deirdre's earlier concerns had revived.

'You think he'd trust us with his Bentley? He must be mad.'

'He wants us. He won't renege.' Michael was confident.

What he failed to say, thinking it more tactful not to, was that Forbes-Clark had been the one to suggest marriage.

'It's commonsense,' he had said. 'You love the girl, and she's nuts about you. Anyone can tell that. And marriage is an honourable estate,' he chuckled, 'because it makes you an Australian, and keeps you safe from any hassle by the immigration department.'

There was no point in spoiling the day by telling Deirdre that, he decided. They were going to stay together, anyway. He'd always hoped they'd get married. This was just advancing matters, and it did make sense like the Doctor said.

As they reached the ground floor, the phone rang. Andrea came out of her tiny apartment to answer it.

'If that's Liddy,' Deirdre said, 'say we got held up.'

'Yes, duckie,' Andrea said, thinking it was a long time since she'd been held up like that, and envying them. But it wasn't Liddy on the phone. It was a trunk call from Cooma, for Michael. First an operator, then a young female voice.

'It's his sister,' the voice said.

'Just a moment.'

She hurried to the front door, but saw the lights of a taxi, and the rear door closing as it drove away. She went back to tell the caller she'd just missed him.

Helen sat in the busy lounge of the Regency Hotel, which was crowded with festive Saturday night dinner parties and cheerful weekend guests. The hubbub of chatter and bright laughter around her added to her sense of bleak despair.

She saw Neil coming down the stairs from his room. *It wasn't your fault*, she had told him, and meant it, but all the same she wished they were not having dinner tonight. It had been stupid to agree. What could they possibly find to talk about all through a painful evening? Him facing charges? Her facing deportation?

'Neil,' she said, when he made his way across the lounge to where she waited, 'I think I should go home. I mean back to the construction camp. I'm sorry, but I don't think I could eat anything.'

'I doubt if I could,' he said. 'But I thought we might try.'

'I just can't. I hope you don't mind.'

'I could hardly insist on us sitting pretending, if you feel this way. Did you talk to your brother?'

'He was out. I'll ring him in the morning, from the camp.'

'What are you going to tell him?'

'To hide,' she said. 'Miki's good at survival.'

'And what are you going to do?'

'I don't know. At the moment, face the drive home, and get some sleep. Then tomorrow, try to think about it.'

'I'm afraid it was a hell of a shock,' Neil said, 'coming like this. Perhaps, after all, it would've been better if I'd written. I tried to often enough, but Sarah persuaded me this would be best.'

They went out of the hotel, to where the jeep was parked.

'Who's Sarah?' she asked curiously. It was a name she hadn't heard before.

'I live with her.'

'Oh.'

It was so casual. Nonchalant. Like a dash of cold water in the face. They reached the jeep and paused there.

'Will you be all right driving home?'

'I'll manage. It's only thirty miles.'

'On a dark road. And not much of one. Rough in places.'

'Please don't worry about me. It was kind of you to come all this way. And I'm sure your friend Sarah meant well. Is she someone you met here, or in England?'

'In Belsen,' he said.

And held out his hand.

She took it, in a state of confusion. She wanted to ask questions, but they were shaking hands.

'Life's a bugger sometimes, isn't it? Goodbye, Helen.'

She said goodbye and got into the jeep, as he walked back to the hotel. Then he stood at the door; she could see him watching her. She felt like crying, but you couldn't do that on a Saturday night in the crowded streets of Cooma – groups of men eyeing her, ready to whistle an invitation – so she started the jeep and drove away.

Chapter 16

Michael was conscious of Andrea Allison's open door, so his replies to Helen were carefully monosyllabic. He liked the elderly actress who was their landlady, but was well aware of her capacity for gossip. She had a wide circle of friends who came to play bridge and drink tea, and news like this would travel fast, so after he realised the seriousness of what his sister was telling him, he spoke in Hungarian.

'I'll be all right,' he said. 'In fact a lot's happened, but too much to explain now. I'll write and tell you.'

'Don't put an address on the letter,' Helen said.

'You think it's that bad?'

'Let's assume the worst, in case. It's lucky you told me the name of the lady who owns the house. That's how I got the number. Will you be staying there?'

'For a while. Deirdre and I might be going up in the world. Also, we're getting married.'

'Michael! When? I mean when did you decide?'

'Yesterday. And I think the ceremony might be sooner rather than later – if you see what I mean.'

'Yes, I do. I wish I could be there.'

'Me too.'

'Will you tell Deirdre about this?'

'Yes,' he said, without hesitation.

'Good. I think you should.'

'I promise,' he said.

'Give her my love. Say I'm glad.'

'I will.'

He glanced at Deirdre, who sat on the first flight of stairs, just above where the telephone hung in the hallway, legs tucked demurely beneath her skirt. They had both spent a restless night, troubled by the urgency of a call from Helen, and she was looking concerned, unable to understand a word of what was being said.

He blew her a kiss, and said in English: 'Helen sends her love. She's glad about our news.'

Deirdre smiled. 'Tell her we'll send her an invitation.'

I haven't told you yet, but there won't be time, he thought, and went back to speaking in Hungarian.

'Why don't you skip, Iluska? Come to Sydney. We'll find you a place to stay.' Even as he was saying it, he knew she wouldn't.

'I'll think about it. I'm not sure that's best.'

'What's better? Being chucked on a boat and sent back? Or put in some illegal immigrant detention centre?'

'It may not come to that.'

'Of course it will.'

The second lot of pips went.

'I'll have to hang up,' Helen said. 'I've run out of coins.'

'Take care,' he said swiftly.

'You too, Mikloska.'

The endearment brought a rush of emotion. It was like an affectionate echo of their childhood, but before he could reply she was gone and a dial tone was all that remained. He hung up, feeling a great tenderness for her, as well as a deep anxiety.

'What's wrong?' Deirdre came down to join him.

'Nothing,' Michael said, aware of Andrea emerging to ask if all was well. Both were clearly curious why he had switched into a foreign language.

'Everything's great. Her arm's better, she's got a new boss, and she's thrilled about us.' Deirdre looked puzzled, aware the news about her arm and the boss had been in a letter weeks ago. She saw his expression, which promised there'd be more to tell, upstairs in private.

'What's "us" mean?' Andrea asked, as he knew she would.

'We're getting married.'

'My dears, how wonderful.'

'What are you doing on Thursday?' Michael asked. 'How would you like to be a witness?'

'This Thursday?' Deirdre stared at him, amazed. 'We were talking of next month. Not that I mind, but what's our rush?'

'I decided I couldn't take a chance,' Michael said.

'Chance of what?'

'Of someone making you a better offer.'

Andrea clapped her hands and pronounced it romantic.

'Sounds just like my third husband,' she said. '*Très gallant* – and always in a hell of a hurry.'

Helen went down to the canteen, where she bought a packet of LifeSavers to get the required change, then returned to the phone box, dialled the number of the Regency Hotel, and asked if Mr Neil Latham had vacated his room.

A woman's voice said she was the relieving receptionist and the assistant manager would be the one to ask. Would she please wait?

She waited, rehearsing an apology for leaving him abandoned there last night, knowing no-one, probably having a wretched meal on his own. She had spent an almost sleepless night, feeling guilty, yet realising it would have been a dreadful and miserable evening. This morning, strangely, she felt fresh and invigorated, and even reassured by her phone call to Michael.

There was something different about her younger brother – her baby brother, she thought fondly – as if he had jumped a few years in his life, had overnight matured and become older. She smiled at the notion of this, recalling how he had always wanted to be older, always lied in the DP camps about his age in the hope that it would make him eligible for America or Canada.

Too old, too soon, she thought, remembering the small boy who used to take off his yellow star of David, and set out to steal food to keep the elderly people in the ghetto from starving. His voice on the phone such a short time ago had triggered off tender memories.

How he was their Mikloska, their little treasure.

Old Mr Gutinsky in Buda, chortling over his cheekiness.

That young Miklos, he makes me laugh, he's a card.

And her acerbic reply – '*He's a card all right*' – desperately worried about the risks he took. The way he enjoyed danger, ran through the streets, a target for any Nazi sharpshooter who wanted to kill someone. But the old people did not listen to her concerns. While they were fond of her, they depended on Michael and they loved him.

In a way, she realised, his marriage might help if migration investigators ever caught up with him. She had a feeling of sudden buoyancy, almost of euphoria. She smiled, thinking she would back Miki against Mr A and Mr B of ASIO any time.

A male voice on the phone asked if she was still there.

Neil, she said, and a moment later realised it wasn't him, and didn't even sound like him. The voice apologised for the delay. He was the assistant manager. Mr Latham had gone, he said. Left quite early that morning, hoping to catch the 8.30 express.

Helen thanked him, and hung up. Two people were queued to use the phone box as she moved away. It would be a long and lacklustre day. She had visualised a picnic, a quite different day to the previous one, perhaps even able to discuss the situation and be relaxed with each other.

She had also hoped he might explain more about the woman called Sarah, whom he lived with, and had met in Belsen.

The train journey seemed endless. He read the Sunday papers for a time. There was an article in one exposing the rise of illegal gambling clubs, and a bland denial by the Commissioner of Police that such places existed, or if they did, were certainly not protected by his elite anti-gambling squad. An editorial derided this statement, claiming any raids by the squad were always known to clubs in advance, and quoted a visiting American judge that Sydney was the equal of Las Vegas as one of the gambling capitals of the world, the only difference being that in the State of Nevada it was legal.

A disgrace, the newspaper trumpeted. Organised crime was running riot in New South Wales, the State of Corruption. Dozens of such clubs existed, where wealthy society people, criminals and show business personalities mixed nightly to gamble safely under police and political protection. The paper, steering a fine line between defamation and the sort of scandal the public savoured, made reference to the well-known Macquarie Street surgeon, Dr Reginald Forbes-Clark, who flatly denied that he was part owner of an infamous den in Kings Cross, known as the Barbary Coast.

Neil put the paper aside, and looked out the window. They were approaching the outer suburbs. It was flat and mainly treeless. Land had been subdivided. A new housing estate was half built; full of small affordable houses with a familiar sign: A SIR CEDRIC LAWRENSON PROJECT. It was a painful reminder of Helen. He tried to think only of their amusing lunch, her transformation, the confident way she had adapted, and not about the remainder of the day.

It had come as too great a shock, told abruptly like that. The news had devastated her. The drive back along the Thredbo River had seemed twice as far, an awful and silent journey in which they could find little to say, and it was then, as a means of breaking the restraint between them, that he had suggested dinner.

That had been a mistake. Leaving her to make a phone call to her brother, while he went to his room to change, it had been almost with relief that he had come downstairs to be told she'd prefer to cancel dinner. Yet as the lights of her jeep drove away he had felt dejected. Unable to eat, he had gone into the bar and sat alone; unable to stand the bar, he had gone to bed and there, unable to sleep, spent a long night wondering how he should have handled it. Perhaps, when you were telling someone their new life was to be wrecked through no fault of their own, there was no easy way.

The train clattered into Central station. Neil walked across

Hyde Park, and boarded a tram near the Supreme Court building that took him into William Street and up the hill to Kings Cross. He got out at the section stop on the corner, and bought flowers for Sarah.

Across the road, in the renowned snack bar, the Hasty-Tasty, Michael and Deirdre were having an early meal with Liddy and her actor boyfriend, Todd Martin, prior to attending a revue at the Phillip Street Theatre, which was to be followed by a party. Michael glimpsed a figure, overnight case in one hand, flowers in the other, starting to walk away into Darlinghurst Road.

'Good Christ,' he said, 'hang on. I'll be back.'

He ran out of the cafe, and began to cross the street. A tram came past the Hampton Court Hotel, the driver furiously clanging his warning bell, and he jumped back only just in time. A car squealed on its brakes to avoid him, and the driver started shouting about lunatics who wanted to be run over so they would get their stupid bloody names in the paper.

In the Hasty-Tasty, Deirdre glimpsed the near accident and ran to the door to yell at him.

'Don't get killed. You're getting married.'

She heard a gust of laughter from the crowded cafe behind her, but was in no mood to acknowledge it, watching anxiously while he let the tram pass, the uniformed driver now also shouting abuse, then dodged his way through the traffic with car horns honking at him until he reached the other side.

He waved to calm her, and looked for Neil. He was too late. A bus was leaving for Macleay Street, and he saw the colourful flowers as Neil swung himself aboard the moving vehicle. For a moment he contemplated trying to catch the bus before it picked up speed. But it was on the far side of the street, and he had to cross yet another line of traffic. The risk wasn't worth it. Besides, what could he learn that hadn't already been told to Helen and passed on by her in the phone call? Although that wasn't the reason why he'd chased him.

He went back to Deirdre, waiting outside the snack bar.

'You're right,' he said, 'I won't get killed. I'll get married.'

'You great drongo,' she said fondly. 'You big dill.'

She bunched her fists and beat him on the chest. He laughed and defended himself by wrapping her tightly in his arms, ignoring the interested audience inside the Hasty-Tasty.

'It was Neil Latham.'

'Was it? Well, he'd do you about as much good as the driver of that tram. You don't really want him to know that you live around here. Not if he's going to be in all kinds of trouble, and might get asked lots of questions.'

'No, you're right,' he said. 'I just feel sorry for him, that's all. He did help us in Milan, when nobody else could be bothered.'

'But you can't help him. From what Helen said, no-one can.'

'I'd still like to have said hello, and wished him well.'

'You're a softie,' Deirdre said fondly. 'You might talk and act rough, but inside you're about as tough as a marshmallow.'

In the end it was ten more days – Wednesday week – before they could be married. It was not just a matter of deciding you wanted to tie the knot; there were formalities. One week's notice of intention to wed. A form to be filled in by the Registrar of Marriages. A birth certificate required by each of them, and in Deirdre's case, being three months short of her twenty-first birthday, parental consent.

'We'll never get that,' she said.

'We don't need it. The Doc's already got a forger busy on my new birth certificate. He can run off a Miller Agricultural Supplies letterhead, and then write a letter from your dad saying how pleased he is you're marrying me.'

'Let's not overdo it,' she laughed. 'He'd die if he knew.'

In due course all the documents were presented and they were married at the Bondi Junction registry office, with Liddy and Andrea Allison as witnesses.

The promised honeymoon at Palm Beach had to wait; not only had Michael not yet had time for driving lessons, but he was already installed at the new club. He was fitted with a white tuxedo, Deirdre with a figure-hugging velvet dress, and even the Doctor's partner, Jimmy Kincaid, who had not welcomed their arrival, had to admit they looked a stylish couple.

The seedy den, formerly known as the Barbary Coast, had been discreetly renamed Maison Lumière; its premises renovated and transformed. The former concrete entrance and dank stairwell now boasted plush carpet. Embossed wallpaper with framed prints of historic Sydney scenes lent an air of decorum. Upstairs, the refurbishment was even more elegant. Chandeliers replaced cheap lightshades. Thick Wilton superseded stained floor coverings. Padded chairs around sturdy gambling tables catered for a more exclusive clientele. Although the club had no official liquor licence, a bar was installed, and experienced staff carefully recruited.

Following the Sunday newspaper article, Dr Forbes-Clark's name did not appear on the lease of the premises, although another document, held in his lawyer's safe, listed him as owning eighty per cent of the club shares, and James Kincaid twenty per cent. On the lease itself, which might be subject to possible public scrutiny, neither partner's name appeared. The lessee was listed as Michael Francis, although Michael had no knowledge of this, and had not signed his name on any paper. The Doctor's forger took care of that small detail.

Deirdre was given a crash course in dealing cards from the shoe. She swiftly learned the rules of baccarat, a duel between the player and the bank. Two cards to the player, two to the bank, with a count of nine or the nearest to it being a winning score. She learned that aces counted as one and court cards and tens were zero. On these rather shallow and simple rules vast amounts were bet. A hundred pounds was commonplace; a thousand not unusual. Outside in the real world, average wages were rising to twelve pounds a week.

In the Maison Lumière, masquerading as a 'social club', the hours were from six in the evening until eight the following morning; if there were players still left at that hour, they were served a lavish breakfast. For Michael, ostensibly the front of house manager, but also obliged to keep watch on Kincaid's well-known propensity for a dip in the till, the hours were arduous, but he thrived on the change in his lifestyle.

He was unfailingly cheerful and well-mannered, even when dealing with drunks and sore losers, and soon became a familiar figure to the regular gamblers and their wives – particularly the wives. Impressed by his virile good looks and his youth, they thought him a distinct improvement on some of the gorillas in dinner jackets whom they'd encountered at other clubs. They spread the word to their friends who came to take a look for themselves, while the males queued up to bet at any table where Deirdre happened to be dealing.

The grapevine let it be known there was a new place at the Cross, which had a bit of style about it. Reginald Forbes-Clark, who prided himself on his judgement, thought he had chosen particularly well in selecting the young migrant and his well-stacked girlfriend. He prevailed on them to keep their marriage a secret within the confines of the club, and in return agreed he could raise Michael's wages to one hundred pounds a week, and offer Deirdre even more sessions.

Before the end of the month his new club was packed nightly. A regular payment to the police ensured there would be no surprises – like unexpected raids. Michael set up 'cockatoos' just in case, one man guarding the front of the building and the main entrance, another in the rear lane, both these sentinels on full-time watch with warning buzzers. Kincaid complained about the unnecessary expense but was outvoted by the Doctor, who declared that while some of his best friends were policemen, with a force as corrupt as Sydney's finest you couldn't be too careful.

Forbes-Clark agreed with Michael that their fashionable clientele, diplomats, businessmen, barristers, judges and their women who more usually graced the social pages would not take kindly to being hauled off in paddy wagons, arraigned, fined, and lampooned in the *Daily Mirror*'s headlines. Jimmy Kincaid merely shrugged and said nothing further, but he was beginning to deeply resent Doctor Reginald Forbes-Clark, and even more so his upstart Hungarian protégé.

Michael was aware of Kincaid's enmity, and knew that some day he could expect trouble from this quarter. Though the thought was never far from his mind, he gave no outward sign. He and Deirdre went looking for somewhere more suitable to live, and found a perfect waterfront apartment at Elizabeth Bay with sweeping views down the harbour to the mansions of Darling Point and the grandeur of Middle Head. The rent was expensive, but they could afford it. In the initial stages, the agent had mentioned an intimidating amount of key money; Michael said he would talk it over with his friend Reggie Clark, and somehow the matter was never referred to again.

He was deliriously happy. Deirdre was courted and drooled over in the club by people whose names were a byword – celebrities from show business and the world of sport, not forgetting millionaire businessmen – but she showed no interest in their advances. She and Michael worked themselves to exhaustion with the long hours, but their leisure time was wonderful, beyond all his dreams. If he had one wish, it was that Helen could be here to see this miracle. He dearly wanted his sister to stand on this balcony with him and watch the view, the busy ferries passing, the passenger liners and cargo ships arriving almost daily from all parts of the world.

It seemed impossible, looking back nearly eight years ago to their escape from Hungary, to recall the sequence of bleak refugee camps, the despairing years of being regarded as sub-human, being despised and overlooked, having to thieve and lie to even manage to survive – until at last, in Milan, an Englishman had listened and said he would help them.

Not only had he done so, but the same man was now in serious trouble, and Michael was distressed, wanting to assist him. But he had no idea how to do this. Or even where to find him. He was aware that none of this astonishing fortune would have happened, but for Neil Latham, and it increasingly occupied his mind. In the meantime, he loved Deirdre and became aware that she looked admiringly each time they passed a showroom where a Jaguar sports convertible was on display. Once they saw one driving by, and she turned to gaze at it.

'Nice car?' he asked her.

'Fantastic,' she said.

The following day he asked the Doctor for a loan against his salary, and went out and bought one, registering it in her name.

Chapter 17

'The court will rise,' the clerk intoned, as the Judge entered.

Neil stood with the others.

Number four court was not made for crowds, nor expecting them. Although less than twenty people were present, there were few spare seats. The Judge wore his wig and scarlet robes, despite the fact that there was no jury.

'All sit,' the clerk said.

Lawyers shuffled papers. One muttered that the accused looked a decent enough sort of bloke, decidedly less villainous than some of their legal brethren and the police. His companion said it was getting difficult to tell the difference between cops and crooks. He was not sure if this meant a better class of criminal, or a shadier type of cop. Meanwhile Neil looked across at the empty seats where a jury might have sat, and wondered if he had been wise about the eminent counsel Henry Falconer had obtained for him.

'You can't trust a jury,' the QC had said. 'Liable to be a bunch of racist pricks. So leave it to His Honour.'

'But what's racism got to do with it?' Neil had asked.

'Well, you helped a couple of Hungarian Jews,' the barrister shrugged. 'Might have two strikes against you there. After all, a jury's twelve ordinary people, supposedly good and true. It's entirely possible they might dislike Yids. And equally likely they might detest Hungarians. Lots of people hate both. Easy to hate, really.'

'Why?' Neil was appalled at the man he had been given to defend him. 'For Christ's sake, why are they easy to hate?'

'Don't get hot under the collar, old man,' the lawyer advised.

'I'm not getting hot under the collar,' he was carefully calm, 'but I don't think I want you to represent me.'

'Rather too late, old chap. I'm your barrister.'

'It's not too late, and you're not my barrister. So sod off.'

'You can't be serious!'

He was from a famous legal family, unused to being dismissed in such terms. His father had been an eminent Chief Justice.

'I'm serious,' Neil said. 'I'd rather plead guilty than have a bigoted bastard like you defend me.'

It had created a minor legal circus that gyrated around him for several days, while the Prosecutor tried to establish whether he was changing his plea. The Crown had a watertight case, and if the accused was dismissing his august barrister and pleading not guilty with no representation, it might cause all manner of complications. Foremost in the Prosecutor's mind was a possible ruling that a fair trial could not proceed until this situation was resolved, which was a nonsense because the case was so conclusive it should only take an hour or two to achieve a conviction. So confident was the Prosecutor, that on the day it was listed for hearing, there was a special Lords Taverner's lunch for which he had accepted, certain this rather seedy matter would be settled by then, and he need not stint on the red wine.

Henry Falconer had been upset, telling Neil his dismissal of counsel had been impulsive and unwise. Perhaps an apology was in order. After all, they both knew there was little defence against the charges, and the reason for engaging the celebrated Mr Tobias Shaw had been for his noted eloquence in pleas of mitigation. And it made sense they had no jury, even if the barrister's remarks had not been in the best of taste. Neil agreed on a trial without a jury, but remained determined about the advocate. Tobias Shaw QC was fired.

Which was why he was now being defended by a very junior barrister named Archie Pringle, while the Crown called their principal witness, Stewart Mitchell.

Sarah slipped into the courtroom and sat unobtrusively at the back, out of Neil's line of vision. He had asked her not to come, and not to offer herself as a witness, for it would revive painful memories and achieve little. But that had been several weeks ago, on the advice of the esteemed Mr Tobias Shaw, who had expressed an opinion that testimony from a survivor of Belsen – a Jewish survivor – would have little impact, and might even be counterproductive.

Sarah had privately been very glad when Neil had sacked his counsel. She had since had a meeting with young Mr Pringle, who was keen and earnest, and whom she liked for his honesty. He doubted if he could get Neil off, for the prosecution felt their case was strong and the charges serious enough to warrant a three-year custodial sentence. Archie Pringle said if he could sway the Judge into anything less than twelve months, it would feel like a victory.

~

It was bizarre, Neil felt, watching this man in the witness box only a few yards away, destroying him. Despite the proximity, their eyes had met only once. Mitchell seemed determined not to look at him during the time he gave his damning evidence. There had been a swift glance at Neil in the dock before taking the oath; since then he had resisted any show of triumph, gazing directly at the Prosecutor and answering his questions, identifying details removed from the original files of the Ferencz sister and brother, and doing his utmost to convince the Judge of his integrity. As the prosecution was staying well away from any mention of two recent convictions for which he had been given suspended sentences, the question of his upright character or his candour went unchallenged.

'And do you know why the accused took it upon himself to do this, against all lawful regulations?'

'Yes, sir. He had a sexual relationship with the girl, Ferencz, who forced him to commit these forgeries.'

You filthy lying bastard, Neil thought, and shook his head so vehemently that the Judge noticed it and frowned at such theatrics.

'Please restrain your client, Mr – er – Pringle.' His Honour seemed to have difficulty remembering the young lawyer's name. 'He will have his opportunity to say whatever is relevant, if you choose to put him in the witness box at a later time.'

'Yes, Your Honour.'

The Judge nodded to the Prosecutor to continue.

'So he was blackmailed?'

'Yes, sir.'

'By this young Hungarian woman?'

'That was the excuse he gave, when I found out.'

At the back of the court, Helen wanted to leap to her feet and rebut the lies. She knew it would not achieve anything, except to draw unwanted attention to herself. She felt angry and sick. It had been futile coming all this way, imagining that she could help.

Stewart Mitchell had managed to show regret and appear almost reluctant to make these allegations against a former colleague. It was a clever performance. Now he waited for the cross-examination.

'You said the accused claimed to have been blackmailed when you found out?'

'Yes, sir.'

'When was that? When did you find out?'

'I can't give you the exact date,' Mitchell said, showing his first trace of hesitation.

'Never mind an exact date. Give me an exact month, or an exact year.'

'It was not recent, if that's what you mean.'

'That's precisely what I mean. It can't have been recent, can it? Not if you spoke to the accused about it, because that was almost eighteen months ago, before he left Europe. Isn't that correct, Mr Mitchell?'

'Yes, I'd say that's correct.'

'This serious matter remained unreported for all that time?'

'I was wrong. It was very foolish of me to try to protect him, but he had been a workmate. A friend.'

'So you didn't find it necessary to bring the matter to attention until a few months ago. What made you change your mind?'

'It was on my conscience. I began to realise it was wrong.'

'Did you, at this time, encounter some trouble of your own?'

Mitchell hesitated. The prosecuting counsel began to rise, but before he could speak the Judge beckoned Pringle to the bench.

'Where are we going with this, Mr Pringle?'

'He has a criminal record, Your Honour.'

'I'll allow it, but I'll remind you we're not in the business of denigrating witnesses unnecessarily, young man.'

'Thank you, Your Honour.'

He turned to repeat the question, but by now Mitchell had been given the necessary time to anticipate it.

'Yes,' he said, 'I did have some trouble, since you ask. I was accused of two black-market offences in Italy, and voluntarily returned to Australia to plead guilty. One was for selling coffee, the other for a few crates of beer. In each case I was given a suspended sentence.'

'Wasn't this in fact the tip of a very deep iceberg?'

'I don't know what you mean.'

'I suggest you do. Years of systematic corruption, which had been carried out in that refugee centre ever since you arrived there?'

'Your Honour,' the Prosecutor started to object, with a gesture that suggested further words were hardly necessary.

'Mr Pringle,' the Judge said, 'we have no jury to impress, and such comments are most unlikely to impress me. If you've finished with this witness, kindly say so.'

'Thank you, Your Honour. No further questions.'

~

The Crown closed its case. The Prosecutor felt he might still have a chance of enjoying the Taverner's lunch, with the news that the defence would not be putting its client on the stand.

'However, we ask that the court hear two character witnesses,' Archie Pringle said.

The Prosecutor sighed, glanced at his watch, and thought nostalgically of the excellent merlot. He had also collected some very good dirty jokes for later in the lunch when they got stuck into the port. Now here was a bloody novice lawyer introducing a couple of people who would drone on, and make absolutely no difference to the end result. With this Judge, the accused would go down for three years, everyone felt quite certain of that.

Henry Falconer did his best. He spoke of Neil's considerable attributes, his ability with languages, his skill at dealing with migrants, his care and deep concern. He recounted the huge amount of samaritan work the accused had done in Germany, as a young soldier in 1945, helping to fight typhus, helping to recruit the medical students when there were not enough doctors, an inspiring and valuable contribution to the massive postwar refugee problem. Many people would have suffered and perished, but for those who cared – like Neil Latham.

Watching from the back of the court, Helen thought that Mr Falconer conveyed the impression of a kindly and sincere man, talking to a Judge who was barely listening. When he left the stand, his glance at Neil seemed like an apology.

'Mrs Sarah Weismann,' the defence barrister requested.

Sarah. The name seemed to hang in the musty courtroom air for a moment, then Helen realised the handsome, middle-aged woman who had been sitting close to her had risen and was walking forward. She glimpsed Neil's reaction, saw him turn in surprise, perhaps even dismay, saw his barrister whisper to him, and Neil shaking his head with what appeared to be angry dissent, but it was too late.

Sarah Weismann was already taking the oath.

The barrister sprang something of a surprise by asking if his witness could proffer certain photographs to the court.

'What photographs?' The Judge sounded testy.

'Pictures that were taken at the time when she first met the accused, Your Honour.'

'Is there some purpose to this?' His Honour was on the brink of a refusal.

'I brought them with me, sir,' Sarah said, 'in the hope they can explain to you what no words of mine could describe.'

Her voice was modulated, the English accented but attractive. She was a well-groomed and elegant woman, which seemed to sway the Judge. Helen watched him reconsider, then nod, and the clerk of the court took a large envelope from Sarah Weismann, and gave it to him. When he opened the envelope, it was clear the photographs had been enlarged. Helen, and everyone else in the courtroom, could see his shock as he gazed at them.

'Where was this?'

'Belsen, Your Honour.'

She waited patiently. The Judge, no longer detached, examined each photograph.

'Who took these?'

'A cameraman with the soldiers, sir. I asked for copies, when I was in hospital. At the time I thought I would die, and there should be some record. I didn't know there were newsreels, or so many dreadful pictures in the newspapers. People had known and ignored our plight for so long, we thought it would be of little interest.'

'I saw the newsreels,' the Judge said, as if they were entirely alone, and judicial protocol was suspended. 'These are infinitely more terrible. This woman, the one in the photograph marked with a cross, this is you?'

'Yes,' she said. 'As you see, Your Honour, we were all naked, our legs and arms like the bones of skeletons. They shaved our heads to get rid of the lice. The sores all over my body, the ulcers – some were from beatings by the guards, some from the bites of rats. There was no medicine or food, no water, no hope, until that young man came with his comrades.'

She pointed at Neil. They could hear the underlying emotion in her voice.

'He could speak German, you see. His officer also spoke the language, but the officer couldn't face us, couldn't bear the horror of us, who looked like walking dead. Or the pits full of bones and bodies; bodies of children and old people, and thousands more that we were told to bury. In the end we didn't have the strength, and so bulldozers were trying to cover these mass graves, trying to hide the crime before the British came.'

Helen sat transfixed, listening. There was absolute silence, the Judge attentive to her every word, occasionally glancing from her to the photographs laid out in front of him.

'In Your Honour's photograph, I was forty years old. I know that I look like a crone of ninety. At the hospital they said I weighed twenty-nine kilos, and seemed surprised I was still alive. I didn't want to be alive. I wanted to die, like my seventeen-year-old daughter had died in the same hut.'

She pointed again at Neil. Helen could see on her face a look of pride. Pride and love.

'He wouldn't allow me to die. First, against orders, he let my daughter be cremated, disposed of with some dignity, instead of being flung among the other corpses. Against orders, Your Honour.' She gave what might have been a semblance of a smile. 'I know. He has a habit of going against orders when it's a simple question of humanity. He used to borrow a jeep illegally, to take me into the countryside, make me sit in the sunshine, to look at fields and church spires, and try to convince me that the world was still a sane place – it was just the people, so many of my countrymen, who had been deranged.

'Now, years later, here in this new country, this new home, the world really is a sane place. I only revisit the past on sleepless nights, or the date of my daughter's birthday. I never look at those photographs. After this I shall burn them. I brought them here today because I thought Your Honour should know how it was, and that this young man, the accused, saved lots of lives, but only the survivors can testify to that – and I testify that he saved mine.

'It's my belief he also saved the lives of this brother and sister, once more against orders, but rules do get broken in places where desperation thrives. I have the strangest feeling, Your Honour, that in those refugees, Helen and Michael Ferencz – two young people rejected and unwanted, about to be left on a human scrap heap – he saw a mirror image of us in Belsen. Perhaps of me. His humanity, his same compassion made him break the rules and commit a crime. I know you can't condone the crime, but I do hope you can understand why he might have done it.'

There was total silence. A woman near Helen blew her nose,

and openly wiped at her eyes. *Thank God*, Helen thought, *that I was present today to hear this.* She wanted to go and put her arms around Sarah Weismann, but knew it would be foolish to identify herself.

The Judge adjourned the court for his deliberations, and said they would resume after lunch. When Helen returned to her seat, she looked for Sarah, but the older woman was now sitting nearer the front, close to Neil and his barrister. She watched as the clerk of the court told him to stand.

The sentencing was brief. His Honour said that while there was cause to question the motives of the prosecution witness, Mitchell, it was apparent that documents had been forged and illegal entry obtained for the two Hungarian migrants specified. What action might be taken in their case was for another authority to determine, in another court.

With respect to what had been said by the character witnesses, he took into account the humanitarian record of the accused, and was particularly appreciative of the statement tendered by Mrs Weismann. It was therefore with some reluctance he was unable to overlook the fact a crime had been committed and laws broken, and the law was the fabric which bound society; without it there lay chaos and anarchy – perhaps even the kind of anarchy revealed by Mrs Weismann in her moving testimony.

For God's sake, Helen desperately wanted to shout, *stop all your preamble and platitudes and tell us! Two years? Three years?*

'It is therefore my judgement that a custodial sentence must be imposed, to discourage such a flagrant abuse of your position of trust, no matter what purpose may have prompted it. I am inclined to believe that consideration for others played a part in your rash action, but rash and illegal it was, and I have a duty to demonstrate that, and to punish you accordingly. You will go to prison for nine months.'

It was over so swiftly. The Judge rising, the court standing as he left the bench, the Prosecutor and his team furious and disappointed. Neil with no more than a moment to thank Archie Pringle, another moment to kiss Sarah; no chance to say what was in his heart, that he would never forget her standing there in the witness box, reliving days of horror, revealing a photograph of herself to the Judge – one he didn't even know she possessed – but an image he remembered of her, naked, skeletal, shaven and filthy. She had come to court and done this to help him, and it was a gesture he would be unable to ever forget, because he knew how much it had cost her.

There was no time to say this. Policemen came to escort him to the holding cell. It was over, and the court was required for another case. He turned for a last look, wanting to reassure Sarah he would be all right, and saw what seemed a familiar figure amid the few people leaving the courtroom. He assumed it was the strain, the relief after so many months of dreading the length of the sentence he might be given. Tension did strange things to the mind. Because for a brief moment, the girl he glimpsed leaving number four court had looked like Helen Francis.

Helen sat in a tiny Oxford Street cafe, little more than a sandwich bar, the closest haven she could find after hurriedly leaving the court precinct. Dreading the judgement, she had been too tense to eat during the break for lunch, and she now needed a cup of tea and a sandwich, and some time to think over what she should do.

Was it safe to go back to Adaminaby? Or would the case be reported in the newspapers, with their names mentioned? Certainly some action would be taken; the judge had promised as much. And the immigration department would know where to find her. Michael had already told her she was mad to think of going back there. He was confident they could both avoid being traced. And he had suggested a solution.

'Get sensible,' he had said last night, while they had dinner and she marvelled at their cosy flat with its harbour views. 'Stay in Sydney. I'll find you a job.' Seeing her wary look, he had put an arm around her and grinned. 'An honest one. I promise, nothing unlawful, not for my Holy Sister. Now Dee and I have to go and earn the rent at the sinful Maison Lumière. You want to come with us, and watch the rich and famous losing their money? See how the other half lives?'

She smiled and shook her head. 'I want to stay and watch the ferries and the harbour lights. Then fall into bed for a good night's rest. Some of us don't travel by first-class sleeper.'

They went off, laughing, saying they'd be back for breakfast. She watched them drive out of the cul-de-sac in the red Jaguar sports car with the hood down. Deirdre drove and Michael played the fool, turning to show his hands raised in a mock prayer, then blowing kisses to Helen. She waved back.

It was another world she was briefly sharing with them; her brother so handsome in his tuxedo, Deirdre looking like a real film star in her evening dress, the smart roadster, the lovely apartment in this expensive district. She was glad to see them so happy, astonished at their affluence, slightly troubled – she knew she couldn't help herself – by the source of so much money from this gambling club.

It had all happened so quickly. A phone call from Michael to say a friend had found the case was listed for that week in the Darlinghurst Criminal Court. If she was determined to risk being present – he thought it a dangerous idea that would achieve nothing – but if she was fixed on it, then please take some extra days because they wanted her to stay with them, to show her around, and Deirdre would meet the train.

She had asked for a week of unpaid leave, giving no reason, and Len Richards had been kind, saying she worked longer hours than most people, and there was no question of it being unpaid; she'd need cash down in the big smoke, and Sir Cedric, who'd sent her flowers, would surely not want to stop her wages for a well-deserved holiday – although, he had grinned, there was no particular reason why he should be told about it. She liked Len; life at the camp had become very different since his advent.

Then, after her arrival, glad to leave the smoky compartment, her first astonishment: Deirdre Miller, from the produce store and the wild hillbilly family, looking gorgeous in smart clothes, almost every man in the rail terminus turning to gaze at her; Deirdre, now her sister-in-law, greeting her lovingly and taking her out to the station concourse where a gleaming red roadster was waiting.

'Whose is it?' Helen asked, as they stopped beside it.

'Ours,' she said. 'Well, mine, so Miki insists.'

The first of many surprises.

The city itself was another, for she had seen it only once, a fleeting glimpse from the back of an open truck, being taken from the docks to Mascot on their first day. She was enthralled by it, the energy and vibrancy, the streams of traffic, the lunchtime streets packed with crowds, the beauty of the harbour.

Later came different surprises. The shock of their jobs in the club, which Michael had not told her about; the large amount of money they earned, all of it in cash, so there was money everywhere, in the linen cupboard, in wardrobes, under mattresses, in the bathroom cabinet.

She begged them to put it in a bank.

'We can't,' Michael said, 'some snooper might want to know where it came from.'

In deference to her worry, Deirdre agreed they should rent a safe deposit box. Thinking about the wads of cash, Helen shook her head. They were just incorrigible. But what a joy it was to see them. Now she wanted to share her relief of Neil's sentence with someone, and it could only be them. For weeks she had been tormented by the thought he could be imprisoned for two or three years. Even having to serve nine months, just for helping them, troubled her.

The waitress came and wiped her table.

'That'll be two shillings,' she said.

Helen paid her, and made her way along Oxford Street. She decided to walk for a while. She needed time to work out what to do, once this holiday week was over. She doubted if she could cut herself adrift and not return to Adaminaby as Michael advised. Breaking her contract, vanishing and becoming illegal; it might be commonsense to him, but she doubted if she could do it.

As she passed the court building, a prison van pulled out. She turned to stare after it, but there was no way of telling who, if anyone, was inside.

The city's main prison, Long Bay, was a short drive from the Darlinghurst court, and the van with three prisoners arrived without incident. Neil, along with two men on charges of armed robbery, was escorted into the reception area, ordered to deposit all his personal possessions for which he was given a receipt, then told to strip and he would be issued with prison clothing.

The senior warder arrived to inspect the three naked men. He told them it was his practice to meet all new inmates in person, so he could assess them. He snapped at them to shower, and to be quick about it. The way he strutted and barked his orders reminded Neil of an army sergeant-major at Aldershot, when he had first joined up. The man had been feared and hated, and had delighted in taunting the new recruits with a regular refrain.

'The only worse bugger than me you'll meet in this bleedin' war is bleedin' 'Itler.'

The memory of his bellow made Neil smile, which was a mistake. He suddenly found the senior warder's face only inches from his, the man's eyes like flint.

'And what's funny, smiler?'

'Nothing,' Neil said.

'Nothing, Mr Steele, *sir*.'

'Nothing, Mr Steele, sir.'

'Then why the little chuckle, eh? Got a small private joke, have we, son? Find all this a laugh, do yer?'

'No, sir.'

'Bit of a fucking ratbag then? Smile at nothing, do we?'

'I'm sorry, sir.'

'You will be, sport. Any more little grins, at me or any of my warders, you'll soon learn to stop smiling. Got it?' he shouted.

'Yes, sir.'

Bleedin' 'Itler, Neil thought, but resolutely kept his face from twitching. It was a bad start. His barrister had said the nine months could even be reduced to six, if he got time off for good behaviour. That might be difficult if a smile was against the rules. He had already been told that Steele's nickname was 'Iron Bar'.

Sleep was long in coming that night. The cell block echoed to the tread of guards, the shouts of abuse. His cell mate was taciturn, fortunately, but had a rasping cough that kept them both awake long after the lights were switched out. Neil had tried to speculate what prison might be like, and attempted to reassure himself it could not be more rigorous than some of the army camps he had known. The worst of those, in the interests of turning civilians into soldiers capable of killing the enemy, had been savage. He resolved to treat it like the army, and if he had been sent to a prison farm that might have been possible. But Long Bay was not like any army camp. Long Bay was a cesspit of hardened criminals, carelessly unsegregated with those who had committed lesser crimes.

In the prison yard the following day, he found himself jostled by a heavily built man. Muscular, his hair cropped, and thick arms covered with tattoos, the bump had been clearly intentional.

'Look out, you careless mongrel,' he said, and as Neil tried to move away, the man deliberately barged into him again.

'I said to watch it,' he said, and suddenly jammed his elbow against Neil's throat, taking him by surprise and pinioning him against the wall of the exercise yard. 'I'm a mate of Stewart Mitchell's, and you're the Pommy prick who got let off light. Stewie said you shoulda got a coupla years. He said to make sure you don't forget him.'

It had been carefully staged. He was winded by a ferocious short arm jab to the stomach. Within seconds they were surrounded by a group busily talking and screening them from the sight of patrolling warders. Hurt by the first blow, then dazed by quick punches to the face, his escape cut off by at least a dozen men, Neil had no chance. In a few minutes he was battered and bleeding.

'Easy, Chigger,' one of the group warned. 'Don't kill 'im.'

'Just warming up,' Chigger said, smashing Neil into the wall, grabbing him by the hair and banging his face against the bricks.

'C'mon, enough.' The others were getting uneasy.

'Bugger you, Chigger, that's his ration. Ease up.'

Neil was on the ground, bleeding. Chigger kicked him.

'That's his ration, but only for today.' He looked down at the semi-conscious and dazed Neil. 'Stewie said to keep on remindin' you what happens to dobbers. You want to dob me in, sport, my name's Chigger Harris. Cell 64. But if you even mention it, we might as well kill you right now, 'cos your bloody life round here won't be worth living.'

He swung his foot again, and laughed as Neil flinched and tried to roll away. He used the toe of his boot to swivel his victim's chin, so that Neil was forced to gaze up at him.

'I don't like Poms, or narks who blow the whistle on their mates. So I warn you now – I'm gonna make you as happy as an orphan on father's day.'

~

Neil was paraded before 'Iron Bar' Steele. 'Fighting already are we, smiler?' the senior warder said, with a frown. 'We get them now and then, difficult men, bad buggers like you. And I don't wanna hear any of your feeble excuses, son. I got ten prisoners who all say that you started it. Any more of it and you'll have a nice long spell in solitary.'

Chapter 18

The cockatoo on watch in the lane behind the Maison Lumière was feeling sleepy. He had been doing this same job for weeks, and it was a chilly night, even with the windows of the car closed. He'd brought a thermos of coffee and a blanket, and thought that since the police were getting a weekly donation, there was no harm in snuggling down for a while. He even reflected on the idea of a quick peek around the corner at Kellett Street, where he knew there'd be tarts on the prowl, and one of the young ones might give him a hump under the blanket for a couple of quid. That would help pass the time. There was a lively little blonde he fancied. If he was in any kind of luck she might come past. He was thinking of this when the back door of the club opened. A shaft of light spilled out into the lane, as the figure of Jimmy Kincaid was framed there.

Pretty silly, the cockatoo thought, *standing like a statue in the flaming lighted doorway. What kind of stupid game is he playing?*

The cockatoo wound down his window, as Kincaid strolled to where he sat in his car. The club door remained open, the light shining out.

'All quiet, Stan?'

'Dead as a bloody graveyard. And cold as charity.'

'You want a young sort to warm you up.'

'Funny, I was jest thinkin' the same thing.'

'Well, if you feel the need, don't be long. And don't tell me.'

Kincaid went back inside and shut the door.

The cockatoo thought it strange. A partner in the club, giving him the green light to go and pick up a girl. He was sure Michael wouldn't like that, and Michael Francis was the one who had hired him. Jimmy Kincaid reckoned it was a waste of money having cockatoos, when they already had the police on the payroll.

An uneasy thought stirred deep in the cockatoo's mind. He got out of his car, strolled to the back door of the club, and carefully tried the handle. It turned. The door was open, left unlocked.

Bloody Kincaid, he thought. *Dirty double-crossing bastard!*

He knew the lighted doorway had been a signal; there was no time to spare. He raced to his car. A length of cord was hooked to a roof rack, and it ran almost invisibly up the side of the building. He jerked fiercely on it, and making certain, jumped into his car, started the engine and drove off. The cord stretched and snapped. Upstairs in the club, the buzzer it set off was like a warning siren.

Michael was there in a flash, switching it off. A glittering crowd of the city's most prominent citizens were on the verge of panic, visualising their names and photos in the newspapers, and he knew he only had moments to calm them. Less than that. He glanced down into the rear lane, saw a wagon arriving, and a large squad of police swarming out.

~

'You weren't supposed to mark his face,' the senior warder said. 'I don't care how important your friend Stewie is, if anyone sees those bruises, shit will hit the fan.'

'My friend Stewie is rich,' Chigger Harris said. 'He made a pile in Italy. If you keep your trap shut, Iron Bar, you get two hundred quid.'

'Two hundred, maybe. But if our smartarse Governor gets to hear of this, I get the bullet. How the hell do we explain the bruises?'

'He fell over,' Chigger said. 'Clumsy on his feet.'

'Don't be a bloody comedian, Chigger. It don't suit you.'

'I'm serious. Twenty blokes saw him trip. Flat on his face, nobody near him – to prevent his fall.'

'Twenty witnesses?'

'Easy. Maybe more. You can't argue with twenty people. Not even the Governor could argue with twenty.'

'I'll take the money – only it's three hundred. Tell your mate Stewart that's the price. And keep your bloody knuckles away from his face.'

They were in the senior warder's room. Chigger Harris had brought cigarettes and a bottle of Johnny Walker Black Label. Lights were out in the rest of the prison.

'Nice drop this,' Steele said.

Chigger refilled their glasses.

The police raid on the Maison Lumière was well planned. A group from the gaming squad came in the unlocked door from the back lane, while a larger bunch of raiders burst in the front entrance, past the bouncer and up the carpeted main stairs. Their only brief problem was a bottleneck caused by the sheer weight of numbers where the two squads met, a collision that created enough delay to impede their forward rush for a few moments, until the tangle was sorted out and they reached the heavy and imposing doors of the club.

They were locked. The brand new gaming sergeant, who had personally organised this operation, was about to hammer on the door to announce the police presence, when he heard massed voices inside.

A large group seemed to be singing *Happy Birthday*.

'Break the fucking door down,' he said to two of his largest, who put their ears to the door and listened. They were not at all happy with their new sergeant, who was going to cost them all a nice regular retainer with this raid.

'It's a birthday party, Sarge.'

'Bollocks,' the sergeant said, and shoulder-charged the doors himself. At that moment they suddenly opened – Michael having by now assured himself that inside all was in readiness – and the sergeant catapulted through. Unable to stop his forward progress, he ended up sprawling on the plushly carpeted floor.

The air was thick with cigar smoke and the aroma of expensive perfume. Men in dinner jackets, women in off-the-shoulder evening gowns, were all singing the final chorus:

'Happy birthday, dear Deirdre,
Happy birthday to you!'

There was a birthday cake with one lighted candle. Deirdre stood beside it, over a hundred people gathered in a semi-circle around her. There were no signs of any playing cards. No trace of baccarat tables. Specially constructed to be instantly dismantled in case of emergency, the baize tops had vanished, the tables transformed. One had a chess set on it, another a bowl of flowers. The unlicensed bar was invisible; folding doors had been snapped shut camouflaging it into a section of the wall, decorated by a screen.

'This is a raid on an illegal gambling club,' the sergeant said, picking himself up to be confronted by an irate phalanx of influential faces.

'It's a private social club, and you've gatecrashed a party for Deirdre's twenty-first,' said a famous radio comedian.

'How dare you barge in and ruin her celebration,' complained a prominent socialite, who glittered all over with diamonds.

'Serving alcohol on unlicensed premises.' The sergeant was determined. He knew there were cards hidden somewhere, but at least he could see a glass of champagne. Any infringement would suffice, giving him an excuse to hold them while he searched the place. He picked up the champagne flute. They all watched while he tasted it and grimaced. It was lemonade.

'The young lady is a teetotaller. It's her night, and that's her choice.' The sergeant recognised a well-known District Court judge, and decided it was time to retreat. He mumbled an excuse about it being the wrong premises, or a case of misinformation, and led his men down the stairs. Behind them they heard a derisive chorus of *Happy Birthday*, and the sound of laughter.

Ten minutes later, with all the doors secured, the cockatoo again on watch in the rear lane and the bouncers in position, the bar was declared open, the baccarat tables reassembled and restored to normal, the cash which had all been hastily stashed inside brassieres and underclothes was produced amid great hilarity, and Deirdre and the other dealers went to work. Her table was more popular than ever. Michael was congratulated on his brilliant idea of the cake and the bogus party. There was a mood of exhilaration among these affluent clients, an atmosphere of almost sophomoric glee at the improvised farce in which they had all participated.

It would certainly do the club's popularity no harm once the story was spread, Michael realised, although an increase in business had hardly been the motive for the raid. While accepting the accolades for his quick thinking, it was hearing street talk about Jimmy Kincaid meeting with the new gaming sergeant that had made him expect trouble all week. Hence the purchase of the birthday cake. Rather than a moment of dazzling spontaneity, it had been a tactic worked out thoroughly in advance.

Kincaid was doing his best to appear delighted at their escape, but the cockatoo's report about the unlocked rear door confirmed to Michael the man's real intention; to cause maximum embarrassment for the club, with arrests and humiliating appearances at the Central police station, where the press would have been on hand to capture some well-known faces, and report a juicy scandal for the tabloids. The incentive was greed, trying to tarnish the club's popular image and squeeze out Dr Forbes-Clark, because it was rumoured Kincaid had a better deal with a prospective new partner.

According to Michael's source, that new partner was a smart operator called Stewart Mitchell. Concealing his shock at the name, realising it was the man who had slandered Helen with his squalid lies, Michael asked for details and was told Mitchell had not long ago come home from Italy, well cashed up, and was looking for the right sort of investment. He wanted a club, a classy place like Maison Lumière, which was the ideal way to launder money.

If it were true, and it seemed likely, Michael knew there was a lot more trouble looming between himself and Jimmy Kincaid.

Helen sipped a cup of coffee, watching what had become her favourite view as a big freighter inched its way down the harbour, and she saw a tugboat, like a vigilant chaperone, steaming out to meet it. Soon the tug would attach lines and usher the vessel past the Garden Island dockyard, then proceed by Woolloomooloo, Mrs Macquarie's Chair and the tram sheds on Bennelong Point, to an anchorage at one of the busy wharves on the far side of the Harbour Bridge. In the past few days she had spent much of her time walking and exploring these places, while still trying to make up her mind what to do.

'Stay,' Michael and Deirdre were both constantly insisting. They wanted her to remain with them, at least until she found a job and could afford a place of her own.

'Don't be a dill,' Michael had pleaded. 'If you go back there, you'll be a sitting duck. Here you're safe. They aren't going to search. We're not important, Iluska. There were no newspaper reports of the trial, no mention of our names. So why go back to Adaminaby and let immigration deport you? Where do they send you? Hungary? You'd be raving mad. Nobody's ever going to kick me out of this country.'

'They can't,' said Deirdre dryly, 'you're the dinkum article, mate, since you married me.'

The tug now had the freighter in tow and was leading it past where she stood watching. Although it was nearly noon, Michael and Deirdre had only just gone to sleep, exhausted after the late night and the tension of the police raid. Recounting it to her when they came home, joking and laughing as they told of the gaming squad's defeat and inglorious retreat, she sensed a feeling of stress in Michael. Despite his bravado, he was worried. She had asked him why, and he'd told her.

About Kincaid, he'd explained, and the rumour he was in a deal with Stewart Mitchell. The name came as a chill to her.

The lousy bastard who lied about you in court, Michael said, sensing her revulsion. He told her it was only street gossip so far, he had no proof, but if it was true there might be ways to put the squeeze on Jimmy Kincaid.

What, she asked, did putting the squeeze on mean – exactly?

Michael had told her that his friend, Dr Reggie Forbes-Clark, was hardly a nobody, not a man to take treatment like this lying down. He was a big wheel who could call up a lot of favours in this town. If Mitchell was trying to get hold of the club, thinking of taking the Doc on, then Mr Bloody Mitchell might end up with a few regrets. He might even end up in deep water with cement boots.

Helen finished her coffee. The tug and the cargo ship were nearly out of sight. She thought about what Michael had said, and felt a deep sense of foreboding. He and Deirdre were so naive – enraptured by a lifestyle that was beguiling, so seductive and unlike anything either had known – that they thought it would last forever. Huge amounts of money, a smart apartment, a sports car to envy. All of it reliant on a criminal doctor, currently their friend, but a thoroughly ruthless man who would hardly be their friend unless they served his purpose. And when that altered – if he had a different purpose – then what?

They were so in love, the pair of them, and so vulnerable.

Like a pair of kids with brand new toys. Gullible and trusting.

She cared deeply for them, and felt afraid.

The prison was burning. Flames were crackling all around him, wood was exploding, dense smoke engulfed him and constricted his throat, choking him; the heat seared his eyes almost blinding him; the blazing gusts scorched the skin on his face, while Sarah's daughter reached out arthritic and emaciated hands, trying to reach him, trying to claw her way out of the fire.

He woke in terror, drenched with sweat, gasping for breath, wondering if he had screamed or shouted. But his taciturn cell mate was lightly snoring, and the adjacent area was quiet. Distantly a warder patrolled, the tread of his boots on the concrete walkway interrupted every few paces as he shone a torch on the occupants of each cell.

It had been a long time since he had woken in such panic and fear. Though not quite the same nightmare this time, it was equally terrifying. He felt the sweat chilling his body and making it clammy, while he tried not to think about the photographs Sarah had shown to the Judge, hoping she had kept her promise and burnt them by now in the backyard incinerator behind the block of flats.

He knew what strength and courage it had taken to bring them to court. So many of the holocaust survivors he had met could not talk about their experiences, let alone speak of them publicly to a group of strangers. The memories were too shocking, too wounding and humiliating to bear. Which made Sarah's act all the more remarkable.

He lay awake in the dark, knowing further sleep was unlikely. He needed to think about his tormentor, Chigger Harris, and what he had been able to find out. There had been another attack this morning, a quick jostle this time, an elbow in the stomach leaving him winded and retching. There was no safety in the prison yard against these kinds of sudden assaults; it was impossible to be constantly on guard, particularly when his assailant was always accompanied by a personal army of supporters. It was going to be a long nine months; his nemesis, the senior warder, had already assured him he would serve the full term, smugly promising there would be no recommendations for good behaviour on his weekly report that went to the Governor.

Although asking questions was neither safe nor popular, Neil had been able to find out a surprising amount about Harris. In the prison population were many who disliked or feared him, resenting his favoured treatment by the warders, and uneasy about the mob who followed him around – 'like a bunch of pet dingoes', one had said – doing whatever Harris ordered. It was the pet dingoes who had formed a protective screen while he'd been attacked the first time. And one of those same dingoes had bumped him in the food queue, spilling his meal all over the floor, attracting the abuse of an orderly who had forced him to clean it up. Fortunately the soup on the tray was only lukewarm, or it would have scalded him.

From another source he had found out Harris was a standover man, serving five years for grievous bodily harm, and had worked for most of the top Sydney crime bosses. The link with Mitchell went back to the early war years, when both had been called up for army service. But their war had been confined to Victoria

Barracks in Paddington, from where they had run rackets together at a time when the black market flourished, especially in cigarettes, liquor, petrol coupons and nylon stockings. According to the rumble around the cells, Harris boasted that his old mate had got an early discharge and scored a cushy job in Europe that nobody else had wanted. Made a heap there.

Now his mate was home and loaded, Harris was onto a good lurk. All he had to do was make life hell for Neil. There was also gossip that Steele was on three hundred pounds to assist. If true, Neil knew he had to do something about the situation, and soon. Or the next nine months would be a nightmare, every single day.

The doorbell rang deep inside the apartment. She could hear it ringing and wondered if anyone was home. Just as she was about to leave, the door opened. Sarah looked at her. After a swift appraising glance, she smiled.

'You're Helen Francis,' she said. 'Am I right?'

'Yes.' Helen nodded.

'I think I saw you in court.'

'You did,' Helen said. 'And I saw you in the witness box. For the past few days, I've been trying to pluck up courage – just to come and say I thought you were brave and absolutely wonderful.'

It seemed quite natural to hold out her arms, and for Sarah to react with equal spontaneity as they hugged each other warmly.

'I could hardly believe it. To sit and watch that judge change his mind,' Helen said. 'He was so cold and remote until then.

I never knew anyone could make such an impression the way you did on him.'

'It was the photographs.'

'They helped. But it was you. Your dignity. Your words. Everyone in the court knew that.'

'Thank you,' Sarah said quietly. 'Now stop spoiling me with such flattery. Come and sit down. Will you have coffee, tea, or a glass of wine?'

'Wine sounds nice. Thank you.'

Left alone for a moment, Helen looked around at the sizeable old-fashioned apartment. She had only a child's memory of their family home in Hungary, the substantial rooms above her parents' pharmacy in the town of Eger, bulky furniture like this, a sense of permanence and safeness – that sadly had not kept them safe. Yet here seemed like a sanctuary, she felt a security she had not known since she was twelve years old. It brought a strange sensation with it, a sudden deep affection for the middle-aged woman returning with a tray on which were olives and two glasses of wine. That was when Helen saw the Menorah.

It was on a table in one corner, an ornamental candelabrum holding nine candles. They had had one at home, where her father was strict about observance, and the feast of lights, as he called it. The nine-day festival of Hanukkah each December, when the Menorah candles were lit, was one of the highlights of their year. But she and Miki had not celebrated any Jewish holy days, not even Yom Kippur, since the night they had watched their parents herded aboard the train that had taken them to their deaths. Their father and mother had been religious, and if that was God's reward for belief, they could do without God.

'I bought this in a shop here,' Sarah said. 'I've never lit the candles, but we had one in Berlin. I bought it in memory of my husband. He was the devout one.'

'Not you?'

'No,' Sarah said. 'Not particularly before the Nazis, even if I paid lip service to the feast days, but never afterwards.'

'It's strange,' Helen said. 'I feel as if . . . as if I've always known you.'

'I knew someone like you,' Sarah said. 'My daughter would've been twenty-five next birthday. How old are you?'

'Twenty-three,' she replied. 'Nearly twenty-four,' she added, and recalling the many times in the past when Michael had used this same tactic to make himself sound older, she smiled. The smile transformed her face. Sarah, who until then had thought her well-mannered and pleasant, suddenly realised she was also beautiful.

They touched glasses, and Helen sipped the red wine. It was mellow, soft on her tongue, and quite unlike the wine they had been served in the ladies' parlour of the pub in Cooma, which was harsh and cheap, and known far and wide as 'fourpenny dark'.

'I like your apartment. Can I call you Sarah?'

'I'd like that. How did you find me?'

'I wrote to Neil at this address.'

'Of course.'

'I feel so guilty that he's in prison because of what he did for us.'

'Well, you mustn't,' Sarah said firmly. 'He'd be worried if he knew that. He made a conscious decision to help you, and it certainly wasn't your fault this happened.'

'Or his,' Helen said, thinking none of it might have happened if Sandor had not killed the Polish SS man. Sandor, at least, was safe. He had done what she always thought he would, returning to Europe to complete his medical degree. His letter had said only that he would not go back to Poland, and she thought it likely he would choose France where he spoke the language.

It had been just a few lines, sent from Fremantle when his ship docked there. He was working his passage, he said, but did not name the vessel or state whether it was a freighter or a passenger ship. Nor, trusting no-one, did he give a forwarding address. Despite this, Helen felt bound by her promise, and would never speak of it. She wished she could; it would be so easy to confide in someone like Sarah.

They went for a tour of the apartment, and then out onto the balcony to admire the view.

'I love the harbour,' Helen said. 'My brother and his wife have a view like this.'

'Your brother's married? And living here in Sydney?'

'Yes. He shouldn't be, but he is. Didn't Neil tell you, after he came back from Cooma?'

Sarah shook her head. In fact, she recalled that Neil had said very little; merely told her he had explained the situation, which, of course, had come as a shock. Nothing about her brother. Not much about Helen herself, come to that. She remembered that he had been quiet for several days after his return, which she had put down to reaction at the unpleasant task of breaking the news to them. Or else his growing concern at his own predicament.

'Where does he live, Helen?'

'Elizabeth Bay.'

'Very grand.'

'It is, I'm afraid.'

'Why do you say it like that?'

'Because I'm worried.'

Sarah glanced at her, but made no attempt to ask any more questions. She was willing to listen, but had no wish to pry.

'About his job, for one thing,' Helen said. 'He works for a man named Forbes-Clark.'

'Not *Doctor* Forbes-Clark? The one who is in the newspapers rather a lot?'

'You mean the one who's notorious. Yes. Michael helps run a gambling club for him. Deirdre – his wife – works there at the baccarat table. The other night there was a police raid . . .'

Once started, she told it all. Her fear they were being used, involved in something that must surely end badly. How she couldn't seem to warn them, and doubted even if she tried, whether they would be prepared to listen. Worst of all, how there was so much money and excitement to tempt them, and they seemed to believe in this wretched doctor, and feel that nothing could harm them.

'I'm sorry,' she said, at the end of it. 'I didn't mean to burden you with all that. But there's no-one else I can talk to.'

'Talk to me about anything you want, my dear. Tell me about you, that's the most important thing. What happens now?'

'I've been trying to decide. In a few more days I must go back to Adaminaby. Michael says I'm crazy, and he wants me to stay.'

'And what do you want?'

'I'd love to stay. But I'm not sure it is right. I suppose I'm straightlaced. That's the expression they use here.'

She hesitated, trying to assemble her thoughts. Sarah watched her and thought no-one this young should look so forlorn.

'I don't want to be put in a detention centre and deported. I think it would be cruel and unfair. But to run away doesn't seem the answer. At least, not an answer I can live with.'

'Deporting you would be very cruel and quite unjust. I wish I could help.'

'Nobody can. I have to make my own choice.'

'Do you want to talk to Neil?'

'He can't help. In Cooma he said that. He told me in the end it was up to me.' Then she added, 'Though I would like to see him, just once, if I'm not going to be allowed to stay. I wish that was possible.'

'It's possible,' Sarah said.

'I don't even know where he is.'

'I do. He's in Long Bay Gaol.'

'Where's that?'

'About an hour's tram ride, past Centennial Park, out towards La Perouse. I telephoned earlier to find out about visitors.'

'Are they allowed?'

'On certain days. Tomorrow afternoon is a visiting time. If you're free, we could go together.'

Helen smiled again.

'That'd be nice,' she said.

Chapter 19

It was a sunny morning, and there were a hundred men in the yard. Later they would be returned to their cells, and another hundred would be sent out. Because of a recent riot in the prison, this drastic reduction of the period they were allowed outdoors had been enforced. They had half an hour of free time, and a further half hour of vigorous exercise. The new Governor was a former amateur athletic champion and a stickler for exercise. It kept men healthy and out of trouble, he was reported as saying. Except that everyone – every single man in the yard – knew that there was going to be trouble this morning.

The dingoes knew it. They were all watching Chigger Harris, awaiting a signal he would give them at any moment. Neil knew it, for there was no mistaking the mood of expectation at breakfast. Word had spread like a brush fire. Rumours were a source of entertainment, and they'd sped about the gaol. All kinds of different rumours.

Chigger was going to put the Pommy in hospital today.

No, he was just gonna duff him up a bit more.

The senior screw, 'Iron Bar' Steele, was gonna start earning his three hundred. Put the Pommy on a charge.

The Governor, Mr Mannix, better known as 'The Archbishop' after Melbourne's Archbishop Mannix, had heard talk.

The Archbishop was in on the deal.

No, the Archbishop was on the prowl.

The Pommy was shit-scared.

So frightened he'd dropped his dinner tray yesterday.

The rumours proliferated, contradicting each other. Tension and expectation grew, and with it a growing anxiety that after all the anticipation, nothing might occur. Time was passing, and their free time was half over. If it didn't happen soon, they'd all be lined up for their bloody exercise; deep breathing, arms in the air, touch your toes, and then running on the spot.

The dingoes saw Neil stroll towards the far corner. Brick walls met there, forming a sun trap. Neil leaned against the wall, like any man trying to get an extra ration of warming ultraviolet, before being taken back inside. The dingoes looked across at Chigger and saw his grin of relish. He scratched his head, which was their signal. They strolled across to form a bulwark between Neil and the other prisoners.

Neil appeared to notice nothing. He seemed to close his eyes, enjoying the sunshine. Through his lashes he saw Harris's bulk push his way through the protective circle. Saw him come close. Braced himself for a blow. Felt instead the surprise as a finger poked him in the chest. He opened his eyes and Harris scowled at him.

'You're in my corner, mongrel.'

Neil said nothing.

'Did you hear me, you prick? This is a sunny spot reserved for me. You're trespassing.' He grinned, as if this was a good joke that he would repeat to his friends and followers later. 'Yeah, and it's a rule round here – trespassers will be prosecuted.'

Still Neil said nothing, staring back at him. Harris's grin started to fade.

'You want to be slaughtered, mongrel? You want to have the crap bashed out of you? Stewie says you're a stubborn bastard. Maybe bashing you ain't the best way, he says. So what you're gonna do is get down and lick my boots. Right now, in front of everybody. On your bloody hands and knees. Now! Or else you'll lick my arse in front of the whole mob before I've finished with you.'

'You know what you are, Harris?' Neil's voice was quiet, deceptively casual. 'You're a prat. Know what that is? A ridiculous piece of work. A drongo in Australian. A bullying sod with no guts. The bloody pits, the dregs. And that's just for starters.'

Chigger Harris was gazing at him open-mouthed, as though his intended victim was insane.

'You're fucking mad,' he started to say.

Neil's hand shot out, grabbing his arm, squeezing a pressure point that momentarily rendered his opponent helpless, then turned him around and put his foot up against the other's backside. He shoved violently. Harris went sprawling face down on the ground. The dingoes tried to move forward, but the allies Neil had gathered were already there to prevent this. Around the yard word spread instantly.

'It's on for young and old.'

They crowded in to watch, preventing the duty warders from a clear view. The warders had been told there might be a small to-do; the Pommy pie-eater was a bowerbird who'd been thieving from Chigger, and old Chig would sort things out. Nobody believed this, but they knew it was an order to turn a blind eye. Which is why, when they saw most of the prisoners crowd the far corner, they dutifully patrolled in the other direction and paid no attention.

Chigger Harris got up slowly, startled. He had expected his dingoes to surround Neil, so he could move in and do him over well and truly, but this hadn't happened. Nobody was making any noise; everyone knew the essential was to stay quiet and watch the show.

'You're a loonie,' Chigger said. 'I'm gunna put you in hospital. That's if I don't put you in the fucking morgue.'

'You're full of talk. All mouth and no brains, Harris. I heard you were a standover man who frightens old ladies. In my opinion, if they swung a handbag you'd run away.'

A couple of men smothered laughter. Harris glared, trying to find the culprits. He knew this smart, talkative bastard had to be sorted out, flattened real quick. He was starting to tarnish Chigger's image.

'You haven't the guts to fight me, Harris. Not without your dingo mates or Iron Bar Steele to protect you.'

There was increased laughter. This was good stuff. Even if the Pommy got half killed in the end, which was more than probable, he'd put on a fair act. Been in the joint less than a week, and already he had found out enough to get Chigger Harris spitting chips.

'Come on, you useless poofter,' Neil taunted him, 'show us your muscles.'

It was a gibe that had to be answered. Harris ran at him and swung his arm with all the force he could summon. If the blow had landed, Neil would have been pulp. But he wasn't there, he was away to one side, where he put out a foot, and Harris flailed forward and fell like an ox. He got up gingerly, more cautious now. But livid.

'Fight, you bastard.'

'I'll fight the way I was taught, you piece of shit,' Neil told him. 'While you were winning the war selling nylon stockings, I was learning this.'

He hit Harris as hard as he could, then weaved and feinted as the other came back furiously swinging punches. The blows all went wild, missing him, and he used the moment to laugh at his opponent, then kick him in the testicles. When Harris screamed and doubled up in agony, Neil began to employ every vicious trick of unarmed combat that *bleedin' 'Itler* had instilled into those recruits who had been marked for special training.

'This is how we'll win the fucking war, lads.'

Elbows, knees, anything was fair in this game. Harris was half blind with blood spreading from a cut on his forehead. Mad with rage, he was unable to lay a hand on Neil. Not once had any of his blows landed, nor had any of his wild kicks connected. But he refused to stay down. He was like a wounded bull in a Spanish *corrida* who could only keep blundering forward; there was no other way, no matter how many lethal sword thrusts he had encountered.

Neil wanted to end it. He'd had enough. Now it was nothing but cruelty for the entertainment of the others. And to hell with the others. Bugger this gleeful prison audience. He hit him savagely, and Harris went down again, rocking in agony on the ground. Then he pulled him halfway to his feet and used his elbow to jab him in the face, breaking his nose. There was a gasp from the watching crowd – but whether shock or approval Neil did not know, nor care. He finally let Harris drop, and this time he lay whimpering and beaten, with blood pouring out of his mouth and nose and spreading across his face.

~

The leisurely tram ride from the city was a delight to Helen. It was one of the unfashionable 'toast rack' trams with open sides and slatted wooden seats, but on a fine day like this it allowed a good view and a breeze to cool them. Even Sarah, who had never liked them much, had to agree to that. Or perhaps it was Helen's sheer enthusiasm that swayed her.

Both were smartly dressed. Helen wore a simple navy dress she had bought that morning at Anthony Horderns.

'Do you realise,' she whispered to Sarah, 'I'm nearly twenty-four and this is the first time I've ridden in a tram?'

'Truly? Not in Europe? Nowhere in Italy?'

'We were mostly in camps. And we never had the fare.'

Today she had left any concern about the future behind. Sarah thought she looked lovely in the new dress, and was enchanted with her. She wondered if Helen had a boyfriend, and felt she must have, although it was strange she hadn't mentioned one.

The conductor clambered along the side and they paid for their tickets. A newsboy, who looked as if he might be playing truant from school, had early afternoon papers for sale.

'Piper,' he called, 'Korea war latest battle. Aussies in action. Readallaboutit!' At the showground stop he jumped off, and they heard his chant. 'Get yer piper. Readallaboutit.'

They went past Centennial Park, and Helen commented on how nice it looked and asked why it was called that. Sarah didn't know, but an Australian couple overheard and explained it was named for the centenary of the arrival of the First Fleet. In addition, on the first of January, 1901, it was the place where Federation had been proclaimed. They were friendly, eager to talk.

'Where do you come from?' the wife asked.

'Adaminaby,' Helen replied, and when they looked blank she said, 'it's down in the Snowy, near Cooma.'

'Cold there,' the husband said.

'Nice in summer though,' Helen told him.

'And what about your mother,' the wife looked at Sarah. 'Does she live there, too?'

'No,' Helen said without hesitating, 'she lives in Sydney.'

'Potts Point.' Sarah, joining in the conversation, was strangely flattered they had assumed Helen was her daughter.

And where were they going today?

'Long Bay,' Helen replied.

'There're two bays, Long and Little,' the husband said. 'Little Bay has the Coast Hospital and some good golf courses. Long Bay only has a prison.'

'We're going to the prison,' Helen said. 'We can't play golf.'

The couple were still chuckling when they reached Matraville, which was where they lived.

'About three more stops. You can't miss it. Great big walls and barred windows. Definitely no bunkers in there.'

The friendly pair waved to the tram, and they waved back.

'I suppose I shouldn't have said that,' Helen smiled.

'My darling, you say whatever you wish. They thought it was great fun, and so did I.'

My darling, Sarah thought. And I only met her yesterday!

Yet it expressed exactly how she felt, and what a joy it was to be with someone like Helen, especially when she cast off the gloom that had oppressed her last night. Today she was bright and vivacious; her eagerness was infectious. Sarah felt a great sense of expectation as they reached their last stop, and realised what it was. Helen's animation. She could hardly wait to get off the tram. And for the first time Sarah speculated on the possibility that this girl was in love with Neil.

Did Neil know, she wondered?

Did Helen?

It was late and most visitors had arrived by now. The senior warder, 'Iron Bar' Steele, was about to give up the whole thing, when he saw two women waved through by the guard on the gate. Both were smartly attired, one middle-aged, the other young and wearing a dark blue dress.

Very nice, he thought, then consulted his clipboard with a list of names and frowned.

'Mrs Weismann?'

'Yes,' the older woman said. 'I'm afraid we're late, but the tram ride was longer than we realised.'

'Senior warder Steele, Madam. I see on my list for today I have only one visitor expected.'

'This is my daughter,' Sarah said with perfect composure, and Helen repressed a pleased smile. 'I do hope it'll be all right.'

'I'm afraid it won't. For either of you.'

'Why not?'

It was the younger woman, sharply disappointed. *Trim, sexy little number*, he thought, *a bit too good for that troublemaker.*

'Why not?' Helen asked him again. 'Why can't we see him? We're only twenty minutes late.'

'If you'll give me a chance, Miss, I'll explain. It's nothing to do with the time you arrived. The prisoner Latham won't be able to see anyone today – or for some time. He's in solitary confinement.'

'He's *what*?' It was the older woman this time. Looking really shocked, the younger one holding her arm as she swayed. 'Did you say solitary?' She almost whispered it, and he felt anxious.

'You all right, Madam?' He didn't want anyone fainting; it was the last thing he needed. He'd waited all this time to tell her, wanting to avoid a fuss, and now wished he hadn't bothered. Better to have left a note, and not gone to so much trouble. 'Are you all right?'

'No,' she said. 'How could I be, when we've been given news like that? Will you please tell us why he's in solitary confinement?'

'I don't have to tell you anything, Mrs Weismann,' he said far more bluntly, because it appeared she wasn't going to faint after all. There need be no kid gloves. 'But I waited to explain, since you've obviously come a long way for nothing.'

'Explain what?'

She sounded afraid, and he enjoyed that.

'Latham attacked and seriously injured another prisoner this morning. He has been placed under guard and charges will be brought against him. I'd say he can expect an extension of his sentence, but that's not up to me. I would certainly doubt if he'll be granted any future visiting rights this side of Christmas. The guard will see you out. The trams run every half an hour.'

'Who did he attack, and why?'

The woman had tears in her eyes. A bloody foreigner, too, with her accent. A migrant. He'd had enough of them.

'That's not information I can give you. It was unprovoked, a vicious attack, and the man he assaulted is in hospital.'

He nodded abruptly and walked away.

'What a pig!'

It was the girl. He knew he had been meant to hear. He turned and stared hard at her. Stared at them both.

'Pretty silly, Miss, a comment like that. Since he's in here, and I'm in charge of discipline.'

'That's obviously a threat, Mr Steele. Please tell me the name of the prison Governor.'

'I think you're the one threatening me,' he retorted, but felt uneasy. It was stupid of him, saying a thing like that in front of them both. She'd even remembered his name.

'Don't worry then, Mr Steele. It's simple enough to find out.'

'Mannix,' he said. 'The Governor is Mr Charles Mannix.'

'Thank you. We'll talk to our lawyer, who will write to him.'

'There's no need.' He tried to control his anger. Bloody chit of a girl, giving him all this lip.

'Oh, I think there's every need. Come on, Mum.'

The senior warder watched them walk away. He felt livid with the world. Furious at the bloody Pommy for belting the shit out of Chigger. Enraged at Harris for being so hopeless. Worried about losing his three hundred quid. And fuming about this damn girl and her threats, with the uneasy feeling she might even mean it.

He went upstairs, where he could see them through the main gate walking towards the tram stop. A taxi cruised past and the girl hailed it. He saw the cab stop, and they got in. *Maybe rich as well*, he thought uneasily, as the taxi drove away.

The idea of Neil being in solitary confinement had devastated Sarah. She was near to collapse. Helen realised this, and hailed the taxi so they could get home swiftly. No long distressing tram journey, no matter what the cost. As soon as they reached the apartment in Macleay Street she made Sarah sit down and rest, and went to the sideboard. She poured a stiff whisky, added a tiny splash of water and gave it to her.

'I know you prefer wine, but you need this,' she said, perching on the arm of the chair beside her. 'Just sip it slowly.'

'Stop mothering me.' Sarah tried to laugh, but it sounded closer to a sob.

Helen was anxious about her. Despite her anger at the prison officer and her anxiety about Neil, she felt Sarah's panic keenly. The day that had begun with such expectation had turned into something ominous and alarming.

'If a man really is in hospital,' she tried to rationalise, 'then perhaps Neil did it. We have to face the prospect that such things could happen in there. But what we need to know is why. Because I don't believe a word that creature said.'

'Nor do I. And I hate to admit it, but I'm still terrified of people like that. All he lacked was a brown shirt with a swastika, or a black uniform and death's-head badges of the *SchutzStaffel*.' The whisky glass shook in her hand as she began to shudder.

'Forget him, Sarah.'

'I can't forget. I've seen too many like him.'

'We need to think. We have to do something.'

'I wish I knew how. It was wonderful of you to try to scare him like that. But we don't have a lawyer. And if we did, I doubt if a Governor of any prison would listen to him.'

The change from the charming, self-assured woman of the previous day was both shocking and painful to see. She was suddenly helpless, unable to cope. She held out her drink to be taken away, as if even the smell of it revolted her.

'We can't do anything, Helen. We won't get in to see him, and no-one will tell us what happened. I thought it would be different here, but it's not.' She put her head in her hands. 'It was bad enough, knowing all these months he might have to go to gaol, but somehow we came to accept that. And in court, it seemed ... civilised. The Judge listened. I felt relieved. Nine months, perhaps only six, it would soon be over. I even felt thankful, because I thought I had helped.'

Helen knelt and held her tightly. She could feel the tremors shaking her.

'You did help. You know you did. And now we have to help again. Because he certainly saved your life, and I feel he saved mine.'

'But how can we help him? And when? You've forgotten – in two days' time you'll be going back to Adaminaby.'

There was a rather long pause, while Helen considered this.

'I don't think so,' she said eventually.

It was dark as night in the cell. No windows or lights, the corridor outside gloomy and full of shadows. It was like being buried, for they had bundled him down steep steps to a cellar, and ever since he had been alone in utter silence. The cell was cramped, with barely room to walk, and contained only a wire mattress and a slop bucket. The bucket reeked, as if deliberately not emptied since the cell's last occupant. He wanted to urinate, and had to feel for it in the blackness, then hold it carefully so he did not spill any. If ever the lights were turned on, Steele would relish evidence he had pissed on the floor, and probably find it a cause for further punishment.

Sometime soon they would have to feed him, although one of the warders had said it would be only bread and water – if they remembered – and there'd be no proper food until he fronted the Governor to have his case heard. He'd asked when that might be, and thought at first they were not going to answer, then the more amenable of the two had shrugged and told him that was up to Mr Steele – who had to formulate the charges – and not to hold his breath. Iron Bar was a busy man, and sometimes these things took a few days. Also, the other warder added, Mr Steele would have to wait until Chigger was well enough to be interviewed, so he could give a proper statement about what might've provoked this savage and unexpected attack. Both warders had laughed at this, switched out the lights and left him to the darkness and his own thoughts.

He was determinedly philosophic, which might have surprised them, had they been aware of it. He had made the decision knowing it would bring trouble, perhaps even an extension of his sentence if the Governor was as biased and dishonest as his warders. But the choice had been made after a lot of thought, and the realisation that at some time during the next few months he would reach breaking point, if Harris and his cronies kept up their daily harassment.

So why endure it for months, then be forced to fight? Why not try to dent the Chigger Harris image, and hope the rest of his time here would be tolerable, even if it was to be a longer period? And perhaps some of those who had fed him information, and helped to keep Harris's dingoes in place during the fight, might even be brave enough to speak up and support him.

In the darkness of solitary, he felt a faint ray of hope.

~

The following morning Sarah telephoned Henry Falconer at his office to ask if he could recommend a lawyer. Helen was relieved at the change in her. After yesterday's shock at Long Bay and the dismaying evening that followed, this morning she had arrived to find Sarah had slept soundly, and was like a different person, no longer helpless and traumatised. On the phone to Falconer she sounded brisk and decisive.

She explained that Neil was about to be charged with assaulting a fellow prisoner, and the senior warder, a Mr Steele, had made some very unpleasant threats. Against Neil, and also against her and a friend. So they needed legal advice on what to do. Whether they could approach the prison Governor, whose name was Mannix. Charles Mannix. If Mr Falconer could call on her after work, she was saying, he could meet Helen Francis, who would confirm the warder's behaviour. Yes, *that* Helen Francis, she said responding to his obvious surprise, and when she hung up she was smiling.

'He'll be here at 5.30. On the dot.'

'Probably to see what I look like,' Helen said, 'after what he heard that creature Mitchell say in court.'

'Well, we'll soon put him right on that.' She studied Helen, who was wearing the same navy dress, and a straw hat that framed her face, with a dark blue ribbon. 'You look like a schoolgirl going for an interview,' she said, and kissed her. 'Good luck.'

Helen ran down the stairs and across the street to wait for the bus. She would need more than luck. They had sat up late, talking over what might be done. They'd discussed plans, before she had made Sarah a glass of hot milk, and suggested bed. Then she had gone back to Michael's flat for a few hours' sleep and a change of underclothes, left a note for them and returned to Macleay Street before breakfast. Sarah's recovery was a great relief, but today would be another difficult day, and regardless of the confidence she had expressed last night, she was not quite sure how to handle it.

The light was switched on, and Neil blinked. Despite the discomfort of the wire bunk, with only a thin blanket spread over the springs, he felt rested and thought he must have slept.

'Is it morning?'

'Lunch time, mate. Sunshine outside. Not a cloud in sight.'

It was the more congenial of the two warders, who opened the cell door and gave him a tray on which was a bowl of thin soup and something that looked like stew. Expecting the prescribed diet of water and a piece of dry bread, this was startling, and made him realise he was ravenously hungry. He had a tin spoon, but ignored it, tipping the bowl of soup to his mouth and consuming it within moments. The warder watched this, not quite friendly, but Neil sensed some change in his attitude.

'I thought it was going to be bread and water?'

'Me, too. Only Iron Bar got a message from the Governor.'

'Message?'

'To feed you proper rations. He won't be hearing the charge for a day or two.'

'Why?'

'Buggered if I know. Only there's various rumours.'

'Like what?'

'Like you got influence with people outside, and the bloody Archbishop is very partial to influence.'

Neil was surprised by the reply. He almost denied he had influence anywhere, then decided it was more sensible to stay silent and look enigmatic.

'That's one rumour. Another is that they're waiting to see if Chigger dies, then they can charge you with murder.'

'That's bullshit,' Neil said between mouthfuls of the stew. It looked disgusting, but because of his ravenous hunger, it tasted delicious. 'Harris won't die. We were trained to kill people, and if I'd wanted to kill him he'd be dead. The idea was to hurt and humiliate him.'

'You hurt him, all right. Trained, eh? Whereabouts?'

'Commando camps in England.'

'Did you get to fight?'

Neil nodded. 'In France and Germany.'

'Yeah?' The warder seemed reluctantly impressed. 'Well, you can handle yourself a bit. Put his weights up, well and truly. Anyway, Mannix says you're on normal rations, and you get a half hour in the small yard later. And Mr Steele's got the shits about it.'

'Good,' Neil said, eating voraciously.

Helen was hungry, but dared not leave in case she missed an opportunity to see him. She looked up hopefully as the secretary approached from the offices in the executive suite, left some messages at the reception desk, then came to where she was sitting.

'I did make it clear that I doubt if Sir Cedric can see you,' she said. 'He has a meeting with bankers, then an appointment at State Parliament with the Minister of Works. You're wasting your time.'

'Is there any reason why I can't wait, in case he can find a spare moment for me?'

'Well, I'm not going to ask anyone to throw you out, if that's what you mean, Miss Francis, but I really am starting to feel that you should go. I could try to make an appointment for you next week. But the week after that would be more suitable.'

'I'm supposed to go back to Adaminaby on Sunday.'

'Then go back, and we'll write to you.'

'But I'm not going back,' Helen said uncompromisingly. 'I can't. And that's why I'm here, because I think it's right I should explain to Sir Cedric.'

'I really don't imagine he'll be interested,' the secretary said with cool disdain. 'If you have a contract, you're obliged to work there until it expires, or else make an application for another job.'

'I know that, but . . .'

'This is a matter for you and your works manager to resolve. Sir Cedric Lawrenson is the head of a very large company, with many thousands of people working for him. He can't be expected to listen to complaints from all and sundry.'

Helen was about to say she was not all and sundry, but the secretary anticipated this.

'The mere fact you met him once, and he asked me to send flowers when you had an accident, hardly qualifies you as someone on whom he should waste his time.'

'I know you have to protect your boss,' Helen said quietly, 'but you're not very friendly, are you?'

'On the contrary, if I was unfriendly I'd long since have had you removed. He won't see you, and it's a waste of *my* time to even be here discussing it with you. Besides, I'm not supposed to be friendly. I'm supposed to be his efficient personal and private secretary – which I can assure you on some days takes every scrap of patience I possess.'

Helen couldn't resist it. 'He's not that bad. I liked him.'

'I didn't say I dislike him. But you try working with him every day.'

Before she could reply, the door to the executive suite opened and a group of men in suits emerged, accompanied by Sir Cedric in shirtsleeves and braces. Helen saw them go to the door, where they all shook hands. He was on his way back when he noticed his secretary, and beckoned her impatiently. Helen began to rise in hope, but he took no notice. She subsided, then realised the secretary was talking quietly to him, indicating in her direction. She stood up again as Sir Cedric walked towards her. He came close, head tilted with an interrogative frown as he studied her. She saw a nod of recognition, a trace of a smile.

'The interpreter. The Hungarian who won't let me fire that loudmouth worker when he calls me names. Yes?'

'Yes,' she said, smiling in return. He sounded the same as he had that day in the freezing cold of the mountains.

'Ilona who became Helen Francis. Because of you, I decided to move them from the tents, down to Adaminaby. Did you know that?'

'I wondered,' Helen said, 'though I didn't like to assume it. And you sent flowers when I had an accident.'

'An accident was it?' He looked at her keenly. 'I think I heard something different about that.'

'It's the past. I prefer to forget what happened, and remember the kindness of the flowers,' she said. 'I wanted ten minutes of your time, but your secretary said it's a bad day.'

'A terrible day. Those men in their suits are bankers, but more like burglars; they want me to bleed, so they can steal my blood. And soon I must go to State Parliament, to the Minister for Works and and kiss his arse. Is that the correct expression? You're the expert.'

'That seems like the correct expression. If you want a special favour from him, it's certainly accurate.'

He laughed aloud. His secretary and the receptionist looked surprised, as if this might be a rare occurrence.

'And now Hungarians come, wanting ten minutes. If you were German or French or Dutch, I don't give you ten seconds. But we're . . . what are we? Do you remember?'

'Aliens from other galaxies,' Helen said immediately, and he laughed again. The distant audience looked even more astonished.

'Correct. So the Minister will have to wait for having his arse kissed. Yes?'

'Thank you, Sir Cedric.'

'Don't thank. We haven't time for thanks. Just start to tell me your problem, and be quick. Ten minutes, yes?'

'It's not easy. It might take fifteen.'

'Bloody Hungarians.' He shook his head. 'They always want a little something extra.'

Henry Falconer arrived punctually at 5.30, bringing with him Archie Pringle, the young barrister who had defended Neil. He explained he had telephoned the lawyer to seek advice on the matter, and it appeared Mr Pringle not only knew the prison Governor, but they belonged to the same golf club.

'Mustn't use it, of course,' Mr Pringle said, adding it would be most improper to exploit the fact he and Charles Mannix happened to be partaking in a four-ball match the following Sunday. He kept an impassive face when he said this, although Helen suspected that beneath it lay a secret smile, and from what she had heard of lawyers they exploited every advantage, particularly a social acquaintance.

If so, she was not going to argue. All she cared about was Neil's safety; she was desperately concerned for him, and fearful of the warder's attitude which had so alarmed her.

'I felt this should be dealt with promptly,' Pringle continued, 'so I phoned the Governor to request an urgent interview on a matter regarding my client, Neil Latham, and a threat made to two lady visitors by his senior warder. I hope you approve of my doing this.'

'Absolutely, Mr Pringle. What did the Governor say?' Helen asked.

Mr Pringle requested they all call him Archie.

'What did he say, Archie?' The young barrister was clearly pleased; he concentrated his gaze entirely on Helen while he answered.

'Charles – er – Mr Mannix was concerned. The warder Steele apparently has a reputation; he's known as Iron Bar, and not for nothing. The Governor will make inquiries. I'm to take a statement from you both, and meet with him and the senior warder tomorrow.'

'Wonderful,' Helen said.

Sarah thought that if she continued to smile at him like that, Archie Pringle was definitely going to ask her out to dinner.

'Short, simple statements, I think,' he said. 'If you write them out, Henry can witness your signatures.'

When the two men were leaving, Pringle suggested he call the following evening, and give them news of his meeting. Sarah thanked him. She and Henry Falconer tried not to smile at each other, as the barrister expressed a hope that Helen might happen to be free, and if so, perhaps they could find a bistro afterwards and grab a bite to eat.

'You've made a conquest,' Sarah said over supper.

'He's very nice,' Helen was carefully prudent. 'And so is Mr Falconer, acting so quickly to engage him.'

Which seemed to Sarah a discreet way of placing the smitten barrister and the upstanding public servant in a niche together, both of them nice because they were helping Neil. She made no comment, but thought it sensible and circumspect, and knew that she was becoming extremely fond of Helen. Her own daughter had been only eleven when they had been dispossessed of their home, and barely fourteen when they had been arrested by the Gestapo. For those dangerous years, they had been forced all the time to remain hidden inside their room, so Trudi's experience of life had ended before puberty began; she had had no chance to live, to ever experience a young man being enamoured of her and inviting her to 'grab a bite to eat'.

Sometimes, although she tried not to think of it, Sarah secretly wished Trudi's life had finished then, instead of the nightmare years in Belsen, being terrified and brutalised. She had seen her die, looking like an old woman at the age of seventeen, and the memory of it was a scar in her mind that still haunted her. In her long convalescence after the war, to protect her own sanity, she had tried to shut it from her consciousness as though she had been childless. And now, in the past few days, as if by a small miracle, here was someone who made her feel maternal – a friend despite their age difference, but also like a daughter lost and recovered. She had forgotten, or perhaps not really known, what a special joy that relationship could bring.

She could only hope that Sir Cedric Lawrenson, of whom she had heard both good and bad – mean as dirt some said, while others claimed he was always on the brink of financial disaster – would fulfil his promise and try to help her. Of this, Helen was in no doubt.

'It was wonderful.' She was bubbling with the excitement of it, eager to share the day's events with Sarah. 'He had his secretary ring the Minister for Works to say he'd be late for his appointment, and then asked her to bring coffee. He has a huge office with thick carpet, and chairs so large and soft I practically disappeared into one. I wish you'd been there! Just to see the secretary's face!'

'Was she cross?'

'A bit, but not very. More surprised, I think, because she was sure he'd throw me out. She got a bit cross later, because it took ages to explain everything – about Neil altering our papers and how he was in gaol and we were likely to be deported. And then I had to tell him about Michael – not too much about him, just that he was doing well financially, but I'd better not mention any names or tell him much more, because it was a bit shady.'

'Very sensible. What did he say?'

'His favourite expression. Bloody Hungarians! We were both laughing, and that's when the secretary came in and said she could hardly ring the Minister for Works again and that he had to go straight away. She was rather bossy, but I think he likes being bossed. So he asked me to come with him and explain the rest of it on the way, and then his driver would bring me home.' She smiled. 'He seemed quite impressed when I said Macleay Street, Potts Point.'

'And you arrived in a chauffeur-driven limousine?'

'A Rolls-Royce.'

'Well, I'm sure my neighbours were also impressed. So would I have been, if I'd been watching. But what can he do?'

'I don't know.' Helen smiled. 'But I told him how much I loved this country, and felt at home here. He said he knew the feeling, and promised he'd help. Just leave it to him. So I said I would.'

Please, Sarah thought, *please God, don't let it be a male boast, some rich man showing off to impress her. For her sake – and for mine. Now I've found someone like this, don't let me lose her.*

'There's one thing I need to talk about.'

Helen, after her early animation, appeared strangely hesitant. They had washed up the supper dishes, and were sitting on the balcony. A ferry was passing on its way to Manly, and the music of the regular trio on deck could be faintly heard from where they watched it.

'I've always loved that sound,' Sarah said, 'since Christoph first brought me here, and I accepted that he wanted to make amends for what his family had done, and this lovely place was mine. After he'd gone, I sat out here and heard the ferry music. I was so happy. Ever since then I'm reminded, whenever I hear it, of that magical time – of what I always felt was the first real day of a brand new life.' She was quiet for a moment, then turned to

Helen. 'You know you can talk to me about anything at all. Whatever it is.'

'If Sir Cedric can help, and I'm able to stay here in Sydney, Michael and Deirdre want me to live with them. They've asked me to move into their spare room. They've even promised to paint it.'

Sarah nodded, expecting this, yet feeling disappointment. But before she could reply the telephone rang. It might have been ringing for some moments; it was not until the ferry music began to fade that they heard its insistent sound.

'I'll get it,' Helen said, and ran, thinking that in a flat this big there ought to be an extension phone, wondering whether she could reach it before whoever the caller was hung up.

'Hello,' she said breathlessly, 'yes, it's me speaking. Yes,' she said after a moment, and sat down on the stool to listen to what he had to say.

Sarah was in the same place, watching the vessels and lights reflecting on the dark waters of the harbour when Helen returned. An air of tension was palpable. Helen took the same chair she had vacated. She looked confused.

'It was him,' she finally said.

'Lawrenson?'

'Yes. What a strange world, Sarah.'

Sarah felt a leaden weight on her heart. She tried to think of what to say, but no words would come. Then she realised Helen had asked a question.

'Have you ever heard of the Hungarian Mafia?'

'The what?'

'Hungarian friends, with other friends in high places. I gather these were politicians. He said he made some phone calls – and drew on a few IOUs, whatever that means.' She could contain her relief no longer. 'I can hardly believe it, but he says it's fixed.'

'Helen!'

'He's guaranteed I'm a good citizen, and two senators, friends of other friends, are going to have a word where it matters. I asked if it was above board, if it was legal, and he told me not to be so stupid. So I promised not to be stupid. Then he said I was a damn sight more use to this country if I stayed here than if I was sent back to Hungary.'

'He's absolutely right.'

'But it is an irony, isn't it? He twists arms and uses influence, and I'm allowed to stay.'

'Because he thinks you're worth it. That's not corruption, at least not to me. It's plain commonsense. Do you have to go back to the Snowy?'

'No. I'm to work the rest of my contract in one of his sites in the suburbs. Next week he'll tell me where. He said he's looking for a difficult spot where I'll have to work hard, and not to expect any more favours. I told him in Hungarian that I loved him – like an uncle.' She laughed and hugged Sarah. 'I can stay. I'm free. Isn't it wonderful?'

'Wonderful. What about your brother?'

'That's the only thing,' she was slightly deflated, 'Sir Cedric said he didn't know him, so he'd help me but wouldn't make guarantees for him. If Michael got into trouble, it could rebound on both of us.'

'Well,' Sarah said, 'from what you've told me of Michael, he sounds as if he can take care of himself. And as he's married to an Australian girl, I doubt if they could deport him, anyway. He'll be glad to have you here, staying with them.'

'But I can't.'

'Can't what?'

'Stay with them. That's what I was about to try and explain before. I don't want to live with them. They have their own life, and much as I love him, it's not my kind of life. I'm going to tell them I'll visit often, but I won't live there.'

'So what will you do?'

'Find a room. I'll have a job. I can afford to rent a room.'

'Will you please come and live here?'

'What? But . . .'

'Please, Helen?'

'But that's what I was trying to pluck up courage to ask you. If I could stay here for a while, at least until Neil comes back to take over the room? I can't think of anywhere I'd rather live, or anyone I'd rather live with. But I didn't want to be pushy and intrude.'

'My darling girl,' Sarah began to say, and thought *there I go again. But I don't care. She is my darling girl.* She reached out a hand, and it was like clutching the hand of someone who was not only a daughter, but a very dear friend. Her eyes were suddenly moist, and she could feel the tears coursing down her cheeks.

'Are you crying?' Helen was dismayed.

'Take no notice,' Sarah said. 'I have this stupid habit. I always cry when I'm happy.'

Chapter 20

The prison yard was packed. It seemed as if they'd relaxed the rule, and let out most of the inmates at the same time, so that when the first of them noticed Neil and nudged others, the silence appeared to spread until he was sure there were two or three hundred prisoners of all ages and sizes staring at him, and hardly a sound to be heard. If there'd been shouts of abuse it would have been only what he expected, but this was eerie. En masse they just stood and looked at him, and it seemed to go on and on.

Altogether he had spent four days in solitary, although Steele's original order that he be kept in the dark on a diet of bread and water had been changed by the directive from the Governor. He had been moved to another cell in the same block, but one with a window and more space, and been served normal prison food. On the fourth day he had been taken to the Governor's office. The senior warder was there, in a state of some hostility judging by his compressed lips and bleak gaze. So, to Neil's surprise, was Archie Pringle, who had brought statements from two visitors who had made a complaint against Steele. Neil had looked on as Pringle gave these to the Governor, who studied them, then questioned Iron Bar.

'You've read these, Mr Steele?'

'Yes, sir. Pack of lies.'

'You didn't make the statements they claim?'

'Of course not. Besides, the girl called me a pig.'

'According to her statement, she made the comment to the other woman. You overheard.'

'I was meant to overhear.'

'And then you told her she was pretty silly, since the prisoner was in here, and you were in charge of discipline.'

'I may have done.'

'And you don't call that a threat?'

'Governor, this is incorrect procedure. You have no right to question me in front of a criminal.'

'Then leave if you wish, Mr Steele. But consider yourself relieved of all duties until I investigate further. Including Harris's assaults against this prisoner, which I propose to examine.'

'You're not going to take the word of some crim against me, I hope. This man viciously bashed another inmate . . .'

'If you choose to remain, then by all means let's analyse that remark. But I've invited Mr Pringle, the prisoner's barrister, to stay purely as an observer, since his client is facing a serious charge.'

'That's highly irregular, sir.'

'A great deal that occurs in this prison is irregular. I was appointed to deal with that. On the matter of Harris, I've already questioned several prisoners and two officers, and I find some curious discrepancies in the accounts of what took place.'

While they had all listened, the Governor read out a statutory declaration, which asserted that Chigger Harris and the senior warder were engaged in a conspiracy, the object of which was to provoke the prisoner Latham into retaliation, which would mean a loss of remission for good behaviour and possible extension of his sentence. Then another, that claimed he was consistently attacked and warders had been told to turn a blind eye to whatever took place.

'Bloody lies,' Steele snapped, barely able to control his rage.

The Governor had then proceeded to read two more depositions.

'Where did you get this crap? It's lies, all of it.'

'Everyone's lying except you? Is that it, Mr Steele?'

'You're new here, *sir.*' He said it like an insult. 'You'll soon learn you're dealing with the dregs, and can't believe all you hear.'

'As I'm in charge, it's my prerogative to choose who I do believe. I questioned Harris, and in my considered opinion he's a dangerous bully who is abusing the system. I'm sending this file to the department for further action, and Harris will be transferred to the security wing at Grafton. You're suspended, pending a full inquiry.'

Neil had seen resentment often enough before, but the senior warder looked as if he was going to launch himself across the desk and attack his younger superior. His face had turned brick red with fury, the muscles in his face working as he tried to control himself. Then, without a word but with a final venomous stare at them all, Steele left the office, slamming the door behind him with such ferocity that a print fell off the wall.

After his departure, learning the identity of his visitors who had made the sworn statements, Neil had realised with astonishment it actually had been Helen he'd glimpsed at the back of the court. And she had come to visit him with Sarah.

There was so much he wanted to know, but he had no opportunity to ask her whereabouts or any other details from Pringle, because a warder arrived to escort him back to his original cell. All he could do was thank the barrister, and express his hope that both his friends would be able to come again to visit him. Perhaps soon.

Not that soon, Governor Mannix had informed him. While a charge was most unlikely, there had to be some disciplinary action, and so he was imposing a month's ban on visitors and Neil would be unable to send letters during that time. Apart from this, the matter would be considered as justifiable self defence, but he said any further displays of unarmed combat, or prisoners dispatched to the hospital, might not be looked upon kindly. Neil was dismissed with a nod and a glance that might almost have contained a trace of admiration.

Now, an hour later, he was turned out into the exercise yard, with half the population of the gaol silently scrutinising him. *All very well for the Archbishop in his office laying down the law*, Neil thought, *but what the hell happens now? Are these all supporters of Chigger Harris? I could be bowled over and stamped on, kicked to pieces in a matter of seconds – and I certainly haven't seen many brave prison officers in this place who'd bother trying to rescue me.*

A voice suddenly called from the crowd.

'Good on yer, mate.'

'You're a bottler.'

More voices followed.

'Yeah. Beauty, sport.'

'Time someone beat the shit out of him.'

'We're well rid of the bastard.'

'Bloody oath we are.'

'Bet Chigger never knew you was a flamin' ex-commando.'

'He'd have shat himself.'

There was general agreement on this, and laughter.

Someone put his hands together and started to clap, and to Neil's astonishment others took it up. Somebody else cheered. Within moments the whole yard seemed to be clapping and cheering. Up on the watchtower gantry, patrolling warders looked down at this display, stone-faced, as if nothing about this place would ever surprise them. Some of the prisoners came forward to pat his back, or nod their approval, even a few for a quick handshake. And then, as suddenly as it had happened, it was over.

The yard returned to normal. Men smoked, chatted, warmed themselves in shafts of sunshine. Chigger Harris was gone, transferred to a tougher prison, and it was clear that no-one was going to miss him. Least of all Neil. Even if the sentence was to last the full nine months without remission, he knew now he could survive. Time would be the only enemy; even the month's ban on visitors was hundreds of hours of monotony, and with it the constant worry of not knowing what was happening in the world outside.

He spent the remainder of the day reflecting on how Helen had come all the way from Cooma to be in court, and had somehow met Sarah. Together they had made the abortive visit to see him, clashing with the senior warder. And Helen had called Iron Bar a pig. The thought of it made him smile. He started to recollect the bright and vivacious girl who had rearranged hotels for him, and the way she had been so entertaining over lunch at the Berridale Inn. Now he wished he had stayed the full weekend, made an attempt to see her again, and tried to get to know her better.

~

It was their second meal at the same restaurant, a tiny French bistro in the heart of the Cross, run by a woman from Normandy and her Australian husband. It was called Colette's Place, Colette being the wife who took the bookings, served the wine, and late in the evening, if her clientele that night was *sympathique*, sat at the tiny piano and sang Edith Piaf songs. Dave, who had been in the RAAF during the war, was surprisingly the chef who prepared the succulent French food. Helen and Archie Pringle enjoyed the place so much on their first visit, that he suggested they must come back again, just to see if the standard was as high the next time, or had they merely been lucky?

She liked Archie very much. He was uncomplicated, and made her laugh. He had kissed her lightly on the cheek after their first date, but had been eager to arrange another, and so here they were, and she wondered where it might be leading.

'They met in France . . .' he was saying.

'Who did?'

'Colette and Dave. You weren't listening to a word I said.'

'No, I wasn't.'

'You don't have to be so honest,' he said ruefully, 'it's a bit bruising to the ego. You're not under oath in the witness box.'

'How did they meet in France?'

'He was in a bomber squadron, shot down outside Rouen. Colette was a waitress in a restaurant, but she was also in the Resistance, and when they located his parachute and found Dave with a broken ankle, she was given the job of looking after him.'

'How did she do that?'

'She had a room upstairs, over the restaurant. She managed to get him there, had the local doctor set it, put Dave in her bed – and as far as I can work out, climbed in after him.'

Helen laughed. 'What about the broken ankle?'

'They were extremely careful.'

'And who taught him to cook?'

'She did. As soon as his ankle was better, Dave kept talking about trying to escape. Going back to help win the war. So she made a pact with him. If he promised not to try to be a hero and stayed with her, she'd get the chef to write out all his favourite menus, and they'd learn to cook them together. She'd come to Australia with him after the war, and they'd open a restaurant. And here it is, and here they are. Nice, eh?'

'What a lovely story. How did you find all this out?'

'I'm a barrister. I practise a lot by asking questions.'

Later, in French, Helen asked Colette if it was all true.

'All true,' Colette told her, complimenting her on her accent.

That night, after the restaurant shut, Archie and Helen were invited to stay and have a cognac. Dave came from the kitchen to join them, a boyish-faced thirty-year-old, who had rushed off to war aged eighteen, determined to be a fighter pilot. He'd failed in that ambition, becoming instead a rear gunner and ending his war in a French farmyard with a busted ankle.

'He's very nice,' Helen confided in French to Colette. 'I'm glad you kept him in bed and he didn't go back to the war. Far too handsome to get killed. It would have been such a waste – of a good cook, too,' she added with a smile. 'But you'd better not tell him all that.'

'I don't need to. He speaks fluent French,' Colette said, and they all dissolved into laughter.

They went back again the following week. Colette and Dave were now their friends, and the restaurant became their regular place.

⁓

When Michael unlocked the rear door of the premises, leaving the sports car parked in the laneway, he instantly knew someone was in the club. He could smell the strong aroma of cigar smoke. He made his way warily up the back stairs, because the club was supposed to be empty. It was only 2.30 in the afternoon, and the Maison Lumière did not open until six.

Part of his regular routine was to conduct a check at this time each day, to ensure the cleaners had been in, the supplies delivered, and all was in order for the opening. He did this after he and Deirdre had finished lunch, leaving her to sleep, and often coming home afterwards to slip under the blankets beside her. She liked to be woken sensually, and then they showered and changed and returned to the club, the start of a long shift that very rarely ended before a champagne breakfast was served to the hardy gamblers and patrons who had survived the night.

He paused outside the ornate doors, and heard the murmur of a voice inside. Someone cleared their throat. The door was unlatched, and gently easing it open he stepped inside.

'Oh, it's you,' he said, without enthusiasm.

Jimmy Kincaid responded with a look of equal dislike.

'Yeah, it's me. Waiting for you, as it happens. I got someone wants to meet you.'

Michael saw a man in his late thirties, well dressed, in casual but expensive clothes and Italian shoes. He had learned to recognise such details, and knew who this was, although they had never met.

'I know you from your photo, the one in your file.' The stranger sounded amused. 'Do you know me?'

'I'd say your name's Mitchell.'

'That's right, kid. I'm the one who can get you kicked out of this country, you and your sister.'

No you can't, Michael thought, but he said nothing. Helen was working for Lawrenson in her new job, and living in Macleay Street. He felt sure she was safe from the threat, but he wasn't going to tell that to this nasty piece of work.

'Did you hear what I said, kid?'

'I heard.'

'One word from me and you're history. Shipped back to some lousy DP camp. But relax, I'm here to talk. We can come to an arrangement. One that'll be good for all of us. You, me and Jimmy.'

'An arrangement? Good for us three?'

'That's right.'

'Will it be good for the Doc? Or is that a silly question?'

'If you mean Forbes-Clark, it's a really stupid question. He's out. I'm coming in. Got the picture, sonny?'

'I got the picture weeks ago. When faithful old Jimmy left the door open for the gaming squad. When I listened to the street talk. When his slimy gaze couldn't look straight at me or anyone else.'

'So what do you say, kid?'

'I say stop patronising me with names like kid and sonny.'

Stewart Mitchell lost his smile. His eyes became bleak.

'I told you he was a difficult young prick,' Kincaid said.

'I might be difficult. I'm not treacherous.'

'So you want to end up back in Europe, do you, sport? Back in shitsville,' Mitchell said. ''Cos I can put you there quick smart, and Forbes-Clark won't lift a fat finger to help you. I knew him when his name was just plain Clark, before he stuck a hyphen on it and became the society abortionist. Reggie's got a lot of enemies, and someday soon one of 'em is going to shoot him.'

'I'll tell him you sent good wishes for his health. And that he should wear his lead vest.'

'Don't be a smartarse. With or without you, this is the kind of club I want to own. Jimmy says he organised it all and runs it, but I think he's full of crap. You're the one who makes this club tick, and you could run it for me.'

'You're right about Jimmy. He couldn't run a shagging contest in a whorehouse.'

'Get stuffed, you bloody Yid,' Kincaid said, aggrieved. 'And bugger the pair of you. Stop talking about me like I'm not here.'

'Shuddup,' Mitchell said, 'or you won't be here. So what's it to be, Mike?'

'I need time to think about this.'

'The club will be mine, one way or another before long, so you better think about it pretty damn quickly.'

'What makes you so sure you can ease the Doc out?'

'Leave that to me. He'll go without any fuss. When people are in my way, they either get out of it or they get hurt.'

Like Neil Latham, Michael thought.

He watched them leave. Appearing calm, inwardly he was beset by questions about what to do for the best. He owed a certain loyalty to Forbes-Clark. He was as big a crook as Mitchell, but the Doc had made all this possible. It had suited him to do so, but their handsome new life had begun the day Forbes-Clark made him an offer he could hardly refuse.

If he had to choose between them, it would be simple. He disliked Kincaid intensely, and didn't trust Stewart Mitchell. But that was not the choice. The choice he had to make was to decide what was safest for himself and Deirdre – and their future. That was all that really mattered. She was all that mattered.

If it wasn't safe, then they'd cut and run. Leave the car, the flat, leave everything if necessary. Go to some faraway place where none of these dangerous people could find them.

Chapter 21

They came after midnight, nearly two weeks later. One of the cockatoos was bribed, they took out the other in the rear lane by the simplest means. A man came running past, sidestepped and knocked him to the ground with a shoulder charge. Another man appeared out of the dark, and held a gun against his head. He had no chance to reach the cord connected to the alarm upstairs, barely time to realise what was happening before they slapped a pad of chloroform across his face. He was dragged unconscious into his car and left there. They did not need to break open the doors; they had keys. The iron bar they carried was for the doorman, who had no opportunity to make a move towards his warning buzzer. He was gagged, tied, and hustled into a broom cupboard, where they stood him upright, dazed and terrified. Before they locked the cupboard door, they dosed him with enough chloroform to render him unconscious until the morning.

It was a Saturday, and the club was full to capacity. Friday and Saturday nights were always well attended by the regular patrons, politicians, socialites, radio stars and wealthy businessmen, especially those with weekenders where their families migrated, which left them free to visit the club escorting ladies other than their wives. After all, what place of liaison could be safer than Maison Lumière?

In addition this particular night was the occasion of the Annual Law Society Ball in the city, and when that ended a flock of legal luminaries sought to prolong the evening by a visit to the premises they'd been hearing so much about, for a few more drinks and a flutter at the tables. All were reassured by the club's reputation for security and discretion. They arrived in thoroughly high spirits, a large throng of dinner-jacketed jurists and their immaculately gowned women, to make it one of the most glittering nights of the Maison Lumière's existence.

Downstairs the initial intruders were joined by others. They brought their equipment in via the back entrance after first barricading the doors to the street, then cutting the wires linked to the entry buzzer. After that they disconnected the phone line. They stood and listened to the steady hum of conversation from the distinguished crowd of people, who were totally unaware of them in the plush premises upstairs.

Deirdre's baccarat table was packed with players and spectators, some to watch the turn of the cards, others there to admire the striking looks and voluptuous figure of the redheaded dealer. She and Michael were both aware exactly why she was employed; Doctor Forbes-Clark had been blunt enough when offering her the job, declaring that he wanted magnets to attract male punters, and Deirdre was a star magnet. But tonight Michael was something of a magnet himself, the centre of a glamorous collection of lawyers' wives, most of them fresh from the Law

Society Ball and new to the club, impressed by the decor, the orderly atmosphere, and their young and good-looking host.

For this is what he had become, particularly as Jimmy Kincaid was rarely present since the afternoon of the meeting with Mitchell. As for Mitchell himself, he had not been sighted in the interim, and Michael had begun to wonder if it was an empty threat. He had debated about confiding in Forbes-Clark, and eventually come to the conclusion that he must. The Doc had listened impassively, thanked him for remaining loyal, and said he would get it sorted out. Since then Michael had heard nothing.

Privately, he and Deirdre had decided on a course of action if there was to be trouble. They would simply vanish. They had taken some cautionary steps already, withdrawing all their cash from the safe deposit, and tightly packing most of it in a shoe box, which they had sealed and asked Helen to keep for them. Being Helen, she had first asked what it contained, and when he said it was just a bundle of private papers, their wedding certificate, and a small amount of cash, she had smiled and looked sceptical.

'If you want me to look after it, then I need to know what I'm safe-guarding,' she had said.

'Well, most of our cash,' he had eventually admitted. 'About three thousand quid. In case we have to make a quick move.'

She had been astonished by the amount, and concerned by his statement. What quick move? Why was he thinking it might be necessary? Michael insisted it was only normal safety precautions, but never having been able to keep a secret from her for long, had finally told her about the meeting with Mitchell, and his ambitions to take over the club. Helen was alarmed. She had agreed to store the package in her room at Sarah's where it would attract no attention, until they needed it.

'You be careful,' she had said, and Michael promised. In the meantime, they had taken other precautions. They had paid their rent two months in advance, and each had packed a suitcase which they left in a locker at Central station, so they could disappear by simply walking out the door. If necessary they realised they might have to sacrifice their car, but only if the threat was real and they were in danger.

One of the youngest of the lawyers' wives was smiling and openly flirting with him when there was a cry of alarm as the door was kicked open. A mob of men – there were at least a dozen – burst in wearing balaclavas that covered their faces, and carrying clubs that looked like baseball bats. A wave of panic spread as they began to methodically destroy the place. The bar was the first casualty. Bottles of liquor were smashed, shelves full of expensive crystal fragmented into splinters of flying glass. The women surrounding Michael, who had been complimenting him on his club, started to scream. Within seconds there was pandemonium; the sound of terror from the crowds of celebrities mingled with the noise of the relentless destruction.

The baccarat tables were bludgeoned and broken. Chairs were flung across the room, and the expensive curtains ripped from their rails. Two of the balaclava-clad figures produced open cans and brushes, and began to deface the walls by smearing them with lurid-coloured oil paint. Another splashed a tin of creosote over the fine wool carpet, with people recoiling from the corrosive smell. When more of the intruders brought buckets of whitewash and started to fling them at random, drenching the frightened women and ruining their expensive dresses, splattering their faces and hair, the terrified shrieking reached a crescendo.

Michael tried to stop one of them, and received a heavy blow to the side of the head from an unseen assailant. He felt numb and sick. Bile rose in his throat. He fell to the floor, and was trodden on by fearful patrons, oblivious of anything except the necessity to escape before harm was done to them, or before the police arrived. A sharp pair of stiletto heels cut his face, as their owner mindlessly fled. In the melee he glimpsed a club being raised and smashing the main chandelier, and he vainly tried to shelter from the shower of glass that cascaded all over him.

He had a last sight of Deirdre, lashing out fiercely as one of the assailants tried to rip off her dress, and the barman bleeding profusely from a head wound as he tried the telephone, jiggling it in futile panic when he realised there was no dial tone. Then the jostling, terror-stricken crowd obliterated his view as they stampeded for the exit. He tried to struggle to his feet, but a baseball bat hit him a numbing blow, and somewhere in the dark he thought he heard Deirdre scream.

RIOT IN GAMBLING DEN proclaimed the excited headlines on the front pages of the Monday morning tabloids, and newsboys in the streets and on tram platforms shouted the refrain and sold extra copies. Sarah's *Herald* was more restrained. CLUB AFFRAY was the heading, which reported that a number of masked men had broken into an illegal gaming club known as the Maison Lumière on Saturday night, and caused a considerable amount of damage. It was believed that many prominent society people and members of the legal fraternity had been among those on the premises at the time, but no arrests were made as the police did not arrive until the early hours of Sunday, and by then the club was virtually empty. They found only an unconscious doorman and a lookout, who had been attacked and chloroformed. No other staff remained, and there was nobody able to identify the attackers.

Sarah read it, and worried for Helen. If she had bought a paper to read on the train to Granville, which was where Lawrenson's were building a new housing estate and where she now worked as the main office secretary and interpreter, then she would already be concerned at not having heard from Michael. After all, it had happened in the early hours of Sunday, over twenty-four hours ago. It was odd that he had not rung, the pair of them being so close, and Michael and Deirdre must surely realise how this news would alarm her.

On an impulse she went to her address book, where Helen had written her brother's number. She dialled it and waited with growing concern as the phone rang and rang – and there was no answer.

Helen had had a hard day. A dispute between a foreman and one of the Latvian carpenters had erupted into a serious fight, and the site manager had called the police. They had arrived already prejudiced and ready to arrest the 'Balt', particularly when he yelled abuse at them in his own tongue. If they could not comprehend the words, the tone of it was unmistakable. Helen had tried to convince them it was a simple disagreement, that with neither being able to speak the other's language these kinds of incidents were inflated, and the Latvian was a good worker who had family responsibilities, with a wife and two children.

'What the hell's that got to do with it?' the younger policeman demanded. 'If he clocks the foreman, then his wife has to do without him for as long as a judge says. A week inside might cool him down.'

'But he didn't throw the first punch,' Helen said, and saw the foreman's angry look. She asked if she could speak to him in private. The young policeman was about to refuse, but the older one nodded.

'Anything to sort it out,' he said. 'Let the young lady have a try. It was only a fight. No knives or guns. No-one got hurt.'

She took the foreman aside. He was quietly livid.

'He threw the first bloody punch,' he asserted, and she agreed it was true, that she'd seen it. 'So why did you say I did?' he asked.

'Because they won't arrest you, will they? They'll take him in, though. You know he's a good worker, and we're short-handed. If he shakes hands and says sorry, can we ask them to drop it? I'll make sure Lawrenson's secretary knows you've been helpful.'

It was a bait. She knew the foreman was ambitious, and any news like this conveyed to the secretary, with whom Helen had become friends after their first encounter, would reach the old man himself.

'Okay,' he said, 'but he's a bad bastard, that Balt.'

She spoke to the carpenter in German. She told him – with some force – to put a smile on his face, make a noise that sounded like an apology, and to shake hands. The Latvian complained that he didn't feel like shaking hands, because the foreman was a miserable bugger. Helen advised him he had ten seconds to do what she'd requested – that she was trying to save his job and keep him out of court – and if he gave her any more trouble he was on his own and could go to hell. So there had been a handshake, a smile, and the police had gone away after telling her some of these migrants were a real pain, and the country would be better off without them.

She sat in the train and sighed. Soon it would be the end of her contract with Lawrenson's. Sir Cedric had asked her to stay on. Learning his secretary Margaret and Helen sometimes had a meal or saw a film together, he'd enlisted her support. Margaret was told to remind her there would be a pay increase and far better conditions, that he was anxious to keep her. Helen knew it, and appreciated the sentiment, as well as being grateful to him.

But she was tired of it. There were too many days like today. The bickering and altercations, the constant animosity that seemed to exist when Australians worked with New Australians; she was worn out with being in the centre of the too frequent disputes. Another job, something entirely different, was what she needed, although as yet she had no idea what it might be.

As she leaned back, thinking of this, she glimpsed the headline. A man sitting opposite was reading the *Sun*. When he folded the newspaper to the sport section, she caught a fleeting look at the front page, long enough to feel the shock of the banner headline: 'CLUB RIOT. GAMBLERS TELL OF TERROR AT MAISON LUMIÈRE.'

Helen left the train at the next stop, bought a paper and, after reading it and ensuring she had enough money for the fare, hailed a taxi to take her to Elizabeth Bay.

They were not there. Almost emptying her purse to pay the cab, she ran inside and up the stairs to the first floor. She rang the bell, knocked repeatedly, and began to feel afraid. After some minutes, a smartly dressed elderly woman came out of the adjoining flat, with a chihuahua on a lead. The tiny dog snarled.

'Cindy, behave! Say sorry to the lady,' the owner instructed her pet, and looked suitably apologetic.

'I'm looking for my brother,' Helen told her, and the woman said she thought she recognised Helen; hadn't she once stayed here with the young couple?

'Yes,' Helen said, feeling desperate. 'Have you seen them?'

'Not today,' the woman said. 'No sign of them.' Then as if seeking reassurance asked, 'We haven't seen them, have we, Cindy?'

Cindy merely bared her teeth and growled, still resentful at her unaccustomed scolding.

Helen ran most of the way home, up the winding incline of Billyard Avenue and the steps that led into Macleay Street. Somehow she knew this was Stewart Mitchell's doing, and she felt a helpless rage against this man whose evil activity seemed to pervade her life.

Why hadn't Michael been in touch sometime yesterday, if this took place in the early hours of Sunday? Where were they? She could only hope they had phoned and left a message with Sarah. But when she reached home, the flat was empty. It was only then that she remembered this was the first day Neil's privileges were reinstated, and Sarah had taken the tram to Long Bay to visit him.

It was a long and slow ride, because somewhere ahead near Randwick Racecourse there had been an accident, and trams were lined up behind each other for about a mile. At least that was the cheery information from the newsboys, making their way along the platforms of the stationary carriages, cashing in on the event to sell the final editions of the *Sun* and *Mirror*, in exchange for reports on the traffic. Not good, they advised. Two trucks had collided, each driver claiming it was the other's fault. They hoped none of the ladies had a hubby at home waiting for his tea.

Cheeky young monkeys, Sarah thought with a smile. She had a soft spot for these children who rode the trams in all weathers, to make only a shilling or two. But the news of the delay concerned her, and she only hoped by now that Helen was home, and that her brother had rung and was safe. She bought copies of each paper. The prose of the evening papers was considerably more florid. The riot had by now become a massive gang war. The devastation was described in detail; smashed chandeliers, paint-desecrated walls, despoiled carpet, and the opulent and palatial premises a veritable sea of ruined furniture and broken glass. There were also hints on the identities of the well-known show business and society figures who had fled from the brutal attack.

Sarah put the papers and her concerns aside, and thought fondly about her visit to Neil. It had been surprising – in a number of ways. Firstly, she had been allowed to sit with him, and he had greeted her with a hug. Expecting some kind of barricade or grill and strict separation, this had been a welcome beginning. It had also been a far longer visit than she thought the rules permitted, and once, when she had thanked a passing warder and wondered if she had overstayed and whether it was time to leave, had been told not to worry about it.

'Not unless you're in a hurry. He's been looking forward to this. The girl couldn't come, eh? Helen – isn't that her name?'

'That's her name. She's working,' Sarah told him.

'Pity. Like to meet her.'

The warder moved away, leaving them their privacy. Neil had smiled at her astonishment.

'What's happened here?'

'The senior warder,' he said. 'It seems everyone hated him, especially the prison officers, and they think you and Helen had a lot to do with getting rid of him.'

'But how extraordinary.'

'Did she really call him a pig?'

'Yes, she did.'

'Wonderful,' he exclaimed, and they both smiled. 'If she comes to visit, they'll queue up to congratulate her.'

'She'll come.'

'Good,' Neil said, and that was all.

He changed the subject. He spoke about the prison routine, how slowly time passed, the daily repetition which was the cause of so much frustration and stress. Fortunately he no longer endured that, because a strange thing had happened. Two Italians, who had been arrested for robbery, could barely speak a word of English, and had endured great difficulty because of their inability to communicate to others in the prison. One day Neil had stopped to speak to them, and the delight with which they heard their own language, and the busy talk that ensued, was noted by a warder who told the Governor.

'I was sent for,' he said, 'wondering if it was more trouble. Instead he wanted to know how I came to speak Italian, and did I know any other languages? Because he had a German in D block, and a Yugoslav, both having a hard time. Could I teach them? Could I?' Sarah watched him, his eyes shining and face animated. 'I could hardly wait to say yes. So we have two hours of lessons in the library each day, and then I'm allowed to stay and set new work for them, and nobody says a word if I spend another hour or two reading books.'

'If I didn't know better, I'd say you were enjoying this.'

'I've learned one thing. That I like teaching languages. And my Serbian has improved.'

'Do you think you'll get remission?'

'Perhaps. The Governor's a fair man but he's tough, and I did cause some rather grievous bodily harm.'

'Justifiably, from what Archie Pringle says.'

'He's prejudiced. But I recommend him, if anyone ever needs a barrister.'

Sarah was determined to say nothing. She had told herself on the way out in the tram, it was none of her business. She would keep silent. But this concerned the two people she loved most in the world.

'Neil, I know I shouldn't say anything, but Helen and Archie seem quite fond of each other.'

'I should hope so,' Neil said. 'Archie's a prince.'

'Oh.' Sarah wasn't sure whether to continue or not. 'It's just that they meet a lot, and have dinner. Once they took me to their favourite restaurant. It's called Colette's Place.'

'Was it nice?'

'Lovely.'

'Good food?'

'Perfect.'

She had found herself describing Colette who sang like Edith Piaf, and Dave who had landed in Normandy with a broken ankle and learned to cook. Neil laughed and said he thought it was splendid. A truly successful love story. He looked forward to meeting them.

His reaction had puzzled Sarah. The quality of the restaurant and its owners was hardly the point she had hoped to make. Or was he, after all, not interested in Helen? Because if she and Archie kept meeting regularly, at least once and often twice a week, it must clearly soon lead somewhere. To bed? Or to marriage? And as much as she liked Archie Pringle, she wanted something better for Helen.

'What is it, Sarah?' He could sense her confusion.

'Nothing,' she had said. Then again her mouth betrayed her. 'I'm so fond of Helen. She's . . . she's like a daughter.'

'I'm glad. Archie told me you'd met, but that's all I knew.'

'There's so much to tell, it would take days. She really is the most wonderful girl. And Sir Cedric Lawrenson has used some sort of influence to make sure she won't be deported.' She told him about Helen laying siege to the Hungarian builder in his office, which made Neil laugh. 'She's a joy. But I'm worried about her brother.'

'Michael. What's happened to him?'

'We don't know. There was a raid on the club, and . . .'

'Club,' Neil had said, 'what club? Don't forget I've been incarcerated in here. All I know is that he left the job at Adaminaby. Have you met him?'

'Oh yes,' Sarah said, 'he's charming.'

'Then he's changed since Milan.'

'What was he like there?'

'Not at all charming. Very bitter and difficult.'

Neil explained it was understandable after the existence they had endured. But he was startled to hear of Michael's extravagant new life and his marriage.

'A country girl,' Sarah said. 'I gather she was something of a rough diamond, but she's certainly polished up well.'

He smiled at that. 'Sounds as if you like her.'

'I do. She's rather stylish. Redheaded. Michael adores her.'

'And Helen?'

'Worries about them both. The job, the people they have to associate with. And today's news is going to upset her.' She told him, as briefly as she could, about the raid on the club. 'I just hope, by the time I get home, there's some word of where they are.'

If I ever get home, she thought, still in the stationary tram only a few miles from Long Bay, but at that moment, to the sound of ironic cheers, the convoy at last began to move. It took a further hour before the traffic chaos extending all the way to William Street was completely disentangled, and it was dark and after seven when she reached the apartment.

She arrived to find Helen frantic. She had phoned Michael and Deirdre's flat several times without success, and tried their actress friend Liddy Samson and their former landlady, Andrea, but neither knew where they might be. Both had read about the raid in the papers and were concerned.

'I think we have to call the police,' Sarah said.

Helen was unsure.

'Miki's told me such horror stories about the police being on payrolls,' she said. 'I wish I knew what *he'd* want me to do.'

'You have to do what's best for them.' Sarah was determined on this. 'If they're hiding, they'd be in touch. They'd want the money in that box they left with you. They'd come here, or ring up. We were home all day yesterday, and I was here till lunch time. Not a word. And by the way, in case you were wondering, Neil's well.'

'I'm sorry,' Helen said. 'I meant to ask. How was the visit?'

'Very different to ours. Nicer atmosphere. And he's got four pupils.'

'Pupils?'

'Migrants. Teaching them to speak English. Let's make some supper and I'll tell you about it.'

The phone rang. Helen picked it up eagerly, but it was not Michael or Deirdre.

'Archie,' she said. 'Yes, of course. I've rung everywhere and . . .' She frowned and started to listen. 'Yes,' she said several times, and finally told him she would be there and hung up.

'You'll be where?' Sarah could hardly contain her curiosity.

'Kellett Street. You know it?'

'Yes. Behind the Cross. Off Bayswater Road.'

'A friend of Archie's lives there, and that's where they are.'

'A friend of Archie's? What friend of Archie's?'

'I don't know. But Michael's been hurt. They tried to call us today. I'm to bring the money.'

'Not on your own, Helen.'

'Archie insists. I have to come on my own.'

'I won't let you.'

'Sarah, I have to.'

'But why?'

'I don't know why. But Archie begged me. And I trust him.'

I wish I did, Sarah thought, her mind filled with doubts. If a friend of Archie Pringle's had been sheltering them, why had it taken so long to communicate? And what friend? Kellett Street was little more than a laneway of once elegant terraces, now notorious as the beat of prostitutes and the haunt of cocaine vendors.

Helen ran to find a warm coat, and to collect the shoe box. She kissed Sarah on the cheek as she headed for the door.

'Let me call a cab,' Sarah said, but it was too late. She heard the latch on the front door click. She ran to the front balcony that overlooked Macleay Street, but Helen was already chasing a bus just pulling away from the section stop opposite. Watching helplessly she saw her jump on board, as the bus went out of sight on its way towards Kings Cross.

Chapter 22

She felt insecure, carrying the shoe box. It seemed to beckon thieves, to invite them, for what kind of fool walked in any street of this district with a sealed box clutched beneath their arm? Particularly this narrow and poorly lit thoroughfare. She wished she had brought a small bag of some kind to carry it, or better still, had emptied the contents and put them in the ample pockets of her old coat. But the street was quiet and virtually empty, apart from two prostitutes loitering for customers in shadowed doorways, and then the reassuring noise of conversation from a coffee shop as she went past it.

Her destination was beyond a cluster of tiny shops and narrow residentials, in a section of the street where the great town houses had been built almost a century earlier, merchants' homes with elegant colonial verandahs, most of them long since divided into cheap lodgings and tiny flatettes, with kitchens that could be concealed in cupboards.

Helen stopped at an entrance, checked the street number, and opened an iron gate framed by ornamental railings. She went to a Georgian front door where a light from the hallway shone through stained-glass panels. There were ten doorbells, and she pressed the one beside the name Archie had given her. In a moment she heard the approach of footsteps inside, and saw the outline of his figure through the glass as he hurried down the stairs.

'Thank God,' he said, as he opened the door, drew her safely inside, and kissed her. 'I got scared when Michael told me what was in that box. I should have come and collected you. No trouble?'

'None. How is he? Where is he?'

'Upstairs.'

'But how did he get here? And whose place is it?'

'First floor. Let's talk there.'

There was a wide, ornate staircase that clearly belonged to a former, grander age, and they went up to the first floor. He tapped on one of the doors, and a young man opened it cautiously.

'All's well,' Archie said to him. 'Don, this is Helen. Helen, this is Don Kavanagh, a friend of mine.'

'I've heard a lot about you.' He was about her age, with neat fair hair and blue eyes. He smiled as they shook hands.

Deirdre came to hug her, and led her to the only bed in the room, where Michael lay. He was conscious, but his face was cut and bruised, and she leaned down to carefully rest her lips on his forehead.

'I know,' he said, and she could tell it hurt him to speak with his badly bruised and swollen mouth, 'you told me to take care.'

'Have you seen a doctor?'

'I'm all right now.'

'You're not. You look like I did, in hospital at Jindabyne.'

'As bad as that?' He tried to manage a grin.

'You must have a doctor.'

'No need, Helen.'

'Miki, there's every need.'

In Hungarian he said: 'Don't keep on about it. Please.'

She wondered why he was so insistent.

'At least tell me what happened. We've been in such a panic, wondering where you were.'

'Someone hit me and I woke up here, late yesterday, with a blinding headache.'

'But how did you get here?'

'Archie saved us,' Deirdre said.

Helen turned and gazed at him. Completely bewildered.

'You did? How?'

Archie shrugged, hesitating before he answered. He appeared tense, and for some reason she thought he seemed embarrassed.

'I was at the club. Among a lot of legal eagles after the Law Society Ball. They decided to go gambling, so I thought I'd tag along. You'd told me all about these two, so I thought why not? It'd be a chance to meet Deirdre and Michael.' He paused, then carefully added, 'Besides, it was only a short walk from Don's, and I was coming here to spend the night.'

Helen barely had time to register what this meant, before she saw Don reach out and take hold of Archie's hand. Archie gripped it, as if it was a lifeline, but his eyes remained fixed on Helen. It was like an electric shock that produced a moment of clarity. Instant revelation, as she saw their clasped hands and understood so many things.

The shy goodnight kisses. The easy and relaxed rapport they had, like a comfortable friendship which had never seemed likely to become anything more emotional.

'I was actually coming for the weekend, which is about the only time we get to spend together. I keep a few clothes here, but we have to be careful. You see, it's illegal – even in private. People talk of changing the law, but nobody does. I'm sorry, Helen. I wanted to tell you often, but I didn't know how. We were such good friends, and I didn't want to risk spoiling that.'

'How could you possibly spoil it?' Helen said, and went to where the two men stood with their hands still linked. She kissed him gently on the mouth. 'Darling Archie, we're friends, and I hope we always will be. Now will you or Don or someone please tell me what did happen?'

'Don and I are going down to the Kellett coffee shop,' Archie said. 'It'll give you some private time to talk together. Then we'll come back and work out what's to be done.'

It was Deirdre who told her. Beginning from the time when one of the raiders had torn off her dress, and tried to get her on the ground, which was when Archie had picked up a discarded baseball bat and belted the man half senseless. Her dress was ripped beyond repair, unwearable, and all she had on beneath was the skimpiest underwear. He had wrapped her in his coat, then improvised one of the torn curtains as a gown for her, after which he went to check on Michael. The club had emptied of gamblers and guests in their panicky flight, and the raiders were on their way out, heading down the stairs smashing whatever remained intact as they went.

Michael was unconscious, and Archie had hoisted him over his shoulder. Deirdre, wrapped in her curtain, had followed them down into the back laneway. By the time they reached Kellett Street, Archie was exhausted, and had asked her to ring the bell.

It would wake Don, but he didn't think he could carry Michael any further, and certainly not lift him unaided up the stairs. So Don had come to the front door, sleepy but immediately taking over and carrying Michael upstairs into the flatette, where they insisted he be put in the only bed.

'It was three o'clock by then,' Deirdre said, 'and I wanted to get a doctor, but Archie said no doctor would come at that hour. We'd have to take him to a hospital. Better to let him rest till morning, then contact Forbes-Clark – because hospitals and most doctors would report a case of assault to the police, which could be a problem. Not only for Michael, but for them. That's when they told me they were . . . you know . . .'

'Lovers,' Helen said, and Deirdre nodded, seizing on the word as if grateful for the definition.

'Yeah, lovers – and that it's against the law – so after the way they'd helped I didn't think we should make them take a risk like that. So Michael was on the bed, and we all tried to sleep in chairs.'

'And in the morning, did Forbes-Clarke come?'

'Archie went to see him. There's no phone in here and the box on the street's been vandalised, so he went to his house. It's only five minutes away, in Roslyn Gardens. I wanted to find a phone to tell you, but Don said it was best to wait till the doctor had been, then I'd have more news. He reminded me I was still only wearing panties and a curtain – so they'd better get me some clothes first. Then Archie came back, and after that we had to stay inside. Keep out of sight.'

'Why?'

'Bloody Forbes-Clark,' she said. 'Double-crossing mongrel.'

'You don't mean he wrecked his own club?'

'Archie was almost there when he saw Clark come out with Mitchell. Neither of them noticed him, so he went into the porch of Andrea's next door, where we used to live. They're real close, those houses, and he could hear part of what they said. The Doctor was pleased at the raid. He'd make a list for the insurance, and they'd get it all back. Shut the place down for a month, give it a new name and re-open. Now that Kincaid was taken care of – that's exactly what he said, *taken care of* – he could accept Stewart's offer of fifty thousand pounds for a half share. He said it was lucky Michael had warned him; it had given them the chance to do their deal and get rid of Jimmy. And now it might be smart to get rid of a couple of others.'

'I bet Kincaid's dead,' Michael said. 'And the others are us, of course, because I know too much.'

'Dear God.' Helen felt ill. 'Are you sure?'

'Archie proved it,' Deirdre said. 'He waited a while, then went and rang the bell. There was a sort of butler, more like a bodyguard. When Archie said it was about Michael, Forbes-Clark was down in a flash. Where was Michael? Was he all right? Archie said he'd been badly hurt, and the Doc said it was terrible, just dreadful the way some criminal gang had tried to ruin him. He was even worried about his partner, Jimmy Kincaid. He hoped no-one had harmed him.

'In the meantime he'd look after Michael; he'd be there in half an hour. What was the address, and what was Archie's name as well? Archie just pushed him flat on his bum and went for it. Ran as fast as he could, in case the bodyguard had heard and tried to give chase, because it's only a street away.'

'Quite a bloke, your friend, Mr Pringle,' Michael said.

Helen could only agree. She reflected that this was a night for some highly illuminating details on her friend, Mr Pringle, not least of which was his almost reckless bravery.

Deirdre said, 'After that, Don was the only one who could safely go to our place to get some clothes for us. He meant to phone you from there, but he spotted two men outside in a car watching the building. They didn't know him, but he thought it best not to hang around too long. He went up to the flat, shoved some clothes in a case, and left by the back stairs.'

'I'll make you a bet,' Michael said, 'someone is still watching the place, waiting for us to come home.'

'What are you going to do?'

'I don't know. Not go back there, for sure.'

'I'll miss our lovely home,' Deirdre said sadly, and Helen felt a helpless anger on their behalf against the man who had caused this.

'So much for the friendly abortionist,' she said bitterly, and was instantly sorry, for Michael nodded in agreement as if no-one could really be trusted, and his rich new life was merely an empty charade. Deirdre, realising this, went and sat beside him like a lioness protecting her cub.

'Where will you go?' Helen asked, but before either of them could reply there was a tap on the door, a key turned in the lock and Archie came back alone.

'They could come here,' Sarah said.

It was an hour later, and they were having a makeshift supper after Helen's return by taxi.

'I thought you'd say that. I even told them you might. But Michael said no, he won't let you run the risk.'

'It's surely not a risk. Not here in Macleay Street.'

'Darling Sarah,' Helen said, 'you look out and see your nice neighbourhood, with interesting shops and pleasant people. But it's not all like that. There are gangs in this part of the city – and gangsters. Half the police force are on someone's payroll. There are people for hire who'd find and kill Michael and Deirdre – if that dreadful doctor ordered it. They have photographs of them both from the club, especially of Deirdre, which could be circulated. Nowhere around here is safe.'

'Is anywhere in Sydney?'

'I don't think so.'

'Then where?'

'Michael's talking of a place in Queensland. It's called Surfers Paradise. Part of an area that's been named the Gold Coast.'

'He should stay away from Paradise and Gold Coasts,' Sarah said with unusual severity. 'He's got a brain, and many talents. He should settle down and use them. So you can stop worrying.'

'If only,' Helen agreed. 'But he never will.'

'Too much wild charm,' Sarah shrugged.

'Too many years foraging for a real life,' Helen said quietly. 'Lying and pilfering to keep us alive. Long ago I tried to change him, but Miki's what he is, and what the fight for survival made him back in Budapest.' She was silent, recalling the fourteen-year-old delinquent dodging shrapnel and bullets, yelling his insults at the *Wehrmacht*. It would always be her abiding memory of him. 'The Gold Coast with a shoe box full of cash – he and Deirdre in their open sports car – that's Michael's idea of heaven. Or should I call it Paradise?'

Sarah smiled. At least the pair were safe tonight, and more

importantly for her own peace of mind, so was Helen. It had been an anxious wait, and well after ten o'clock before she had heard the sound of the cab stopping and had hurried to look down at the street. Relief had been replaced by a moment of dismay. All she could see beside the waiting taxi was the sight of Archie Pringle and Helen locked in an embrace.

Oh well, she'd thought, repressing her disappointment, there was no accounting for emotions or personal choice, and it was none of her business. She'd switched on the hall light and opened the door, as Helen came hurrying up the stairs.

'I love Archie,' she had announced, and hugged Sarah.

'That's nice, dear.'

'I love him very much. And I like his boyfriend, too.'

'What, darling?'

'Don. Archie's lover.'

'Oh . . .'

'Oh?' Helen had smiled. 'Is that all you want to say, Sarah?'

'I think so, for the moment. Have you eaten?'

'No, and I'm starving.'

'Why don't I cook while you tell me about Archie and Don. Not forgetting Michael and Deirdre. Tell me all that happened.'

Helen had explained everything that had occurred since the raid on the club, and how Archie had surprised them by coming back alone from the coffee shop.

'He came to tell us he and Don had made a decision. Michael and Deirdre need a place to hide until they can leave Sydney, so Don's moving into Archie's apartment, never mind the risk of neighbours finding out about their relationship. Archie was sweet, he made them promise not to go outside, and Don will come every day to bring them food and the newspapers.'

'How marvellous of them,' Sarah said. 'And very courageous.'

'It is, isn't it?'

'What about Michael? Does he need a doctor?'

'He refuses. Says he's too tough.' She smiled and could hardly wait to add, 'but Deirdre might. She's pregnant.'

'Helen!' Sarah was torn between delight and her concern for their situation. 'Are they pleased?'

'Ecstatic. Six months from now. Neil will be out of gaol, and I'll be an aunt. You'll be an unofficial great-aunt.'

'How lovely,' Sarah said, 'to be a great-aunt. If they go to their Paradise, their Gold Coast, do you think we could visit there?'

'I think we must. After all, we're family. That child is going to need us.'

They both laughed and Sarah felt an extraordinary sense of happiness. *We're family*. She had had none for so long, and now she had Helen as a surrogate daughter, by their mutual consent, and so by extension she had a family again. What a strange day, she thought. So full of anxiety and stress, and at the end of it, relief and such utter joy.

It was sometime later, preparing for bed, that she remembered the date, which made it even stranger. It was exactly eight years since she and the last Belsen survivors had been discharged from hospital. Neil had borrowed a jeep and driven her across Hanover and the British occupation zone, to the ruins of Berlin. After he had helped her find temporary accommodation, she remembered how they had bade each other farewell and she had stood watching as he drove away, feeling a deep sense of loss and wondering if they would ever meet again.

~

Neil had forgotten the date. There was no particular reason why he should remember. His concern was centred on counting the days of this year's calendar, ticking off the slow moving weeks of his nine-month sentence, which meant a total of two hundred and seventy-three days, unless, in the meantime, the Governor chose to recommend his early release.

He had no idea if this would happen. The injuries inflicted on Harris would count against him. A decision would be taken by the Prisons Department. No bureaucrat who resolved such matters would know that gaols allowed terrorists like Harris to function, not only allowed it but tacitly accepted the violence as a part of the system, almost by acceptance as a part of the punishment. He recalled people saying about various cases, 'Five years: he got off easy', and wondered if they had ever spent a week forcibly incarcerated within their house, let alone a real prison. On the other hand, he was teaching English to his four foreign students, and the Governor had come to inspect their progress, stayed to watch and take part in a lesson, and declared himself well pleased.

He was also forming ideas about the future, since the chance of working with the immigration department again seemed unlikely. He knew Henry Falconer would gladly have him back, but Henry had no real power when it came to such decisions. Neil himself had a number of suggestions, but they would wait. Now that he was allowed visitors at last, he hoped Helen would come soon, because he kept thinking about her, and wanted to tell her his ideas, and ask her if she thought they might work. He realised with surprise that her opinion was important to him.

He also kept being reminded by the warders that they wanted to meet and congratulate her on the demise of senior warder

Steele – the bloody Iron Bar – and apart from that, she sounded like a real good sort. What's more, they said, with all these bloody migrants, a girl named Helen Francis sounded like a proper Aussie sheila, and that's what we needed. Late at night, lying wide awake and thinking with amusement of these typical chauvinist comments, Neil remembered her and the way her bright laughter had enlivened the restaurant at Berridale, and was inclined to agree with them.

He was sure of one thing; he wanted to see her again.

Michael was restless. After two more days, with Deirdre making him remain in bed, and Don bringing them meals morning and night, he was sick of being cossetted.

'Let's get the hell out of here,' he said. 'Go up to this beach place, Surfers Paradise. I'll find a job, and we'll have about three kids.'

'All right with me,' Deirdre said, 'but let me have one first and see what it looks like. Suppose we have a kid who looks like my dad?'

'Im-bloody-possible,' Michael said, and proved he felt much better by cajoling her into the bed and making love until the tenants of the flatette next door banged on the wall and told them to shut up.

'There you are,' he said, 'I can still get you going.'

'You're a bastard, Miki,' she said with tremendous affection. 'Such a lovely bloody bastard. I could stay in bed with you going at it like a pair of rabbits forever, but we have to be practical.'

'Why?' Michael asked. 'I like the other idea best.'

'Stop it,' she giggled. 'Be sensible. Let's get out of this city.'

'Okay,' he said. 'You pack the clothes that Don got us from the apartment. We won't go there to pick up any more, it's too risky. We've got the cash, and all we need is the Jag.'

'I'll collect it,' Deirdre said.

'*I'll* collect it,' he corrected her, 'then I'll pick up our stuff in the locker at Central. Give me an hour, then be packed and ready. Soon as I'm back, I'll toot. We shove the cases in, and we're away like bats out of hell. Right?'

'Right,' Deirdre said. She felt like going back to bed with him, but thought they should be sensible.

Ten minutes' walk to pick up the car, Michael estimated, then Central station and back to Kellett Street. They'd be across the Harbour Bridge and up the Pacific Highway before noon; he'd phone Sarah and tell her, so she could pass messages to Helen and to Archie. It was best to get out of here, now that they knew the sort of shit Forbes-Clark had turned out to be. He'd liked the Doc, had thought him a sort of friend and trusted him, but it went to prove you could never tell.

A pity after things had gone well for so long, but they had a good wad of cash to see them through, and the Gold Coast sounded like his sort of place. Deirdre and he in the open Jag, heading for the sun. Lucky he had fluked finding a garage for the car just days before the raid because in this neighbourhood it would probably be without any tyres, or even its seats and the engine by now. Just like the vehicles in Budapest, he thought in a moment of memory.

Deirdre and he and the baby, on their way to a place called Paradise. Impossible to believe such a future back there in

Budapest, stealing loaves of bread and running from the fat German corporal with the rifle. He thought about the close shot that had chipped the statue beside his head; now, almost eight years later, he was nearly rich, very much in love, and going to be a dad.

He smiled at the thought and quickened his pace.

The watcher sat by the window in the demolished and ruined club. He was bored stupid with waiting. He had been given a photo of Michael Francis, but felt sure they were all on the wrong track. If he was this geezer Michael, he'd be in Melbourne by now, which was a big enough city to hide in, and with the right connections there was no way any Sydney urger could find you. But that was only his opinion, and he'd been careful to keep it to himself. The Doc was paying good money for this caper, enough so he and his girlfriend could afford a bit of a splash, maybe a luxury cruise to Hong Kong, or one of them Asian cities.

He glanced down at the laneway, and at the rows of garage doors. A bit like an English mews it seemed to him, because although he was from Belfast, he had spent time in England – done time there, too, only nobody here knew that – done two in the Scrubs for grievous bodily, and a few other matters, so it seemed best to emigrate, and getting into Australia was dead easy if you were white and British, which was why he had come here. It had cost him some dosh for a new passport, but worth it to get away from the smog and cold and English coppers. Only there wasn't a lot of work, after all the promises, so Forbes-Clark and this deal had come at a useful time, the best offer he'd had, though he couldn't say he liked the Doctor all that much.

He heard footsteps, and glanced down. Just a bloke on his way through to Bayswater Road. Another bloody false alarm. Then he became alert as the man stopped, took out a key and unlocked one of the garage doors. He grabbed the photo that had been circulated and studied it. He was still not quite sure until the garage door swung open and the Jaguar sports car was revealed.

'Holy shit,' he said, and took the gun. He thought it best to be cool, give himself a proper target, wait until the driver backed the convertible, then got out to shut the garage. He waited, nerves twitching. The convertible reversed, the driver left it idling and closed the garage door. As he returned to the car, the gunman slid the window open, aimed and shot. He missed the first time, and felt a moment of panic so intense that he fired again, and kept firing until the chamber of the gun was empty, and the man – just a boy really, he thought – was sprawled across the Jaguar with blood covering the seats and all the rest of the car, so that it looked like a slaughterhouse.

He used the phone line that had been restored inside the club, and said it was done, and the price was two thousand pounds. He was told that was the agreed amount, and it was in a package waiting for him in the flower shop across the street.

'It had better be,' he said, but never got to smell the flowers. While he was crossing the road, a sniper, alerted and waiting, steadied his aim and carefully shot him. It was two days before the police linked the death of the killer in the main street, to the violent murder of a young man identified as Michael Francis, shot dead alongside his sports car outside the laneway garage.

Chapter 23

The Waverley Cemetery must once have been a site of rare beauty, a quiet and select resting place, but was now overcrowded and cluttered with marble obelisks and memorials of crumbling sandstone. Deirdre had chosen it for the view. Situated at the edge of the sea, on a headland high above it, the vista beyond the acres of graves was truly spectacular, with rolling blue water stretching out to the horizon – and further – far across the Pacific. But the mass of headstones, thousands of them, some cracked, with names worn to near obscurity by the wind and passing time, others untidy with lichen or disfigured by weeds, were to Helen deeply depressing.

She came here rarely now. Months ago, in her initial shock and overwhelming grief, she had come constantly to bring flowers and tidy the grave. Sometimes Sarah had accompanied her, sometimes a heavily pregnant Deirdre, both anxious about her and aware these unduly frequent visits were an obsession. The grave, new and neatly pebbled, needed no tidying. Often the flowers were still alive from the previous occasion.

She knew of their concern, and the extent of her own despair. The paralysing horror of Michael's violent death – after they had survived so much violence and escaped so many deaths, only to meet it here in the place where they had sought sanctuary – had brought her to a confused state of anguish that at times threatened to engulf her and make a return to normal life impossible. Helen had always thought she was strong; she knew now she might not have survived these months without the strength of Sarah, whose own suffering had been so deep, or the support of Deirdre who had lost so much.

She placed the fresh flowers against his headstone, plucked at a tendril of grass that threatened to encroach, then rose and looked down at the grave. He had been tall and strong; this grave seemed too tiny for him, dwarfed by the many large shrines, the ostentatious vaults and family crypts, some of them absurd with angels and embellished with pompous or pathetic verse.

At least Michael had been spared that. They had all agreed on simplicity, just his name, and the dates – MICHAEL FRANCIS 1931-1953, the heartbreakingly brief twenty-two years he had lived. *No memorial*, she thought, *for Miklos Ferencz*, but this was best, and one day when he was old enough to understand, Deirdre would bring her son here to meet his father. Their baby son who was also named Michael.

She walked down to gaze at the view, deciding she would not come again, at least not until next year on the anniversary of his death. It made her too despondent, started her speculating on what might have happened had they ever been allowed into Israel, or gone to Canada or America, or even remained in Hungary? The thoughts disturbed her because there was no sense in such conjecture. She wished she could cry instead of constantly tormenting herself by dwelling on these alternatives. Tears would be such a relief, but in all these months no tears would come.

Only regrets, while she remained sick at heart and never stopped thinking of what might have been.

If only they had decided to leave the car behind. Or if Deirdre had gone to collect it, would the assassin have shot her? Or even supposing they had never moved into their room in Roslyn Gardens, and had not met Forbes-Clark . . .

Futile surmising. It only unsettled her and made her angry, because the killing was so pointless. Michael had represented no danger to anyone. He had intended to leave the city with Deirdre and seek their distant Gold Coast. He wanted only to flee and find a new life. At least in the end – by a bitter irony – the murder had caused the downfall of the Doctor and Stewart Mitchell, who would otherwise have become partners in the gambling club, continuing to bribe police and enjoy the laxity of the law while they proceeded to enrich themselves.

Out at sea a yacht was in full sail, adding to the splendour of the view. Far below her, closer inshore, a fishing boat was anchored, and she could hear excited cries and see a rod bending. One of the fishermen was hastily winding in the line, until there was a glitter of sun on the threshing silver scales as a fish was landed. *Poor thing*, she thought, and wished she could weep – for the fish and for her dead brother.

'At least they got the bastards, Miki.'

She realised she had said it aloud, but it didn't matter; there was no-one close enough to hear, or to wonder if she was crazy.

Both men were in prison, awaiting trial for murder. Not for the death of Michael; that could never be proved. But a gunman, the one paid to take the phone call, then shoot the hired killer, had been caught and gave Queen's evidence in a vain attempt to save himself. Turned informer and named both men. At the committal proceedings, represented by the most expensive lawyers that money could buy, it seemed for a time as if the guilty men might avoid justice. But Jimmy Kincaid's body had been found, those paid to dispose of him had talked, and everything had begun to unravel. Now Forbes-Clark and Mitchell with their various accomplices were in the remand section at Long Bay. Archie had sought another interview with the Governor, and secured his assurance there would be no chance encounter there with Neil.

Dear Archie, she thought. He and Don had been such a help, especially to Deirdre in the dreadful days afterwards, and later until the baby had been born two months premature. *Thank God*, she thought, *that in the sixth month Sarah had insisted on Deirdre coming to stay with them in the flat – as though she might have had some premonition.*

It had been almost midnight when Helen remembered being woken by Deirdre, her face damp with sweat, her eyes scared, all the courage she had shown since the day of the funeral suddenly turned to terror, because it was too soon and could not, should not, be happening this early.

But it was happening; her bed was soaked where her waters had already broken, and the pains were sharp and steadily increasing. By the time an ambulance arrived, Deirdre was fighting not to scream. Gasping, she told Sarah she didn't want to wake up the neighbourhood.

'Never you mind the neighbourhood,' Sarah had told her, 'I'll explain to them. You scream as loud and as long as you need to.'

So Deirdre had screamed and lights had gone on in the flats downstairs. Sarah had hurried down and told everyone to relax, a baby was on the way, and eventually ambulance men had carried a stretcher downstairs, with the neighbours waiting at their front doors to wish Deirdre well. And Helen and Sarah had ridden with her in the back of the ambulance to St Luke's, with the siren blaring, both of them trying to make cheerful and optimistic remarks, but each frightened and not wanting to express their fear that she might lose the baby.

Yet after all the night-long drama, it had been late morning before a nurse had come to announce the birth of a boy, and that despite his early arrival, and the fact he would spend his first few weeks in an incubator, mother and son were both well and wanted to see them. Later that day Archie had come to the hospital, and Helen smiled as she remembered his joy, his moment of pride when Deirdre had asked if he would be the baby's godfather.

She watched the yacht sailing into the distance. The fishermen had hauled in their lines, and were pouring themselves glasses of beer prior to cleaning and gutting their catch. Now she was ready to face the long walk back through the jungle of tombstones.

'They got them, Miki. It'll be life imprisonment.'

She felt good saying it aloud to him. It was time to go home.

Sarah was full of news. Deirdre had called in and spent a few hours with her. After lunch they'd bathed the baby together. Such a fragile little thing still, but getting much stronger, and such good lungs. Wonderful noisy lungs. And fine hands. Perhaps an opera singer, or a concert pianist?

'You're a romantic,' Helen told her, and made them tea.

'There's something else,' Sarah said, and there was a tremor in her voice that caused Helen to turn in surprise, concerned about her.

'What else?' One look and she knew. '*Neil?*'

'On Friday.'

'But that's wonderful,' she said, then realised the immediacy of it. '*This Friday?*'

'Yes.'

'Who told you?'

'Archie rang up. He kindly offered to drive out and collect him if we wished.'

'No, we'll meet him.'

'That's what I said. I felt sure you'd want to. Only I forgot my new student. I have him for a piano lesson on Friday.'

'I thought that was on Thursday.'

'I made a mistake. Friday. So you have to go alone.'

'Sarah,' Helen said suspiciously, 'I don't believe you.'

'I'm a liar?'

'No, a matchmaker.'

'And if this name is true, could there be a match?'

'I don't know,' Helen said, after reflection. 'It takes two.'

'You mean I should stop asking such awkward questions.'

'I mean that if I knew the answer, I'd tell you.'

'Ten o'clock, Friday morning. Don't be late.'

'I promise not to be. Wouldn't it be awful,' she could not resist the impulse, 'if there was a tram strike?'

'Helen! Don't say such things!'

They both laughed. Helen put her arms around her, and rested her cheek against Sarah's.

'Such news. I'm surprised you're not awash with tears.'

'I've got none left,' Sarah said. 'I had the best cry of my life earlier, after Archie rang. Just as well our nephew had gone.'

'At two months old, do you think he'd have noticed?'

'Of course he would. His great-aunt, behaving like a fool. He'd have noticed. He's a smart boy, that one.'

'Takes after his dad,' Helen said, then suddenly, unexpectedly, the tears she had been unable to shed until now overwhelmed her. She clung to Sarah, sobbing helplessly, unable to stop. Sarah held her tightly, trying to comfort her, and thought she had never heard such sounds of loss and bitter grief.

The tram went along Anzac Parade past Randwick racecourse, through Kingsford, Maroubra Junction and Matraville, and she began to see the familiar street names, then Pioneers Park, the rifle range, the Malabar public school, and finally the stop she knew so well, outside the walls of Long Bay.

She had been coming here almost weekly for five months, ever since their first dismaying reception, sometimes with Sarah, sometimes alone. While she liked the clattering old toast rack trams, she hoped never to come on this route again.

The warder at the gate greeted her. They all knew her and had ever since she first came alone to visit Neil.

'G'day, Helen.'

'Hello, Jack.'

'He's waiting. All packed. We'll miss yer.'

'You say that to all the girls,' Helen said, and he laughed.

'I don't know any other girls who called Iron Bar a pig,' he said, grinning.

'My claim to fame around here, is it?'

'Not a bad one, kiddo. He's jumpy, young Neil is.'

'Jumpy?'

'Takes 'em like that sometimes, Graduation Day. Said you might come to collect him, but he wasn't sure. Said you had to work.'

'I took a sickie,' Helen said, and waited while the warder put through a call, and then joined her again.

'On his way now. Only be a minute or two.' He looked at her and said: 'We'll sort of miss him.'

'Do you think he'll miss you?'

He shook his head and grinned.

'Not if he's got any sense. But he ain't really a proper crim, if you know what I mean. I don't think he did much harm, did he?'

'None whatever,' Helen said.

'They reckon he forged some papers.'

'For me and my brother. So we could come here.'

'Is that a fact?' He was astonished. 'I never knew that. And you and him, well . . . I mean, it's a kind of love story, ain't it?'

Before Helen could attempt to reply, they heard a nearby door slam and the sound of approaching voices.

'Well, it is,' the warder said quietly, aware of the voices. 'I mean . . . we all know he's nuts about you.'

'You all know that?'

The voices were closer. The warder spoke hurriedly.

'It's obvious. He'd be happy when you were due, miserable after you'd gone. Real worried about you when your brother got killed. In here we get to know a bit about people. And that bloke's gone on you. Honest.'

Helen had no time to do more than gaze at him, before she

saw Neil coming through the entrance. They stopped about a metre apart.

'Sarah here?' he asked.

'No, just me,' she said.

'They call it Graduation Day.'

'So Jack's been telling me.'

'So long, mate,' the warder said. He shook hands. 'I'll always remember the day you sorted out Chigger Harris. I think we all will.'

He nodded at Helen and shook hands with her, too. 'Good luck.'

'Thank you,' she said, and he smiled. The door clanged shut and they were alone outside the prison walls.

'I thought you'd be at work,' Neil said.

'I'm leaving work,' she replied. 'I went to see Sir Cedric, and said I'd agreed to stay longer because I liked him, but now I had to leave. I told him I want to teach.'

'Teach what?'

'English. Teach migrants.'

'But that's what I've been doing in here.'

'I know,' Helen said, 'that's what gave me the idea. It seems to me if people can understand each other, then they can live better together.'

He turned in surprise. 'I once said something like that to Henry Falconer. It was about the children. Being laughed at in school, being thought thick because they couldn't understand English.'

'And if they do learn, they can teach their parents.'

'I think I said something like that, too.'

'We seem to have the same sort of ideas,' Helen said, and took his arm. He was acutely aware of her hand tucked against his body.

'We do,' Neil said. He felt strangely tongue-tied. A veteran of a few intense love affairs – Caroline, Lucy, one or two less significant others – he hardly knew what to say next.

A tram was coming. They had to run across the road to catch it. They found an empty compartment and sat together on the bench seat. The tram, at this time of day, was virtually deserted. He was aware of her arm, as she replaced it inside his, and he drew a deep breath and prepared to speak. But he was too late.

'I love you,' she said. 'Jack, the warder, who seems to be a student of human nature, says you're fond of me. Gone on me, he said. Well, I wanted to tell you in Milan that I was a bit gone on you, but you weren't there. I think you were gone on someone else.'

'I think I was at the time,' he said.

'Gone off with her. And I was left like a shag on a rock.'

'Where did you pick up all this lovely slang?'

'From Miki,' she replied. 'He felt it made him an Australian.'

'And so he was.'

'He'd have liked that.'

'Just as we are. You and I.'

'Yes. I hope so.'

'You know what that expression means in England? A shag on a rock?'

'Yes,' she said. 'Making love on an uncomfortable surface. To put it politely.'

Their laughter drowned the sound of the conductor who coughed to attract their attention.

'Fares, plizz,' he said.

'I think we're getting married,' Neil announced.

'Yeah?'

'I just had to tell someone, and you're the nearest.'

'Good luck, but you still gotta pay your fare,' the conductor said, and gave them their tickets and the change. He glanced at the girl, then at the man enviously. *He won't need no luck*, he thought, *not with a sheila who looks like that.*

They watched him swing his way along the footboard, wishing for a more gracious audience.

'Sarah will be pleased,' Neil said. 'Shall we go and tell her?'

'I think Sarah might already know,' Helen smiled. 'Let's go home and celebrate with her.'

She leaned against him, and he put his arm around her. He hoped it would stay there forever. It was his first day of freedom, the best moment of his life, as the tram clattered through the junction, taking them away from the prison towards the future.

Author's Note

This book had its origins long ago, when I first saw the Snowy Mountains Scheme and met people who had worked on it. There was to be a radio feature, which for lack of funds never happened, but as the proposed writer I was enriched by material that has remained with me ever since. I spent time in what is now called Old Adaminaby, before the waters of Lake Eucumbene covered it, visited work camps, met Poles, Czechs, Estonians, Hungarians and Yugoslavs, some of whom had spent years in Displaced Persons camps after the war, for in 1945 they no longer had a country, and could not find a home.

The characters in *Against the Tide* came here after that war seeking refuge, during the largest population growth in the history of Australia. It is ironic that in the two years of research and writing this book – 1997 to 1998 – our country encountered the most virulent campaign against immigrants and immigration since that post-war era.

The parallels with that time are interesting. In those days we were told we were importing *undesirable citizens*, people who would never fit our way of life. They were abused and called *reffos*, disliked because they were not Anglo-Saxon, feared because extremists said they would take jobs and spread disease. Over two million of them left ruined countries to start a new life, transported on overcrowded ships, billeted in remote army camps, discovering they had been misled about what they would encounter here.

They had been promised paradise; they found something far less. The Australia of the 1950s was a very different landscape to the country of today. Credit for the change to a more vibrant society is due in no small part to those migrants, who endured prejudice and stayed here. They, and especially their children and grandchildren, are an integral part of the fabric of our nation. It would be difficult to imagine this country without them.

This is a work of fiction. There was corruption in post-war Europe's refugee camps, but the Milan Centre and its officials are imaginary. The Lawrenson Company, the Maison Lumière club, and events in Adaminaby are also fictional, although Kings Cross and some of the characters who inhabited it may resemble certain notorious figures of the time. Many of them were larger than life, and difficult to forget.

My thanks to Mary and Brian Wright who provided me with an insight into the United Nations relief work, by introducing me to Fedora Gould Fisher's biography *Raphael Cilento*. It was from her book I first learned how medical students were brought in to help the survivors of Belsen, and she kindly allowed me to make use of this little-known event.

Once again it has been a great pleasure to work with Ali Watts and Saskia Adams at Penguin Books. And finally, though it is many years since we met, my gratitude to Rachel Skinner, formerly an agent with Rick Raftos Management and now living in New York, who encouraged me to write this and other early novels. It was a career move I have never regretted.

Peter Yeldham
pyeldham@bigpond.net.au

Also by Peter Yeldham

Barbed Wire and Roses

The First World War, everyone said in 1914, would be over by Christmas, and Stephen Conway rushes to enlist. Leaving behind a new wife and a baby on the way, he soon finds himself in the trenches of Gallipoli. Four horrific years later, Stephen is the only survivor of his platoon. Shell-shocked and disillusioned, and during the heat of battle on the blood-stained fields of France, he mysteriously disappears.

More than eighty years later, Stephen's grandson Patrick finds a diary that leads him to Britain and France on a journey to discover what really happened. It is a journey during which he unexpectedly finds love, and the truth about his grandfather's fate that is even stranger and more shocking than he imagined.

Based on true events, this is an unforgettable novel of courage and survival from a master storyteller.

'Five stars. A heart-wrenching account of our young Anzacs'
ADELAIDE ADVERTISER

'A gripping tale of romance and mystery'
WEEKLY TIMES

The Murrumbidgee Kid

'Belle Carson was a good-looker, the best looker for miles around; even those who didn't like her (which included most of the women in town and quite a few of the men) had to admit that. But they also agreed she was as nutty as a fruitcake, and the bush telegraph – which spread any gossip the least bit unusual or outrageous – frequently carried news of her.'

Belle longs for her young son, Teddy, to achieve the success that eluded her on the stage and screen. Determined to pursue this dream, she abandons her devoted husband and their Murrumbidgee River home for a more vibrant city life. But Belle's obsession leads her and Teddy – whom the press christens 'the Murrumbidgee Kid' – into a world where nothing is safe or familiar. And from her carefully hidden past a threat soon emerges to make their precarious lives even more vulnerable . . .

From rural Gundagai to the bright lights and shady underbelly of 1930s Sydney, this is a beautifully written and absorbing story about an unconventional family's coming-of-age.

'a strong and entertaining story'
THE AGE